Someone
Like You

Center Point
Large Print

Also by Victoria Bylin and available from
Center Point Large Print:

Until I Found You
Together With You

**This Large Print Book carries the
Seal of Approval of N.A.V.H.**

Someone Like You

VICTORIA BYLIN

CENTER POINT LARGE PRINT
THORNDIKE, MAINE

ISBN: 978-1-68324-034-1

Library of Congress Cataloging-in-Publication Data

Names: Bylin, Victoria, author.
Title: Someone like you / Victoria Bylin.
Description: Center Point Large Print edition. | Thorndike, Maine : Center Point Large Print, 2016. | ©2014
Identifiers: LCCN 2016014678 | ISBN 9781683240341 (hardcover : alk. paper)
Subjects: LCSH: Large type books. | GSAFD: Love stories. | Christian fiction.
Classification: LCC PS3602.Y56 S66 2016 | DDC 813/.6—dc23
LC record available at http://lccn.loc.gov/2016014678

For my husband . . . Always!

I will give you a new heart
and put a new spirit in you;
I will remove from you your heart of stone
and give you a heart of flesh.
Ezekiel 36:26

One

Zeke Monroe appreciated a good joke, and this one was on him. Grinning, he crossed the plush charcoal carpet in his office to a desk the size of an aircraft carrier. A new Han Solo action figure guarded his pencil cup, and a handwritten sign was taped to the back of his massive leather chair.

"Starship Command," he read out loud. "Captain Zeke Monroe to the rescue."

Chuckling, he peeled off the sign. Everyone on the Caliente Springs management team knew he appreciated a silly prank now and then, and in the eight months he'd been general manager of the historic California resort, he had come to call them all friends.

Which made the task before him daunting at best: save Caliente Springs from bankruptcy, or allow two hundred people to lose their jobs.

People like Ashley, the CS marketing director, whose daughter suffered from severe asthma.

Or Javier, a college kid who helped support his family by working as a concierge.

And Mrs. Jenson, the gift shop clerk who joked—maybe—about living on cat food without her small paycheck.

Four months from now, the historic resort

needed to be booked solid with guests, weddings, and conferences, or they'd all be out on the street. No way would Zeke let that happen.

His gaze shot to the window that faced the distant brown hills. The rolling landscape was lovely, especially at sunset, but he would have preferred a view of the entire resort. Caliente Springs was huge, a conglomeration of the five-story main hotel, three single-story buildings that offered garden rooms, a cluster of luxurious cottages behind a security gate, and top-notch recreation facilities: golf, tennis, three swimming pools, game rooms, a gym, restaurants, a fishing pond, hiking trails, and an equestrian center.

Zeke loved this place, but it was falling apart. The roads constantly needed repair, and the majority of the guest rooms screamed 1990, with dark green accent walls and dusty rose tile. Trendy? Definitely not. But he was working on modernizing everything from the décor to the business model.

He dropped onto the chair and tried to open his desk drawer to check his to-do list. Something caught inside, so he pried at it with a letter opener. When the jam sprang loose, the "Chicken Dance" song crowed from the birthday card he'd been given last week from the marketing department. A grin spread across his face. Who could *not* laugh at the "Chicken Dance"?

Irene, his executive assistant, hobbled around

the corner. "If I wasn't having a hip replacement next week, I'd invite you to polka with me." Dancing wasn't his thing, but he'd do it for Irene. "Bring on the Oompah band."

Irene patted her bad hip. "I'll leave the dancing to you. In the meantime, while I'm out, I've written instructions for whoever fills in."

"Thanks."

"About the business cards—" She arched a brow at him. "Have you decided which one to use?"

"No."

Irene, silver-haired, with reading glasses on her nose, waited in that motherly way that mixed patience with silent urging. A week ago, she'd given him a sheet of paper with three versions of his name. It was still on his desk, front and center, face-up, with his doodling all over the page.

She peered at him over her wire-framed glasses. "Is there a problem?"

"A big one. I don't know which one to use." Being named after a biblical prophet was a problem for a man wrestling with his faith. Being named after two of them, as in Ezekiel Amos Monroe, was just plain inconvenient. Zeke couldn't even hide behind a normal middle name. He lifted the sheet with the three versions and studied it.

Irene sat in the guest chair. "Try reading them out loud."

He started with the card he was using now.

" 'Zeke Monroe, General Manager.' " Simple. Unpretentious. Exactly who he was. But old nicknames slapped at him, like Zeke the Freak. Or worse, Zeke the Meek, the name he'd been handed back in college by a self-absorbed jerk named Hunter Adams.

Irene waited for the next one.

Zeke crossed it out while he read. " 'E. A. Monroe, General Manager.' Forget it. People will think I'm Elizabeth or Emily and trying to hide it."

Irene nodded. "Yes. Forget that one."

Using his pep-talk voice, he read the last name on the list. " 'Ezekiel A. Monroe, General Manager.' " It was a preacher's name, assigned to him before he even drew his first breath.

His gaze flicked to the edge of his desk and the photograph taken ten years ago with his dad at their mission church in Chile. Arms linked, they grinned into the camera, father and son, preacher and protégé. But not anymore. Memories of his dad, and one quarrel in particular, still pricked his heart.

Thrusting those memories aside, he compared the names from a business perspective alone. Ezekiel A. Monroe would be a constant reminder of his dad, but it also made him sound older than thirty-one. He was a decade younger than most men in his position, so sounding older was an advantage.

He circled *Ezekiel A. Monroe*, slid the page

to Irene, and leaned back in his chair. "That's it."

She peered down, tipping her head to see the paper. "That wasn't so bad, was it?"

Excruciating. But Zeke just smiled. Becoming Ezekiel again, even on paper, struck him as a fitting way to end a morning spent emptying his parents' storage locker. Seventeen boxes sat in the back of a U-Haul in his driveway, waiting to be unpacked and the contents sorted. Two of them belonged to Zeke and held mementos from his college days. The other fifteen belonged to his parents. He should have unpacked them two years ago after the memorial service, but he just couldn't. Those boxes would still be in storage if the lease hadn't expired.

Irene, lowering her chin, peered over her glasses again. "I have to tell you something else."

"What is it?"

"Ashley called a few minutes ago."

Ashley Tate. Attractive. Single. Ambitious but unreliable because of her asthma-afflicted daughter. "What happened?"

"She can't make that three o'clock meeting with the event planner scouting us out for Carter Home Goods."

Carter Home Goods, a newcomer in the home-based business industry, sold household gadgets and décor at home parties much like the company Thirty-One sold personalized canvas tote bags. The Carter catalogs showed up in the lunchroom

11

now and then, and Zeke had read about the growing company on a business blog. Larry Carter was a strong Christian who rewarded his employees with perks like vacations. An event planner from Dare to Dream Events was coming to scout Caliente Springs as a potential site for those vacations as well as for Carter's annual sales conference.

The Carter account alone wouldn't save Caliente Springs, but it was the kind of repeat business Zeke needed to land in order to pull the resort out of the red. He dragged his hand through his hair. He wasn't gray yet, but at this rate, he'd have streaks of silver before he knew it.

"What happened this time?" he asked.

"Her daughter's in the ER again. She's sorry, Zeke. But you know how it is for her."

Single moms. They gave him a headache when they missed work, but he loved kids and respected the women who raised them on their own.

Irene lowered her voice. "Ashley's worried you're going to fire her."

"No." Not even close. "Tell her I said she's too good to lose. I'll cover the meeting."

"You're a good man."

Hardly. At least not by his father's standards. Zeke had disappointed both God and his earthly father more times than he cared to admit, but he loved people and he loved his work. The CS employees were like family to him. He picked up

12

a pen to make some notes. "Fill me in. Who's the contact?"

"Her name is Julia Dare."

The pen tumbled out of his hand. "Julia *Dare?*"

"That's right." Surprise leaked into Irene's voice, and nothing ever surprised Irene. "You must know her."

"I do. Or I did."

Irene waited for more, but Zeke wasn't about to explain Julia Dare to Irene, or to anyone else for that matter. He picked up the pen and jotted her name on a turquoise Post-it Note—her favorite color. *Julia Dare.* Brunette hair that bounced when she walked. Stunning brown eyes that saw into his soul. A heart that cared about everyone who crossed her path. Even him, at least until she dumped him.

Irene arched a brow at him, then looked pointedly at the Post-it, where he'd written Julia's name three times.

He tossed the pen aside. "So where am I meeting her?"

"The concierge desk."

"Perfect. Which room is she in?"

"418."

Newly refurbished. Modern electronics. Spacious, with a view of the golf course and the mountains. "Good choice. Email me Ashley's proposal. I'll read through it before the meeting."

"It's already done."

"Thanks. Just one more thing. Did Ashley order a gift basket for the room?"

"Yes. I already checked."

The rattan baskets were filled with crackers, cheeses, a bottle of wine, and the hotel's famous chocolate chip cookies. "Add a bag of mini Milky Ways."

"The candy?"

"Exactly." Mini Milky Ways. Julia's favorite. She and Zeke had shared more than a few bags of them during their senior year at UC Berkeley.

"I'll take care of it."

"Anything else?"

"John Rossmore called." The resort's golf pro and Zeke's friend. "He wants to talk to you about more water for the fairways. The drought—"

"I know. It's killing business." It was killing a lot things—the landscaping by the front gate, the budget because of the increased cost of water, even the local aquifer. As for the fire danger, it was high, and something Californians lived with like Midwesterners lived with tornados. "What else?"

"Kevin in maintenance received the third pool fence bid. You're scheduled to meet with him tomorrow at 8:30. His office."

"Good."

"And Chet wants to know if you're inspecting the trail loop tomorrow."

Chet Smith, a wizened old cowboy, supervised

trail rides and dude-ranch-style camping trips. Zeke loved the old man, but the stable ran at a big loss and was perpetually on the chopping block. "Reschedule the ride. I need to concentrate on the Carter meeting."

"Will do."

He glanced at the antique wall clock made from the stump of a California oak, symbolic because the tree had been cut down to make room for the original Caliente Springs lodge. If he hurried, he could unload the U-Haul sitting in his driveway before he cleaned up for the meeting. He pushed the chair away from his desk. "If that's all—"

"One more thing."

Ignoring Irene was always a mistake, so he shifted the pen back to the pad of Post-its. "What is it?"

"Ginger called this morning." Irene sounded grim, a bad omen because Ginger and her twin brother, George Travers, co-owned Caliente Springs. "She wants the numbers for July."

Zeke sighed. "They're not due for another week."

"I know."

"Why do you think she's asking?"

"Just to be difficult?"

Irene liked Ginger as much as Zeke did, which wasn't much. He felt bad about his uncharitable attitude, but Ginger pestered him about every little detail. George, on the other hand, was a close friend and the reason Zeke had been hired as GM. George loved Caliente Springs and wanted it to flourish. Ginger loved it too, but she wanted to sell the place and be done with the financial drain.

"She'll get them," Zeke said. "Any other surprises?"

"Not yet."

"Good. I'm outta here." He walked with Irene to her desk, then took the employee entrance to where he parked his hotel SUV and headed to the manager's residence, a small bungalow on the backside of the CS property.

Six years had passed since he'd seen Julia Dare, or Jules, as he used to call her. He looked forward to seeing her again, catching up on old friends, and hearing about where life had taken her. She had hurt him, but she crossed his mind often. No surprise there. A man didn't forget the first woman he had ever loved.

Julia Dare steered her eight-year-old Outback through the wide valley that led to Caliente Springs, her fingers light on the wheel as a Christian station played music through the speakers. She knew her four-year-old son, Max, was in good hands with her mother, Ellen Dare, at the Los Angeles home where Julia had grown up. The three of them had been living together since Julia left Max's father six months ago.

Max was the light of Julia's life, but his father,

Hunter Adams, was the bane of her existence. Her son needed a father and Julia wanted a husband, but she had never married Hunter, and it was hard to believe she had ever loved him at all.

But that was over now, and she was starting again as a new Christian. All that mattered was living her faith, making Dare to Dream a success, and being a good mother to Max.

The surrounding hills, washed out by drought and bright sun, were the color of the Cheerios she and Max had eaten for breakfast. She missed her son terribly, but owning a business required sacrifices. And risk. And good judgment. The Carter Home Goods account was her first big break, and she was determined to recommend the best possible location for their needs.

The owner of Carter Home Goods was an old golf buddy of her dad's. Benjamin Maxwell Dare had died during Julia's senior year of college, and since then, Mr. Carter and his wife had stayed in touch with Julia and her mom. She was touched—and grateful—that he'd come to her with this project, and she intended to earn his loyalty.

This was Julia's third resort visit this month, and she hoped it would be the last. Her mother loved Max as much as she did, but leaving him still cut a hole in Julia's heart. The time he spent with Hunter cut an even bigger hole, one lined with trepidation, because she didn't trust Hunter's judgment. At the last stop for gas, she had taken a moment to skim the multiple texts Hunter had sent while she was driving up Highway 101, each one choppy with impatience.

Call me.

Need to talk re: the weekend.

R u driving? Pull over. Shouldn't take long.

As soon as she reached her room at the resort, she needed to call him.

She steered onto a horseshoe driveway in front of the five-story white stucco building surrounded by palms and conifers. A low-peaked roof shaded both the cars and flowerbeds full of birds-of-paradise, ivy, elephant ears, and lilies of the Nile.

A parking valet helped her out of her car, another retrieved her suitcase from the trunk, and a bellhop escorted her to the lobby. She checked in at a polished oak counter manned by a sharp, friendly receptionist, and five minutes after arriving, she walked into an air-conditioned room that smelled like vanilla. A gift basket on a table caught her eye, and she went to inspect it.

Healthy snacks and gourmet cheeses. Thumbs up.

A bottle of wine. Classy.

The hotel's famous chocolate chip cookies. Yum.

Miniature Milky Ways? Her mind shot back in time to a man with dark blond hair, startling blue eyes, and a natural confidence that put everyone around him at ease, including her. The years peeled away, leaving behind a host of bittersweet memories. *Zeke Monroe*. A strong Christian who had planned to enter the mission field with his parents. A man dedicated to feeding the poor and saving souls. He had tried to save her soul too, but it hadn't worked. Instead she had tarnished him. Julia stared at the bag of Milky Ways, her heart aching with regret. She was no longer in touch with Zeke, and that was for the best.

Very gently, she placed the bag back on top of the cookies. As tempting as Milky Ways were, she couldn't bear to taste the memories. Wherever Zeke was, she hoped he was happy.

She picked up her phone to call Hunter but paused to look at the photograph of Max on the screen. With his dark hair and brown eyes, he took after the Dare side of the family, but he had Hunter's chin. A sweet glow filled Julia's chest, but it faded when she pulled up Hunter's newest text.

Hey babe. Julia shook her head. How many times did she have to tell him not to call her that before he would respect her request? Where are u? I'm free on Saturday. Let's get together. You me and Max.

Julia typed back. Can't. Will still be at Caliente Springs. He knew her schedule; he just didn't respect her enough to remember it.

While waiting for a reply, she swiftly put on a

tailored red dress with side belts and gold buttons. Her favorite. The red made her dark hair almost black, and the gold matched her light brown eyes.

Hunter's text came through. Ok. So just Max and me.

She tapped in, Plans?

This time Hunter answered immediately. TBD.

"To be determined" could mean anything from McDonald's to a day at Castaic Lake racing around on Hunter's speedboat. An image flew through her mind of Hunter putting Max on water skis, even though Max could barely dog-paddle. There was also the bike in her mother's garage, far too big for Max and another gift from Hunter. In spite of the training wheels, Max had toppled hard while pedaling fast to impress his daddy. The scab on his elbow was still as thick as a nickel.

She couldn't let Hunter take Max for the day without knowing his plans, so she called him. It went to voice mail, but two minutes later, her phone meowed with the ringtone she had assigned to Hunter to amuse Max.

"So," she said, trying to sound friendly instead of controlling, one of his complaints about her, "what does TBD mean?"

Hunter chuckled. "Babe, you worry too much."

"I'm a mom. It's my job."

"And I'm a dad." Hunter's tone took on an edge. "I love Max as much as you do. He's my mini-me."

Coming from Hunter, Julia hated that expression. Max was a little boy, not a clone of his dad. There was no point in quarreling, so she kept her voice even. "What do you have in mind for Saturday?"

"How about the zoo?"

"It sounds fun." And far safer than the speedboat. "I won't be home until late afternoon. I'll tell my mom you're picking him up."

"I'll text her."

"All right." But Julia would call her mom too. She didn't trust Hunter to stick to the plan, and she didn't want her mom to be caught in the middle. "What time will you bring him home?"

"Come on, babe. Relax."

"I wish you wouldn't call me that."

"Come with us. It'll be fun."

"I told you. I can't." Even if she were home, she'd say no. A family date would send the wrong message to Hunter, the master of the yo-yo relationship, and it would confuse Max, who was still adjusting to his parents being apart.

Hunter's gruffest voice came over the phone. "I know you love me, Julia. I love you too, and we both love Max. I want us to be a family. I want—"

"Hunter, stop."

"We should have gotten married when he was born."

As if the choice had been hers! She had brought

up marriage and even made a fun little proposal when the pregnancy test came out positive, but Hunter put her off with a long engagement and plans for a big wedding. A year passed and they delayed the wedding two more times. When he wanted to delay it a third time, she finally saw the truth: He valued the show of a wedding more than he valued marriage. Or her.

"Babe, are you there?"

"Yes. I'm here."

"I love you, Julia. Just say the word, and we'll head to Vegas."

In your dreams, pal. "That's not going to happen."

"Why not?"

"You know why." They were talking about her faith, something Hunter didn't respect. Knowing how he felt, she muttered good-bye and ended the call.

After six years, she knew Hunter well. The counselor she saw after leaving him thought he had narcissistic tendencies. In Greek mythology, Narcissus was a man in love with himself and incapable of truly loving others. *"Narcissists feed on people,"* the counselor had told Julia. *"They love you for what you give them. If you reflect Hunter back to Hunter, he'll love you. If you don't, he'll lash out at you."*

Julia could cope with Hunter's demands, but how did she protect Max from a father who couldn't love his son the way a boy needed to be loved?

She didn't know, and she was running late for the meeting with Ashley. She dabbed on lipstick, picked up her portfolio, and rode the elevator to the lobby. Heels clacking on the marble floor, she walked to the concierge desk. She didn't see Ashley anywhere. Not a good sign for a hotel that sold itself on customer service.

Wearing a slight frown, she approached the concierge, a young Hispanic man with the spit-shine polish of a U.S. Marine. He greeted her with a smile. "Good afternoon. How can I help you today?"

"I'm looking for Ashley Tate."

"You must be Ms. Dare."

"Yes, I am."

Behind her, a mellow tenor voice rose above the dull hum of the lobby. "Hello, Jules."

Jules. Only Zeke Monroe called her by that name. Slowly, her heart pounding, she turned and saw a man in a heather gray suit. A man with Zeke's broad shoulders, those unforgettable blue eyes, and dark blond hair streaked gold from the sun. The Milky Ways suddenly made sense.

Somehow she unglued her tongue and managed a single word. *"Zeke?"*

His grin widened. "The same."

"How—what—"

She gaped at him as he closed the space between

23

them. The moment called for a handshake, but her body swayed toward his, as if her muscles remembered what her heart needed to forget. His arms slipped around her and they hugged with a stiffness born of too many memories.

She broke away, but even as she started to pull back, their hands met and their fingers entwined.

"I can't believe this," she murmured.

"Neither could I when my assistant told me you were here." He flashed the relaxed smile that used to put her at ease. "It's great to see you."

"Same here."

Except acid burned in the back of her throat. Back in college she had betrayed Zeke with Hunter, and he didn't know it. The three of them had worked together at St. John's Refuge House. Zeke as a paid assistant manager; Julia as an intern for a sociology class; and Hunter, a law student, as a legal aid volunteer. There was no excuse for what she had done, only the pathetic explanation that she'd been dazzled by Hunter's confidence and seduced by a cynicism that, at the time, had matched her own.

Zeke gave her hands a gentle squeeze and let go. "You're here on business. Let's go to my office and talk about Carter Home Goods. We can catch up on the personal stuff after that."

Two

Zeke glanced at Julia's left hand. No wedding band. No rings of any kind, and she looked great in red. The dress skimmed above her knees and showed off long legs that ended in high heels instead of the ballet flats she wore in college. Her eyes were the same light brown, a honey color, but her hair was different. Tamer than he recalled, but still shoulder-length and full of loose curls.

"Well." She rested her arm on the leather portfolio hanging from her shoulder. "I'm starting to recover from the shock. How did this happen?"

Zeke reached in his coat for a business card. "I'm general manager."

"Really?"

"Really."

When he held out the card, she pinched it with her manicured fingers, read it, and studied him with a look that mixed surprise with admiration. "This place is light years from St. John's, but in a way it makes sense."

"How?"

"You're still taking care of people."

Food. Shelter. Respite from the demands of life. Call him Martha Stewart, but he was at home in the hospitality industry. "It's a good fit. Bigger, obviously, and we have more balls in the air. I wouldn't have known you were here, except Ashley had a personal emergency."

"Oh no." Julia's dark brows collided. "Is she all right?"

"She's fine. Her daughter has asthma."

"Rachel."

"That's right." Kudos to Ashley. She'd made a strong connection with a potential client. "They're at the ER now, so I'm filling in. When I heard your name, I couldn't believe it. You look the same, Jules."

"Thank you. But I go by Julia now."

"Of course." She'd grown up and so had he. Berkeley was a long time ago. He indicated an alcove off the lobby. "This way."

They fell into step, crossed the lobby, and walked into a nook with vending machines, pay phones, and a door marked "Private" with a keypad lock. Zeke punched in the numbers and opened it wide. "My office is at the end."

As they walked down the corridor, she skimmed the names and titles stenciled on the glass doors. "I thought you were in Chile with your parents."

"It's a long story."

They passed human resources, marketing, and guest relations. Housekeeping and accounting were located down a different hall along with the chief maintenance engineer and the food services manager. Zeke's office was at the intersection of the two corridors. When they

26

reached his door, he held it open while Julia walked into a sitting area with leather chairs, an oak table, and western art on the walls.

Irene was seated behind the reception counter and working on a spreadsheet, probably the report for Ginger. When Zeke made the introductions, Julia extended her hand, something not everyone did for an administrative assistant.

Irene's gaze shifted to Zeke. "Ashley called a few minutes ago."

"How's Rachel?"

"Out of danger. They gave her a breathing treatment and sent her home." Irene focused on Julia. "Do you know about Ashley's daughter?"

"I do. It's rough."

Zeke broke back in. "Send balloons to Ashley's apartment. Something fun."

Irene gave him a smug smile. "I knew you'd say that. The Disney Princess balloon bouquet is already on the way."

"Thanks." As usual, Irene was two steps ahead of him. He rapped his knuckles on the wood counter, then aimed his chin at the short hallway. "My office is this way."

Julia led the way down the carpeted hall but stopped at the open door on the left. She peered inside, unsure.

"This is it." Zeke reached past her and pushed the door another inch.

She took several steps inside. Turning in a

slow circle, she surveyed the desk, the corner windows, the diplomas and awards, and his personal artifacts on the bookshelves, including his collection of geodes, hollow rocks split in two to reveal colorful crystals.

He propped a hip on the corner of his desk. "Look around. You'll see a few things you recognize."

She murmured something that sounded like *more than a few,* then approached the shelf holding an irregular-shaped geode with a turquoise center. "I gave this to you."

Memories of their only Valentine's Day slammed into him. She had packed a picnic, and they'd hiked to the middle of nowhere in Muir Woods, a stunning forest of redwoods, clover, and lush ferns. When he spread the blanket he kept in his old pickup on the ground, she set down the wicker basket and faced him. A kiss. Two kisses. He had restrained himself, mostly. He remembered everything about that day—the fog lingering in the tops of the redwoods, the sun breaking through the silver mist, the crisscross of shadows and refracted light.

Don't go there. Zeke swallowed hard.

Julia turned away from the geode and focused on the wall displaying his diplomas and awards. She read each one, then approached his desk, where Han Solo stood ready for battle next to the pencil cup.

"You're still you," Julia said. "But you've changed."

"A lot."

"Me too. More than I ever imagined."

That turquoise geode. Her heart pounded against her ribs, shooting her back to St. John's and the first time she saw Zeke. Tall and muscular, he'd been wearing a dark blue T-shirt, Levi's, and work boots. It was the middle of September and the first day of her internship. She'd been searching for the office when he saw the lost look on her face and approached.

"Can I help you?"

"I'm the new intern. I'm looking for Zeke Monroe."

"That's me."

When he smiled, she had melted into a puddle of hormones. But that was ancient history. They were very different people now, and she needed to focus on doing her job.

Except when she turned to Zeke, he was opening a mini fridge next to his desk. "How about a Sprite?"

Her beverage of choice. He knew that. "No, thank you."

He closed the fridge without taking anything for himself and rocked back on his heels, his hands in his pockets the way she'd seen a hundred times before. *Focus on the job.* But what popped out of her mouth was a question. "How did you end up at Caliente Springs?"

"That's another long story."

"Tell me."

He indicated she should sit in the guest chair at his desk, then he dropped down in his own bigger chair. "Have you heard of Home and Hearth?"

"It's a charity, isn't it?"

"Yes, nationwide. About twenty years ago, a business mogul named Harlan Jones turned a run-down motel into a homeless shelter, called it a campus, and ran it like an assisted-living facility. Add in vocational training and a code-of-living contract for the residents, and you have Home and Hearth. Some residents stay a very long time. Others recover from whatever life handed them and move on."

"What a great idea."

"I worked at the LA facility during grad school. That's where I met George Travers. He's on the national board of directors, but he's also hands-on. He spent a lot of time with the residents."

"I've heard of him. Country music, right?"

"One of the Travers Twins," Zeke explained. "He and his sister Ginger were big back in the eighties."

"My mom was a fan. She still keeps his old vinyls on a shelf. Back then, he was a heartthrob."

Zeke grinned. "He'd object to *back then*."

"My mom would too."

"How is she?"

"Good." Julia didn't dare say more about her family because of Max and Hunter. "What's the connection between George and your job?"

"He and Ginger own this place. When I finished my MBA, I moved into management at Home and Hearth and worked as West Coast director. George poached me away about eight months ago."

"I'm impressed." Her own career path had been a downhill slide from ambitious do-gooder to unemployed temp to struggling business owner. "But what happened to going back to Chile?"

Looking down, he picked up a geode paper-weight and rubbed the coarse exterior with his thumb. "I'm not the same person I was in college, but there's another reason. A sad one. My parents died in a plane crash."

"Oh, Zeke." Sorrow rocketed along every nerve, a mix of empathy for Zeke and the old grief for her dad. "I'm so sorry. When did it happen?"

"Almost two years ago."

"Two years or two months—it still hurts."

"You know how it is."

Their eyes locked, and in the way of the couple they'd been in Berkeley, they recognized the memory of Julia getting that awful phone call from her mom. Her father, an insurance broker, had suffered a heart attack at the office. Zeke took her to the airport, then drove to LA to be with

31

her. She had leaned on him with all her might in those dark days.

It was later, when the shock wore off, that she had accused him of shoving religion down her throat.

Zeke set down the paperweight. "What about you? Dare to Dream is based in LA, isn't it?"

"Yes. I moved back home with my mom. It was good for both of us." And Max, but she kept that detail to herself. "There's not a lot to tell." At least not a lot she wanted to tell. "I've worked some different jobs. Event planning suits me, so I started Dare to Dream."

He waited for more.

"I like it." She reached into the portfolio. "Carter Home Goods is my first big client, and I'm on a tight deadline. Could we get started?"

"Of course." He hooked a thumb at a flat screen on the wall. "Ashley planned to start with a PowerPoint presentation, but I'm more hands-on. How about a tour?"

"Sure."

"You might want to change into something more casual. We're going to do some walking."

"No, thanks." The red dress made her feel professional, and she needed that barrier between herself and Zeke.

He glanced at her shoes. "If you're sure—"

"I am."

He picked up a two-way radio off the charger on his desk and raised it to his mouth. "GM to Valet."

"Yes, sir. Valet 3 here."

"My SUV's in the employee lot. Would you bring it around front?"

He clipped the radio to his belt and came around the desk. Together they headed to the lobby, where the revolving door spilled them out onto the sidewalk. The smells of mulch and car exhaust blended together in the heat, along with a hint of Zeke's aftershave, something smoky and dark and new to him.

A white SUV zipped up the road and stopped in front of them. A valet hustled to open her door, but Zeke waved him off. "I've got it."

"Yes, sir."

Hearing Zeke called *sir* was as surreal as standing in his office. He held out his hand, indicating the portfolio on her shoulder. "I'll put that in the back."

"Thanks."

After she handed it to him, he opened the door, and she climbed into the vehicle as if they were going on one of the long drives they used to take in college. Like a slap, the A/C cleared her mind of the past and she stared out the windshield.

Zeke put the portfolio on the backseat and came around to the driver's side. When he glanced at her, she saw a gleam in his eyes and knew the question he was about to ask, because he had asked it so many times before. "A/C or windows?"

"Windows."

33

"I thought so." He powered down all four windows, drove to the main road, and started a sales pitch that mirrored the CS website. "There's no smog here, and the climate's great all year round. For drivers, we're centrally located between LA and the Bay Area, and the San Luis Obispo Airport is just thirty minutes from here."

"It's a great location," she agreed. "I'll be straight with you. I've visited two other resorts. They were nice, but Caliente Springs has more to offer than either of them."

"Glad to hear it."

"Of course, cost is a factor."

"We'll talk about that tomorrow." Slowing the SUV, he pointed to a wrought iron gate made of elaborate scrolls. "The cottages are that way. Did Ashley tell you about them?"

"A little. They're luxurious and secure."

"And perfect for a CEO who wants some privacy. Let's take a look." Zeke steered to the gate, punched in a code, and drove down a winding road to a cul-de-sac with five houses well spaced and angled for privacy. He stopped in front of the first one. "The cottages all have gourmet kitchens, media rooms, and three bedrooms with Jacuzzi tubs on the patios. Even the most dedicated CEO needs to get away from the crowd."

He slowed the SUV to a crawl, giving her time to take in the pretty houses, the chirp of birds, and the rustle of a breeze through the oak trees. Julia couldn't remember the last time she sat under a tree and simply breathed. "This is lovely."

"We work hard to keep this area pristine."

A question struck her. "Where do you live?"

"There's a manager's house on the backside of the golf course." He steered out through the gate. "It comes with the job."

"You must put in a lot of hours."

"I do, but it's hard to call what I do 'work.' I spend my time with great people in a beautiful place. We have our share of challenges, but I can't imagine doing anything else."

"It suits you."

Zeke gave the SUV a little gas. "We'll check out the golf course next. You probably know from the website that the resort covers seven hundred acres, including green space. We rent golf carts for guests to use to get around, plus there's a shuttle. We're big, probably bigger than the other places you visited."

"That's a plus. Carter Home Goods is expecting three hundred sales reps, mostly women. This is a combo sales meeting and reward, so the reps are invited to bring spouses and families."

"We're perfect for that sort of thing. We offer golf, tennis, horseback rides, and lazing by one of the three pools."

Julia liked what she was hearing. "Golf is important. Mr. Carter plays almost every day."

Zeke slowed as they passed a green where a man

in vintage tweed knickers and argyle socks was lining up a putt. A second man waited in the rough. Club in hand, he was dressed in orange and yellow plaid pants, a white shirt, and a matching bowtie. A plaid beret topped off the outfit.

Zeke turned to her, his expression deadpan. "As you can see, we're serious about our golf—and our plaid."

Julia smiled. "Yes, I can see that."

"Fashion demands aside, we'd be glad to set up lessons or even a tournament to keep family members entertained."

Zeke parked in a half-empty lot, picked up his radio, and led her toward a low building with a wide overhang. When he opened the glass door, she stepped into an air-conditioned shop full of irons and putters, accessories, and plenty of plaid.

A man with sandy brown hair approached with his eyes on Julia. "Good afternoon. I'm John Rossmore, golf pro."

Julia shook his hand. "It's nice to meet you."

Zeke introduced Julia as the CEO of Dare to Dream Events. "I told Julia you'd be glad to arrange a tournament for her group. She's—"

His radio cut him off with a crackle and a gruff voice. "GM, this is Cowboy."

Zeke raised the radio to his mouth. "Hey, Chet. I'm in the middle of something. Can this wait?"

"No, sir. It *cannot*. We have a 911 at the stables."

Three

Julia braced herself for news of an accident or a fire. In the current heat wave, a single ember could set the hills ablaze. The Smokey Bear sign outside the resort was set on red, and the drought conditions were the lead story on every newscast in Southern California. Her stomach flipped at the thought of smoke and scorched earth, lost jobs and even lost lives.

Zeke pressed the radio button. "I hear you, Cowboy. What's the problem?"

"It's that confounded goat."

Goat? Surely she had misunderstood. Brows tight, Zeke raked his hand through his hair. "I'm on my way."

A grunt rattled across the radio. "That nasty old thing has to go. I don't give a hoop-dee-doo who owns her. Get her outta here, Zeke. Or I'll have the last word."

"Roger, Cowboy."

"I'll feed her to the buzzards!"

"Give me five minutes." Zeke clicked off the radio. Looking pained, he faced Julia. "I'm sorry, but I have to handle this. How would you like to tour the clubhouse with John? Maybe take a golf lesson? If I'm not back in an hour, he'll take you to the hotel."

His suggestion made sense, but something in his expression made her feel like the girl in Berkeley who had thrived on adventure. "I'll go with you."

"Are you sure?"

"Positive."

They said good-bye to John and returned to the SUV. As soon as Julia fastened her seat belt, Zeke zipped out of the parking lot and headed west to a fork in the road. "I'm sorry about this. If Ashley were here, you'd have her undivided attention."

"Things happen. I'm just glad it's not too serious."

"Oh, it's serious all right."

"A goat?"

"A mean goat." Zeke's jaw hardened. "Ladybug is a menace, but she's owned by Ginger Travers. Ginger keeps her because she has a calming effect on a horse named Clipper. Most people have dogs or cats for pets, but not Ginger. She adopted Clipper from a racehorse rescue opera-tion. Ladybug was part of the package."

"Cute name." Julia pictured a little white goat in the spirit of *The Three Billy Goats Gruff*, a story she occasionally read to Max. "I take it Chet isn't fond of Ladybug."

"No. And neither am I."

He made a right turn, drove up a long driveway, and parked on an apron of hard-packed dirt. A short man with a fringe of white hair under a straw cowboy hat strode toward the SUV, his bowed legs churning up dust. Zeke climbed out and so did Julia.

The cowboy, presumably Chet, tipped his hat to her but made a beeline to Zeke. "That goat leaves or I do."

"What did she do this time?"

"She ate the seats off the Gator." Chet hooked a thumb at a small utility vehicle with a flat bed, off-road tires, and two torn-up seats. "This is the *third* time."

"I know—"

"If you don't stop her, I will." The cowboy's face was as red as the bandanna hanging out of his hip pocket. "They'll be serving goat stew in that *or-ganic* restaurant of yours."

Julia traded an amused glance with Zeke. Out of respect for Chet, they both held back grins.

"So where is she?" Zeke asked.

Chet flung his gnarled hands up into the air. "If I knew where she was, I'd have her lassoed by now. No doubt she's somewhere she doesn't belong, eating everything in sight. Try that *or-ganic* garden. I have a trail ride coming in— six horses with four adults and two kids. I'm shorthanded as it is, Zeke. You know that."

"I'm working on it."

"There's no way I'm goin' on a goat hunt right

39

now. If you want Ladybug, you're gonna have to round her up yourself."

Zeke lowered his chin. "I get it, Chet."

The old cowboy didn't seem to hear him. "I don't give a rip who that nasty thing belongs to. Ginger Travers or the president of United States, or John Wayne himself. That old thing—"

"Chet. I get it. That's enough."

"Sorry, boss." The cowboy turned to Julia and tipped his hat. "And apologies to you too, miss. But that goat gets on my last nerve."

As he stalked off, Zeke gave Julia a rueful look. "This isn't the side of Caliente Springs we usually show to guests."

"No points off. I promise."

A familiar twinkle returned to his eyes—the one that looked into her heart and read her thoughts. Six years had passed, six years full of tragedy and triumphs, and yet they were still attuned to each other's feelings. One side of Zeke's mouth hooked into a grin, a sign that he remembered too. It didn't seem possible, but she was close to choking up with the sweetness of it.

Swallowing hard, she pushed her emotions back into her chest. "Can I help you look for Ladybug?"

Zeke shook his head. "You're here for a business presentation, not a hike around barns and corrals. I'll take you back to the hotel."

"You'll lose time. I'll wait in the car."

40

"Are you sure?"

"Positive. I'll check messages on my phone."

Zeke helped her into the SUV, gave her his cell number in case she needed him, then strode past a row of covered stalls, dust puffing under his black oxfords. Even in a suit, he looked like he belonged here.

That was Zeke. Comfortable in his own skin. In charge. And ready to fight for a good cause.

Julia picked up the phone and shot a text to Ashley. Hugs to you & Rachel. Single moms unite!

Next she texted her mother. How's it going? Love to you and Max.

Waiting for replies, she relaxed against the seat and closed her eyes. The smells of hay, horses, and summer filled her nose, and she dragged in a lungful of warm air. It felt good to let her guard down for a moment.

Her phone signaled a text. Expecting her mom or Ashley, she lifted it off her lap, saw Hunter's name, and sighed. The message started with a link to the Encino Hills Academy, the private school they had discussed for Max and the school Hunter attended as a boy. Julia didn't like the idea, in part because Hunter would use the high tuition to manipulate her. She wanted to send Max to the school run by her church, where he'd be with his friends. It was accredited and considered excellent.

The rest of the text said, School meeting. Monday at 9. Can you make it? Need to know now.

As if she had no other obligations! She needed to submit the Carter proposal before Tuesday and was planning to spend Monday at her computer. A playdate for Max was already arranged. Hunter's presumption galled her, but the text was typical of the conflicts that came with co-parenting. His way or her way? What was best for Max, and how did she measure it?

Before she could decide, something slammed into the back of the SUV.

Her gaze swung to the side mirror, where a large brown goat, presumably Ladybug, stared back at her. The goat was about the size of a Great Dane, silky brown with patches of white, and eyes the exact the color of her coat. Two short horns curved back on the top of her head, and a pair of long, floppy ears grazed her rhinestone collar.

Julia called Zeke on his cell. "Unless you have more than one brown goat, Ladybug just butted the car."

"I'm on my way."

With Julia watching in the mirror, Ladybug veered to the right and trotted toward the long driveway. "Uh-oh. She's leaving."

"Which direction?"

"Down the driveway."

"I'll hurry, but I'm almost at the garden."

Julia climbed out of the SUV and slammed the door. "She's headed toward a storage shed. I'll follow her."

"Don't. She's dangerous."

"I'll keep my distance." With the phone to her ear, she followed Ladybug, narrating her progress to Zeke as she trailed the goat for about fifty feet. "She stopped at a hedge of some kind."

"Julia, I mean it. Stay back."

"Don't worry. I will." She could run in her heels if she had to, but why take that chance? "She's eating leaves off the hedge."

"Good. I'm almost there."

"Oh dear."

"What?"

"She's looking right at me." Julia backpedaled a few steps. "She's coming this way." At a trot . . . an enthusiastic trot, with her eyes glued to the shiny gold buttons on Julia's dress. "I'm going back to the car." She turned and walked as fast as she could, keeping the phone to her ear as she glanced over her shoulder. "My word! She's fast."

"Hurry, Jules. Get to the car."

Ladybug bleated repeatedly, like a freight train working up speed. Julia's breath came in matching pants that carried over the phone.

"Julia. Talk to me."

"I'm—I'm running."

Zeke muttered something Julia couldn't hear.

"She's gaining on me!"

43

The SUV was just ten steps away. Then nine, eight. With her eyes focused on the door handle, Julia lowered the phone and made a final sprint. Ladybug bleated behind her. Just as Julia grabbed for the door handle, the goat snagged a mouthful of fabric and tugged. As the dress ripped, Julia spun and lost her grip on her phone. It flew up in an arc, sparkled in the sun, and landed at Ladybug's cloven hooves.

Julia dove for it but fell short. On her hands and knees, she crawled forward, eye-to-eye with Ladybug as the goat snatched up the phone and crunched down on it.

"Bad goat!"

"Maaaah. Maa—AAAH!" Ladybug screamed at her, sounding more like a person than an animal. Julia had never heard anything like it.

She leapt to her feet, dashed to the front of the SUV, and scrambled onto the hood, losing her shoes as she climbed. Ladybug snagged one of them, worked her jaw a couple of times, then spat out the leather and bellowed at the top of her lungs.

"Julia!" Zeke was running at full speed, his coat flapping behind him and his eyes full of determination to save her. "Are you all right?"

"That goat ate my phone!"

"Don't move. I'll get her."

Julia hoped he lived to tell the story and pulled her feet all the way up onto the hood of the SUV.

Zeke snapped some leaves off a shrub, then approached Ladybug with a gold lamé leash hidden behind his back. The goat stared at him with an air of superiority, bleated once as if to scold him, then walked docilely toward him and nibbled the leaves.

"Good girl." Zeke reached for the collar, but Ladybug twisted away from him, spat out the leaves, and grabbed the flap of his coat instead. Legs splayed, she tugged with all her might.

"Hey—" He tried to pull the coat out of her mouth, but Ladybug pulled harder. The fabric let loose with a long, slow rip. Muttering to himself, he grabbed her collar and hooked the leash into place. Ladybug stepped back as far as the short line would allow, but Zeke, now looking at Julia, kept a grip on the handle. "I've got her. It's safe."

Julia wasn't so sure. Ladybug had circled behind him. Head down, she took aim at his backside. "Zeke! Watch out—"

Whump!

His hands shot out to break the fall, but he still landed on his belly in the dirt. Muttering and sputtering, he managed to hold on to the leash as he lumbered to his feet. Dust was everywhere— on his chin, his face, all over his pants and the torn coat.

"Oh no!" Julia cried. "Are you all right?"

"Just another day on the job," Zeke deadpanned. When Ladybug let out another man-killer

45

scream, Zeke broke out laughing, and so did Julia. She laughed so hard her ribs ached and tears pushed into her eyes. Those tears were born of more than laughter; they sprang from the desire to live life to the fullest. Deep down, in the most tender part of her heart, she longed for more moments like this one, where she could be herself with a man who knew how to love and laugh. She yearned for that kind of relationship, but she was terrified of repeating her mistakes. A lump shoved into her throat, a plug that bottled up her crazy, confused feelings.

Zeke gave Ladybug a very dirty look, then wiped the dust off his coat and shortened the leash. Ladybug's screams dwindled to pathetic bleats.

"She nailed you," Julia said with a big grin.

He just shook his head. "When you write up the Carter proposal, make sure you include goat hunting as a new sport."

"Oh, I will."

Their eyes met, his twinkling and hers too, until he broke the silence. "I'm going to tie her up. Stay put."

"No problem!"

Zeke led Ladybug to a split rail fence and tied the leash in a knot. The goat protested with more pitiful bleats, then discovered some weeds and snagged a mouthful.

Zeke strode back to Julia. She scooted to the

edge of the hood, but when she reached for his hand, her silky dress glided over the paint and she picked up speed. Instinctively she grasped his shoulders. Gripping her waist, he lifted her up and spun her around until she landed gently on the ground and stepped back.

Their gazes matched and held for what felt like six years. She recalled walking down Telegraph Avenue, where sidewalk vendors and street people made every day a circus. She'd been so full of big ideas back then. More than anything, she had valued personal freedom and self-definition. Zeke, far more pragmatic, had majored in business.

"Why not religion?" she had asked him once.

"I'm a preacher's kid. I've read the Bible my whole life. With a business degree, I can bring some practical know-how to a church or a ministry like my dad's. That's what I was born to do."

But here he was now, at a resort that didn't look anything like a church. There was a story there, but if she asked him about it, she'd have to tell her own. It was best to stick to business.

Cramming the past back into its proper place, she offered a wry smile. "I guess this ends the tour."

"For today, yes. But I hope Ladybug didn't scare you off completely."

"No." She glanced down at her torn dress flapping at her knees, then remembered—"My phone!" She spun around, spotted the device ten feet away, and hurried across the rough ground. Her bare foot found a rock. Yelping, she hopped on one leg until she lost her balance.

Zeke grabbed her arm, steadied her, then picked up the phone and inspected it front and back. "The screen's cracked, but the SIM card might be all right."

"I hope so." Julia needed her business contacts, but mostly she wanted the countless photographs of Max.

Zeke dropped the phone in his pocket. "The hotel will replace it along with your dress and shoes. Did Ladybug get anything else?"

"That's all."

Zeke collected the shoes and handed them to her. "I'll cut a check for the clothing. But you need the phone now. How about a trip to San Luis Obispo?"

"Hmmm."

"We can grab dinner away from the hotel."

The trip would be private and personal. Just them, the past six years, and the things she didn't want to tell him about Hunter. She didn't want to risk that conversation, but she needed her phone. She tried to say yes, but all she could manage was another indecisive "Hmmm."

Zeke waited a moment. "Was that yes or no?"

"Both."

Something bright flashed in his eyes. "You

always did confuse me, Jules."

Especially at the end, when she broke off their relationship with vague allusions to needing emotional space instead of the truth that she had started to date Hunter. "I was confused about a lot of things back then."

"So let's be confused at the Apple Store." He held up the phone to show her the cracked screen. "My goat just ate your phone. I owe you a new one, plus an upgrade for your time and trouble."

She owed Zeke too—gratitude for his prayers six years ago, amends for her arrogant attitude at the time, and maybe a confession about Hunter, though she wasn't sure about that last item. "All right. We'll go."

He raised the radio to his dusty face. "GM calling Cowboy."

Static crackled until Chet answered. "Cowboy here."

"Ladybug's in custody."

"Well, hoop-dee-doo," Chet grumbled, "but I can't fetch her right this minute."

"I'll put her in her pen." Zeke signed off and lowered the handheld radio. "I'll take care of Ladybug, then we'll go back to the hotel, clean up, and head out."

Julia climbed into the SUV to wait, drumming her fingers as Zeke coaxed Ladybug to follow him. While he was gone, she made plans. When she reached her room, she'd call her mom from the hotel and give her Zeke's cell in case of an emergency.

Hunter presented a different problem. He was waiting for an answer to the school question, but Julia wasn't ready to commit to anything. She didn't want to annoy Hunter, but sometimes life happened. For once, he would just have to wait.

Four

Zeke parked the SUV in his private spot behind the main hotel, took Julia to her room via a service elevator, and headed toward his office to check in with Irene before going home to change clothes. With clean Levi's and a fresh shirt, he'd be ready for the trip to San Luis Obispo.

And dinner with Jules.

She was a lot more than an old friend. He had loved her enough to consider marriage, though he had struggled terribly with the differences in their worldviews. Those differences didn't matter to him now. When it came to Christianity, Zeke considered himself a has-been. He had tried his best to be a model Christian in college, but somehow he could never work hard enough or love God enough. Even now, an admonition from his father played through his brain. *"Son, if you love Jesus as much as I think you do, you won't let Him down. We obey Him because we love Him."*

But Zeke had failed to obey, first by dating Julia, a non-Christian, then by sliding down a slippery slope that had ended in her bed. After that, rebellion set in and he stopped trying so hard. Did that mean he didn't love God enough? What did a man do when he tried his best and failed, or when he was so sick of *trying* he couldn't stand to open his Bible or even pray?

Zeke didn't want to think about those things right now. Frowning slightly, he strode through the door to his office.

Irene turned from the computer and gaped at him. "What happened to you?"

"Ladybug."

A rumbling chuckle, the one made famous by George Travers, came from behind him. "She nailed you, bro."

George stood with his thumbs hooked in his belt, one knee jutting, and a brown blazer pulled back to reveal a washboard stomach beneath a thin T-shirt. For an old guy, he was in great shape. Zeke was no slouch himself. When you ran a resort with a first-class fitness center, you used it.

He offered his hand to George. "It's good to see you. What's up?"

"A wedding."

Zeke's brows shot up. "Yours?"

George snorted. "No woman in her right mind would put up with me."

"Then who?"

"A sweet little girl named Tiffany Ann Reid. Her daddy, Tom Reid, was the best friend I ever had. Ginger and I are Tiff's godparents. Tell me, Zeke, have you ever made a promise to a dying man?"

"No." Unless he counted the promise he had made to his father a month before the plane crash. *"All right, Dad. I'll go back to church."* But he hadn't done it, and he wouldn't. Zeke had disappointed God too many times, failed too profoundly and too often—and too willingly—to pretend he was someone he wasn't.

George stood ramrod straight. "Tom died of leukemia. Before he passed, I promised him I'd keep an eye on Tiff. Her mom is gone too."

"I'm sorry."

George wiped a guitar-calloused hand through his iron-gray hair. "She just got engaged to a kid named Derek. Ginger and I don't see eye-to-eye on a lot of things, but we both want to give Tiff a real wedding."

Zeke turned to Irene. "Looks like you'll be busy when you get back from medical leave."

A skeptical hum came from her lips. "We'll see."

"You *are* coming back, right?" Zeke couldn't afford to lose her, not with Caliente Springs struggling like a dinosaur in a tar pit.

Irene reassured him with a smile. "I'll definitely be back. Just not in time for the wedding."

George put his hands on his hips. "Irene already heard the story. Let's give her ears a rest and talk in your office."

Zeke led the way down the hall, ushered George inside, and went to the mini-fridge. The fridge was well stocked with soft drinks, water, and liquor for guests who imbibed. "How about something to drink?"

George grunted. "You know I gave that up."

"The whole world knows. I was offering you a Coke."

"I'll take it."

He handed an icy can to George, chose water for himself, and guzzled half the bottle. The chair creaked as he sat. "So tell me about this wedding."

"Here's the thing." George steepled his fingers over his chest. "Like Irene said, Tiff's in a hurry."

"Pregnant?"

"No. Just young and in love. Her boyfriend's in the Coast Guard. He's leaving for Alaska in a month."

"A month?" Stunned, Zeke lowered his chin. "Are you saying what I think you are?"

"Yep."

"You want us to put on a wedding in less than thirty days?"

"Yes, sir. I do."

"How many guests?" Maybe it was small.

"Up to five hundred."

"*What?*"

"You heard me." George reclined back in the chair, his shoulders relaxed while he tapped his fingers together. "I promised Tiff I'd stand in for her daddy, and she wants a wedding with all the bells and whistles. Ice sculptures. A fancy dinner. Dancing, but don't worry about that. I've got the band covered."

"You're crazy." Not that being crazy mattered to

54

George. His pre-sobriety stories made Zeke laugh until his sides hurt or put painful lumps in his throat. Somehow it was all the same with George. "A month isn't much time for people to plan. What about invitations?"

"Tiff's making calls as we speak. Formal invitations can go out a little later."

Was a huge, high-class wedding even possible on such short notice? The hotel was only moderately booked, but accommodations for another five hundred people? Plus the wedding itself. Mentally he ran through a list of banquet rooms and ceremony sites, catering options, staff requirements, flower suppliers, and a dozen other needs.

It wasn't the first time he'd been asked to stretch his resources. As general manager, he led a staff of approximately two hundred people, including a tier of high-level managers directly below him, several salaried administrators, and hourly employees like maids, clerks, and grounds crew. But like most businesses in tough economic times, the employees, including Zeke, were already working at maximum capacity.

On the other hand, George was his boss and a good friend. "I'll make it work. I don't know exactly how, but we have a good team."

"I admit it's a tall order, but you know what the Good Book says. All things are possible with God."

Zeke didn't want to hear about God, especially from George. With nine years of sobriety and the bold declaration that Jesus Christ was his Lord and Savior, George lived with a freedom Zeke didn't understand. The singer cussed now and then, lost his temper in traffic, made sarcastic remarks, and didn't give a rip what people thought of him. At least most people. There were some men in George's life, like the chaplain at Home and Hearth, who'd been known to rein him in.

To Zeke, a kid who'd been taught that his behavior was his witness, George's flagrant humanity mixed with his bold faith was confusing. So was his trust that God ordered his steps like David described in the Psalms. In Zeke's experience, God expected a man to pick up his cross and carry it until he dropped from exhaustion.

Needing to clear his mind, he took a long swallow of water, then set the bottle down on the desk. "Let's leave God out of this."

"Fine. Suit yourself." George let the challenge hang in the air. He and Zeke had this conversation frequently, and it always ended the same way—with Zeke irritable and George quiet.

Nonplussed as usual, George tossed a scrap of paper down on the desk.

Zeke saw Tiff's name and number, and put them in his phone. "I'll call her first thing in the morning."

"Good, because there's a little more at stake than a nice wedding for a sweet girl."

With George, surprises were never good. Zeke froze with his phone in hand. "What is it?"

"Ginger has a stake in this too. She and Tiff's mom were thick as thieves. Bev is gone now, and Ginger's like a second mom to Tiff." George's eyes glinted. "Bev hated me."

"Great."

"I don't blame her." George chugged the last of the Coke, crumpled the empty can, and tossed it in the trash. "I was a bad influence on Tom."

Zeke could imagine.

"So here's the deal. Ginger doesn't think we can pull this thing off. I told her we could, and she and I reached an agreement. If Tiff's wedding is spectacular enough, Ginger will give up the notion of selling Caliente Springs."

"Why?"

"Because she's a good businesswoman. If you can pull this off, word will spread that we're a premier place for weddings, and business will pick up. At least that's the hope. Deep down, Ginger loves this place as much as I do. She doesn't really want to sell. She just wants to stop losing money."

Zeke dragged his hand over his dusty neck. "I wish you'd just buy her out."

"I can't. The money's not there." George's music still sold but not like it used to. And he still performed, but in small venues instead of arenas. Years of hard living and hard drinking had taken a toll on his bank account, though he sobered up before he lost everything. He was more than comfortable, just not rolling in dough like Garth Brooks.

Zeke kept his voice even. "So we pull off the wedding or lose Caliente Springs."

"Exactly." Leaning back, George laced his hands behind his head and stretched. "Hire a wedding planner, someone who knows the ropes."

Julia's face flashed in Zeke's mind. With a flick of his wrist, he woke up his computer, went to the Dare to Dream website, and angled it so George could see a slide show of wedding images, along with Julia's name prominently displayed on the bottom of the screen. "What do you think?"

George watched a few frames and grunted. "All that froufrou looks alike to me. Who's Julia Dare, and how do you know her?"

"We were friends in college. Now she's an event planner, and she happens to be here on other business."

"Hire her."

"Maybe." Zeke clicked through another wedding album. The photos looked great, but pictures could be deceiving.

"The way I see it, God just tossed you a life rope."

It was just like George to give God credit for a

coincidence. Zeke turned from the computer. "I'll talk to her."

George pulled his six-foot-five frame to its full height. "How about dinner? We can throw some steaks on the grill and shoot some pool." He lived in the Travers family mansion located behind the same gate that guarded the cottages. With six bedrooms, five baths, a swimming pool, and some of the oldest trees on the property, the house was George's personal oasis, though he shared it with Ginger when she visited.

"It's tempting," Zeke said. "But I can't."

"So what's up?"

Zeke told him about the Ladybug incident. "I'm taking Julia to get a new phone. The drive will give me a chance to find out more about her wedding experience."

"Sounds like good timing." George rapped his knuckles on the desk. "I'm outta here. We'll cook those steaks another time."

"Sure. How long are you staying?"

"Just tonight. I leave tomorrow for a show in Reno."

"That reminds me." Zeke opened a desk drawer, lifted out one of George's 8x10 publicity photos, and slid it across the desk. "Julia's mom is a fan. How about an autograph?"

"My pleasure." George selected a Sharpie from the cup on Zeke's desk. "What's her name?"

"Ellen."

"You know her?"

"We met when Jules and I were dating." Zeke liked Ellen a lot, in part because she and Julia were a lot alike. "She's a widow now. Her husband died in the middle of Julia's senior year."

George scrawled out a few lines, signed his name, and capped the pen. "If you knew this girl's mom, it must have been serious."

"Yes and no."

"What kind of answer is that?"

The same kind Julia gave him back at the stable. "We were serious, but neither of us expected it to last. It didn't. End of story."

"I don't think so."

"What do you mean?"

"I can see that gleam in your eyes." George paused. "I might even say . . . she's got your goat."

Zeke groaned. "That was awful."

"Yeah, but someone had to say it."

It was time for payback. Zeke put his hands on his hips and rocked back. "It figures it would be an old goat like you."

George roared with laughter. "You win, Zeke. And right now, this old goat needs to hit the road."

Zeke stole a glance at the clock. He had thirty-six minutes before he was supposed to meet Jules. If he hurried, he could make it with five seconds to spare. "I'll let you know what Julia says about the wedding."

"Sounds good."

The instant George left, Zeke hurried home. Feeling a little like Superman ducking into a phone booth, he changed clothes in record time, sped back to the hotel, and knocked on Julia's door, all with a minute to spare.

Five

Three hours after the debacle with Ladybug, Julia walked out of the Apple Store with Zeke at her side, the latest iPhone in her hand, and a smile on her face. The new phone was fully restored from the undamaged SIM card, partially charged, and protected by a shock-proof OtterBox case.

While slipping the phone into her purse, she stepped with Zeke to the curb of the busy parking lot. "Thanks. I'm back in business."

When a car whizzed past them, he rested his hand lightly on her back to guide her away from it. "The drive here wasn't bad either. It gave me a chance to sell you on Caliente Springs."

"Which you did. Thoroughly."

The decision to recommend Caliente Springs over the other resorts she had visited turned out to be easy. Zeke's passion for the hotel and its guests impressed her, and it was perfect for both a large conference and employee vacations. The next step was for Julia to meet with Ashley tomorrow as planned to discuss details like meeting rooms and menus. Next, she'd email her recommendation to Mr. Carter. If he liked what he read, he and his wife would visit CS themselves.

Thinking of the Carters, she tipped her head up to Zeke. "Do you play golf?"

"Badly. Why?"

"You should brush up. Mr. Carter will want to play at least a few rounds."

Zeke winced as he opened her door. "I'm taking lessons from John, but right now I'm awful at it."

"You'll get better." When he grimaced, she punched his arm. "Look at the bright side. You get to wear plaid pants."

"Lucky me."

Chuckling, she climbed into the SUV. Zeke was rounding the hood when her phone signaled yet another text from Hunter. Earlier, when the Apple guy handed her the phone, she checked quickly for messages and saw three from him, each more curt than the last. She sympathized with his desire to pin down a time for the school meeting, but she couldn't finalize the schedule until she checked with her mom. That call needed to wait.

As Zeke opened his door, she tapped a quick text to Hunter. Can't talk. Will call tonight. Then she slipped the phone into her purse.

Zeke turned the ignition and rolled down the windows just the way she liked. "Now that you're back in business, I'd like to talk to you about another possible job for Dare to Dream."

"Sure." Her phone dinged again. This time she ignored it. "What's up?"

"A big wedding at the resort." He hesitated. "It's complicated, and with Irene out, I'm looking for someone to coordinate it." After a glance in the rearview mirror, he backed out of the space. "I thought we could discuss it over dinner."

A pleasant warmth rippled through her, but she hesitated. Dinner would lead to those personal questions she wanted to avoid. On the other hand, she enjoyed Zeke's company, and he'd said the magic word to an event planner: *wedding*. When her stomach rumbled, the scales tipped. "Dinner would be nice."

"So what sounds good?"

Before she could answer, her phone signaled another text. Frowning, she checked it and saw Hunter's ID. Again? Seriously? Trying not to grimace, she texted back, LATER.

Zeke paused with his foot on the brake. "I know you have a business to run. If you need to take care of that, go ahead."

"It can wait."

"Whatever you need to do. I understand being on call." Zeke braked at the parking lot driveway and signaled a left turn. "How does Mexican sound?"

"Great."

"Formal or casual?"

"Casual."

Zeke smiled at her in that familiar way. "I knew you'd say that."

She smiled back, her pulse thrumming with a little too much pleasure for a business meeting, but just the right amount for a woman enjoying the company of an old friend.

Zeke steered into the afternoon traffic, thick with commuters and students from the university. "If you're up for a drive, there's a taco stand at the Pismo Beach Pier. The food's super spicy. You'll love it."

He would know. In Berkeley, she had fussed all the time about the bland Mexican food in the Bay Area. "That sounds good."

"So tell me about Dare to Dream." He kept his eyes on the road. "How long have you been in business?"

Julia relaxed against the leather seat. "I started it a few months ago with help from my mom. She runs a flower shop now and works with me on the side. We plan weddings, conferences, family reunions, anything that needs coordinating. I love it."

Zeke made a right turn onto a four-lane highway that headed toward the sinking sun. "It's not easy to get a business on its feet."

"No."

"How big is your client base?"

"Not big, but we're working on it. My mom's shop has a great reputation and a solid customer base. That gives us some exposure in the wedding market, and she's not shy about telling people about Dare to Dream. Mr. Carter, for instance. He's a family friend. And I—" She hesitated. "I have some contacts of my own." *Through Hunter.* She'd done some event planning for his law firm.

"What made you go into business for yourself?"

"The need to eat?"

"That works." He maneuvered around a lumbering RV and settled into a faster speed in the left lane. "When we left Berkeley, you were planning to work for a year, then go to grad school."

Julia stiffened. Those plans had changed because of Hunter. "That's right."

"Did you go?"

"No."

Zeke didn't know anything about that year, because he had been in Chile. The few emails they'd exchanged were short, until she stopped answering altogether, mostly because she didn't want Zeke to know about her relationship with Hunter. In Berkeley, the two men had clashed badly.

"What changed your mind?" Zeke asked.

Hunter. He'd been in his last year at Boalt, the UC Berkeley School of Law. Somehow her ambitions had been absorbed into his, though at the time she didn't realize it.

Zeke was waiting for an answer. All she could do was shrug. "I just lost interest."

"It happens. So what did you do then?"

"I stayed in Berkeley for a while and worked as

a checker at a grocery store. It wasn't glamorous, but it paid the rent."

"What about St. John's? Did you stay involved?"

Her breath ballooned in her lungs, as if she were with Zeke in the St. John's parking lot, watching him play basketball with the boys who gathered at the portable hoop. Most of the time she just watched and cheered, but one day he was in his office and worried about something. She had grabbed the basketball and said, *"Let's play."* They hadn't kissed at that point. But after the game, he took her out for a milkshake. They had talked for three hours, and when he walked her back to her car, he kissed her for the first time.

"Julia?"

Warmth shot to her cheeks. "Sorry. My mind wandered."

"St. John's? Did you visit?"

"No. I thought about it, but I never did."

"Me either."

His voice came out rough, like hers. They sat in silence for a quarter mile, both staring through the windshield.

Zeke broke the silence first. "What did you do next?"

"I moved back to Los Angeles." First to her mother's house, then in with Hunter. She'd been in love with him then, and in spite of twinges of doubt about their relationship, she had chosen to go with the flow and let Hunter set the course.

She hadn't meant to move in with him, but her possessions migrated one by one to his condo. After a year, she changed her address on her driver's license.

"What did you do before Dare to Dream?"

He was interviewing her for a job, but their history meant she needed to include more detail without being too personal. "I planned campaign events for a mayoral candidate." Hunter's father had pulled strings to get her the job. "Over the course of the campaign, I arranged everything from fundraisers to rallies to thousand-dollar-a-plate dinners. Unfortunately, the candidate lost."

"Too bad."

"If he'd won, I'd be working in the mayor's office." Instead she had hit the pavement with her résumé, found nothing, and been criticized by Hunter for not making more contacts of her own.

Zeke pushed his sunglasses higher on his nose. "What did you do after the campaign?"

Got pregnant by accident. Cried in my mom's kitchen. But that had come later. "I talked to a couple of headhunters, but they weren't interested. I needed to do something, so I worked as a temp."

"Admin stuff?"

"Everything." She rattled off the computer programs she knew. "When it comes to office work, I'm a Jill-of-all-trades."

"That's an asset in my book." He drummed his fingers lightly on the steering wheel. "Back to

Dare to Dream. How many weddings have you planned now?"

"Just three." Four if she counted the one for herself that didn't happen. "I love weddings. Big or small, it doesn't matter as long as the day is special to the bride and groom."

"Tell me about the biggest one you've done."

Julia grinned at the memory of Mark and Gina, a couple in their thirties with the money to splurge. "We started with a terrific venue, a 1940s mansion in Pasadena." The place she had picked for herself and Hunter. "The bride and groom loved old movies, so we went with a classic Hollywood theme, an evening ceremony, and spotlights to create the atmosphere of a movie premiere. It was a lot of fun."

"How many guests?"

"Around two hundred." To Julia, that was huge. "Mark and Gina wanted it casual with lots of dancing, so we served buffet style. No wedding is perfect, but this one was close."

"So what was the glitch?"

"You mean glitch*es*." Julia could smile now, but it wasn't funny at the time. "The flower girl helped herself to her mom's lipstick. Bright red, of course. That was a mess, but it wasn't as bad as what the groom's dog did."

"Oh no."

"Yep. Right in the aisle."

Zeke winced, but his eyes were twinkling.

"No dogs at this wedding. At least that I know of."

"And no goats, I hope."

"No goats. That's a promise."

A chuckle spilled from her lips. As different as she and Zeke had been in college, somehow they saw humor in the same things. Apparently they still did. Julia blew out a small breath. "The lipstick mess and the dog were trouble at the time, but those are the best stories. Now Mark and Gina laugh about it."

Someday, maybe she'd laugh at her own wedding in that way. But that day was far away, if it ever happened all.

Five minutes after they arrived in the town of Pismo Beach, a grid of narrow streets lined with restaurants, tourist traps, art galleries, and specialty shops, Zeke bought tacos from an outdoor stand. With Julia holding the soft drinks, he led the way to a south-facing bench on the pier, and they sat. So far, he liked what he was hearing about Dare to Dream and hoped Julia would be interested in planning Tiff's wedding.

Julia was on her third bite when her phone chirped with a text. Grimacing, she set the taco on the orange grease paper, wiped her fingers, and tapped out a reply.

Zeke didn't mind waiting. In fact, it felt good to soak in the fading sun. Below them, the pylons creaked with the slosh and roll of waves. To his left, an Asian woman was fishing with a friend, chattering in the singsong cadence of her native tongue. Zeke wasn't on speaking terms with God, but he still relished the majesty of a beautiful sunset.

The breeze lifted Julia's hair. The six years since Berkeley had softened her face, and her body too. Everything about her was somehow fuller than he remembered, as if she had ripened like a grape on a vine. They were different people now, but Julia was even more beautiful to him. What that meant, Zeke didn't know. But he was willing, even eager, to give those old sparks a chance to rekindle.

Julia sent the text, picked up her taco, and finished it. "We were talking about your need for a wedding planner. I'm definitely interested. When is the big day?"

"September twenty-second."

"Next year?"

"No. Next month."

Her brows shot up. "That's"—she counted on her fingers—"four weeks and two days. It must be small."

"No."

"How many guests?"

"Up to five hundred."

She gaped at him. "How is that even possible? Wedding venues like Caliente Springs are booked a year in advance."

"I wish we were. The resort has had some tough times. We're older. Out of date. We're not on the cutting edge, but I'm hoping to change that. This wedding could put us on the map."

"But five hundred people in a month?" She shook her head like a doctor giving grim news. "You know that's insane, don't you?"

"It is, but there's a lot at stake." Between bites, he told her about George's promise to Tiff, Ginger's involvement as a stand-in for Tiff's mom, and the resort's financial woes. "If I don't pull off this wedding, there's a good chance CS will end up on the chopping block. I love my job, but what's even more important are the two hundred people depending on me. We're like family."

She stared down the coastline again, her thoughts hidden until she shook her head. "I'd like to help, but—"

Her phone interrupted for the second time in five minutes. With her jaw tight, she mumbled an apology, rushed a reply, and took a breath before facing him. "Where were we?"

"You were about to turn me down." And he couldn't let that happen. "Do you have other commitments?"

"A few, including Carter Home Goods. But that's not the problem. I live three hours away. My contacts are all in Los Angeles."

"Mine aren't."

She blinked a couple of times. "You mean the hotel."

"Exactly." He raised one hand and counted off the benefits. "Catering. A choice of beautiful sites for the ceremony. An in-house florist. A staff at your beck and call."

"Hmmm."

"The big pieces are in place, but I need someone who can coordinate the flow. Plus, you have to get along with Ginger and George."

"And Tiff. Don't forget the bride."

"See? You're helping me already." Just like she had helped him at St. John's with paper work and grant proposals. "I really do need your expertise. About compensation—what do you charge?"

She gave him a *you're crazy* look. "For a massive wedding in a month? A million dollars."

"Done."

"In that case, sign me up." She bumped his ribs with her elbow as if they were in college again. "Being serious here, my fee for a wedding with over a hundred guests is fifteen percent of the total cost."

"George can handle that."

"I haven't said yes."

"No, but you want to." He needed to sweeten the pot. An idea hit him that seemed perfect, especially with Julia's background as a temp. He stood and faced her with his hands laced behind his back. "Let's negotiate."

73

"I don't think—"

"Hear me out." He kept his voice light. "With Irene on leave, I need an assistant, and you have all the right skills. How about this: You plan Tiff's wedding *and* fill in for Irene. You can work on the Carter account for Dare to Dream, plus I'll throw in a suite for the duration of your stay."

Julia gawked at him, her mouth agape. "I have to admit, it's tempting."

"So what's stopping you?"

"It's a wonderful offer, Zeke. But . . ." She drew in a long breath as if to steel herself. "I can't just pack up and move for a month. I have a son."

"Wow." That was all he could say. *Jules with a child.* He hadn't considered that possibility. Surprised but not shocked, he dropped back down on the bench.

She scooted a few inches away. "His name is Max. He's four. His father and I weren't married. That's over now."

She held his gaze, but a haunted light filled her eyes. Did she think he'd throw stones at her for having a son outside of marriage? In the past, he might have. But not anymore. He'd lost the right to feel superior to anyone, especially her. "Jules, I—"

"Don't say anything yet." The breeze caught her hair and lifted it away from her face. "I don't want to talk about Max's father, but there's something else you deserve to know."

His imagination drew a complete blank. "What is it?"

"I'm a Christian now."

"A *Christian?*"

"Yes." Her hands finally unknotted, and she sat back as if a weight had been lifted. "Kind of a surprise, huh?"

A big one. Zeke dragged his hand through his hair. "Wow," he said again.

"I feel the same way."

"I bet."

"It's a long story, and I don't want to tell it right this minute. But I need to thank you for the things you said to me back in Berkeley, and for praying for me. I argued with you at the time. I'm sorry now—for everything. I think you know what I mean."

Memories crashed down on him. That night in his apartment. The vanilla candle burning in the smoky dark. The agony of fighting temptation until he just couldn't fight anymore. He had resisted making love to her as long as he could, but in the end, nature was just too strong, or his faith too weak. Or maybe God was just too demanding.

The old anger boiled up in him. Struggling to compose himself, he pushed off the bench and strode to the railing.

Julia's steps hammered behind him. "Zeke, I—I don't know what to say. This is—I didn't plan— It just—"

He broke out laughing. Not at her, but at the irony of their present circumstances. Julia was full of life and hope. And Zeke was . . . he didn't know exactly. Backslidden? Burned out? Weakwilled and unworthy? All of the above, he decided. They had flip-flopped. But she didn't know it, and he didn't want to tell her.

"Jules, forget it."

"But—"

Turning, he took her hands in his and peered into her eyes. "The honest truth is, I don't regret a thing. What happened between us was my choice as much as it was yours. A man never forgets that first time, and he sure doesn't resent the woman who gave it to him."

"Oh." She blinked a couple of times. "But you're a Christian, the strongest one I know. You were waiting for marriage. I took something special from you without knowing the value of it."

"Jules. Drop it." He let go of her hands.

"You're upset."

"A little." No, a lot. The war between the Christian man he had tried to be and the flesh-and-blood man he really was had turned him inside out. The war was over, his heart toward God hard and unfeeling except when someone like Jules or George hit it with a hammer. "My reaction doesn't have anything to do with you. What happened between us—*all of it*—is in the past. I think we both want to keep it there."

She nodded furiously. "Yes. Definitely."

"Good." He indicated the bench he'd been watching out of the corner of his eye. "Let's sit back down before someone swipes your purse."

"Oh!" Julia spun around. "I can't believe I left it."

He guided her back, and they sat in the same places but farther apart. Zeke draped one foot over his knee and deliberately wiped his mind clean.

"Going back to the job offer. It still stands."

Julia shook her head. "I can't do it. Not with Max. My mom watches him for me."

"So bring them."

"Really?"

"Sure. Why not?" Zeke liked kids. "The hotel has a lot of activities for children. The three of you can stay in one of the cottages."

"Are you *serious?*"

Four of the five cottages were empty now and likely to stay that way. "Yes, I'm very serious."

Suddenly a cat meowed . . . in Julia's purse. Zeke didn't mind unique ringtones, but he was tired of her phone interrupting them. Judging by Julia's frown, the person texting had decided to call. She was probably dealing with a bridezilla of a client.

"Sorry. I have to take this." She snatched up the phone and walked away. When the phone meowed a second time, the breeze muted the cat sound but not the angry thump of Julia's steps.

Zeke used the moment to check his own phone for messages. Nothing needed a quick reply, so he put it away and watched Julia pace along the railing, the phone to her ear and her thumb hooked in her back pocket. When she pivoted, he saw the furious slant of her brow. A client wouldn't do that to her, but something personal might, like a Godzilla of a boyfriend. Because of the ringtone, Zeke dubbed the guy Catman.

The wind calmed, and the flags stopped snapping in the breeze. Silence engulfed him until Julia hissed into the phone. "I told you. I'll call you tonight. . . . Yes. School is important. I get it."

School. Zeke added Max's father to the list of possible monsters blowing up Julia's phone.

She ended the call but lingered at the railing. When she returned to the bench, the emotion was stripped from her face. Zeke handed her the Styrofoam cup of Sprite.

"Thanks." She sat and took a long sip through the straw. "Sorry for the interruption."

"Are you all right?"

"I'm fine."

"You look a little rattled."

She took another sip of the drink. "It was Max's dad. We don't always see eye to eye. Thanks for trying to help, but I don't want to talk about him."

Neither did Zeke. In his opinion, Catman

was a first-class jerk. "Then let's talk about Tiff's wedding."

Her fingers squeezed the edge of the bench, curling until they were bone white. "I wish I could do it, Zeke. I really do. It's just—"

"Don't answer now." *Maybe* beat a flat-out *no* any day of the week. "Think about it, okay?"

"All right. I will."

Six

Julia spent the next day with Ashley. They visited an array of meeting rooms, discussed scheduling options, and considered different meal plans. The accounting department crunched some numbers, and Julia spent the evening in her room, working on the proposal for Mr. Carter.

Zeke called once to check on her, but the conversation was all business. She didn't see him again, but on the morning of her last day at Caliente Springs, a concierge delivered a package to her room. It held a check to cover the cost of the dress and shoes and an autographed picture of George Travers doffing a black cowboy hat. Zeke's note read: *It was great to see you again. Give my best to your mom.* He signed it with a "Z" just like he used to sign notes in college.

Julia thought about the job offer all the way home. She longed to say yes, but what about the impact on Hunter? He saw Max often and tried to be a good dad. She wanted to honor that desire, even if they disagreed on just about everything.

The last miles slid by until she steered down the off-ramp leading to her mom's house in a typical suburban neighborhood. At a red light she glanced at her phone. No messages. No calls. No word from Hunter since that awful argument on the pier.

Julia didn't regret a thing about that afternoon. Hunter needed to respect her boundaries, and telling Zeke about her faith had felt good. While talking about the past was awkward, it had to be done. If she took the job, she would tell Zeke about Hunter as soon as possible.

Home at last, she pulled into her mother's driveway. It was almost six o'clock, and she expected Max to be home from the zoo. Anticipating one of his hugs, she passed through the garage to the kitchen and set down her suitcase.

"I'm home," she called out.

No answer.

"Max?" Skimming her eyes over the empty sink and clean counters, she wondered if Max was still with Hunter. Annoyed, she plopped her purse on the table.

Her mom breezed into the kitchen. Dressed in jeans and a tailored blouse, her brown hair dyed to hide the gray, and blessed with good skin, Ellen Dare looked closer to forty than to her real age of fifty-three. "Hi, sweetheart."

They hugged quick and tight. "Where's Max?" Julia asked.

"With Hunter. They're still at the zoo."

Both women looked at the wall clock. Whenever Hunter took Max, Julia hammered down times and activities. Because of the fight on the phone, they hadn't confirmed like they usually did. For all she knew, Hunter and Max were careening around Castaic Lake on that awful speedboat.

"Did Hunter say when they'd be back?"

"No, and I didn't ask." Ellen's brows furrowed. "I thought you arranged the visit as usual."

Julia hated putting her mother in the middle. "We had a fight on the phone. I was meeting with Zeke and couldn't talk. Hunter didn't like that, and now he's not speaking to me."

"I wish—" Ellen waved her hand as if shooing a fly. "Never mind. I was about to say something unkind."

"Well, I'm already thinking it. Hunter's acting like a child."

"I wish this were simpler."

"Me too. But so far, we've worked things out."

And avoided court and custody issues. That was important to Julia. On his own, Hunter paid child support, which she tried not to need, and they arranged visits casually. So far, so good. But he was on his best behavior because he wanted her back, and Julia was trying hard not to antagonize him. A month in Caliente Springs would test their boundaries.

Eager to unpack, she reached for her suitcase and turned to her mom. "Come with me. I have a surprise for you."

"What is it?"

"You'll see."

With Ellen in her wake, Julia went to the old bedroom where she had cried over skinned knees and crushes on boys. Living at home again embarrassed her, but she was grateful for a place to heal. A little melancholy, she heaved the suitcase onto the bed, extracted the manila envelope holding George Travers' picture, and handed it to her mom. "This is for you."

Ellen slid the cardboard out of the envelope, saw the photograph, and burst out laughing. "Where did you get this?"

"George and Ginger Travers own Caliente Springs. George lives there. Zeke must have asked him for it."

Ellen looked down again, angled her head to read the autograph, and gasped. "I can't believe this."

"What does it say?"

" 'To Ellen Dare, Proverbs 3:5–6, Stay brave, George Travers.' " She looked up at Julia, a sheen bright in her hazel yes. "That's my verse. How did he know?"

"I have no idea."

Only a few people knew it, but the reference to the verse about trusting God and not one's own understanding was tattooed on Ellen's left shoulder, something she'd done in the throes of grief for her husband. What a terrible time that had been for them all—Ellen, Julia, and her older brother, Michael, a soldier stationed in Texas. Julia had offered to move back home, but her mother insisted she finish her senior year.

Zeke had tried to comfort her, but she'd been put off by his glib talk of her dad being in a better place. *"I don't want to hear about eternity. I miss my dad now."*

"I know you do, Jules. But heaven is a real place."

"You don't know that."

He had looked at her with those soulful eyes, kissed her forehead, and told her he would pray for her.

"Thanks a lot."

She didn't care about prayer at that moment. All she had wanted was to hear her father's voice one more time. That was when Hunter started joking about Zeke the Meek. To her shame, she had joined in. A few days later, she went with Hunter for coffee, then dinner, all behind Zeke's back.

Remorse crawled up her neck like a slow-moving fire. If she had listened to Zeke back in college, her life would have been far simpler. On the other hand, she wouldn't be the person she was now. And of course there was Max, the light of her life.

"Julia?" Ellen was still waiting for an answer about George's choice of Proverbs 3:5–6.

"Maybe he just likes the verse."

A silly grin spread across Ellen's face. "I used to have a terrible crush on him, but then he took that bad turn."

The entire world knew the rest of the story. The

Travers Twins broke up because of George's drinking and drug use. Ginger never performed again, but he went solo and became a platinum success. Even so, he was more famous for his womanizing, car crashes, and two trips to the Betty Ford Center. That was all nine years ago. He was sober now and a Christian.

Ellen slipped the picture back into the envelope. "This is a treasure. Thank you. And thank Zeke for me."

"I will." Julia lifted the plastic bag holding her laundry. "So what do you think of the job offer?" They had discussed it earlier on the phone.

Ellen sat on the bed. "I'm all for it. In fact, I talked to Winnie about it yesterday. She'd be glad to take over the shop for the next month."

"Really?"

"Yes, but this is your decision."

Julia dumped the dirty clothes in a laundry basket, watching them tumble while she considered the possibility. "I'd have to talk to Hunter. I don't think he'd like it."

"Probably not."

"I don't want to rock the boat, you know?" She lifted the red dress out of the suitcase and held it up to inspect the skirt. Amusing memories of Zeke and Ladybug washed over her, but the dress was beyond repair. Sighing, she set it aside and lifted out the remaining clothes. "The bottom line is Max and what's best for him."

"*And* what's best for you." Ellen's chin lifted with defiance. "You're young. You have the right to move on."

"Mom. Please. Don't go there." Julia wasn't ready to date, not even someone like Zeke, who respected her and made her laugh. Avoiding her mother's gaze, she zipped the empty suitcase.

Ellen held up her hand as if taking a vow. "I won't lecture, honey. I promise. Tell me about Zeke instead. I always did like him."

"I like him too," Julia admitted. "But just as a friend, so don't get any ideas."

"Why not?"

"I'm not ready for a relationship. And there's Max. How do I date without the risk of him becoming attached?"

"You can't," Ellen admitted. "But if you don't take a chance now and then, nothing will ever change. I miss your dad every day, but life goes on."

Julia's gaze shifted to the photograph of her parents on her nightstand, the one taken at their twentieth high school reunion. She adored that picture. "I miss Dad."

"Me too."

Julia lifted her makeup bag out of the suitcase. "You know, if I have the right to move on, so do you. Dad would want you to be happy."

"I *am* happy." Leaning back against the pillows, Ellen tucked her feet under her hips. "I have a good life. Not a single complaint—except for hot flashes and chin hairs. And those fifteen extra pounds. And while I'm at it—"

Julia laughed. "How about the fact your daughter and grandson took over your house?"

A few years ago, Ellen had converted Julia's old bedroom into an office. Now her desk and filing cabinet were crammed into the master bedroom, Max's toys were always underfoot, and last week he'd flushed a rubber whale down the toilet to watch it swim.

Ellen smiled in that calm way Julia envied. "I'm glad you're here and you know it. This house was too quiet before you came home."

"You're just saying that."

"It was. That first year without your dad was awful."

"I remember."

There had been so many questions, so many painful decisions. How much life insurance was there? Did Ellen want to stay in the house? What did they do with Dad's golf clubs? Only Julia liked the game, mostly because of the memories of lessons from her dad, but the clubs were too big for her. In the end, her brother sold them on eBay.

Ellen turned to Julia. "I survived, and you'll survive the trouble with Hunter. You just have to stay brave."

"And trust God."

"Lean on Him." Ellen tapped the shoulder with her tattoo. "Trust in Him with all of your heart."

Julia's soul fed on those words. When it came to being a Christian, she was a babe in the woods. All she could do was read her Bible, pray, and trust the God she didn't fully understand.

Her mom, who could read her like a book, waited a full minute before surrendering to the urge to give motherly advice. "Say yes to the job. Personally, a month at Caliente Springs sounds wonderful."

Julia thought so too, but she wasn't ready to decide. Rather than debate, she gave her mom a smug smile. "You just want to meet George Travers."

Ellen laughed. "Sure. Why not?"

"Seriously?"

"Good grief. No." Ellen held up the envelope with the photograph. "For one thing, he's photo-shopped. And I'm not."

"You look great."

"I'm past all that, but you're not. A month at a resort could be just what you need for a fresh look at life."

Julia gnawed her lower lip. "It would be good for business."

"And for you." Envelope in hand, Ellen pushed to her feet. "Are you hungry? I'll fix you a sandwich."

"Let's see what's up with Max first." Julia

fired off a text to Hunter. How's the zoo? ETA?

His reply came immediately. Can't talk. Later.

It might as well have said *Payback,* because that was what he was doing—making her wait the way she had made him wait two days ago. She showed her mom the message.

Ellen scowled at the screen. "He's toying with you."

Tit for tat, that was Hunter.

"I think I'll work on the Carter proposal. If Hunter doesn't answer before I'm done, I'll call him."

The clothes dryer gave an obnoxious buzz. With the picture of George Travers in hand, Ellen headed for the door. "I need to hang that stuff up. But Julia?"

"Yes?"

"Think about Zeke's offer."

Knowing the dryer would spin another five minutes, Ellen detoured to her bedroom. Julia was right about the room being crowded, but the physical clutter didn't make Ellen's heart stumble nearly as badly as the clutter of memories. The scent of Ben's aftershave was long gone, but sometimes, like now, she inhaled and pretended to smell it. A few of his shirts still hung in the closet, and once in a while she wore one around the house.

Her chest ached with the loneliness of someone

who had been loved well but left behind. The sorrow never left completely, but she didn't mind it all that much. It kept Ben close.

Even now, as she set the photograph of George Travers on the dresser, she imagined Ben at her side, elbowing her and calling her a middle-aged fangirl. He didn't go for country music at all. He'd been a Springsteen kind of man. *Born to Run* had been his personal anthem.

"Where did the years go?" she said out loud. And how many good ones did she have left? Julia was right. Ben would want her to marry again. She was young for a widow, but no one could replace Benjamin Maxwell Dare, not even George Travers.

Ellen picked up a photo of Ben and kissed his face. The glass was cold beneath her lips, but she imagined being in his arms.

Swallowing hard, she set the photograph back in its place of honor between formal portraits of their children. There were snapshots too. Pictures from Christmases, birthdays, and vacations. And of course there were photographs of her grandson. She loved Max to pieces, but she didn't like Hunter at all.

With her throat tight, Ellen looked back at Ben. "I wish you were here, honey. You'd know what our girl needs."

The face in the glass smiled at her.

"She misses you. So do I. But I have a good

life, thanks to you." Life insurance mattered when a man died young. Ellen loved her kids, her grandson, and her home. And she still loved Ben.

Feeling a bit superior, she slid the photograph of George Travers out of the envelope. He smiled up at her, a finger on the rim of his black hat. His eyes, dark blue and sultry, testified to his star power.

Ellen wasn't impressed. "Forget it, cowboy. My heart belongs to Benjamin Dare, and it always will."

Seven

Curled on the sofa with her laptop, Julia hit Send on the proposal recommending Caliente Springs to Carter Home Goods. Two hours had passed since she first sat down, and she was now furious with Hunter. Fed up, she snatched up her phone and texted him. Where are you?

No answer.

Maybe he was driving and couldn't respond. Or maybe he was teasing her like a cat with a mouse. Churning inside, she strode to the living room window and separated the drapes. Dusk pressed against the glass, and the streetlights glared white through the trees. Every child on the block knew the rule: when the lights came on, it was time to go home. Her phone hadn't chirped or meowed, but Julia checked it anyway, her imagination on fire with pictures of Hunter's Lexus upside down with the wheels spinning.

Unable to resist a minute longer, she called Hunter.

One ring.

Two rings.

She lost count until a female voice told her the subscriber's voice mail was full. Her hand shook as she ended the call. Hunter checked his voice mail all the time. Was someone else worried and leaving messages? If he'd been in a wreck with Max, would his parents call her? They hated her now.

"Julia?"

She spun around and saw her mom wearing an expression as tight as her own. "I haven't heard from him."

Ellen twisted the switch on a hurricane lamp. Yellowish light hurled circles on the carpet and walls, intersecting to make arcs and ovals. "I'm concerned."

"Me too."

She turned back to the window, opaque now because of competition from the lamp. Instead of the street, she saw a movie of her fears play on the black glass, including the fear she refused to voice to anyone, even her mother. Hunter's family was wealthy. If he wanted to take Max and disappear, he could do it as easily as he bought groceries.

But he wouldn't do that to her.

Would he?

The grandfather clock gonged eight times. It was Max's bedtime. He needed a bath and a story, a kiss good-night, and his favorite stuffed bear.

Julia banged her fist on the doorjamb. "I can't stand this."

Her mom stood behind her, silent, probably praying, until Hunter's black Lexus swept around the corner. Julia jerked open the door but stopped on the edge of the concrete step. If she attacked

Hunter, he'd lash back. Forcing cool air into her lungs, she unknotted her fists and choked back the sour taste of helpless fury.

Hunter climbed out of the car, turned, and stared at her. He wasn't very tall, but his posture exuded power. So did his expensive clothes, the razor cut of his light brown hair, and the intelligence gleaming in his green eyes. A long time ago those eyes had beguiled her; now they teased and toyed with her, with Max as the prize.

Fuming, Julia waited while Hunter lifted Max out of the car, swung him in the air, and laughed when Max flung out his arms and made airplane noises. *Joy,* but at what cost? Hunter's values were light years from hers. What would they do when Max was a teenager? What would Hunter teach him about girls, money, and cars? Unconsciously, she raised her hand to the base of her throat and pressed.

"Mommy!" Max shouted. "We went to the zoo."

"That sounds fun." Faking a smile, she lowered her hand and came down the steps. Hunter set Max on the ground and opened the trunk.

Max charged up the walk and flung himself at her legs. "I saw the elephidents."

"Oh wow!"

"And the hipp-motomoses."

Julia laughed, but it hurt. Max would talk about this trip for days, and she hadn't been there.

Ellen joined them. Grinning, she ruffled Max's

hair. "Hey, kiddo. Let's go inside. Grammie wants to hear about the elephants."

Max turned toward Hunter, now approaching with a huge bag from the gift shop.

Julia murmured her thanks to her mother, placed her hands on Max's shoulders, and waited until he looked up. "It's bedtime. Give Daddy a hug and go with Grammie."

"No!"

Shocked, Julia drew back. She couldn't possibly allow her son to behave that way. "Max. Look at me."

He lifted his chin, smirked, then looked pointedly at his feet—his father's mini-me, ignoring her the way Hunter had ignored her texts and calls.

Julia shifted her gaze to Hunter, saw a smirk, and knew he was inwardly laughing at her. Angry words boiled up in her throat, but she swallowed them. Instead she placed a finger on Max's chin and tipped up his head. His eyes popped open, but he closed them again, squeezing the lids as tight as he could.

Julia placed her hands on his shoulders, gently but with authority. "Max. Open your eyes."

Silence. Not even a twitch.

"You have three seconds to open your eyes, or you'll be in time-out tomorrow. No games. No toys." She took a breath. "One. Two—"

Hunter cut her off. "Come on, Julia. He's just

revved up. We had a great time. Don't ruin it."

Just revved up? Hopped up on sugary soda and cotton candy was more like it. And revved up or not, she loved Max too much to let him turn into Hunter. She couldn't discipline her son and cope with Hunter at the same time, especially with Hunter armed to the hilt with toys from the zoo, so she cut her losses.

"We'll talk later," she told Max. "What did you like best?"

"The gift shop." He grabbed the bag and held it like a trophy.

Hunter laughed, but Julia saw no humor at all. By indulging Max with several souvenirs instead of telling him to pick one, a rule they had agreed upon, Hunter had undercut her authority. His extravagance turned her into the bad guy, which was both unfair and wrong. The rules protected Max.

Ellen took the shopping bag and reached for her grandson's sticky hand. "Come on, kiddo. I bet we can find a book about elephants."

Max scooted happily toward Ellen, but he stopped midway and faced Hunter. "Daddy, can you stay?"

"No, son." Hunter dropped to a crouch, putting himself eye to eye with Max. "That's your mom's decision."

Max swiveled his head back to Julia and looked up, imploring her with his eyes to do the impossible. "Mommy, can Daddy stay with us?"

Julia didn't resent Max's desire for a father, but she was furious at Hunter for using Max to manipulate her. Refusing to let even a flicker of ambivalence show, she shook her head. "No, Max. We've talked about this."

"But—" His bottom lip wobbled.

Hunter pulled him into his arms. "Hey, Max, don't cry. This is between Mommy and Daddy. I'll see you in a few days. I promise."

The hug ended with Max sniffing back tears and Hunter giving him a pat on the shoulder.

Ellen took Max into the house, leaving Julia alone with Hunter. If she took one false step, the fragile peace they maintained would disintegrate. But what did she do about his manipulation, the way he blamed her for their separation? If she fought too hard, they might end up in court with a judge deciding how to raise Max. She couldn't allow that to happen, because a judge would see the good man Hunter reflected to the world, not the one who twisted truth to his own advantage. She couldn't compete with Hunter's income, polish, or charm. And without a successful business, she couldn't provide for her son.

God? Is this from you? Are you telling me to take that job with Zeke?

Her eyes caught on the mulberry tree, and she recalled the day her father had cut it down to nothing but the trunk and the three main branches.

"Daddy, it's going to die."

"No, Princess. Just watch. A year from now it'll have all new growth. In a few years, it'll be stronger and prettier than ever."

That was her life—a tree hacked to three main branches—Max, her mother, her new faith. And like that tree, she was going to come back stronger. If Hunter didn't approve of her decision to spend a month at Caliente Springs, so be it.

Determined to hold her ground, she faced him. "We never finished talking about Max and school. I'm sorry about the other night, but it couldn't be helped."

A smirk lifted his lips. "So what happened?"

A goat ate my phone. I haven't laughed so hard in ages! And then . . . Julia shoved the picture of Zeke's shining eyes out of her mind. "My phone needed to be replaced. A trip to the Apple Store wasn't on my schedule, plus I was in a meeting with a big account. You know how that is."

He preened with the ego stroke. "Yeah, I get it. But I needed to talk to you. One minute, that was all I needed. When you didn't give me an answer, I confirmed the school meeting for Monday at nine."

"I'll be there." The one-sided decision was just like Hunter, but tonight Julia could use it for leverage when she brought up Caliente Springs.

Hunter stuck out his hand. "Peace?"

Julia stared down at his smooth fingers. The

handshake was an old custom between them, the way they used to end silly quarrels. If she didn't shake his hand, she'd look petty. If she did, he'd hold on a little too long. She flipped a mental coin and shook back.

"Peace."

Hunter grinned. "You're forgiven for the phone tag."

Julia lifted her chin. "So are you."

He laughed, not at the joke but at her. Every cell in her body rebelled, but she sealed her lips. This wasn't the first time she'd taken a mental punch from Hunter, and it wouldn't be the last. She was in his good graces, so she took advantage.

"I have some news."

"Oh, yeah?"

"I'm coordinating a wedding near San Luis Obispo. Have you heard of Caliente Springs?"

"It's a nice place. Old. But it used to be classy."

"I'm going to be working there for a few weeks. I thought I'd make it a vacation for Max and my mom." She saw no reason to mention Zeke.

"Nice." Hunter sounded pleased, even impressed. "I hope you have a good time."

"We will. About your weekends—"

"Don't worry about next Saturday." He shoved his hands in his pockets. "Jeff Donahue is in town. We're getting together for drinks. I'll come up to Caliente Springs the Saturday after that. The three of us can spend a weekend together."

No, a thousand times no. A family-style weekend with Hunter was out of the question. It sent the wrong message to Max, and she especially didn't want Hunter treading on Zeke's territory. "That won't work. I'll meet you in Santa Barbara. We can trade him off there."

His full lips pulled into a mocking smile. "So you're willing to meet me halfway after all."

"Hunter—"

He held up one hand. "I know. You think it's over between us. But Julia, it's not. You still love me. I know you do. Let's run off to Vegas and find one of those wedding chapels. Don't you think we owe it to Max?"

Julia owed her son the best life she could give him, and a loveless marriage struck her as the wrong place to start. With her throat tight, she glanced at the full moon shining through the tree branches. If she didn't get Max to bed soon, he'd be cranky for church.

Schooling her features, she looked back at Hunter. "I have things to do. I'll see you Monday."

"All right. I give up, but just for tonight." After a seductive look, one she didn't return, he climbed into the Lexus and drove off.

Julia went inside and headed for the bathroom. Max was still in the tub, kicking his feet and making motorboat sounds, while her mother used a cup to rinse baby shampoo from his spiky hair.

"I'm going to take the job," Julia said.

Ellen paused with the cup in the air. "That's great. When do we leave?"

"How about Monday afternoon?"

"Perfect."

"Good. If you're okay with Max, I'll call Zeke now."

When Ellen nodded, Julia went to her room, closed the door, and took her phone out of her pocket.

Eight

Zeke thoroughly enjoyed Saturday nights at Caliente Springs. Green spotlights lit up the junipers and palms visible through the lobby's glass walls, piano music spilled out of a dark lounge, and though the crowd at the steakhouse wasn't as big as he wanted it to be, an air of contentment mixed with the aroma of good food as he walked down the main aisle.

He didn't need to be here tonight, but he enjoyed greeting guests as they dined, especially when he ran into frequent visitors like the Davidsons, a couple in their mid-forties who visited the resort every few months.

Zeke approached their table with a smile. "Tim, Lacie, how are you?"

"Excellent." Tim extended his hand and they shook.

Lacie piped up. "We're celebrating our tenth anniversary."

"That's great. Congratulations." One bucket of champagne, coming right up.

Caliente Springs had money trouble, but being cheap wasn't in Zeke's nature. Like his dad used to say, *"Give and give big, son. You'll never regret it."* That was one of the things about his dad that Zeke admired.

He chatted with the Davidsons for another minute, then left when the waiter arrived with a sizzling chateaubriand. After a word to the maître d' about the champagne, he visited a few more tables, checked with the night desk manager, then went home.

It was a little before nine o'clock when he pulled into his driveway, opened the big garage door, and saw the boxes from his parents' storage unit—the two from Berkeley bearing his own scrawl and the fifteen others numbered in his father's precise printing.

No one would ever mix up a "1" with a "7" when Reverend Jacob Monroe was in charge. Most people scribbled words like *Kitchen* or *Linens* on dented cardboard, but Jacob Monroe's boxes were clean except for the number. Knowing his dad, Zeke expected to find an inventory list in Box No. 1. For the second time in an hour, he heard his father's voice. *"You better get moving, son. Those boxes won't unpack themselves."*

No, they wouldn't.

A vibration from his phone yanked Zeke back to the present. On Saturday night, a call usually meant a problem with a troublesome guest. He raised the phone, expecting to see the security department number, but the caller ID showed *Julia Dare.*

He accepted the call fast. "Hey. What's up?"

Her voice fractured into disjointed syllables.

"Hold on, okay?" He climbed out of the SUV and walked down the driveway with the hope of finding a stronger signal.

"Zeke? Are you there?"

"Yes. I'm here."

A coyote howled in the distance. Another one joined in the song, then another. The notes blended into a lonesome chorus that echoed with beauty, longing, and all the tones in between.

The soft intake of Julia's breath wafted into his ear. "That's incredible. Where are you?"

"At home."

"It sounds like the coyotes are in your front yard."

"They're closer than I'd like. With the drought, they're looking for food near the resort."

"That's scary."

"Only if you're Ladybug. She better be nice to Chet, or she'll end up like that goat in *Jurassic Park*."

"That's awful!"

"Don't worry. I'm Ladybug's guardian angel."

"Guardian angel, huh?"

Zeke flinched. "Bad word choice. I traded my halo for that MBA."

A thoughtful silence told him she was getting ready to ask what he meant. He didn't want to explain his fall from grace, especially to Jules, who had known him in the days when he believed he could stand up to giants. Now he'd do well to save a rickety old resort from bankruptcy.

Hoping she was about to take the job, he squeezed the phone. "So you called . . ."

"Yes, but before we talk business, I want to thank you for the autograph. My mom loved it."

"Glad to do it."

"And second"—she paused for two beats of his heart—"I'd be delighted to plan Tiffany's wedding as well as fill in for Irene."

He let out the breath he'd been holding. "That's great. It'll be nice to see Ellen again and to meet Max. When can you start?"

"I'd like to drive up Monday afternoon and start work on Tuesday."

"Could you make a three o'clock meeting on Monday with Tiff and Ginger?" He'd scheduled it when he called the bride on Friday morning.

"Maybe. But it'll be tight. I can't leave here until at least eleven o'clock. Plus we'll be traveling with a four-year-old. That means stopping a few times."

"I don't want you to rush." Ginger was a stickler for punctuality. If Julia arrived late, she'd torpedo herself. "I'll push the meeting back to four."

"That would be better. Where should I meet you?"

"Go to the concierge desk. Javier will take you to the cottage, then he'll bring you to the conference room."

"That sounds good."

Better than good. With Jules in the picture, Zeke could roll off some of the load, but he also needed to prepare her. "I don't want to prejudice you, but Ginger can be demanding."

"No problem," she assured him. "Part of my job is negotiating between family members, suppliers, and anyone else who's involved. Emotions can run high during the planning phase. Think of me as a go-between."

"Thanks, I will."

"Let's get started," she said. "If you give me Tiff's number, I'll call her tomorrow."

"Hold on." He pulled up the number in his phone and read off the digits.

"Got it. What's the groom's name?"

"Derek Wilkins."

"Is that D-e-r-e-k, or Derrick like an oil derrick? Or something entirely different?"

Zeke mentally applauded her attention to detail. "D-e-r-e-k. And Wilkins is standard."

They ran through a few more details, with Julia quizzing him and Zeke telling her all about Caliente Springs as a wedding venue. Just like at St. John's, they traded ideas with ease.

Before Zeke realized it, they were talking about the kids who had gathered for basketball at St. John's, including a twelve-year-old prankster who poured a tube of glitter on the visor of Zeke's truck. Julia had been riding with him when they both noticed flecks of silver and gold on the dashboard. When he lowered the visor, the pixie dust blew everywhere—his hair, his face, all over the truck.

"Do you remember the glitter episode?" he asked.

Laughter bubbled out of her. "I'll never forget it. You should have seen your face."

He and his truck had sparkled for weeks, and he'd been dubbed "Glitter Man" by the kids and the staff.

Such good times, at least when he didn't think about the kids who ended up in trouble in spite of his effort to reach them. Or about the guilt that came from sleeping with Julia.

He wasn't the first man to fall in that way and he wouldn't be the last, but he had expected more from himself, and he was sure God did too. As for his earthly father, Zeke hadn't mentioned Julia to his parents even once. A lie of omission, but when he went back to Chile after Berkeley, he just couldn't do it. For the three months he'd stayed with them before returning to the U.S. for grad school, he'd lived a lie. Finally, unable to stand himself, he told his father he didn't want to be a preacher anymore. That quarrel still rang in his ears.

Julia's laughter over the glitter incident faded, leaving them in silence until a coyote repeated its lonesome song.

"Zeke?"

"Yeah?"

"This might be terribly presumptuous of me, but I'll feel better if I just come out and say it."

"Sure. What is it?" He paced along the driveway, his leather soles slapping against the concrete.

"We had some great times and you're as wonderful as I remember, but . . . well, I'm not interested in dating right now. I'm focusing solely on my business and being a good mom to Max."

She was smart to draw lines. The way people at CS gossiped, Zeke needed to draw lines too. "We're in complete agreement here. Friends only. Thanks for being up front."

"I probably didn't need to mention it, but—"

"No, I'm glad you did." Especially since his own rules didn't quite fit. He didn't date employees, but Julia was a contractor and her own boss. "Anything else?"

"Just one thing." She hesitated. "I don't want to dwell on the past, but there's something I'd like to . . . to clarify. But not right now. It's late and I'm tired from the drive home."

He was curious, but Julia's needs came first. "That's fine. Just let me know."

"I will. Thanks."

"Anything else?"

"No, that's it. I'll see you Monday at four o'clock sharp."

Julia gave Zeke a cheerful good-bye, leapt to her feet, and did what Max called her happy dance, the one where she pretended to wave pom-poms. Planning a massive wedding in thirty days would test her skills, but she thrived on challenge.

"Mommy!" Max's muffled voice came through the closed door.

Before she could open it, he barged in and charged at her with his *Cars* pajamas sticking to his damp skin. Dropping back on the bed, she pulled him into a hug. A bath usually calmed him, but not tonight.

Ellen, red-faced from the steam and chasing Max, arrived in the doorway. "Did you speak to Zeke?"

"It's all settled." She told her mom about the plan to leave Monday. "Should we take your car? It's more reliable."

"That's fine. I'll tell Winnie tomorrow and forward the house mail to the shop." A relaxed smile arched her lips. "I'm looking forward to it."

"Me too."

Julia kissed the top of Max's wet head. "Guess what? We're going on a vacation."

"Yay!" He did his own happy dance, waving his arms and stomping his feet while shouting "yay" over and over, though he didn't really know what a vacation was.

Julia rolled her eyes at her mom. "I'll finish bedtime."

"Good luck!" Ellen blew a kiss to Max, traded a sympathetic look with Julia, then slipped down the hall, no doubt ready for some peace and quiet.

Julia led Max to his room, listening as he talked a mile a minute. They all paid when Hunter indulged him in too many treats, but Max paid the highest price of all. When he didn't get enough rest, he was prone to the sniffles, and sniffles led to ear infections.

Swallowing her frustration, she tucked him into bed and took *Goodnight Moon* off the shelf. She read it in her most soothing voice, and eventually Max yawned. Relieved, she closed the book, turned out the lamp, and folded her hands for their bedtime prayer. When Max did the same, Julia's heart swelled with a mother's love. "Father God, Max and I thank you for today."

"And for the zoo. And for elephidents."

"And for Grammie."

His fingers, laced loosely on his chest, tightened into a fist. "And for the stuff daddy bought me."

Julia appreciated his gratitude, but she wanted Max to have a more grounded perspective on blessings. "Thank you, God, for the food we eat. And for the roof over our heads. And for loving us."

"And for Daddy and Mommy and for—for—" His eyes popped open. "I want Daddy to live with us."

They had this conversation often, and Julia

struggled with it every time. Wishing life didn't ever have to hurt, she smoothed Max's hair. "I know you do, honey."

"Why can't he?"

When Max was older, she'd answer every question he asked. But now he needed words he could understand. "This is a decision for grown-ups. What you need to remember is that Mommy and Daddy both love you. And so does God."

"Can I pray for God to bring Daddy back?"

The words cut straight to Julia's heart. This was the first time Max had mentioned praying to God on his own, and she desperately wanted to give him good answers. Did she tell her son he could ask God for anything, but that sometimes the answer was no? It seemed like sage advice, so that was what she did.

Max, his expression solemn, closed his eyes again. "Please, God, I want my daddy to live with us. And God, I want Mommy to be nice to Daddy. I love her lots and lots."

Lord, help me. Julia would give anything to fix the mess she'd made for Max, but she didn't have that ability. All she could do was trust God with all her heart like Proverbs said. Surely He knew what was best for this innocent child, her, and even Hunter.

With her chest aching, she said, "Amen," kissed Max's warm forehead, and went to start packing for a month at Caliente Springs.

Nine

Zeke was in the maintenance garage on Monday afternoon when his cell phone buzzed. Hoping it was Julia reporting her travel progress, he stole a glance and saw a message from Rhonda, the administrative assistant filling in for Irene.

Ms. Travers is here. PLS CALL.

The caps put him on full alert. After a word with Kevin Dailey, the head of maintenance, Zeke stepped out of the staff meeting and called Rhonda from the hallway.

"What's going on?"

"Ms. Travers wants to see you before the four o'clock meeting. I told her you were up in maintenance, but she said to call."

Zeke glanced at his watch. Ginger was an hour early. "Where is she?"

"The conference room. It's already set up."

That was a plus. "Is Tiff with her?"

"No."

That was a minus. "Tell her I'm on my way."

Zeke hung up, strode to his SUV, and arrived at the main hotel in nine minutes, just long enough to imagine a dozen reasons why Ginger had arrived early. He parked in his usual spot, grabbed a quick drink at the water fountain, and rounded the corner into the conference room.

Ginger stood at the window, her back to him and her eyes on the straw-colored hills. Tall and slender, dressed in an ivory pantsuit, with her short hair colored to platinum perfection, she possessed the poise of a star and the command of a CEO, one who didn't mind wielding the ax.

"Hello, Ginger."

She faced him wearing a wistful expression, blinked to erase it, and frowned. "I'm not happy about this wedding."

George and Ginger disagreed on just about everything, so Zeke had navigated these waters before. "That's between you, George, and Tiff."

"Yes, it is. And I'll get to that later. I came early to speak with you about something else."

Preparing for a debate, either an old one or something new, he nodded crisply.

Ginger turned back to the window but didn't speak. Zeke followed her gaze to the boisterous clouds towering in the brilliant blue sky. Below them, the hills were a lifeless brown.

She gave a slow shake of her head. "This place is shriveling in front of my eyes. George thinks you can turn it around. I don't."

"It's my job to prove you wrong." He kept his voice light, but they were dueling nonetheless.

She sized him up with a long look. "I know you have four months left on your contract, but I want to start the sale process now. That means finding a real estate broker."

"What does George say?" As co-owner, he would need to sign any official documents.

"You know George. He has no business sense, but I intend to persuade him. This place is a money pit."

"It won't be in a year."

"You don't really know that."

"True," he said. "But we have a good shot at pulling in Carter Home Goods. We're looking at their annual sales meeting plus a large number of employee vacation packages."

Ginger's eyes lit up, but the spark dimmed instantly. "I admire your optimism, Zeke. But it's not enough."

"It's a start."

"Maybe, but I'm afraid you're the little Dutch boy with his finger in the dike. I want this place to succeed as much as you do, but I refuse to waste another cent on a lost cause."

Zeke propped a hip on the table. "You can't give up yet. We have employees who have been here thirty years. Women like Irene—"

"I know that."

"Sorry. It's just—"

"Don't you think I care?" Ginger's voice rose with each word. "I do. But I can't wave a magic wand and fix the problems."

Zeke backed down. There was no point in antagonizing Ginger, and she was right to be worried. Summer occupancy was down from last year, and the fall quarter was under-booked. Water and landscaping costs were through the roof, and most of the guest rooms were in desperate need of a facelift. The answer to the problem was capital, but borrowing wasn't an option. George hated debt as much as he hated drinking.

Ginger breathed a sigh. "Ideally we'll find someone who appreciates the character of this place. The right buyer might even expand it. Jobs could be saved, not lost."

Zeke doubted it. In his experience, if CS was sold to a big corporation, there would be cuts to staffing and benefits. His job would be the first one to go. As a single man without a family, he could start over anywhere, but what would happen to employees like Ashley, John, and Chet?

Ginger surveyed the table neatly arranged with writing tablets, pens bearing the resort's logo, and a tray holding bottled water. Brows furrowed, she glanced at the wall clock. "It's almost four. Have you heard from Tiff?"

"Not since Friday."

"Maybe she's come to her senses."

Before he could reply, footsteps tapped down the hall. Zeke hoped it was Julia, but Tiff zipped through the door and flew into Ginger's arms.

"Aunt Ginger, you look great."

"Thank you, honey. So do you." Ginger hugged her hard and long, but when they broke apart, the steel returned to her silvery blue eyes. "Darling, are you sure about this wedding?"

"Positive."

Ginger's nostrils flared. "I'm sorry to say it, Tiffany dear, but I'm not."

Zeke didn't want to be caught in the middle. "If you'll excuse me—"

"Sure," Tiff answered. "Is Julia here yet? We talked yesterday for *three* hours. She's great."

Zeke glanced at the clock. It was ten minutes to four, and he hadn't heard from either Julia or Javier, who had instructions to text Zeke the instant she arrived. "She'll be here any minute," he said with more hope than confidence. "If you two are settled, I'm going to take care of a few things."

"We're fine," Ginger answered. "This will give me a chance to talk some sense into Tiff."

"Aunt Ginger!" Tiff laughed, but there was an edge to it.

The instant Zeke stepped into the hall, he checked his phone for a text from Julia. Seeing nothing, he went to his office, called Javier, and learned that she hadn't arrived. He skimmed the messages written by Rhonda, glanced again at the clock, and shot a text to Julia.

Where are you?

When she didn't reply, the acid in his stomach burned even hotter. It wasn't like her to be late. Car trouble? Kid trouble? He blinked and imagined fire trucks, flashing lights, and twisted car frames. With his phone dark in his hand, he recalled a January night at St. John's. Julia had been in a hurry to leave, but he'd been caught on the phone. Rather than wait for him to walk her to her car, a St. John's policy, she handed him a note. *Have to go. Will call when I get home.*

Except she didn't call. Two hours later, after frantically driving through the grid of streets between St. John's and her apartment, an area known for violent crime, he found her car with a flat tire and Julia locked inside with a dead phone.

She had flung herself into his arms, called him her hero, and whispered *I love you* for the first time.

I love you too, he whispered back.

They had stood under a dim streetlight, wrapped in each other's arms, until he reminded her that he needed to change a flat tire.

Six years, yet he remembered every detail of her face, that kiss, following her home, and taking the flat tire to a gas station to be patched.

A slow breath hissed from his lips. Julia would always be special to him, but the past was the past. Annoyed with himself, he shoved up from his desk chair. There was no real reason to worry about her, at least not yet, so he returned to the conference room.

When he stepped inside, Tiff and Ginger were seated across from each other, Tiff with her back to the door and Ginger facing forward. Guessing he'd have to play referee, Zeke sat between them at the head of the table.

While Ginger drummed her fingers, Tiff scrolled through social media posts on her phone. Zeke watched the clock, staring as the long hand swept away another minute and made Julia officially late.

He opened his mouth to make excuses, but Ginger stopped him with a withering look. "Your wedding planner is late."

"She'll be here." Zeke said it more for his benefit than Ginger's.

Air hissed through Ginger's nose. "Tiff and I made it on time. It's a matter of *planning*."

Tiff passed her aunt a bottle of water. "I'm sure Julia's on her way. Who cares about five minutes anyway?"

Julia did, and so did Ginger. The clock swept away another two minutes.

To distract Ginger, Zeke looked out the window. "It sure is hot today."

"It's August," Ginger shot back. "Of course it's hot. Don't try to distract me with the weather. How did you meet this woman?"

"She's the event planner representing Carter Home Goods." That didn't seem like enough, so he added, "We were friends in college."

"USC or Berkeley?"

"Berkeley."

Ginger shoved the water aside. "Did she learn to tell time, or just how to change the world?"

Zeke was used to Ginger riding him, but he couldn't tolerate the disrespect to Julia. He opened his mouth to defend her but sealed it when his phone flashed with a text from Javier.

In the same instant, Julia charged into the room, out of breath, her face as pink as the tunic top that capped off her black pants, which were creased from the drive. Fresh lipstick hid some of her nervousness, but the messy bun holding her hair told a different story.

Zeke stood to greet her.

Inhaling deeply, she splayed her fingers at the base of her throat. "I am so sorry to be late. There's no excuse—"

"Forget it." Tiff stood and hugged her, awkwardly because Julia was still holding her purse and portfolio.

If he downplayed her late arrival, maybe Ginger would drop the scowl. "We're glad you made it."

"Yes. At last." Julia blew out a breath that lifted a wisp of her hair. "I had a meeting this morning. It ran late, plus my son woke up with a fever. It's been crazy, but that's no excuse. Late is late, and I apologize."

Ginger studied her with a cool stare, her chin raised and her shoulders back. She didn't say a word.

Tiff nodded like a bobblehead. "Stuff like that

happens to me *all* the time. Uncle George says I'll be late to my own funeral."

Zeke stifled a groan. Just what he needed—a bride with a punctuality problem, a stand-in mother of the bride with a stopwatch, and a wedding planner with a sick child. As important as this meeting was to him personally, he couldn't help but worry about Max. He'd ask about him later and in private.

"Shall we get started?" he said.

Tiff sat, but Julia stayed on her feet, turned to Ginger, and waited for Zeke to make a formal introduction. Smart woman. Ginger would recognize the respect.

"Ginger," Zeke said, "this is Julia Dare, owner of Dare to Dream Events."

Julia dipped her chin as if she were meeting royalty. "Miss Travers. It's an honor to meet you."

"Thank you, dear." Condescension dripped from every word, but if Julia noticed, she ignored it.

Zeke indicated she should sit. As the chairs dragged on the carpet, all eyes turned to Julia. More composed now, she pulled a computer tablet out of the portfolio along with three folders sporting the Dare to Dream logo. Zeke opened his and found a slick brochure, a Dare to Dream pen, notepaper, and a "save the date" magnet trimmed with polka dots.

Tiff held up the magnet. "Cute."

Ginger slid her unopened folder six inches away. "This is all very nice, dear. But let's be serious for a moment."

Zeke interrupted. "Ginger, Julia's doing her job."

"Her job is irrelevant." Ginger shot icy daggers at him first, then Julia, and finally at Tiff, though the daggers at Tiff melted instantly and put a sheen in Ginger's eyes. "Tiffany, dear, someone has to be realistic. You and Derek are rushing into this."

Tiff returned Ginger's tough look with one of her own. "I love Derek and we want to get married. I thought you liked him."

"I do."

"Then why aren't you happy for us?"

Zeke stole a glance at Julia. Her expression stayed neutral, but she was listening and watching, ready to jump into the fray if needed.

Ginger sat taller in her chair. "You're too young to get married."

"I'm twenty-two. My mom was twenty-one when she married my dad. They had a good marriage too."

"Yes," Ginger admitted, "but there's no reason for you to rush into this."

"I admit, the *wedding* is rushed," Tiff said. "But we're not rushing into marriage. We've been together two years now."

Ginger, using one pink fingernail, nudged the Dare to Dream folder another inch away. "Even if I agreed that marriage at your age is wise, you can't pull off the wedding you want in just a month."

"I think we can," Tiff argued. "And there's no choice about the date. Derek leaves for Alaska on October first. I want to go as his wife. I also want the dress, the flowers, and all those special moments. My mom and I used to talk about it, so this is for her too. Is that wrong?"

"No, honey. It's not wrong at all." Ginger's face softened, maybe with memories. "Your mom was my best friend. I *want* you to have that special day. I just don't think we can pull it off so quickly. We need time to plan. Why not just live together?"

Tiff shook her head. "That's not what I want."

"Ms. Travers?"

All eyes turned to Julia.

Ginger glowered at her. "What is it?"

"A month isn't much time, but I'm convinced we can give Tiff the wedding she wants. Let's look at the resources we have." Julia lifted the remote off the table, turned on the wall monitor, and made a few swipes on her tablet. A list like the one he'd rattled off at the pier appeared on the screen. "We already have the big pieces in place."

Ginger read the list twice. "This is nice, but it's

not enough. What about invitations? They should have been sent months ago."

"We'll get to the invitations in a minute," Julia replied. "First I'd like to settle a few things."

"Such as?" Ginger's voice was acid.

Julia met her gaze with a strong one of her own. "The wedding is set for Saturday, September twenty-second. Tiff and Derek both want an outoor ceremony at sunset, so I'm suggesting six o'clock."

She clicked to a photograph Zeke recognized from the hotel website. It had been taken from Golden Point, a lookout that offered a spectacular view of sprawling meadows and the rugged mountains to the east. When the sun hit at a certain angle, the earth and sky shimmered with beams of yellow, orange, and pink light.

"This is Golden Point," Julia explained. "Tiff and Derek want to take their vows here at unset. It's beautiful, but we might have access problems. With Zeke's help, I plan to scout out other sites and consult with everyone. Since the invitations will direct guests to the main building, we can make the final choice later."

Julia focused on Ginger, silently inviting her to share an opinion. When Ginger answered by arching her brows, Julia turned to Zeke instead. "Does this seem reasonable so far?"

"Very."

They traded a familiar look, the one where they

did a Vulcan mind meld of sorts, then she clicked the PowerPoint to a screen that read *Invitations & Guests*.

"Ms. Travers mentioned invitations. This is where we break the rules for the sake of expediency. We'll send traditional paper in the next twenty-four hours, but Tiff is already calling, texting, and emailing."

Ginger scowled at Tiff. "You're doing this too casually."

"Ms. Travers?"

Zeke hoped Julia had her protective shields up, because Ginger stared at her with laser intensity. "Let me guess. You're going to tell me times have changed, and this is the *right* way to do things."

"No. I'm not."

Zeke didn't envy Julia. Somehow she had to please Tiff while appeasing Ginger, who had no interest in being appeased.

Julia passed out paper samples. They were white with gold embossing, very classy and traditional. "Tiff and I discussed the invitations yesterday. The address list is ready to go, but we can add anyone you or Mr. Travers would like. If you approve of what Tiff and Derek chose, and if we skip hand calligraphy, the invitations can be in the mail by five o'clock tomorrow."

"But still—" Ginger grabbed her own pen, not the one from Julia. "This is just so rushed. Guests need time to plan."

Zeke was tired of Ginger's fault-finding, but Julia seemed nonplussed, maybe even a little smug, when she exchanged a look with Tiff.

"Are you ready?" Julia asked her.

"I am." Tiff laced her hands against her chest. "I hope you like the invitation, Aunt Ginger, because it's straight from my heart. My mom and dad would like what I wrote. I hope you do too, because this is the invitation I want to send."

Julia clicked the remote, and the screen went to words written in a traditional font.

Mr. George Travers and
Ms. Ginger Travers
Honorary Parents
Request the joy of your presence
At the marriage of their goddaughter
Tiffany Ann Reid
Daughter of the late Tom and
the late Laura Reid
To
Derek M. Wilkins
Son of William and Susan Wilkins
Etc.

Zeke choked up when he read the words *Honorary Parents*. With his own mother and father in heaven, he knew how it felt to miss important people on important occasions.

The silence suffocated them all until Ginger snatched a tissue from the box on the table and pressed it to her eyes. "Tiff, dear, I'm honored. You're the daughter I always wanted to have."

"So you're okay with everything?" Tiff sounded far younger than her twenty-two years.

Ginger dabbed at her tears, showing the side of her that rescued ornery goats. She loved Tiff fiercely, and it showed when she narrowed her gaze at Julia. "You've impressed me, Julia. I admit it, but I'm also skeptical. Can you guarantee me that Tiff's wedding will be worthy of this beautiful invitation?"

Ten

Julia was too much of a professional to be bullied into making a promise no human being could keep. Ginger Travers was everything Zeke had implied, and everything Tiff had described in yesterday's phone call. Poised. Polished. And a human bulldozer.

"I can only promise you this," Julia replied. "I'll do my very best to make this wedding everything Tiff and Derek want it to be."

Tiff placed her hand over Julia's and squeezed. "Thank you."

Ginger studied her a moment longer, then acquiesced with a nod. "All right then. This wedding has my full support."

Tiff launched out of her chair, hurried to Ginger, and wrapped her in an awkward sitting-down hug. "I can't thank you enough. And Uncle George too. I don't know what I'd do without you."

Julia felt the same way about her own mom. Ellen had supported her through all the ups and downs of the past few years by doing what she was doing this very minute—staying behind in LA to take Max to the pediatrician. This morning had been terrible. Between Max's sore throat and fever, Hunter's late arrival to the school meeting, and working until three in the morning on today's presentation, she could barely hold back an eye-watering yawn.

Fighting the urge to slouch, she turned to Zeke. When his eyes met hers, they traded a smile. She started to relax until she realized Ginger was watching them. She broke Zeke's stare with a crisp nod, and they both turned to Ginger. Tiff went back to her seat, and Ginger picked up the Dare to Dream pen to make a note.

Julia indicated the invitation on the monitor. "If we all agree, I'm going to send this to the printer right now."

"Go for it," Tiff replied.

"This is final," Julia reminded her. "So read it carefully for typos, especially the names, date, and time."

Four pairs of eyes studied every letter. When Tiff, Ginger, and Zeke each signaled their approval, she emailed it to the printer.

For the next hour, they hashed out details. Ginger skimmed the invitation list, added a few names, and promised to email additional addresses to Julia by the next morning. Tiff reported on the bridal party. The bridesmaids and groomsmen were all confirmed, and her wedding dress was in her closet. When Ginger asked about bridesmaid dresses, Tiff showed off a selfie with her three friends wearing matching rose-gold sheaths.

"Did we miss anything?" Julia asked with one eye on the clock. By now, her mom and Max would be back from the doctor.

"That's it." Tiff pushed her chair back and stood. "This is fun. Let's all have dinner together."

Julia opened her mouth to decline and almost yawned. Zeke saw it and answered for them both as he stood. "Thanks, but Julia and I need to go over a few things."

"Of course." Ginger joined Tiff at the door.

Zeke told Julia he'd be back, then escorted the other two women to the lobby. The break gave her a chance to call her mom. Ellen picked up on the second ring.

"How's Max?"

"He's doing just fine. Dr. Barrett prescribed the dreaded pink medicine." Amoxicillin. Max hated it. "Tylenol is helping, but you know how he gets."

"He wilts." A piece of Julia's heart wilted too. "I wish I could be there."

"We're fine," Ellen replied. "In fact, we're curled up on the couch watching *Cars*."

His favorite, along with *The Incredibles*. "I don't know what I'd do without you, Mom."

"You'd find a way."

"Maybe, but it wouldn't be easy." She'd still be working as a temp. Rent, food, and daycare would devour her budget, and she'd be using Hunter's support money to live on instead of depositing it in Max's college fund. That money came with strings and gave Hunter power over her decisions, so she was glad not to need it.

Thank you, God, for taking care of us. Her throat tightened with love for Max and her mom, and the sad awareness that Hunter wanted to be a good dad but didn't know how.

Julia let out a breath. "Can I talk to Max?"

Ellen chuckled. "He's already grabbing the phone. Here you go."

"Mommy?"

"Hey, big guy. How are you feeling?" She spoke in her mommy voice, the next best thing to a hug.

"My ear hurts."

"Again, huh?"

"Yeah. But Grammie says it'll get better, then we can go on vacation with you. I want to go swimming. Grammie says there's a pool with a slide."

"Yes, there is."

"Mommy?"

Her son's voice, even nasally, was music to her ears. "Yes, honey?"

"I miss you lots."

"I miss you too." She blew a loud kiss into the phone. It was a game between them, one he'd outgrow all too soon. She heard footsteps, looked up, and saw Zeke waiting in the doorway with an amused smile on his face. "I have to go now," she said to Max. "Give the phone to Grammie, okay?"

Zeke signaled that she should take her time, but she was too self-conscious to talk to Max in front of him. She needed to tell Zeke about Hunter, and this seemed like a good time.

Ellen's voice came on the line. "Julia?"

"Zeke is back. I'll call you later, okay?"

After a quick good-bye, she set down the phone, looked at Zeke, and opened her mouth to say, *"Oh, by the way, do you remember Hunter Adams?"*

But when her gaze met his, she lost herself in his twinkling eyes. No wonder he'd been dubbed Glitter Man in college. Everything about him was shiny, strong, and ready to fight for his cause.

A long time ago, that cause had been *her*. She didn't realize it at St. John's, but when they first met, Zeke had tried to be Jesus to her. He never intended to date her. When she started to flirt with him, he invited her to a campus group called Bread on the Water and introduced her to several of the girls. She became part of the group, but she didn't make the faith leap. She might have, but when her dad died, she abandoned those friends.

Even so, Zeke stuck with her. He let her rant about God and fate until she was hoarse. They were in love. But for Julia, that love had been the "just for now" kind she used to believe in. For Zeke—

"Julia?" His voice pulled her back to the present. "Is everything all right?"

No, it's not. I hurt you and I lied. You deserve to hear the truth, and I need to tell it.

Her throat tightened, but she managed to nod. "I'm fine. Just tired."

He propped one hip on the conference table. "We can talk about ceremony sites later. You must be exhausted."

"I am." She leaned back in the chair. "It was an awful morning. I'm sorry I was late. Ginger was probably counting the seconds."

"Every one of them, but she's happy now. You nailed everything."

"The meeting turned out well in the end." Excellent, actually. "Now I just have to pull off the wedding of the century."

"We."

"We?"

"As in you and me." Zeke smiled. "I'm not going to leave you alone to square off with Ginger. She's demanding, but she means well."

It was just like Zeke to see the good in everybody. In Berkeley he had even been decent to Hunter, though he often gritted his teeth at Hunter's mocking. Eager to unburden herself and be done with it, she opened her mouth, but Zeke spoke first.

"I overheard you talking to your mom. Are she and Max here?"

"They stayed behind in LA." She told him about the ear infection and the trip to the pediatrician. "We've been through this four times now. I don't know what I'd do without my mom. Like today—she took over so I could be here."

"We need to get Max signed up for the children's program. I'm sure we have something for his age group."

"That's great."

"We can talk more tomorrow. Right now, you need to get settled." He lifted the two-way radio to his mouth.

"Zeke?"

"Yes?" His eyes met hers, but he went ahead and pushed the radio button. "GM calling Javier."

The concierge answered immediately. Zeke directed him to escort Julia to one of the cottages, then he faced her. "What's up?"

Oh, by the way sat frozen on her tongue. She couldn't bring Hunter up now. "What time should I be in the office?"

"The work hours are nine to five-thirty, but that's flexible."

"Is that when you come in?"

"It varies." He pushed the door wider for her. "We're a 24/7 operation. If I work late, I sleep in. Tomorrow's an early day."

"How early?" If she was going to fill in for Irene, she needed to know Zeke's habits.

"Six o'clock for a golf lesson."

"Mr. Carter would be impressed."

"Not with my swing, but I'm working on it."

He ushered her through the door to the lobby. Javier greeted them, and Zeke handed her off with the promise he'd see her tomorrow. Outside, the valet was waiting with her car and a vehicle for Javier.

When Julia saw the cottage, she fell in love with it. White stucco with a red tile roof, surrounded by bottlebrush and pink hibiscus in full bloom, the house promised respite. As soon as she climbed out of her car, she snapped a picture and sent it to her mom and Max.

Javier cleared his throat. "May I show you the house, Ms. Dare?"

"Yes. Thank you."

He unlocked the door and pushed it wide. Julia stepped past him into the entry, inhaled deeply, and smelled lemon furniture polish. With her heels clicking on the Spanish tile, she took in textured walls, dark ceiling beams, and over-stuffed furniture that made her want to flop down and kick off her shoes.

"It's lovely," she said to Javier.

He gave her a quick tour of the three bed-rooms, showed her the kitchen, and ended in the dining area where a gorgeous flower arrangement decorated an oak table designed to seat six. A card with her name on it poked up from the mix of lilies, roses, and carnations.

When Javier left to get her luggage, she plucked the envelope from the holder, opened a card with the CS logo, and saw Zeke's familiar handwriting. *Welcome to Caliente Springs. We hope you enjoy your stay.*

The note was signed with his full name and title, and below it were similar notes from the maid assigned to the cottage and the head concierge. Zeke probably signed these cards by the dozen, but somehow this one felt special to her.

She propped the note up on the table, then sniffed a rose. That *Oh, by the way* conversation needed to happen, but it was far more pleasant to enjoy the flowers, the cozy house, and the sweet anticipation of planning a beautiful wedding.

Eleven

Julia arrived at the office shortly before nine o'clock the next morning, heard the intercom give a two-ring blast, and picked it up. Fortunately, she knew the phone system from her temp days. "Julia speaking."

"Who?" A male voice. Not Zeke.

"My name is Julia. I'm filling in for Irene."

"I heard about that. I'm Kevin, the maintenance manager. Would you tell Zeke the backhoe broke down again? He'll know what it means."

"Sure thing."

She didn't see a phone message book, so she jotted a note on a pink Post-it. Before she finished, the intercom rang again.

This time it was Katrina Andersen, the woman who ran Katrina's Kitchen. She welcomed Julia, asked about Irene, and left an invitation for Zeke to sample the autumn specials before she ordered menu inserts.

When a regular phone line rang, Julia grabbed her third Post-it Note. Fifteen minutes later, a clothesline of pink squares hung from the bottom of the computer monitor.

Zeke, dressed in khakis and a white golf shirt, strode through the hall door, saw the Post-its and lifted a brow. "You've been busy."

She unstuck the notes and handed them to him. "They're all for you. We'll need to talk about how you handle calls, messages, that sort of thing, but Kevin's message seems the most urgent."

Zeke grimaced. "The backhoe again?"

"He said you'd understand."

"Unfortunately, I do. It breaks down all the time, and we're not budgeted to replace it for another two years." He skimmed through the notes and set them back on her desk. "This can all wait. Before you settle in, let's go meet some people."

A veteran at learning new jobs, Julia picked up a notepad and pen and followed Zeke down the hall. For the next hour, they walked around the main building and greeted key staff members. Zeke rattled off names, giving her tidbits about each person and patting that person on the back at the same time. Almost everyone asked about Irene's surgery, scheduled for later that day.

Julia couldn't help but be impressed by Zeke's easy ways. Just like at St. John's, he made people feel important. The last stop was Katrina's Kitchen, where they sampled fresh pumpkin bread and left with full cups of coffee.

When they returned to Irene's desk—her desk now—Zeke told her to make herself at home. "Ashley'll be here soon. She'll train you on the hotel software. In the meantime, feel free to pester me if you have questions."

"Thanks."

He started to walk away but stopped midstep. "Does today remind you of anything?"

"My first day at St. John's?"

"Exactly."

Julia lifted the paper coffee cup in a kind of toast. "To the Caffé Med."

Zeke toasted back. "As I recall, we solved the world's problems at that back table in the balcony."

"Everything except global warming," she teased back. "That was beyond us."

They both smiled at the memory and maybe at the hubris of thinking they could save the world. She and Zeke used to leave St. John's together and go to the Med to study or meet up with friends from Bread on the Water. They'd shared a lot of good times in that old café. Hard times too.

Their gazes lingered for a few more seconds. She wondered if he was going to say something else, but he turned abruptly and went to his office.

Julia dropped onto Irene's chair, surveyed the contents of the desk, and tried not to think about Berkeley and how sure of herself she'd been when she transferred to the huge school as a junior. Before that, she had commuted to Cal State Northridge near her parents' home. The school was comfortable, but she'd been bored with her high school friends and hungry for adventure.

Well, she'd had the adventure. Been there. Done that. Had Max to prove it. If she'd learned one thing since becoming a mom, it was that love wasn't the fickle thing she used to imagine.

Holding in a sigh, she downloaded Tiff's wedding files from Dropbox. As promised, Ginger had emailed a list of names to be added, including notes like, "Aunt Ethel is in a wheelchair" and "Uncle Gene is allergic to shrimp." The menu issues were predictable. Finding a ceremony site that could accommodate five hundred people in various stages of health was another problem altogether, a huge one she needed Zeke to help her solve.

She worked on the wedding until after five o'clock. Zeke was in and out all day, but there wasn't time to talk except for a quick word when Irene's husband called. She was out of surgery and doing well.

On Wednesday afternoon, Ellen and Max arrived and settled into the cottage. Julia finished Tiff and Derek's website, prepared for a Carter Home Goods Skype meeting on Thursday, and met with Zeke to make a list of possible ceremony sites. He blocked off Friday afternoon for taking her around to check out some of the options.

Busy days. Rushed conversations. She still hadn't told Zeke about Hunter. Between his schedule and hers, the opportunity just hadn't presented itself.

On Thursday, Julia looked at the clock and wondered if she could work the conversation in that day. Or maybe not. They were supposed to pick up her mom in five minutes for a quick look at the Travers family mansion. The back patio was a potential site for the rehearsal dinner, and Julia wanted Ellen's ideas. Max, fully recovered, was participating in the hotel's children's program.

The glass door to the office suite swung wide. Holding it open, Zeke stood in the threshold. "Would you mind meeting me at the house? I have to swing by the pro shop."

"Not at all." The mansion was located behind the same gate guarding the cottages.

Zeke took off, and she called her mom.

"I'm on my way."

"I think I'll walk," Ellen said. "It's a gorgeous day, and the house isn't far."

"Sounds good. I'll see you in a few."

Ellen loved Julia and Max to pieces, but after the ear infection, ten screenings of *Cars*, packing for a month-long trip, and making a long drive with an impatient four-year-old, she craved solitude. Inhaling deeply, she left the cottage in a rush but slowed when she imagined Ben's voice in her head.

"Where's the fire?"

"Not under you, slowpoke!"

They'd traded that jibe a million times. She looked up at the clouds, blew him a kiss, and resumed her brisk pace with the hope of burning off yesterday's French fries.

The Travers' mansion, white stucco and shaded by giant oaks, loomed in the distance. Seeing it gave her a little thrill. She felt teenage and silly, but she enjoyed the little rush that came when she thought of that signed picture of George Travers.

Expecting Julia and Zeke any minute, she decided to walk up the long driveway and wait for them on the porch.

Tires squealed on the concrete driveway. She whirled, expecting to scold Zeke for speeding, but instead of a hotel SUV, she saw a white Corvette charging straight at her. She bolted for the lawn, but her toe caught on a brick and she went down in a heap. Brakes screeched in her ears. Hot exhaust filled her nose, and pain shot through her head and right leg. A peculiar numbness overtook her mind, a feeling she recognized as shock.

A car door slammed, then a man in cowboy boots and a black shirt dropped to his knees at her side. "Don't move, miss. You're hurt."

That voice . . . it seemed to come from a dream. In spite of her dizziness, she turned her head and looked into a pair of brilliant blue eyes set in a craggy face. Blinking, she saw stars, or more correctly, one star. George Travers was peering down at her. Worry was etched across his brow, and he was . . . taking off his shirt?

This couldn't be happening. George Travers? Her teenage crush? Her heart did an odd little dance as if she were sixteen again, which she wasn't. Not by a long shot.

She tried to sit up, but he laid a hand on her shoulder and gently pressed her back to the grass. "Stay still, darlin'. You're bleeding."

Ellen could barely think, let alone move. Her head was pounding now, and she couldn't stop staring at George Travers. *The* George Travers. Ben would have teased her unmercifully about her tongue-tied reaction. She was too old to be a fangirl, but George Travers was better looking now than he had been thirty years ago. And in better shape too. His shoulders were broad enough to cast a long shadow, one that protected her from the sun and shaded her eyes from the glare.

She opened her mouth to speak, but she could only stare at the white T-shirt hugging his chest. He either chopped wood for fun, or he worked out in a gym.

Not the least bit self-conscious, he wadded up the black shirt in his hands and wiped blood off the side of her face. "You smacked your head pretty good."

"I'm—I'm all right." She reached to hold the shirt for herself.

He let it go, studied her for a moment, then took his phone out of his pocket. "I'm calling 911."

"No. Don't. I'll be fine in a minute." She managed to sit up to prove it, but a wave of nausea leveled her and she lay back down. Her ankle throbbed with every beat of her heart, and so did her head. "I can't believe this."

"Me either."

Fighting nausea, she closed her eyes and moaned. "This is a dream, or you're really George Travers."

"It's not a dream. And if I may be so bold—" His voice took on an edge. "Who are you? And why are you in my driveway?"

"It's a fluke."

"Uh-huh." His tone made her feel like a groupie. "You just happened to go through a locked gate and walk half a mile?"

"No." She looked up, felt blood ooze, and pressed the shirt tighter against her scalp. "My daughter's planning Tiff's wedding. I'm helping her. She'll be here any minute with Zeke."

"You're Ellen." He sounded pleased.

"That's right." She felt even more ridiculous. "Thank you for the autograph. It was very nice of you."

The steely glint in his eyes transformed into a lively twinkle. "Glad to do it, Ellen."

Her name lingered in the air, soft and resonant like a song lyric. A sweet shiver rippled through

her, which was absurd, considering the circumstances. Still queasy, she pressed the shirt more
firmly against her scalp and tried to move her
ankle. Pain shot up her leg, and she winced.

George peered into her face. "I'm taking you to
the ER."

"No." Not a hospital. Since Ben's death, she
couldn't stand them.

George put his hand on her shoulder. "Ellen,
darlin', we aren't negotiating. You could have a
concussion, and that ankle is swelling into a tree
stump. You need a doctor."

"You're right. It's just—" She couldn't finish.

George took out his phone again. Before he
could use it, Julia pulled up behind the Corvette.

Flinging open the car door, she cried out.
"Mom! Oh my word—"

"I'm all right. Really."

Julia skidded to her knees, stared into Ellen's
face, then placed her hands on the bloody shirt.
Ellen lowered her arm.

"What happened?" Julia asked.

"It's crazy. I was—I mean—and then . . ." Ellen
looked to George for help.

"She surprised me." His eyes met hers and
held tight. "I came around the corner like Richard
Petty, and she ran to get out of the way." He
indicated the row of bricks lining the driveway.
"She tripped and went flying."

Julia gripped Ellen's hand. "Mom, I know how

you feel about hospitals, but we're going right now."

"No."

"Yes," Julia said.

A white SUV pulled up behind Julia's Outback. Zeke climbed out and strode toward them. After George filled him in, he crouched next to Julia. "Ellen, it's good to see you, but I'm sorry about the circumstances. We'll get you taken care of."

Julia turned to him. "The Carter meeting is in an hour. I hate to miss it, but I have to take care of my mom."

"I'll handle it."

"What meeting?" George asked.

Zeke told him about the Carter account. "We're Skyping this afternoon to work out some details for Mr. Carter's visit."

Ellen shook her head. "Julia should be there. The Carters are old family friends."

Julia scowled the way she did at Max. "Mom, forget it. There's no way I'll leave you with a broken ankle."

"It's not broken."

"You don't know that," Julia insisted.

"Ladies!" George put his hands on his hips. "There's a simple answer. I'll take Ellen to the ER. Julia, we haven't met, but I'm George Travers." He offered his hand.

"Yes, I recognized you." She shook back, then

145

gave Ellen a smug little smile. "My mother's a fan."

Ellen turned six shades of red. "Julia, really."

With an even brighter twinkle in his eyes—they were more silver than blue—George looked down at her, winked, then faced Julia. "It just so happens that I'm a fan of beautiful women, so your mother and I are on equal footing."

Good grief! He could certainly turn a phrase, but Ellen didn't feel beautiful at all. She felt like a fool. A fool in pain and bleeding all over George Travers' shirt. A fool who *did not* want to go to the hospital with a stranger, especially a stranger who was famous and more handsome now than he was on the covers of his old CDs.

But Ellen needed to consider her daughter and grandson too. Julia had an obligation to Zeke, and the children's program ended at three o'clock. If Julia took Ellen to the ER, they'd have to bring Max. Not a good place for a four-year-old. Ellen hated moments like this one, when she felt helpless and middle-aged. And alone.

Torn in two, she looked up at George. His eyes met hers, and somehow she knew he understood, because he too was middle-aged and a little worn out by life.

"I'll go with you," she told him. "Thank you."

George and Zeke helped her up, each one taking an arm. Julia reminded her to take her health

146

insurance card. Ellen almost snapped back that she wasn't a child, but without the reminder, she would have forgotten. As George helped her into the Corvette, Zeke left for the office, and Julia went to the cottage to fetch Ellen's purse.

Five minutes later, Ellen was on her way to the ER with George as a chauffeur, her foot on a pillow, and a fresh towel to hold against her scalp.

"This is crazy," she said. "I'm supposed to be helping Julia, not the other way around."

George stared out the windshield, his chin slightly raised. "God works in mysterious ways."

Ellen thought so too, but she couldn't speak over the lump in her throat. Those mysterious ways included Ben's death. She was done grieving him in that initial, razor-sharp way, but at times like this, when she was alone and in need, the grief expanded like a water balloon, heavy in her chest and ready to break.

George steered around a wide curve. When the road straightened, he glanced at her. "You can tell me to mind my own business, but I have a heart for a certain subject. May I ask you a question?"

She couldn't imagine what he'd ask. "Sure. Why not?"

"Are you a believer, Ellen?"

"Yes. I am." Considering George's music and his reputation for being blunt, the question didn't surprise her, nor did she consider it intrusive. Her faith defined her, and she had a tattoo to prove it.

"Then you know what I'm about to say." He kept his eyes on the road. "God's got this covered. He knows what you're going through—all of it."

It was the kind of thing Ben would have said. "Thank you. I needed the reminder."

"I need it every day. You probably know my story."

"Most of it."

"Just so you don't get your news from the *National Enquirer.*" He said it with such disdain that she hurt for him.

"No," she said. "Your songs tell your story. My daughter was right when she said I'm a fan. I enjoy all your music, both old and new."

"It's been a long, hard road. But here I am now, mistakes and all. We worship a pretty amazing God."

"Yes, we do." And she had to admit, George Travers was a pretty amazing man.

He stopped the Corvette in front of the glass wall of the emergency room. "I'll get a wheelchair."

Ellen took in the smoky glass, the red signs, and the people hurting the way she had hurt for Ben. "No. I can't. It's just—" She bit her lip.

George laid a hand on her shoulder. "What's wrong, darlin'?"

"I'm fine. It's just—" She couldn't bear to think about Ben, so she searched for an excuse. "I hate wheelchairs."

"That's easy to fix. You can lean on me instead."

Lean on me. Ben used to say that to her. Tears rushed into her eyes, and she relived the day of the heart attack, the terror and the stunned prayers, the five days of hope that had ended with a flat line on the heart monitor.

She fought a sob, but it broke free and she began to weep. Babbling apologies, she explained the tears to George.

"Ah, darlin'. I'm so sorry."

He put his arms around her and held her while she cried. George's aftershave wafted to her nose, and the warmth of his skin pressed through the T-shirt. He wasn't Ben, but he radiated a kindness exactly like Ben's. George held her close, saying nothing yet somehow telling her he understood. He wasn't Ben, but he came closer than any man she'd ever met.

Twelve

The Carter video conference included Zeke, Julia, the Carter Home Goods sales VP, and Mr. Carter himself, each at their respective computers. The meeting ended on a high note with plans for Mr. Carter and his wife to visit CS late the next week for a look at the resort and that dreaded round of golf.

As soon as Julia disconnected the call, Zeke joined her at her desk. "Great job."

She gave him a cheeky grin. "Break out the plaid, because the golf course will matter to Mr. Carter."

"No plaid," Zeke joked back. "I'll eat enough humble pie when he shoots par and I shoot 150."

"I'll go with you," Julia offered.

"You play?"

"A little. My dad used to take me to the driving range with him on Saturday mornings. And then—" She looked away, unable to meet his gaze. "I played with Max's dad and his parents."

Catman. Every time Julia mentioned him, a shadow passed over her face. Zeke was curious about him, but he wasn't comfortable asking questions. That conversation would cross boundaries, and he was already struggling to think of her merely as a friend.

He gladly changed the subject. "Any word from your mom?"

"No, and I'm worried. If she broke her ankle, it could need surgery. And if she needs surgery . . ." Julia chewed her lip.

"You might need to go home."

"Yes."

"Ellen comes first."

But his stomach did a flip. In just a few days, he'd come to rely on Julia the way he relied on Irene. Except he didn't think about Irene when he went home at night, or when he woke up, or when he looked in the mirror and shaved. Or when he—*Stop it.* Zeke flexed the muscles of his self-will, but thoughts born of strong feelings put up a fight, a battle he knew well.

Julia lifted her phone, called her mom, then grimaced when the call went to voice mail.

Zeke took out his own phone. "I'll call George."

One ring later, George's drawl rumbled in reply. "Glad you called. I heard Ellen's phone go off, but I didn't want to dig in her purse."

"Hold on." Zeke set the phone on the counter. "You're on speaker so Julia can hear."

"Hi, George." Julia smiled her appreciation at Zeke. "Thanks for taking care of my mom. How is she?"

"Just fine. Her head's stitched up, and they're X-raying the ankle now."

"That's good." Relief washed the tension from

Julia's face. "Did the doctor say anything about a concussion?"

"She has a goose egg, but they're not overly worried. You'll have to wake her up tonight, but that's just a precaution. The ankle's a bigger question. As soon as we know something, I'll call you or Ellen will."

Julia turned to Zeke but spoke to George too. "I'm going to pick up Max and head to the hospital."

Zeke nodded his agreement. She didn't know it, but he was going with her.

"I have another idea." George's voice crackled with static. "Why don't you two hang loose for a while? Ellen could be released in five minutes or five hours. I'll call you the minute we know what's next."

Zeke thought it was a good plan, but the decision was Julia's.

Her brow furrowed even deeper than before. "My mom hates hospitals."

"I know," George said. "She told me."

"She *did?*"

"I know about your dad's heart attack. I'm sorry for your loss." George paused in a respectful silence. "I'm looking out for her, honey. You don't need to worry."

Julia paused. "I don't know what to do."

She didn't let go of responsibility easily. Zeke knew that about her, so he answered George for her. "We'll wait in my office. Call as soon as you know something."

After quick good-byes, Zeke turned to Julia. "George is a good man."

At one time, Zeke would have added *in spite of his past.* But it was that colorful past that made George the man he was now. He wasn't proud of his so-called glory days, but he didn't shy away from them either. George was simply . . . George. A man who fell short but loved God with all his heart.

Zeke had once loved God with that same passion. At St. John's he spent countless hours trying to help people reboot their lives. Some responded; most didn't. The failures wore Zeke down. When he stumbled with Jules, he hit hard and failed to get back up, mostly because he'd been sick to death of trying to be a good man, carrying the weight of the world, failing God, his earthly father, and himself.

"Zeke?" Julia looked at the broken pencil in his hand.

He looked at it too, unaware that he'd plucked it out of a cup on the counter and snapped it in half.

"What's wrong?"

"Nothing." He tossed the pieces in the trash.

Julia glanced at the wall clock. "I have to pick up Max. You didn't bargain for an afternoon with a four-year-old. Maybe I should wait at the cottage."

"No way."

"But—"

"I like kids." She already knew that about him, but he wanted to reassure her. She still seemed nervous, so he reached for the hotel phone and called Brittany Thompson, the assistant rec director leading that day's children's program. "Hey, Brittany. It's Zeke. Do you still have kids there?"

"Just Max."

"Good. I need a favor. Julia's here and waiting for a phone call. Would you bring Max to my office?"

"Sure."

When he hung up, Zeke expected Julia to relax. Instead her brows cinched into crooked lines. She seemed to be thinking about something, so Zeke let her think. They weren't in any hurry. He dropped down onto the leather sofa, and Julia walked over and perched on the edge of a chair.

"There's something I'd like—"

Her cell phone interrupted with a message. With her sentence hanging, she jumped up to check it.

"Your mom?"

"No. A wedding photographer."

"So you found someone?"

"Not yet and I'm desperate. I better call this woman now."

With the phone to her ear, she sat at the desk

and picked up a pen. "Hello, Ruth? This is Julia Dare . . . Yes. The Travers wedding." Technically, she was arranging the Reid-Wilkins wedding, but the Travers name gave her leverage. "That's right," she said into the phone. "That wasn't a typo. It really is September of this year. Three weeks from now."

Looking at Zeke to include him, she rolled her eyes toward the ceiling. "Yes, I know it's short notice. Is there someone you could recommend?" She scribbled a name or two, ended the call, and came back to the sitting area.

"I'm worried. I've called at least twenty photographers and no one I trust is available. Food gets eaten and flowers wilt, but photographs end up on mantles and nightstands. We need someone with an artistic eye, someone who can capture the romance."

Without thinking, Zeke gave her shoulder a squeeze. She stiffened but relaxed with the next breath. She wasn't unhappy about the touch, and neither was he.

She offered a rueful smile. "I don't suppose you have a fabulous photographer at your beck and call?"

"No, but the resort uses a local guy on occasion."

"Does he do weddings?"

"I think so."

Hope flashed in her eyes. "We need someone

artsy but not weird. Someone who's creative and good with people."

"This guy isn't weird." Boring maybe, but not weird. "Let's check out his website."

They were moving to her computer when the glass door flew open. A little boy with Julia's dark hair burst into the office, leaving two smudgy handprints on the glass. He stopped dead in his tracks when he saw Zeke.

Julia pulled the boy into a hug. "Hey, big guy. How was play time?"

"Fun."

Brittany smiled down at him. "We painted pictures of dinosaurs. Didn't we, Max?"

"Yep. Mine's green."

With her hand light on Max's shoulder, Julia turned him to Zeke. "Max, this is Mr. Monroe. He's my boss."

Suddenly shy, Max buried his face against Julia's leg. He was a cute kid with his mother's brown eyes. If he resembled his dad, Zeke didn't see the likeness.

Zeke wanted to make friends, but he respected Julia's rules, so he whispered to her, "Do you mind if he calls me Zeke?"

"That's fine."

He dropped to a crouch, one arm draped over his knee. "Hey there, Max. My name's Zeke. It's a funny name that starts with Z like zebra."

Max peeked over his shoulder. "My name starts with M."

"Cool," Zeke replied. "Which dinosaur did you paint?"

"A T. rex."

"That's my favorite."

"Oh, yeah?"

"Yeah," Zeke replied. "He's the biggest."

When Max eased away from his mom, Zeke knew he'd made a friend. *Cute kid.* No wonder Julia was proud of him. Someday Zeke wanted a son of his own, but first he needed a wife. He had dated a lot before coming to CS, but no woman fascinated him the way Julia had . . . and still did.

Don't go there.

But it was too late. When she tousled Max's hair with her long fingers, Zeke's chest tightened the way it did in Berkeley when they were in love. The thought didn't scare him a bit. In fact, he rather liked the idea of testing those murky waters.

He waited while she arranged for Max to attend the next day's children's program. As soon as Brittany left, he made an offer that a hungry woman with a four-year-old boy couldn't refuse.

"How about a picnic in my office?"

Julia hesitated. "Are you sure? We can be a handful."

"I'm positive." He walked around her desk to

the hotel phone. "You skipped lunch, and I have a hunch Max can always eat. We'll order from Katrina's. What does everyone want?"

Max called out first. "Chicken nuggets."

Jules went next. "A turkey sandwich on sourdough—"

"With extra tomato?" Zeke finished.

She laughed. "I can't believe you remember that."

There were a lot of things Zeke remembered, including the way she pulled her hair into a ponytail on a hot day, or how she dabbed French fries in ketchup. When it rained, she closed her eyes and listened. And when it was sunny, she closed them even harder and basked in the warmth on her skin.

He cleared his throat with a rumble. "I remember a lot of things."

"So do I. You're going to order a cheeseburger well done."

"Burnt to a crisp."

A wistful smile crossed her face. "Some things don't change, do they?"

"No. But others do, and that's okay." His gaze flicked down to Max.

Instead of bantering back, Julia gnawed on her lower lip.

Max tugged on her arm. "Mommy, let's play."

Kids . . . they had more energy than lithium batteries. While Julia distracted Max, Zeke called the restaurant and placed their order. When he finished, he came back around the desk. "Hey, Max. How would you like to see a dinosaur egg?"

His eyes popped wide open. "Really?"

"Sort of." He told Max about the geodes. "Some are hollow and look like miniature caves. Others are solid. Those are thunder eggs, but my dad called them dinosaur eggs. Let's go look."

Max peered up at Julia, asking for permission or maybe reassurance.

She patted his shoulder. "Let's all go."

They walked to Zeke's office with Max gripping Julia's hand. Zeke led the way to the shelves and hoisted Max to his hip.

The boy pointed at the biggest geode, a mix of yellow and white that resembled a raw egg. "Wow!"

Zeke traded a smile with Julia. Before he could think, his gaze dipped to her lips. He looked up fast, but their gazes met and held. In the span of a blink, six years melted away, and Zeke found himself holding Max even tighter.

Julia's phone rang with the opening notes of *Amazing Grace*. A little clumsy, she snatched it from her pocket and held it to her ear. "Mom? How are you?"

Zeke watched her expression for clues.

"So it's just a mild sprain." She gave him a big thumbs-up. "Are you on your way back?"

He expected her to indicate her mom's answer with a nod or a shake of her head. Instead, her brows shot up. With her mouth agape, she pointed at the phone as if to say, *You won't believe what I just heard!* Curious about the drama, Zeke carried Max to the couch and gave him paper and some colored pens, then sat next to him, listening while Julia finished with Ellen.

"No, mom. Don't hurry. We're having a good time. Text me when you're close, okay?" She ended the call with "I love you," lowered the phone, and slapped her hand over her heart. "I can't believe this."

With George involved, Zeke could believe anything from a concert in the waiting room to pizza delivered to the entire ER. "What happened?"

"George is taking her to IHOP."

"IHOP?"

"You know." She waggled her brows. "The International House of Pancakes . . . for dinner."

"So?"

"I think it's a date."

Zeke rubbed his chin with his fingers. "It's a date, definitely. But only if you're over fifty-five."

She hummed. "My mom's fifty-three. How old is George?"

"Sixty-four."

"That seems so . . ." She shook her head.

"Old?"

"Yes, but I was going to say far away." She dragged the guest chair at his desk closer to the couch and sat. "I hope it *is* a date. My mom says she's happy, but I think she's lonely. My dad was a great guy."

Zeke recalled the Thanksgiving he spent with her family. Benjamin Dare had greeted him with a handshake that nearly broke his fingers and a look that said, *Mind your manners with my daughter.* Then he invited Zeke to watch football as if he were one of the family.

"I liked your dad a lot."

"He liked you too." Julia lowered her gaze to Max, who was scribbling with all his might. Her mouth pulled into a sad smile. "I named Max after him."

Zeke recalled the funeral notice with her father's full name, *Benjamin Maxwell Dare.* "It's a fitting tribute."

And one that made him wonder about Max's dad. Had he asked Julia to marry him? And if he did, why did she say no?

Thirteen

The food arrived and the three of them ate at the coffee table. While Max and Zeke debated the merits of burgers versus chicken nuggets, Julia argued in favor of turkey sandwiches. The only tension in the room was in her mind, where the *Oh, by the way* speech waited patiently to be delivered. If Max fell asleep, she could tell Zeke in a bland tone that wouldn't wake her son or stir up too much drama.

When Max yawned, she stacked the ketchup-stained plates, then fetched the sweater she kept at her desk and covered him with it. "Someone's sleepy," she murmured.

Zeke yawned too, either to influence Max or because he was worn out from an early golf lesson and a busy day. Max slumped against Zeke's side, and they both closed their eyes.

She didn't have the heart to disturb Zeke, especially to deliver a speech that would taint the day, so she kicked off her shoes, hugged her knees, and considered how much they had both changed. His features were sharper now, more acute, as if parts of his youth had been chipped away. Julia too had endured the hammer and chisel of change. She didn't trust her heart at all, but she knew God loved her. She could barely fathom it, but Zeke did. He loved God more than any person she knew.

Her phone broke into her thoughts with a text. As Zeke and Max opened their eyes, she skimmed it. "It's my mom. They'll be at the cottage in about twenty minutes. I better go."

Zeke lumbered to his feet and stretched.

Julia turned her attention to Max. "It's time to go. Say thank you to Zeke for lunch."

Max's lower lip pushed out. "I want to see the rocks again."

"Not now, big guy."

His face puckered into a pout. Julia couldn't blame Hunter for this one. Max was tired, fussy, and acting like a four-year-old.

Pushing to her feet, she held out her hand, a clear signal to obey. "It's time to go."

He made a mad dash for the bookshelf holding the geodes. "I want to see the red one again."

She marched after him. "No, Max. It's time to leave."

Ignoring her, he pushed up on his toes, grabbed a shelf for leverage, and tried to climb.

Zeke bolted forward and swept the boy up to his hip. "Hey, Max. Your mom makes the rules."

"No, my daddy does." Max wrenched around and stared at her, Hunter's mini-me in every way.

Zeke put Max down but kept a grip on his hand. "Your mom makes rules too. Good ones

163

that keep people safe. You don't want Grammie waiting outside, do you?"

Max thought a moment, then shook his head.

"Now—" Zeke waited until Max met his gaze. "You and I are going to open the door for your mom, because that's what guys do for girls."

The idea seemed to hang in the air, then Max nodded. "Okay, but can I come back and see the rocks?"

"That's up to your mom."

Max spun toward Julia. "Can I?"

"May I," she corrected. "And yes, you may, but only if it's okay with Zeke."

Max scampered to the door, stopped short, and turned back to Julia. "You go first cuz you're a girl."

Smiling her gratitude to Zeke, she stepped through the door and waited until Max scrambled past her and out of earshot. There wasn't time for the full conversation about Hunter, but she could start it. Dreading the entire prospect, she forced the words from her tight lips. "I want to tell you about Max's dad. Not right now, but soon."

Zeke glanced at the back of Max's head. He was six feet away, pretending to be a T. rex. "Anytime."

"Maybe tomorrow. At lunch."

"Mommy!"

Zeke answered for her. "Hold on, Max. She'll be right there." He lowered his voice again. "Whatever works for you. Just let me know."

"Thank you."

"In fact"—he sounded dead serious, but his eyes twinkled—"when your mom's up and around, how about dinner at IHOP?"

Julia couldn't help but smile. "If you're under fifty-five, that's not a date."

"Then we'll go somewhere else." His voice came out husky, just the way she used to love.

Idiot. She had no business blurring the lines between them.

Sobering instantly, she dropped the smile. "Just to be clear, this won't be a date. It's more of a—"

Confession.

"Mommy, hurry." Max started to bounce on his toes. "I have to go potty."

Zeke laughed. "Someone needs you. We'll sort out the details later."

It was just like Zeke to put Max first. And her too. No pressure. Just patience. "Thanks for everything, Zeke. You made today easier than it should have been."

"I'm glad."

"About tomorrow morning . . . I can't leave Max with my mom on crutches. Is it okay if I work from the cottage?"

"No problem."

"Mommy!"

"Go," Zeke said, chuckling a little.

Julia thanked him with a quick smile, hurried to Max, and led him out the door to the ladies' room, listening to his protests that he was a big boy and could go to the men's room by himself.

"Not today," she told him.

He gave in, but Julia ached with the knowledge of how badly Max needed a father. Someone like Zeke who'd teach him to hold open a door. Hunter would teach the same lesson, but when he did something nice, he expected to be admired for it. Zeke didn't think that way. He put others first, which made her want to put *him* first. Or second, right after God.

When Max finished, Julia led him to the sink to wash his hands. She waved her own hand to turn on the automatic faucet, then held Max's hand under the soap dispenser. His stubby fingers were covered with white foam and water when her phone meowed. Stifling a sigh, she instructed Max to finish rinsing and took the call.

"Hunter, this isn't a good time."

"It'll just be a minute."

"What is it?"

"My plans changed. I thought I'd spend the weekend with you and Max."

"Here?"

"Sure, why not?" He sounded pleased, as if he'd bestowed her with an honor. "We can hang out at the pool."

"No. I'm working."

"Not on Saturday."

"Yes, on Saturday." His tone irked her. "That's

when the bride and her stand-in mom will be here." The faucet stopped. Julia started it again to keep Max occupied. "This isn't a good time for you to visit. My mom sprained her ankle this afternoon. She's going to need me."

"I think it's a perfect time. I can take Max off your hands."

The offer made sense, but she didn't want Hunter to visit Caliente Springs. She was free from him here, except for the techno-leash. "It just won't work."

"Come on, Julia. Be reasonable."

"I am." At one time in their relationship, she would have appeased him. Today she felt bullied.

Max cupped his hands under the faucet to make a fountain. Water sprayed everywhere, which he thought was hilarious. She couldn't turn off the automatic faucet, so she moved his hands, which made the water splash on her beige slacks.

She spoke to Max instead of Hunter. "Let's dry your hands—"

"What's going on?" Hunter demanded.

"Hold on." She set down the phone and led Max to the automatic dryer. After two swipes of her hand, it roared to life. She picked up the phone again. "Sorry. We're in the bathroom. The faucet went a little wild."

"Where are you, anyway?"

"Just leaving the office."

"And you took our *son* to the ladies' room? You

baby him, Julia. He's old enough to use the men's room."

"He's in a new place and it's unfamiliar." Did Hunter have to criticize everything she did? Apparently so.

"Let me talk to him."

As if she didn't have enough to juggle. "His hands are wet, and we need to leave. We'll call you tonight."

Max turned to her, his face bright. "Is that Daddy?"

"Yes, honey." Julia ignored his still-wet hands. "We'll call him after we take care of Grammie."

"I want to tell him about Zeke and the rocks."

Julia held her breath. *Please, God. Strike Hunter deaf for that one word.*

Hunter chortled into her ear. "Did he say *Zeke?*"

"Yes."

Hunter laughed even louder. "I haven't heard that name since St. John's. Zeke Monroe was a real wuss."

Julia couldn't let the insult slide. "Well, he's not a wuss now. He's the general manager of Caliente Springs." When silence crackled in her ear, she indulged in some gloating. For once, she had surprised Hunter. "I'll call you later. We can make plans for the weekend after this one."

"I'm busy then."

Julia doubted it. As usual, he was manipulating the circumstances to his liking.

"This weekend, babe. Plan for Saturday."

"Hunter, no."

The phone went dead in her ear. Shaking with anger, she leaned against the counter and massaged her temples. Across from her, Max waved his hands at the dryer. It roared to life and blasted hot air. What if Hunter showed up tomorrow instead of Saturday? The thought of him surprising Zeke sickened her. She needed to talk to Zeke now, at least briefly.

Gripping Max's hand, she headed back to the office. If she left Max at her desk, she could tell Zeke quickly with the promise of a full explanation later.

She was almost at the door when her mom texted. At the cottage. Forgot my keys!

Pulled in four directions—between her mom, Zeke, Hunter, and Max—Julia decided her mother needed her most.

Gripping Max's hand, she headed to her car, aware that Hunter hadn't asked a single question about Ellen and her injuries. If that was how he treated people in need, what kind of father was he to Max?

Not the kind she wanted.

But what could she do about it? Hunter's DNA trumped all her instincts to cut him out of her life. She could only hope God's mercy, and especially his love, trumped Hunter's DNA.

Fourteen

On Friday afternoon Zeke pulled his SUV into the driveway of Julia's cottage. Apparently IHOP did count as a date, because George's Corvette was there. He was looking after Ellen and Max so Zeke and Julia could scout ceremony sites as planned. If Julia was up for it, they were also free to have dinner away from Caliente Springs.

As Zeke braked to a halt, the cottage door opened and Julia stepped onto the brick path. Sunglasses in place, she cut across the lawn with a white sundress swishing around her tanned legs. A man couldn't help but notice a pretty woman, and Zeke noticed.

He climbed out of the car, intending to open the door for her, but she waved him off and climbed in on her own. The instant the door latched shut, she burst out laughing.

"What is it?" he asked.

"My mom and George! They're acting like teenagers. You should see the flowers he sent."

Zeke backed out of the driveway. "Knowing George, they're over the top."

"Completely. He sent three dozen of the most perfect yellow roses I've ever seen. My mom knows flowers, and she's impressed. Yellow might stand for friendship, but three dozen? That says something else entirely."

"George doesn't hold back."

"No, and I like that about him." Julia pushed her sunglasses higher on her nose. "You know that sports saying 'Go big or go home'? That reminds me of George, and it's what we have to do for Tiff's wedding."

"Especially the *big* part." Zeke turned right at the gate. "The number of guests is going to limit the options for the ceremony site. What's the RSVP count?"

"I spent the morning making calls to the people who haven't responded yet. Counting guests and plus-ones, we have three hundred and seventy yes's, forty no's, and thirty-eight people who are still deciding."

Zeke did some quick arithmetic. "If we plan for four hundred and fifty guests, we should be safe."

"I think so too." Julia reached into the portfolio she carried everywhere and took out a notepad. "Which site are we visiting first?"

"Golden Point."

While Zeke drove, they chatted about wedding plans. A quarter mile past the stable, he turned right on a road that sloped uphill and ended in a round parking area. An arrow-shaped sign marked the spot as Golden Point and pointed to a dirt path.

Julia studied the ground with a critical eye. "I

don't think Aunt Edith will be up for off-roading in her wheelchair."

"We can take her in a golf cart," Zeke offered.

"Maybe."

They walked down the path, each commenting on the pros and cons of the site, mostly the cons. When they reached the concrete pad, Zeke assessed the size while Julia eyeballed the chipped brown paint on the metal rails. Together they stepped to the edge and took in the tranquil view.

Zeke nodded toward the mountains just east of the resort. "When the sun hits at a certain angle, the minerals in the rock catch the light and shimmer gold. It really is beautiful."

Julia let out a sigh. "The sunset won't matter if we can't seat four hundred and fifty people up here."

"No. It won't."

She paced off the concrete pad in both directions, measuring with her own steps. "It'll be tight. But even if the chairs fit, we're forty yards from the parking area. That's a long walk in high heels on a rocky dirt path."

Zeke thought a minute. "It's not in the budget, but we could consider laying down asphalt."

"Just for Tiff?" Julia shook her head. "That's too much to ask."

"Not if the investment pays off. If this wedding leads to several others, the benefit will outweigh the cost."

"You have a point." Julia glanced again at the view. "But it's a big project and time's running out. Let's check out the other sites. What's next?"

"That little lake I told you about."

Ten minutes later, Zeke turned down a narrow road marked by two stone pillars and a sign that said *Diddly Down Lake*.

"It's named after George and Ginger's first big hit," he explained.

"Cute." Julia perked up. "So far, so good."

The SUV's tires crunched on old gravel. "We use the lake to irrigate the golf course. The oak trees are nice, and the ground is level. Those are both pluses."

"Is it romantic?" Julia peered ahead through the windshield. "We need a spot that's sigh-worthy."

"You'll have to be the judge of that." Zeke was far more concerned with logistics and safety for a big crowd, especially when the SUV bounced in a pothole. "The parking lot is a decent size. Big enough for vans from the hotel and limos for the family, but it's in pretty bad shape."

Julia was already eyeballing the lake. "No one will care about the parking lot. Let's check out the view."

Side-by-side, they walked along a path littered with twigs and debris. Zeke swept at the mess with his foot and sent a dozen acorns skittering in the dirt. "The grounds crew can sweep this all up and put down some DG."

"What's that?"

"Decomposed granite. It'll give us an even surface."

Julia looked up into the branches. "The shade is nice. And I like the symbolism of old trees."

They passed out from under the canopy and stepped into the sun. The lake, more of a pond because of the drought, reflected the sky and clouds. Julia studied it with a practiced eye. "It's pretty but not stunning. We would need to do something special . . . something crazy." She spun to him. "I've got it."

"What?"

"Swans!"

"Swans?"

"If we put a hundred of them on the lake, it'll be unforgettable."

Zeke scratched under his chin. "I'll call Rent-A-Swan right away. Seriously, where do you get a hundred swans?"

"I don't know," she admitted. "But what do you think of adding two black ones? They'd symbolize Tiff and Derek, and people could look for them. It would give them something to chat about. I really like this idea."

Zeke's mind was stuck on finding the swans, not to mention the problem of wildlife regulations, feeding a hundred swans, re-catching a hundred swans, and generally putting up with a hundred swans. He couldn't imagine what they'd do to the golf course.

He dragged his hand over the back of his neck. "Swan wrangling isn't exactly my area of expertise."

"Mine either. But I love the whole idea. Could we check it out?"

Her sweet smile undid whatever doubts he had. For Julia and Caliente Springs, he'd put on his superhero cape and take on swans, bureaucracy, and anything else in the way. "I'll make some calls."

She faced the lake and closed her eyes. "I can see it perfectly. A flock of swans. Or a bevy. Whatever they're called. The sun reflected on the water." She inhaled deeply. "The smell of grass and—" Her eyes popped open. "Oh no." She sniffed the air like a deer scenting danger.

"What?" Zeke sniffed too. "Oh."

They turned to each other and spoke at the same time. "Skunk!"

Julia pinched her nose. "Ew."

"No kidding." Zeke's eyes were watering like faucets. "There must be a den nearby."

When he pressed his hand to his face, Julia burst out laughing. "Can't you just see it? Derek standing by the lake in his tux. Tiff coming through the trees in her beautiful white gown . . . and the guests all sitting here with handkerchiefs to their noses."

Zeke cringed and laughed at the same time. "We can forget Diddly Down Lake."

Gripping her hand, he led her back down the path strewn with acorns that rolled like marbles. Slipping and sliding, they grabbed each other like circus clowns and laughed even harder. When they reached the safety of the parking lot, he put his hand on the small of her back. For a moment they studied each other and the laughter faded.

With her fingers laced behind her back, she blinked twice, then glanced down and to the side. He knew that look. She was working up the courage to say something, but apparently she changed her mind, because she simply exhaled.

"Let's check out the last spot. It's the garden by the main building, isn't it?" she said.

"I have another idea."

"Good, because we could use one."

"It's not about the wedding," he said. "Let's go for a drive. We can have dinner together."

Julia was determined to have the *Oh, by the way* talk tonight, and a coffee shop with bright lights struck her as the best place for it. After all the talk of Tiff's wedding, the swan idea, and giggling about skunk smells, she needed a dose of reality.

She reached for her phone. "I'd like that a lot, but I need to check with my mom and George."

"He's fine with it."

She took a moment to process what Zeke had said. "Oh, I get it now."

"What?"

"George paid you to kidnap me so he can flirt with my mom."

"You figured it out," Zeke teased as he helped her into the SUV. "Ellen better watch out, because you know George's reputation. He's up to no good."

"For my mom's sake, I hope so." Julia wasn't free to enjoy a romance of her own right now, but Ellen was. *Go for it, Mom!*

While Zeke drove toward the coast, they chatted about everything from the wedding to his golf lessons and the unrelenting drought. As they approached the town of Pismo Beach, she expected him to ask her about dinner, but instead he drove down a narrow road that ended at a parking booth. He paid the attendant, rounded a curve that ended at the sand, and stopped to take a tire gauge out of the glove box. Unless there was a Denny's down the beach, they weren't going to a coffee shop.

She glanced quizzically at the gauge. "What are you doing?"

"Letting air out of the tires."

"Why?"

"You'll see."

While Zeke circled the SUV, crouching by each tire, Julia peered down the beach littered with vehicles. A sign told her this was part of the famous Pismo Beach recreational vehicle park.

Zeke climbed back in the car. "Here we go." Pressing the accelerator, he launched the SUV onto the sand. Not fast, but the slip and slide of the tires made her feel like they were dancing.

Moving with the rhythm, she turned to Zeke. "You surprised me."

"Good."

"Why did you let the air out?"

"It helps with traction. We'll have to stop to put in air before we hit the highway home, but it's worth it."

Julia wasn't so sure. For the *Oh, by the way* conversation, she would have far preferred the harsh glare of overhead lights to the romantic glow of a sunset.

"So," she said, trying to lighten the mood, "is there a taco stand around here somewhere?"

"No taco stand. I have firewood and a picnic basket in back." He glanced at her shoulders, bare in the sundress. "And a couple of hoodies."

"So you planned this."

"Yes." He kept his eyes straight ahead. "We went on a few picnics back in Berkeley. I thought you'd enjoy the spot I have in mind."

They rode down the beach in silence, her fingers knotted on the seat belt strap. Zeke finally backed up onto dry sand and parked.

In five minutes, they were sitting shoulder to shoulder on a Mexican blanket, their knees up and toes buried in the sand. The fire was laid and ready to light. The picnic basket was behind them, unopened except for the can of Sprite in her hand and the bottle of water in his. In front of them, the waves washed up and down the shore, a backbeat to the hoarse squawking of the seagulls.

Neither of them spoke. It wasn't the least bit awkward, but the *Oh, by the way* speech was about to change everything.

Julia took a breath, let it out, and eased an inch away from him. "I want to tell you about Max's dad."

Zeke had planned a picnic for this very reason. Julia needed both privacy and the promise of no interruptions when she told her story.

The sun sat on the horizon, an orange ball shimmering against turquoise sky and blue-gray water. Focusing on the distant swells, Julia raised her chin like a prisoner about to walk the plank in a pirate movie. Whatever she had to say couldn't be that bad. Single motherhood was practically the norm now. But a shiver ran through her, either from the faint chill in the breeze or something dark and internal.

Zeke pulled matches out of his shirt pocket. "I'll light the fire. You talk."

Shifting his weight, he knelt in front of the pile of wood and struck a match. The kindling caught fast. Flames shot from the bottom and licked the bigger pieces of construction scraps and split pine. A minute later, Julia still hadn't spoken, but the fire was burning strong enough for Zeke to sit back down.

She hugged her knees to her chest. "When my dad died, it was awful. You probably remember how hard it was for me."

"I remember everything." Her tears dampening his shirt. How he had pushed heaven at her. The fights that came later.

"You were good to me, Zeke. But I lashed out at you. I was confused—"

"And hurting."

"Yes, but that's no excuse for the way I behaved."

He didn't see the tie to Max's dad, only his own failings. When Julia had needed a shoulder to cry on, instead of listening, Zeke sledgehammered her with his faith. He was so sure of himself back then, Mr. Perfect Christian who knew the rules but couldn't keep them.

Next to him the fire burned brighter as the sun dropped lower. A stream of smoke poured off a log, filling his nose with the pungent scent of change.

"It was a rough time for me." Julia dug her toes deeper into the sand, curling them so that two little mountains bulged. "I didn't realize it then, but it was easier to be mad at you than to admit how helpless I felt."

"I get it. Sometimes life stinks."

"But still—"

"Jules, go easy on yourself." He wished he could take his own advice, but he thought of the boxes in the garage and heard his dad's voice telling him to try harder, do more, be better. "What happened is in the past."

"Well, not exactly."

"I'm confused."

She looked him square in the eye. "Do you remember Hunter Adams?"

"Of course."

Hunter Adams had been a thorn in Zeke's side, and that was putting it mildly. As hard as Zeke had tried back then to turn the other cheek, Hunter Adams was the one human being who got thoroughly under his skin. Homeless guys who reeked of sweat and booze? No problem. Low-end hookers with haughty eyes? No problem. But if you put someone like Hunter in his path, an arrogant jerk who looked down on everyone, Zeke wasn't so sure about turning the other cheek.

It didn't help that Hunter had ridiculed him mercilessly with those silly nicknames. There had been a peculiar, even twisted, rivalry between them, one that tested every ounce of Zeke's Christian charity until Hunter bad-mouthed a client. When Zeke corrected him, Hunter had goaded him into an embarrassing shouting match. Another defeat for a man determined to control his feelings and turn the other cheek.

Why would Julia bring up Hunter now? A chill of premonition shivered down his spine. Steeling himself, he turned his head in her direction.

She met his gaze with an unblinking stare. "Do you remember how confident Hunter was? How sure of himself?"

"I'd say arrogant."

"So would I—now." She paused, studying him even more carefully. "But at the time, he seemed to have all the answers. And I wanted that security."

A log snapped and hissed. A wave rolled up the sand, coming closer than the one before it. Knowing what she was about to say, he said it for her.

"Hunter is Max's dad."

"Yes." Unable to look him in the eye, she swung her gaze back to the fading sun.

Zeke stared at the horizon just as blindly, his mind spiraling back to those last days in Berkeley, in particular the misty May night she had asked him to meet her at Caffé Med. She'd waited until after finals to do it—a small mercy, considering she'd torn his heart out.

"It's over, Zeke. I appreciate everything you ever did for me. I really do. But we don't see the world the same and we never will. It's best to go our separate ways."

He didn't fight with her. His plane ticket to Chile was booked for two days later, and they had been at odds since her dad's funeral.

That final good-bye hadn't been a surprise, but now, as his mind drifted back to that time, fresh details snapped into place. Julia chatting with Hunter. The way she propped a hip on Hunter's desk. Her guilty look when Zeke walked in on them sharing a private joke.

His stomach twisted into an unforgiving knot. But that knot was honest, and he was done sugar-coating his life. With his stomach burning, he faced facts. "He's the reason you dumped me."

Wincing, she hung her head to the side, her hair falling to make a curtain that hid her face but not the quaver in her voice. "That's partially true. You and I were . . . we were arguing all the time."

"I remember."

"I started seeing Hunter before we officially broke up. It wasn't deliberate. I had lunch with him a few times, then dinner. I didn't tell you. I knew it was wrong, but at the time it seemed okay." She dragged a finger through the dry sand, watching as it caved in on itself. "Nothing physical happened until you were in Chile, but I still betrayed you. When Hunter made fun of you, I didn't defend you. Instead I joined in. I hope you can forgive me, because I feel terrible about how I treated you."

He picked up a charred broom handle and stabbed at the logs. Once. Twice. A third time. Embers shot to the darkening sky and exploded into painful memories. He had been so sure of himself when they first met. She wasn't a Christian then, and his upbringing taught him not to be unevenly yoked. He tried hard to put up walls to protect them both, but the walls crumbled one at a time until he fell into bed with her.

A groan crawled out of his throat. There was no excuse for Julia's betrayal, but his own slate was far from clean. He was the last man to pick up a stone and throw it.

"Zeke—" Her voice cracked. "I'm so sorry. You must hate me."

"Hate you?"

"Yes. I cheated on you. I lied—"

He dropped the smoking broomstick in the sand. "For both our sakes, let's get everything out in the open. I'll be honest. It hurts. I didn't like Hunter then, and from what I saw the other day on the pier, I won't like him now. He's a jerk. But the past is the past, and you have a wonderful little boy who deserves the best life you can give him."

Julia finally turned to him, her eyes damp with tears. "I'm so glad you feel that way."

"I do. Hunter's a problem, but Max is a great kid."

A human being with a personality and ambitions of his own. A blend of his parents but still himself.

Before they left the beach, Zeke wanted to bury the past completely. "Just to finish up, what happened after I left Berkeley?"

She told him about going with Hunter to Los Angeles, the unplanned pregnancy, the three cancelled weddings, and her decision to finally break up, move out, and move on.

"That was six months ago. All I want now is to be a good mom to Max and to make Dare to Dream a success. You have to laugh at the irony here. I spent three years planning my own wedding and it never happened. Now I'm planning Tiff's in thirty days."

"If you ask me, you dodged a bullet."

"By not marrying him?"

"Yes."

"I think so too. But it's hard with Max. Whether I like it or not, Hunter is part of my life." She hugged her knees again. "Like this weekend. He's coming up here. I asked him not to, but he hung up on me."

"Does he know I'm here?"

"Yes."

"That's fine," Zeke replied. "There's no reason the three of us can't be civil, even friendly."

"No reason except Hunter." Julia visibly shuddered. "If you want to avoid him, we're trading Max off at Katrina's at noon."

Saturdays were busy for Zeke, but if he wanted to be part of Julia's life, he'd be wise to keep the peace with Hunter. Extending an olive branch was the right thing to do. "There's no reason for me to avoid him. In fact, I'd like to say hello."

She lifted an eyebrow at him. "Are you sure?"

"Positive."

A faint sigh slipped from her lips. Relaxing, she stretched her legs out and leaned back on her arms. "I used to have all the answers about everything. Life. Love—"

"Global warming."

"Exactly." She gave him a sad smile. "Hunter knocked the wind out of me. I'm just now learning how to breathe again."

The breeze lifted wisps of her hair, revealing both her strong cheekbones and a new fragility. An old ache started deep in Zeke's heart. He recognized the longing to be strong for her. The instinct to protect her. The desire to connect to this beautiful woman in a beautiful way. He had loved her deeply.

Looking at her now, with his pulse thrumming and his chest tight, he was afraid he still did.

Those feelings cried out to be explored, but now she was a Christian and he was damaged goods. In the deepest part of his soul, someplace dark and childlike, where monsters lived under the bed, he wanted the faith of the little boy he'd once been. Julia couldn't give it to him. He knew that. But somehow, looking at her in the fading light of the fire, he wanted to search for that faith on his own.

He stood abruptly and offered his hand. "It's a warm night. Let's be brave and get our feet wet."

Fifteen

When Zeke tugged on her arm, Julia leapt off the blanket with her heart as light and soaring as a helium balloon. The weight she had carried since seeing Zeke in the hotel lobby was gone now. He knew everything there was to know about Hunter, and her conscience was clear.

He rolled his Levi's up to his knees, and with her hand tucked in his bigger one, they walked toward the water. Pismo Beach was long and shallow, the kind of shore where waves stacked on waves and broke gently. She stayed close to his side, reveling in the contrast of the shame she'd felt an hour ago to the forgiveness and grace lifting her heart now.

With their fingers entwined, they stepped from dry sand onto the cold, flat apron left by the last wave. Thirty feet in the distance, a wave broke with a rumble and sped toward them. Holding tight to Zeke's hand, she braced for the shock of cold water covering her ankles. When the wave hit, she did a little dance complete with a chorus of "Oh-oh-oh!"

Zeke caught her by the elbow. Chuckling while she splashed, he held her steady as the retreating water sucked sand from beneath her feet.

Before she knew what was happening, they were facing each other. His hands slid up her arms, and in the next breath his face was an inch above hers. When she looked into his eyes, her breath caught while her heart pounded madly. Slowly, giving her time to change her mind, he matched his lips to hers.

The kiss was small and sweet, but it recalled a thousand that were big and bold. When he lifted his head, she froze with her face still raised to his. His mouth dipped back to hers and he kissed her again, lingering until she pulled back.

With her pulse racing, she searched his eyes and saw everything she could ever want in a man. Passion. Integrity. Respect. The faithful heart of a man who put God first.

Zeke rubbed her back the way he had in college. Old feelings came alive, and she dared to wonder about a fresh start. But then the present crashed into the past. Hunter wouldn't like it if she started to date again, and he'd be especially hostile if that man were Zeke. On the other hand, she couldn't allow Hunter to dictate her choices. Like her mother said, she needed to be brave. But fear boiled out of a crack deep in her psyche. If she upset Hunter, he'd use Max to manipulate her the way he had with the zoo trip.

Trusting God with her own well-being was one

thing. Trusting him to protect Max required a depth of faith beyond Julia's experience.

Weak and still shaking, she took a big step back. "I shouldn't have done that."

With one brow arched, he shoved his hands in his pockets. "Why not?"

"A lot of reasons." She didn't even want to breathe Hunter's name. "My life is complicated. Max. My business. My mother too."

"And Hunter," he said for her.

"Yes."

Another wave, a big one that would eat the ones in front of it, roared toward them. Quick as a blink, Zeke snatched her hand and guided her higher up the beach.

Facing her, he clasped her cold arms with his warm fingers. "You're in limbo right now. I get that, so I'm going to be very direct. I have feelings for you, Jules. Strong ones. I want to give those feelings a chance to grow, but you have responsibilities and so do I."

"I feel the same way." Her voice quavered.

"So let's take our time. Tonight doesn't have to change anything. First and foremost, we're friends."

She tried to nod, but her brow lifted in doubt. Friends didn't kiss the way they had just kissed. Not once, but twice. That second kiss was still burning through her.

"I know what you're thinking." His mouth

hinted at a smile. "Friends don't kiss the way we just did. So let's draw some lines." He dragged a toe in the wet sand. "The first line is for Max. He comes first. Always."

"Yes."

"You make the rules concerning your son, and I'll follow them to the letter. Kids are vulnerable. No matter what the future holds for you and me, I don't want Max to be hurt."

Her biggest concern, and it was Zeke's biggest worry too.

He drew a second line parallel to the first. "This is the 'we work together' line. Caliente Springs goes wild with gossip. You don't need that kind of attention, and I don't either. I'm in the public eye there. People watch, including Ginger, so we need to be ultra-professional."

"Especially about Tiff's wedding. We can't let anything interfere with it." So far, he was reading her mind.

He took another step back, drew a third line longer and deeper than the others, and stared at it for several seconds. The angle hid his face, but she saw tension in his neck and jaw. When he looked up, the light was gone from his eyes. "That third line is for me. It's a reminder that we're not the same people we were in Berkeley. You've changed. So have I."

His bleak tone bothered her. She knew how she had changed, but Zeke was the same good man he'd always been. Tonight, even with all the turmoil, he'd put her first.

Before she could ask him what he meant, he aimed his chin at the fire. It was smaller now but still burning bright. "I'm starved. Let's eat."

Close but not touching, they walked back to the blanket. A land breeze blew her hair back and chilled her skin. Before adding wood to the fire, Zeke helped her into a hoodie and put on one himself.

While he stirred the embers, she opened the picnic basket, saw hot dogs, and smiled. "You're cooking dinner for me."

"Hot dogs," he said with his trademark grin. "My specialty."

They'd done this before at St. John's, only instead of cooking for two, he had cooked for two hundred at a fundraiser. He fed a lot of people that day, rich and poor alike. But that was Zeke. He took care of people. And tonight he was taking care of her.

Snuggling into the hoodie, she dared to hope that today was indeed the start of something brand-new.

Ellen was seated on the sofa next to George with an empty popcorn bowl between them. The closing credits for *The African Queen* scrolled on the flat-screen TV, and her foot was propped on a pillow on an ottoman. Still aglow with the happy ending for Charlie and Rose, aka Humphrey Bogart and Katharine Hepburn, she turned to George.

"Good movie," he said.

"It's old."

"It's a classic," he replied, his voice pitched low. "Those just get better with time. Don't you think?"

Ellen paused. "Yes. I suppose they do."

They weren't talking about the movie anymore. They were talking about themselves in the same clever way she used to talk with Ben. She couldn't help but like George. He understood her in ways no one else did, and looking into his eyes, she—

Julia's key rattled in the front door.

Ellen startled like a teenager caught on the couch with a boyfriend, which was ridiculous. She was decades past acne.

"I'm back," Julia called from the door.

George lumbered to his feet. "Looks like it's time for me to head out." Aiming the remote, he clicked off the movie.

Julia walked in, saw the fading screen, and looked first at Ellen then at George. "Don't leave because of me."

"The movie just ended," he assured her.

Ellen expected him to say good-bye and head for the door, but he didn't budge. Instead he crooked a brow at her the way Humphrey Bogart teased Katharine Hepburn for sitting primly in the *African Queen*.

Julia cleared her throat. "Thanks for helping out tonight, George. I really appreciate it."

"My pleasure."

When he still didn't move, Julia excused herself, went to the kitchen, and turned on the faucet to make a curtain of white noise.

Ellen focused on George. He took two steps, stopped in front of her, and looked down. She stayed on the sofa and looked up.

Those eyes were the same ones she'd mooned over as a teenager. Only now they were wiser, twinkling with mischief, and challenging her with a look that made her toes curl.

Ellen hadn't kissed a man since Ben. The few times she had dated, she dodged that awkward moment. But tonight was different. The kiss hung between them, waiting to be taken or given. The choice, she realized, was hers. George was giving it to her out of respect for her grief and maybe for Ben.

The temperature in the room shot to 150 degrees. The change had nothing to do with Ben *or* George. She was having a hot flash, the kind that made her drip like a mop. She usually joked about having a personal summer, but she couldn't bring herself to make a crack about hormones to George.

"Good night," she said in a too-high voice.

Instead of leaving, he planted his big feet in front of her, reached down, and trailed two fingers down her cheek. "Good night, darlin'."

Perspiration beaded on her brow. Hot flashes were unstoppable. In another thirty seconds she'd be a puddle. Hoping George would take the hint, she glanced at the door.

"I'll let myself out," he murmured.

He left, but Ellen stayed on the sofa with both the hot flash and his touch burning through her.

"Mom?" Julia stuck her head out of the kitchen. "Are you all right?"

"I'm fine." Ellen hoisted herself up on her crutches. "Did you have a good evening?"

Julia pulled in a ragged breath. "I need chocolate."

So did Ellen. Still perspiring, she hobbled into the kitchen, where Julia was seated at the table with the open bag of Milky Way Minis. While Ellen maneuvered into the chair, Julia counted out three for each of them.

"I told Zeke about Hunter. He took it well."

"I thought he would."

"I'm the one who's tied in knots." She shoved the bag of candy to the side. "Zeke's a good guy."

"Your dad liked him a lot." Ellen wished Ben were here. He'd know what to say to their daughter, though he'd tease her terribly about crushing on George.

"I like him too," Julia said in a low voice. "But I'm scared."

"Of what?"

"I was so wrong about Hunter. I don't trust my judgment anymore. And now there's Max to consider. If Hunter thinks I'm dating someone, I'm afraid he'll use it against me."

When it came to giving Julia advice, Ellen prayed a lot more than she talked. But tonight she had something to say. "You can't let him control your life."

"I know that."

"Yes, but—"

"Mom, don't." Julia slumped back in her chair. "You know what will happen. If I do something Hunter doesn't like, he'll twist things around and Max will end up in the middle."

"What I know is this." Ellen tapped the tattoo under her sleeve. "We can trust God, or we can live in fear."

Wearing a slight but deliberate smirk, Julia handed Ellen another Milky Way. "For the record, I think George is perfect for you."

Ellen didn't want to talk about him, especially with another hot flash climbing up her neck. When it came to men and dating, Julia lived in a different universe. She took the future for granted, while Ellen coped with the fragility of every breath. She wasn't afraid of loving again the way Julia was; she was afraid of losing the people she loved.

Julia grinned. "You're blushing."

"I am not." She fanned herself to prove it. "It's a hot flash. I had a Coke during the movie. You know what caffeine does to me these days."

Ellen waved her hand even harder to fight the perspiration, but it didn't help. She was a pinprick away from a fight or maybe a crying jag. She didn't want this turmoil, and she didn't need it. She was done with the drama of love, except for old movies and the Hallmark Channel.

She snatched up a napkin and blotted the perspiration from her face. "Hot flashes are miserable."

Julia fetched a glass from a cupboard, filled it with ice water, and handed it to her.

"Thanks." Ellen drank it down. "I'm going to church with George on Sunday morning. Why don't you come with us?"

Julia let out a frustrated sigh. "I'd love to, but Hunter's leaving Sunday. We're trading Max back at checkout time."

"Hunter again."

"Always." Julia stood and put away the candy. "I'm beat. Do you need anything before I go to bed?"

"No, I can manage."

"Be brave, Mom. It's what you'd say to me." Julia kissed Ellen on the cheek. "I'm going to check on Max."

Ellen watched her leave, her own heart full and aching. She and Julia were friends as well as mother and daughter, sisters in Christ now, and joined by a history as complex and beautiful as a tapestry. She hoped Ben was watching from heaven, because he'd be proud of their daughter.

"*I am, Ellie. I am.*"

"I miss you," she said out loud.

Ben didn't answer back, not even in her mind. But somehow she knew he was proud of her too, and that he'd like George Travers very much.

Sixteen

Whoever thought golf at dawn was enjoyable was crazy. Zeke would have gladly slept in this morning, especially since the memory of sand between his toes had kept him awake half the night. He and Julia were good together, still. But now she was a Christian and he was . . . adrift. Friendship only made sense, but his heart and body were having trouble believing it.

On the driving range for a golf lesson with John, Zeke raised the club, swung, and topped the ball. It dribbled onto the grass, painfully short-fallen, like Zeke's walk with God.

"Do you know what you did?" John asked about the bad swing.

"Pushed up on my toes."

"Watch your hips too."

Zeke tried again. This time the ball went sideways. The golf date was set for Thursday, along with dinner with Mr. and Mrs. Carter, himself, and Julia. Technically, it wasn't a date, but she'd be wearing high heels. Maybe a little black dress and the red lipstick he liked.

He swung and missed the ball completely.

"You got distracted," John remarked.

"A little." More like a lot.

With John offering advice, Zeke refocused and

banged out three buckets of balls until the last shot finally flew straight and true, an encouraging sign and a good way to end the morning.

John clapped him on the shoulder. "You'll get it."

Zeke shook his head. "I'm going to humiliate myself with Carter and you know it."

"Yep," John said with a grin. "He's going to beat the pants off you. But who cares? Enjoy the game."

"I'd enjoy bringing in his business a lot more."

John reached for the club in Zeke's hand. "We're behind you, Zeke. The whole staff is pulling for you."

"Thanks. It's mutual."

John took care of the clubs, leaving Zeke to hop on a golf cart and head out to the fourteenth hole. Because of a sprinkler malfunction, the green itself, a complex mix of sod, sand, and drainage, had nearly died yesterday. Pete Martin, course superintendent, was out there now with a crew and a water truck.

Zeke pulled the cart up next to Pete, greeted the two workers with a wave, and took in the improved condition of the grass. "It looks a lot better."

"Yep." Pete didn't say much in general.

Confident the green would survive, Zeke thanked him for his fast response, waved to the workers, and drove the cart along the dried-out fairway. The natural landscape would bounce back from the drought, but the golf course looked awful. Mr. Carter would notice that.

With the weight of two hundred jobs on his shoulders, Zeke went home, showered, and put on a suit. While tying the tie, he wondered how Superman managed to change clothes in a phone booth. Then again, superheroes didn't need to worry about practicalities.

When Zeke arrived at the main hotel, he checked Hunter's reservation himself. Everything was in order, so he headed to his office to work until noon, when he planned to greet Hunter in the lobby.

As he dropped down at his desk, his phone flashed with a text from Julia.

Another photographer crashed & burned. Will you be in the ofc @ noon? Hoping for someone local.

Seeing Jules appealed to him a lot more than meeting Ginger at the stable, reason unknown, but he was stuck. He texted back. Sorry, can't. Mtg w/ Ginger. Later?

Can't. Food tasting.

After that?

Can't. Dessert tasting.

After that???

She texted back an emoticon pulling its hair out. ACK! Let's try for tomorrow morning.

Sure. Text me when you're up.

A smile lifted his lips. If she wanted to come to his house, he'd cook her breakfast. It would be a nice follow-up to the hot dogs, but in the next breath he dismissed the idea of another cozy meal together, one where she'd ask him questions. She had opened up to him, and he owed her the same respect, but he squirmed at the notion of telling her about his loss of faith.

Maybe, if he found it again on his own, he could skip that confession altogether. But how did he find it again? What did a man do when he'd read the Bible through ten times, heard a thousand sermons, sung all the songs, and prayed a million prayers?

Disheartened, he set the phone down, refocused his mind, and plowed through his email until close to noon.

Not sure what to expect from Hunter, Zeke put on his coat, walked into the lobby, and headed for Katrina's Kitchen. Between the crisscross of guests and staff, he saw Hunter standing stock-still, his hands in his pockets and his eyes locked on the revolving door at the front entrance. A languid blink erased all emotion from his face except for a trace of disapproval.

Zeke never had liked the guy. At St. John's, homeless people in need of legal help received it, but many of them remarked on Hunter's attitude, as if he were holding his nose while he met with them. He still wore that superior look. It grated on Zeke, but he was determined to put the old hostility aside. For Julia's sake, the best strategy was friendship, so Zeke crossed the lobby with relaxed strides.

When Hunter spotted him, his eyes narrowed. Most people would have taken a few steps and met Zeke part way, but Hunter waited like a king holding court. Zeke was accustomed to dealing with difficult guests. It was part of the job.

He put on a smile and thrust out his hand. "Hunter Adams. Welcome to Caliente Springs."

"Hello, Zeke." Hunter offered a flimsy hand-shake as if Zeke weren't worth the effort of a strong grip.

"You must be waiting for Julia."

"*And* my son."

Hunter was doing more than claiming Max and Julia. He was warning Zeke to keep away. That wasn't going to happen, unless it was Julia's choice.

Hunter glanced pointedly at his watch. The rudeness didn't matter to Zeke, but Julia did. Determined to be courteous, he handed Hunter his business card, the one with his full name. "Call if you need anything."

Without sparing a glance, Hunter slid the card into his pocket. "Thanks."

Zeke walked away. Being dismissed irked him, but he was determined to show goodwill to Hunter. Using the back entrance to the restaurant, he found Katrina and told her to charge Hunter's lunch to his personal account.

Katrina promised to make the arrangements, then pointed to the biggest walk-in freezer. "I hate to tell you this, but that one's acting up again. Maintenance looked at it this morning, but they can only do so much."

Zeke glanced at the dingy steel door. The freezer was ancient. "Is it working now?"

"Yes. But it needs to be replaced."

Zeke mentally ran through the budget. The freezer wasn't slated to be replaced for another year, and the cushion built into this year's budget was long gone. Plus, he needed to consider paving the path to the lookout. "Let's give the repair some time. If the freezer goes out again, I'll do some juggling."

"Thanks, Zeke. If anyone can do it, you can."

"We're a team." He meant it.

"Do you have another minute?"

"Sure. But just one."

"I'll make it quick." Katrina told him about the new chicken-and-apple soup she was adding to the autumn menu. He told her it sounded delicious, said good-bye, then spotted the cook, a man named Jack-T with a booming voice and a colorful past.

Zeke called out a greeting. "Thanks for making those cheeseburgers well done."

"You mean burnt." Jack-T's laugh barreled out

of his chest. Just to show off, he flipped a burger high.

The cook reminded Zeke of the men at St. John's. Like everyone else, Jack-T needed this job, and Zeke was determined to save it for him. He just wished he really had superhero powers, because with the drought and broken freezers, he needed help.

With Max in hand and his backpack on her shoulder, Julia hurried into the lobby, where she spotted Hunter staring at the revolving front door. She was five minutes late. Not the end of the world, but she braced for a snide remark.

"There's Daddy!" Max pulled out of her grip and ran to Hunter, nearly bowling over a guest in his eagerness.

When Hunter swooped him into the air, Max giggled and clung to him. Julia's heart jammed into her throat. Sometimes she wondered if she was being too hard on Hunter. He really tried to be a good father. On the other hand, she knew his personality. If Max displeased him, Hunter would hold back his love the way he used to do with her.

Not anymore. Her mom was right. She kept a solid two feet between them. "Hello, Hunter."

"Julia."

Still holding Max, he leaned in to kiss her, something she had told him repeatedly not to do, but old habits were hard to break. Forgiving him, she dodged and offered her cheek. The kiss, as light as it was, made her queasy.

Easing back, Hunter placed his hand on the small of her back. "I've missed you."

She scooted away from his touch, but what did she say? *I'm sorry to be blunt, but I don't miss you at all.* Sometimes the truth couldn't be told because it was just plain mean, but neither would she pretend to feel something she didn't.

To avoid a losing battle, she changed the subject. "How was the drive?"

"Nice."

"It's a beautiful day, but we need rain." The weather seemed like a safe topic. "Max is happy to see you."

"Yeah!" Max bounced on Hunter's hip.

Grinning, Hunter winked at his son. "We're going to have a good time, aren't we? How about going to the pool?"

"I like the one with the slide." Max wiggled sideways to find her. "Mommy, come with us."

"No, sweetheart." She hated moments like this one, where she was forced to crush her son's hopes or perpetuate a lie. "This is Daddy's time. You two will have fun."

Max screwed up his face. "But—"

"Mommy's right," Hunter said. "This is guy time. But I bet she'll have lunch with us if we say please."

Julia barely stifled an angry reply. Why did Hunter do this to her? He knew she was working this afternoon. She frowned at him, but he set Max on his feet and stepped back, leaving her to deal with their son alone.

She put on her strong mommy face, a look that meant business. "I'm sorry, Max. But Mommy needs to work."

Max's whole face drooped. "Can you work later?"

He wasn't manipulating her like Hunter did, and he wasn't being bratty or demanding. He was just a kid who wanted his parents to be together. Guilt swamped her. How could she say no?

Hunter broke in. "We'll keep it short. I promise."

Max bounced on his toes, pleading with his eyes. Love for him mixed with the guilt, and she thought a prayer. *I need help, Lord. Yes or no?*

Turning slightly, Hunter whispered in her ear. "Before you decide, I want to tell you something."

"What is it?" She braced for a false promise, maybe a bribe of some kind.

"I've been going to church."

Her mouth fell open. She snapped it shut, but old conversations played through her head, the ones where Hunter belittled her new faith and called her weak-minded.

Stunned, she gaped at him. "Are you kidding me?"

"I'm dead serious."

"When did this start?"

"Two weeks ago." He looked a little sheepish, or like a wolf in sheep's clothing. "There's a church near the law office. I've been feeling pretty down, mostly about us, and I decided to give church a try. I liked it."

She didn't know whether to trust Hunter or not, but in good conscience, she couldn't slam the door on him. "This really is a surprise."

"A good one, I hope."

"Well . . . yes."

How could it not be? And yet a gut feeling held back any real sense of joy. If Hunter was manipulating her, he'd sunk to a new low. She didn't know what to think.

He spoke in a murmur just for her. "I thought the three of us could go to church tomorrow."

Julia loved church—the singing, the teaching, the holiness of prayer, even the weak coffee afterward. She wouldn't know anyone at George's church, but she was sure she'd feel at home. Hunter deserved a chance to join that family, not because he had earned it, but because Jesus had died for him too.

"Tomorrow is fine," she said. "In fact, we can meet my mom and a friend of hers. He goes to a church in San Luis Obispo." Julia decided to leave George's name out of it for now. His star status would detour the conversation.

"Perfect." Hunter placed a hand on Max's shoulder. "Did you hear that, son? We're all going to church tomorrow."

Max spun toward Julia for an explanation, so she told him they were going with Grammie and George. "It's not our regular church, but I think you'll like it."

"We're going with Daddy?"

"Yes, we are." Somehow she kept her voice light.

When the hostess approached, her eyes swept from Hunter to Max and back to Julia. "Three for lunch?"

Hunter looked at Julia, his brows slightly arched with a reminder that she hadn't yet said yes.

She took in Max's eager face, the menus in the hostess's hand, and looked again at Hunter. "I'll stay. But we need to keep it short."

"Thanks." There wasn't a trace of arrogance on his face, only a wistful smile.

Hoping her decision was the right one for Max, she followed the hostess through the maze of tables. Hunter, a step behind, put his hand on the small of her back.

As she turned to scowl at him, Zeke strode out of the kitchen. His gaze went straight to her back, then rose to her face.

Seventeen

When Zeke saw Hunter put his hand on Julia's back, he didn't like it a bit. The scowl on her face said everything. She didn't want Hunter to touch her, and Hunter didn't respect that boundary. Zeke's fists knotted at his sides, but Julia took care of herself by brushing Hunter's hand away.

Love your enemies. The Bible verse echoed in Zeke's mind, but he couldn't bring himself to love Hunter. He could have faked it, but he was done lying to himself and to God. The truth was that he wanted to kick Hunter out of Julia's life the way he wished Adam had kicked the snake out of the Garden of Eden.

When the trio arrived at a booth, Max slid in first. Julia sat next to him, forcing Hunter to sit alone. Zeke reached the restaurant entrance, turned, and saw Max talking a mile a minute and Julia staring at him over Hunter's shoulder, anguish plain on her face. When her gaze met his, he nodded as if to say, *I understand. He's Max's dad.*

She nodded back, almost imperceptibly, then raised the menu and hid behind it.

Leaving her sickened him. No man liked to feel helpless, and that was particularly true for a man raised to play the hero.

Zeke was late for his meeting with Ginger, so when he arrived at the stable, he parked next to her car and strode toward Chet's office, a route that took him past Ladybug's new pen. So far the goat hadn't escaped, but she screamed obnoxiously at guests. Most people found the screech amusing, and Chet had put up sign that read *Ladybug, The Singing Goat*. Zeke braced for a bone-jarring serenade as he passed, but the pen was empty.

Chet barreled around the corner, his face red and his fists knotted. His Resistol hat shaded his eyes, but his jaw jutted like the prow of a battleship. Whatever he had to say, it wouldn't be good.

Zeke dragged a hand through his hair. "Please don't tell me Ladybug's on the loose again."

"She's with Ginger," Chet said with a growl. "And if you don't stop Ms. Travers' crazy plan, I'll quit on the spot."

"What plan?"

"She's bringing in another goat."

"What for?"

"She didn't tell me. But I think she wants to breed the stupid things. If she turns this place into a *goat farm,* I'm outta here faster than you can shake a stick."

Was goat breeding a new craze that would earn income, like raising alpacas for their fiber? Zeke had checked into that one. He'd do anything to save Caliente Springs, even breed goats.

"Is she bringing in a male?"

"I don't know, but I heard her cooing to Ladybug about being a lonely old lady. Goats don't get lonely. They get mean."

Zeke didn't know what goats felt, but he knew people. Ginger had endured more than her share of hurt, a lot of it due to George's drinking and the ruin of her career. Many years ago, she had also been married and divorced. Ladybug wasn't the only lonely old lady who liked to sing.

Zeke focused back on the goat breeding. "Let's get the facts. This might be a false alarm."

"It better be!" Chet's voice rose to a near shout. "I have a good mind to tell Ms. Travers to—"

Zeke spotted Ginger rounding the corner of the barn. "Chet, wait."

"—pack up her goats and—"

Ginger sauntered up to Chet. "And do what with my goats?"

Beet red, Chet yanked off his hat and held it over his heart. "I apologize for my rudeness, Ms. Travers. And for the disrespect."

"Apology accepted." Ginger's eyes twinkled at him. "Now, tell me what I should do with my goats."

"Well, since you asked . . ." Chet gave Zeke a look to include him. "In my opinion, goats don't belong here. We're an equestrian operation, not a farm. Goat breeding doesn't fit with our typical duties."

"I'm not breeding them."

"Then what's the plan?" Zeke asked.

When Ginger hesitated, Chet slapped his hand to his forehead. "No, Ms. Travers. Don't do it."

"Do what?" she asked.

Chet gave a pitiful shake of his head. "You're going to start an orphanage for animals and call it a petting zoo. Ducks, sheep, critters no one wants. If you're thinking about llamas, forget it. They spit."

Zeke ruled out the idea instantly. "There's too much liability. The insurance costs would—"

A smile softened the lines around Ginger's mouth. "Gentlemen, relax. We're talking about just one goat, not a petting zoo. A friend of mine is losing her farm to foreclosure. She was able to sell her horses, but no one wanted Annie. She's an orphan and just a baby."

"Aw, crud," Chet muttered. "We're doomed."

Zeke felt the same way.

"Annie is precious." Ginger's voice came out with a lilt. "And she desperately needs a good home."

Who could say no to a baby goat? Not Zeke. And neither could Chet. Little Orphan Annie already had them wrapped around her cloven hoof.

Ginger's gaze flitted between them before landing solely on Chet. "I know Ladybug's a nuisance, but Annie won't be any trouble at all.

She's very sweet, and Chet, you have a gift with animals. I've seen it."

The cowboy scuffed a boot in the dirt. "That's kind of you to say, Ms. Travers."

"It's true."

Chet gave Zeke a helpless look. They'd been steamrolled by Ginger and they knew it.

Zeke jumped in. "What do you say, Chet? Can we handle another goat?"

"Sure. Why not?"

"Oh good." Ginger clasped her hands at her trim waist. "Barbara's bringing Annie tomorrow. If Ladybug takes to her the way I expect, they can share the same pen."

Chet grunted. "I don't know about that."

"I think they'll do just fine," Ginger said. "And if they don't, would you build Annie her own pen?"

"You know I will."

Ginger smiled her appreciation. "You do a great job, Chet. How long have you been at Caliente Springs?"

"Fourteen years." His drawl stretched over a decade of memories.

Ginger's expression turned as wistful as his. "We wouldn't have made it this far without you."

"Thank you, Ms. Travers." Standing tall, he fingered the brim of his hat. "It's a pleasure to work for you and your brother." He gave Zeke a nod. "And for this guy too."

As general manager, Zeke saw himself as the boss and a servant, someone who led by example. The responsibility weighed on him, but he loved what he did. "Thanks, Chet."

The old cowboy excused himself and left.

The instant he was out of earshot, Ginger faced Zeke. "I know you think I'm a hard-hearted old woman."

"No, I don't." Not only had she put up with George at his worst, she'd forgiven him for ruining her career. They sparred all the time, but underneath the jabs there was real love.

Ginger swept the stable area with her eyes. "I can't let this place go bankrupt."

"It won't."

"You sound so sure, but you've seen the guest count. You know what's happening as well as I do."

"Yes, I do." He'd earned every letter in his MBA. "And I'm still convinced we can turn the resort around."

She skimmed her eyes over the pipe rail stalls that were as old as the resort, and the ten layers of paint that covered them. "A year from now, this place will be even more run-down. When Barbara asked me to take Annie, she was in tears. Do you know what she said?"

"No." He wasn't going to like it either.

"She said she wished she had sold sooner. She fought hard, and in the end she lost everything. I can't let that happen."

Bile rose in his throat. It tasted of fear and failure, and he nearly choked on it. The broken freezer, the drought, the old barns glued together with twenty coats of paint. Every day was a battle with the forces of nature and the economy, things a man couldn't control. Maybe he really was the little boy with his finger in the dike. Or maybe he needed to work harder to bring in new business.

"You have a point," he said. "It would be foolish to go bankrupt. I won't let that happen."

Her gaze swept over the barns, the Gator with its duct-taped seat, and finally to a corral in the distance. "I want to believe you, Zeke. But there's a fine line between hope and foolishness. George still refuses to even talk about selling. I'm determined to change his mind."

"So I have some time."

"Unfortunately, yes." Ginger sighed. "You know George. He's stubborn."

Ginger was fighting an uphill battle, but so was Zeke. Even with the hope of the Carter business and a wedding boon, he needed to do more to give Caliente Springs a boost over newer resorts. But improving the old place took money, and the money just wasn't there.

Ginger's phone signaled a text. She read it and smiled. "Tiff's here, and Derek just checked in. I'm meeting them for the food tasting. Will you be there?"

"No. Julia can handle it."

"I like her a lot," Ginger admitted. "She's smart and efficient. *And* diplomatic. I'm not easy to deal with, you know."

Zeke smiled. "I'm too smart to agree with you."

Ginger gave an easy laugh. When she wasn't being difficult, she was fun to know. "Are you free tonight?"

"I can be."

"Why don't you come to the dessert tasting? It's at the house at seven. Derek's parents came up from San Diego for a few days. George will be there, and so will Ellen and Julia. We'd love to have you join us."

Zeke jumped at the chance to spend time with Jules. "Thanks. I'll be there."

Ginger clicked the remote to her hybrid sedan. Zeke opened the door, but she stopped before climbing in. "You're a good man, Zeke."

He waited for the *but*. It always came, either from his father or his own conscience.

"When the time comes, George and I will help you find a new position."

He thanked her, but as soon as she drove off, he gave in to a frown. No way would he give up on saving Caliente Springs and those two hundred jobs, including his own. The thought of storing his diplomas and awards in boxes like the ones in the garage cut him to the heart. He loved this place, the people, even the problems.

Love. It coursed through him with a richness he'd once felt while living as a Christian, but even then he had sometimes wondered if that feeling was genuine or an old habit.

God, are you listening?

Zeke doubted it. Why would God listen to a man who didn't love Him enough? A headache broke just above his eyes. Ignoring it, he headed back to his office.

Julia dampened a corner of her napkin and dabbed a smear of hot fudge off Max's face. She would have said no to the big dessert, especially if Hunter planned to take him swimming, but when Hunter suggested it, the delight on Max's face had stopped her.

"Let's get the show on the road," Hunter said to him now. "Are you ready for the pool?"

"Yeah!"

Julia opened her mouth to caution against swimming too soon after lunch, but Hunter was already telling Max they needed to wait an hour before hitting the water.

"We'll check out my room first," Hunter said. "You can see the goodies that came in the gift basket."

Goodies from Zeke . . . like miniature Milky Ways.

Hunter signaled for the check, took his platinum

American Express card out of his wallet, and tapped it on the table.

Their waitress approached with a broad smile. "You're all set."

Hunter's eyebrows pulled together. "But the check—"

"It's taken care of." The waitress glanced at Julia, recognized her, and said, "Mr. Monroe treated your family to lunch today."

Dread trickled down Julia's spine. Hunter was the guy who always grabbed the check. She used to think he was generous, but now she saw the habit as manipulative. No matter where he was, he needed to be the star, and Zeke had just stolen the show.

Hunter shoved the card back in his wallet and removed some cash instead, presumably to leave a tip. So far, so good. When a person received a free meal, leaving a generous tip was polite and appropriate. Julia let out the breath she'd been holding, but then she saw a hundred-dollar bill in Hunter's hand.

He held it out to the waitress, making sure everyone saw Ben Franklin's bald head. "Thank Mr. Monroe for us. And this is for you."

The waitress gaped at the bill, covered her mouth with one hand, then turned to Hunter with her eyes popping. "That's too much."

"Take it. I insist."

"But—"

"Take it." He slipped the money into the pocket of her red apron. "You took good care of my family today."

His family. By blood if not by law; by obligation but without real love. The word *ex* severed some ties but not all.

The waitress recovered a bit. "Thank you, sir. It's been a pleasure."

She might have gushed longer, but Hunter dismissed her with a nod. When she was gone, he hiked up one hip and put away his wallet. "I suppose we need to thank Zeke the Freak."

The silly name-calling irked her. It also set a bad example for Max. She leaned forward so only Hunter could hear. "Please don't do that."

"Do what?"

"You know what." She kept her voice low, but the effort scraped at her throat.

"What I know"—he set both hands on the table, his eyes burning into hers—"is that Zeke Monroe has a thing for you."

"He does not." *A thing* didn't begin to describe the feelings growing between them, but she wasn't about to enlighten Hunter. "Zeke and I are friends. Get over it."

Hunter snorted. "Right."

If she continued to argue, he'd fight even harder. Faking an air of aplomb, she slid out of the booth. Max followed with his backpack on his shoulder. She took his sticky hand, and the two of them headed for the lobby, staying three steps ahead of Hunter.

He caught up to them at the bank of elevators, halted behind Max, and gripped the boy's shoulder. Julia held tighter to Max's hand. Crowding her from behind, Hunter touched her back yet again, but he lowered his hand before she could react.

His breath grazed the shell of her ear. "What time should Max and I pick you up for church?"

She yearned to cancel, but if she did, she'd be a hypocrite. Plus Hunter would use the broken promise against her. "I'll text you later."

"You're not going to back out are you?"

"No."

"So what time?"

"I don't know yet." Just once, she wished Hunter would accept what she said without badgering her for details. She couldn't win, so she faced him. "There are two services. One is at nine-thirty and one is at eleven. I don't know which one my mom will pick. And I don't know where the church is. It could take fifteen minutes to get there or it could take thirty. Like I said, I'll text you."

Hunter glared at her. "You're mad. What did I do now?"

You keep touching my back. You stand too close, and you can't say thank you to anyone. Max loves you, and you're teaching him to be rude and ungrateful.

There was no point in having the same old argument, so she kept her eyes on the numbers above the elevator. "This isn't the time."

"Then when is?"

Never. They'd had this conversation before, when she'd been trying to salvage their relationship. Repeating it proved Einstein's definition of insanity—doing the same thing over and over and expecting different results.

The elevator started down, so she hugged Max and told him to have a good time. Max hiked up one shoulder as if the backpack weighed a hundred pounds.

Hunter took it from him, leaning toward Julia as he hoisted it onto his arm. "This is about the tip, isn't it?"

If she said yes, she'd sound petty. But if she denied the truth, she'd be a liar. She took cover in neutral territory. "The waitress appreciated it. You'll be the talk of Katrina's Kitchen."

His eyes flashed with pleasure, or maybe victory. "Good. I hope Zeke the Freak hears about it."

Julia's blood pressure rose a notch. She couldn't win and was sick to death of holding back every drop of anger.

When the elevator dinged, she muttered good-bye, but as she turned, she spotted Ginger walking toward them and waving.

"Julia!"

Of all the bad luck. Julia was happy to show off

Max, but Hunter was a wildcard. Sometimes he mocked her in front of other people and acted like it was funny. Other times he preened over her. Either behavior sickened her.

The elevator was filling up, but Hunter didn't budge. His gaze was on Ginger, impressively dressed in tailored denim and striding toward them with the air of a star.

Julia put on her game face and waved. When Ginger joined their little group, Julia made introductions. "Max, this is Ms. Travers."

Ginger bent down and smiled. "Hello, Max. It's nice to meet you."

Suddenly shy, Max leaned against Julia. After an understanding smile, Ginger turned to Hunter, who thrust out his hand.

"Ms. Travers. It's a pleasure. I'm Hunter Adams. Max's dad."

"It's nice to meet you too." Ginger accepted the handshake with her usual grace. "Thank you for sharing Julia with us. She's doing a wonderful job."

"I'm sure she is." He flashed a smile in her direction. "Julia's a talented woman."

So he'd chosen to preen. *Jerk!* In private he belittled her for starting Dare to Dream Events. He didn't have the right to piggyback on her accomplishments now, but all Julia could do was smile benignly.

Ginger turned to her. "By the way, Tiff and I

checked out the website for Hot Pink Photography. A friend of hers suggested it, and we liked what we saw."

"I'll get in touch with the photographer."

"Good, because time is running out." Ginger turned back to Hunter. "I hope you enjoy your visit."

"I'm sure I will." He puffed out his chest. "After the week I put in at the office, I can use some R&R."

"What do you do?" Ginger asked politely.

"I'm an attorney. Real estate. It's my father's firm. He's been in practice for years. "

Ginger cocked her head, her eyes sharp. "I don't suppose you know someone who'd like to buy this old place?"

"Maybe."

Julia's stomach started a slow drop to the floor.

Hunter faced her with a mocking gleam in his eyes. "You remember Uncle Maury."

"Of course."

Maury Applegate was an old friend of Hunter's parents, an uncle by affection, and one of the most successful housing developers in California. If Maury Applegate wanted to buy Caliente Springs, he could do it.

Hunter cocked one brow at Ginger. "If you're serious about selling, I'll call my uncle today. He's always looking for the next big project."

Ginger's mouth fell open. "Well, yes. Thank you."

Hunter took out his phone. "What's the best way to reach you?"

As they exchanged numbers, another elevator dinged and the mirrored doors crawled open. Hunter brushed a wet kiss on Julia's flushed cheek. Her stomach burned until it cramped, and her fingers turned to ice. When Max dashed into the elevator, Hunter and Ginger followed while talking in low tones. As the doors closed, Hunter faced forward. The last thing Julia saw was a smirk on his face.

She pressed her hand to her chest. *Calm down. Breathe deep.*

Zeke needed to hear the news so he could do damage control, so she hurried to his office. The lights were on in the reception area, but his desk was empty and his computer dark. She couldn't radio him. The whole staff would hear and be curious. She considered calling his cell, but she didn't want to explain on the phone. The conversation would have to wait until tonight after the dessert tasting.

Turning to the window that faced the hills, she prayed for the strength to trust God and not her own understanding, because Zeke's two worst enemies had just formed an alliance, and she'd unwittingly been the catalyst.

Eighteen

Zeke's conversation with Ginger stayed in his mind all afternoon. From the stable he went to the pro shop to check with John about the Carter reservation for Thursday, then he visited the maintenance yard to consult with the road crew about laying asphalt at Golden Point. Last, he responded to a call for assistance from security chief Rex Hayden. A teenage boy had vandalized a candy machine, and his parents were accusing the maid who saw him of lying.

Zeke didn't make it back to Katrina's Kitchen until after five p.m. Free at last, he headed toward Katrina's cubbyhole of an office to pick up the receipt for Hunter's lunch. As he passed through the back entrance, he met Jack-T in street clothes.

The cook clapped him on the back. "Zeke, my man."

"Hey, Jack-T."

"That friend of yours"—Jack gave a slow shake of his head, whistling for good measure—"he blew Shirley into next week."

The so-called friend had to be Hunter, and Shirley was a waitress. Zeke didn't know what to imagine. "What happened?"

"He tipped her a C-note."

"Really." It was statement, not a question.

"He sure did." Chuckling, Jack-T slipped by Zeke and reached for the doorknob. "Gotta run, man. But we're all hoping your friend comes back tomorrow for breakfast, lunch, and dinner."

Jack-T left, but his laughter stayed in Zeke's head long after the door swung shut. By trumping the meal with a massive tip, Hunter had thrown down a gauntlet. Zeke could absorb the insult, but if Hunter caused real trouble for Julia or Max, Zeke would be at her side with swords drawn, tasers hot, and shields up.

With his jaw tight, he headed to his office, sat at his desk, and woke up his computer. There were twenty-six emails, including one from Ginger. He opened it first.

Met a friend of yours today. Hunter Adams. He knows of a potential buyer for CS. Be prepared for a possible VIP visit from Hunter and Maury Applegate. I expect to hear from Hunter re: the exact date early next week. I know how you feel about this, Zeke. But I'm sure you'll be thorough, fair, and professional.

Zeke's pulse jackhammered in his veins. He needed a plan. Calling Julia was out of the question, because there was a chance she was at the Travers mansion preparing for the dessert tasting. He'd see her tonight, but he'd have to wait to speak with her.

Shifting to Plan B, he Googled Maury Applegate. Hundreds of links rolled onto the screen, each with phrases like *commercial property investment* and *redevelopment guru.* There were also titles like president, CEO, and Chairman of the Board. All that plus pictures of him at big-name charity events.

Zeke drew back, launched out of the chair, and strode to the window overlooking the hills. His vision narrowed to a distant oak, and for a moment he couldn't force air into his lungs. It was ridiculous, even appalling, to think he could lose Caliente Springs so easily. His jaw tightened until his teeth ached. He didn't want to go to war with anyone, but when an enemy showed up in the camp, a dedicated leader stood up to him.

Determined to be that kind of man, Zeke returned to his desk and read news stories and posts about Maury Applegate until it was time for the dessert tasting.

He went home first, changed into casual clothes, then drove to the Travers house, determined to keep a professional air. A rental car and Ellen's Camry sat in the driveway, but there was no sign of Julia's Outback. If she'd ridden with her mom, Zeke would have a good reason to drive her home.

He rapped twice on the door. George opened it but stepped out to the deck. "We need to talk."

"Hunter Adams?"

"That's the guy." George closed the door behind him. "You must have read Ginger's email."

"Unfortunately."

"Have a seat." George indicated the swing at the far end of the deck, out of sight from the front windows and shaded by the elongated eaves.

Zeke leaned against the railing, his hands braced at his sides and one foot tapping.

George sat on the swing, rocking gently while the chains creaked. "So did you Google Maury Applegate like I did?"

"For an hour straight."

"He looks like the real deal."

"I think so too." Zeke pictured the short man with a round belly, a fringe of white hair, and a goatee. "You should know something else. Hunter, Julia, and I knew each other back in college. There's some history here. It could be awkward if I let it, but I won't."

George's eyes narrowed. "Ellen told me the whole story. She's not fond of Hunter."

"Yeah, neither am I." Less now than ever before. "So what do we do?"

"Talk to Julia. See what she knows about this Applegate character, and then be ready for a showdown."

"I will. But I hope it doesn't happen. Hunter's a piece of work."

George grunted. "I'm going to meet him tomorrow."

"How?"

"Church. He's taking Julia and Max. They're meeting Ellen and me at Hilldale for the nine-thirty service."

Zeke gaped at him. "Hunter in church? You're joking."

"Nope."

Either Hunter had turned over a new leaf, or he was even more deceitful than Zeke thought. If he was sincere, the situation could change 180 degrees. Julia might even feel obligated to give Hunter a second chance. Zeke's stomach burned at the thought, but it was possible, and even desirable, considering Max.

George cleared his throat. "Why don't you come along tomorrow? Give Hunter something to think about."

Zeke opened his mouth to say, *Sure, why not.* But the words stuck in his throat. "No, thanks."

"It's your choice," George said, backing down as usual. "Let me know if you change your mind."

They had this conversation about church often, and it always ended the same way. George let the subject drop. Zeke, however, continued to think about that promise to his dad that he'd go back to church. But he couldn't keep his word without feeling like a hypocrite, and he refused to put on a mask even for one day, not even to glean information about Hunter and Maury Applegate.

He followed George into the house and down a hall that led to a living room straight out of an old *Bonanza* episode. A leather sofa faced a rock fire-place, a wagon wheel lamp hung from the ceiling, and watercolors of wild mustangs added adven-ture to the white plaster walls. Off to the side was a den with a flat-screen TV, sound equipment, and a collection of Travers Twins memorabilia. George called the den his personal lair.

The women were crowded together on the sofa, looking at a computer tablet and cracking jokes. They didn't hear Zeke and George enter, but Derek approached with the look of a man who needed to talk about football instead of flowers. Derek's father, an older version of his son, joined them.

Derek offered his hand to Zeke. "Thanks for making the wedding happen so fast. Tiff and I owe you."

"Julia's the one to thank." Zeke raised his voice so she could hear the compliment.

"Don't believe him," she told Derek. "Zeke's the powerhouse around here."

He didn't feel that way with Hunter and Maury breathing down his neck, but he bantered easily until Ginger clapped her hands for attention.

"Who's ready for dessert?" she asked.

"I am." Derek looped an arm around Tiff and hugged her.

"Me too." George abandoned the men, joined Ellen, and helped her with her crutches.

Derek's parents paired off, and they all followed Ginger into the dining room, leaving Zeke and Julia alone.

He crossed the room in four long strides. If all they could manage was a whisper, he'd take it. "Jules—"

"Zeke, I'm so sorry. Ginger told me about the email."

The guilt in her eyes cut him to the core. Only the awareness of the others kept him from taking her into his arms. "It's not your fault."

"But—"

"We'll talk tonight."

She nodded furiously, then glanced into the dining room where Ginger was peering at them through the wide doorway.

Zeke gave Ginger a nod, then turned back to Jules as if they had been conducting everyday business and not trading secrets. "Let's check out those desserts before George gets to them."

She gave him a grateful look, and they joined the others around a table covered with tarts, truffles, pastries, macaroons, and chocolates. For the next hour, they all enjoyed the samples while Julia made notes. When the tasting was finished, she assembled the group in the living room to announce the selections.

"With approval from Tiff and Derek, the

dessert buffet will include chocolate truffles, both white and dark chocolate; raspberry tarts; rainbow petit fours; and old-fashioned chocolate chip cookies."

Derek and Tiff traded a kiss, and the gathering migrated to the living room. After a round of hugs, Derek's parents left with their son and future daughter-in-law.

George hooked a thumb toward his den. "Anyone up for a movie? Ellen and I are going to watch an oldie with John Wayne."

When Zeke, Julia, and Ginger all made excuses, Ellen nervously tried to talk them into staying. The twinkle in George's eyes hinted at why. A movie night was closer to dinner at IHOP than a romantic date, but it was close enough to paint a blush on Ellen's cheeks.

Zeke leaned close to Julia. "Your mom would love to be rescued, but we need to talk. Can I drive you home?"

"Definitely." She cleared her throat. "Mom? Zeke just offered me a ride. Can you drive the Camry, or should I—"

George opened his mouth, probably to say he'd take Ellen home, but Ellen cut in. "I'll be fine. It's my left ankle, and the cottage is just down the street."

Zeke glanced at George, who looked even more pleased than before. He liked a challenge, and Ellen was giving it to him. Zeke said good-bye to Ginger next, fully aware of the hard stare that cut through him and straight to Julia. If Ginger thought his relationships with Julia and Hunter would interfere with his job, she could relax. Zeke intended to play fair even if Hunter didn't.

Ellen focused on Ginger. "Are you sure you don't want to stay? We could out-vote George and watch a chick flick."

Ginger gave George a look that said, *You owe me,* then pretended to stifle a yawn. "It's been a long day. You two enjoy yourselves."

Zeke palmed his car keys and turned to Julia. "Are you ready?"

She hugged Ellen good-bye, said something Zeke couldn't hear, then picked up her portfolio and hurried out the door.

Nineteen

Julia made a beeline for Zeke's SUV, her portfolio heavy on her shoulder and her thoughts racing.

Zeke caught up to her halfway down the drive-way, opened the passenger door for her, then climbed into the driver's side and backed out to the street. "Considering how much this place loves gossip, I'd rather not have my car in your drive-way on a Saturday night. Let's go to my house."

"That sounds good." Her lungs were about to burst with the need to unburden herself. "I'm so sorry about Hunter. I led him here. I even introduced him to Ginger."

"Forget it."

"But—"

She started to argue, but he surprised her by pulling to the side of the road and cupping her face with his hand.

"I don't care about him, Jules. I really don't."

"But—"

"I *do* care about you." His warm fingers trailed down her face, releasing her. "He's Max's dad, and he came to see his son. There's no reason for you to feel guilty about any of this, okay?"

She tried to nod but couldn't.

"No guilt," he repeated. "None."

"But—" She choked up.

Zeke's mouth lifted into the hint of a grin. "Let's leave the 'buts' to Ladybug."

Julia didn't know whether to laugh, cry, or groan, so she did all three.

Zeke gave her shoulder a reassuring squeeze, put the vehicle in gear, and pulled back onto the road. "I don't want to dwell on Hunter, but I'd like to know how he and Ginger teamed up."

She told him about the conversation in the lobby, including Hunter's smirk in the elevator. "I didn't hear about Maury's possible visit until I arrived at the house and Ginger thanked me for introducing her to Hunter. It was awful. He made it sound like we were still together, but I set her straight."

Zeke drove slowly, his eyes on the road as they passed the sign for Golden Point. So much still needed to be done for Tiff's wedding, and now Hunter was a distraction. "So tell me about Applegate."

"He and Hunter's father are old friends. Hunter even calls him Uncle Maury." So had she during the engagement. "I hate to say this, but he's a nice man. I liked him a lot."

"So he's not a total shark."

"No."

"What do you know about his business?"

"He started in the nineties by flipping houses.

235

Houses turned into apartment buildings, and single buildings turned into entire blocks. Most of the areas were on the verge of becoming slums. Maury would buy the buildings, level them, and put in new units from scratch."

"Apartments?"

"And condos."

Zeke turned onto the street that led to his house. "Caliente Springs doesn't fit that model, but the redevelopment angle makes me worry."

Julia tried to think like Maury. "Do you think he'd put in an outlet mall?"

"I doubt it. We're too far from the 101, and I don't think he'd buy a golf course just to bull-doze it."

"Maybe I can find out more tomorrow." She hated what she needed to tell Zeke next. "Hunter's going to church with us."

"George told me." His jaw tightened, but his voice stayed level. "So is he a Christian now?"

"I don't know, but he asked to go with Max and me. If he's sincere, I'm glad. We're meeting my mom and George at Hilldale Community."

Zeke let out a slow breath. "I know the church."

"Do you go there too?"

"No."

That was all he said, but they were approaching what had to be his house, a large, tile-roofed bungalow that matched the hotel architecture. It was at the end of a cul-de-sac, both part of the resort and an oasis for a hardworking general manager.

Zeke pushed the remote on the visor, and the garage door lumbered up. "Let's finish this inside."

Julia started to say yes, but her eyes caught on a wall of cardboard boxes inside the garage. "What are those?"

"Boxes."

She started to make a joke about his obvious answer, but the grim set of his jaw stopped her. Instead she climbed out of the SUV and followed him into the garage, where the cartons were numbered in someone's precise writing but stacked out of order. Off to the side were two boxes that didn't match. They were both labeled *Berkeley* in Zeke's sloppy printing.

Curious, she turned to him. "Are those what I think they are?"

If Zeke had been thinking ahead, he would have taken Julia through the front door. But this was the way he always came into the house, and he'd been distracted by their conversation. The way she was looking at the boxes labeled *Berkeley* hit him in the solar plexus.

She glanced up at him, her eyes bright and full of mischief. "Can we look?"

He hesitated. When he packed those two boxes, he'd been feeling sentimental. "It's just stuff."

"But it's your stuff."

She could have said *our stuff,* because that was what most of it was. She didn't know that, but Zeke did. He was already fighting old feelings for her. Attraction. That longing just to be with her. The irresistible pull of his eyes to wherever she was. The Berkeley box was a powder keg of memories. But was it Pandora's box or the gateway back to his lost faith?

He wouldn't know unless he took a chance. "This'll be interesting."

He set one of the cartons on the workbench, slit the tape with his pocketknife, and lifted the lid. The smell of vanilla from a half-burned candle wafted out of the box and knocked him into the past. He and Jules had burned that candle together, and on one night in particular. *That* night. When their gazes met, he knew she was remembering too. The air between them thickened into a jarring silence.

Hoping to erase the awkwardness, he reached into the box and lifted out a manila envelope he knew would change the subject.

"Here," he said. "Open it, but be careful."

She peeked inside, broke into a smile, and slid out a farewell card from the kids he used to play basketball with. It was made of black construction paper and decorated with a pound of glitter.

Julia laughed. "Glitter Man to the rescue!"

Wayward sparkles of silver and gold flew between them. When one landed on her cheek, Zeke tried to wipe it away with his thumb.

"You have some too." She reached up to dab it from his chin but stopped with her hand an inch shy of his jaw. Something akin to shock filled her eyes, but her hand didn't move.

Zeke reached up and snagged her fingers in his, brought them to his lips, and kissed them. His voice came out rough. "We were good together, weren't we?"

"Yes."

"We still are." Feeling a little steadier, he let go of her hand.

The old guilt for sleeping with her hammered at him. So did resentment, because the harder he had tried to resist temptation, the more profoundly he had failed. *Why, God? Why did you make it so impossible?*

Zeke loathed himself for failing, and if he wasn't careful, he'd fail again. Not physically. He fully understood and respected the boundaries of Julia's faith. The danger lay in the cry of his heart to love her again.

Alone with her, he faced up to the truth that had started on the beach. Without a faith of his own, he wasn't the man she needed or deserved. To be that man, he needed to find his way back to God. But how? What did he do or say when the last thing he wanted to do was hit his knees?

Zeke didn't know, but one thing was certain. If he didn't stay behind those lines in the sand, they'd both get hurt, especially Jules.

He took a small step back. "Sorry. I got distracted there."

"Me too." Her cheeks were as pink as her lips. "We need to stay focused on the wedding and the mess with Hunter."

"Especially the wedding." Zeke jammed his hands in his pockets. "I don't know what I'd do if you weren't here."

"You'd manage."

"I don't know how."

In less than a week, she had sent out five hundred invitations, fielded more than four hundred RSVPs, set up Tiff and Derek's website, arranged the food tastings, scouted ceremony sites, searched for a photographer, consulted with the hotel florist, and worked with the facilities department on the reception. There were also plans in the works for a classy rehearsal dinner at the Travers mansion with a menu to put Wolfgang Puck to shame. *And* she had moved heaven and earth to obtain five hundred customized votive candles for wedding favors.

Zeke couldn't begin to count the hours she'd spent on the phone with Tiff and Ginger. And then there was the time spent on the Carter proposal, screening his endless phone calls, and just being part of the busy, friendly CS team.

He eyed the glitter still on her cheek. "I may be Glitter Man, but when it comes to getting things done, you're Wonder Woman." She even looked a little like Lynda Carter but younger, shorter, and a lot less 1975.

Julia rolled her eyes. "I'll leave saving the world to you."

Zeke was about to suggest they go inside when Julia stood on her toes and took another envelope out of the box. This one had his name on it in her writing.

Her mouth fell open and she laughed. "Is this what I think it is?"

"Valentine's Day." The only card she ever gave him, because his birthday was in late July.

Stepping back, he watched her read what she'd written—a poem about love being just for now because no one knew what tomorrow held. At the time he'd choked up, both because she loved him and because the sentiment was so far from his Christian faith. Then there was the line about his smile lighting up her heart like a thousand suns. Bad poetry? Definitely. But he had treasured it even more for its sincerity.

Reading the inscription now, she groaned. "This is too cheesy for words. Burn it. Please!"

He snatched it from her. "No way."

"But it's awful!"

Zeke gave her a cheeky grin. "Let's just say poetry isn't your strong suit."

"You know"—she propped her hands on her hips—"the card *you* gave me was just as mushy."

He remembered that card in all its painful glory, both the picture of a young couple holding hands and what he'd written. *I love you, Jules, and I always will. You've changed my life in beautiful ways.* He had struggled with what to say then, and he was struggling now.

The silence returned with a roar, thickening until she let her arms fall to her sides. "That was a long time ago, wasn't it?"

"We were different people."

"Yes," she said, confident now. "But do you want to know something?"

"Sure."

Her mouth lifted into a faint smile. "Cheesy poetry aside, I admired you then, and I do now. You put others first, always. You go the extra mile even when it costs you something. A lot has changed in our lives, but you're still Glitter Man to me."

So spill your guts, Glitter Man. Tell her you lost your faith. But he didn't want to be a cynic to her, not when her own faith was so new.

He tried to close the flaps of the box, but Julia turned and peered inside again. "Let's see what else we can dig up."

Zeke didn't want to dig up anything. But she reached into the box before he could stop her and pulled out a box set of *The Lord of the Rings* movies.

"We watched these together, all three at once with the Bread on the Water crowd. That was fun."

Not for him. Knowing he was sinning by sleeping with her and lying about it, he'd been riddled with guilt through all three movies.

Julia might be enjoying this jog down memory lane, but Zeke was squirming. It was impossible to stop the excavation, so he quickly shoveled out the remaining college shirts and old books.

To his dismay, one of those books was his Bible. He tried to slide it under the T-shirts, but Julia glimpsed the worn black leather cover, complete with his full name embossed in gold. The Bible had been a gift from his parents for his sixteenth birthday.

"Your Bible . . ."

"Yeah." He left the book on the workbench with the rest of the stuff, including the candle with its burned wick. There was a lot of history in those two items. A lot of failure on his part—a battle waged, lost, and declared pointless. His personal Vietnam.

Julia riffled through the pages he'd marked up with colored pencils, then looked into his eyes. "It seems strange that you packed this away."

Zeke shrugged. "I was moving. You know how it is."

"But you carried this Bible everywhere."

She sounded doubtful and rightly so. He'd just lied to her, but he didn't want to confess he'd lost his faith out of fear that he'd disillusion her.

He aimed his chin toward the door. "Let's go inside. I'm thirsty."

Her face softened and she gave a little shrug. "It's been a rough day for both of us. How about we go inside and work on finding a photographer? Ginger gave me a new lead."

Relief settled into those deep cracks he couldn't seem to fill. It was just like Jules to know he needed a break and to give it to him. "That sounds good. I take it the local guy didn't impress you?"

She made a face. "Sorry, but he's Mr. Boring. All grip-and-grin and Last Supper poses. We need someone with a flare for romance."

She headed to the SUV, fetched her portfolio with her computer tablet, and followed him into the kitchen.

While he pulled bottles of water from the fridge, she wandered into the spacious living room with its beamed cathedral ceiling. "This is a far cry from your place in Berkeley, isn't it?"

"Light years." Eager to return to less sensitive topics, he carried the water bottles to the coffee table. "Let's see this photographer Tiff likes."

Julia dropped onto the couch and retrieved her

tablet from her purse. Zeke sat next to her, and they checked out Hot Pink Photography, a boutique studio run by Chelsea Robertson, a woman with a flamboyant pink stripe in her auburn hair.

"She does great work," Zeke remarked when Julia finished skimming the galleries. "Is she available?"

"Yes. She's waiting to hear from me, but what about George? Do you think I should send him the link?"

"Forget it," Zeke said. "He'll leave it to Ginger. Besides, I have a hunch he's nowhere near a computer right now."

Ellen thought George's den was a charming mix of a movie theater, a museum, and a cozy home. Four recliners complete with cup holders faced a monster-sized flat-screen TV, and the walls were decorated with memorabilia from his career. The touch of home came from the Sherpa blanket he draped over her legs at the start of *Rooster Cogburn*, which he suggested because it starred John Wayne *and* Katharine Hepburn.

She sat in one of the middle recliners with a Diet Coke in hand. George was in the seat next to her, stretched out with his cowboy boots crossed at the ankles. When the closing credits rolled, she let out a contented sigh. "Good movie."

"It's a favorite." He turned off the DVR, stood, and offered his hand to help her up. When she took it and maneuvered to her good foot, he held on even tighter. "How would you like the ten-cent tour?"

"I'd love it."

"Good, because there's something in particular I want to show you."

When she reached for her crutches, he offered his elbow. "It's crowded over there. Can you manage if you hold on to me?"

"Yes, I think so."

Fearing a hot flash, she curled her fingers around his arm. He tucked his free hand over hers and led her to a wall decorated with album cover art and gold and platinum records. When Ellen commented on particular songs, George told her stories about writing or recording them. He also shared the history of the five guitars on the wall, including the first one he ever owned.

"I'm impressed," she told him.

"Don't be. Not by all this. It just about killed me."

She tightened her grip on his elbow, leaning on him but also inviting him to lean on her.

Another wall displayed dozens of photographs, and he guided her to it. "What I want you to see is over here."

In the middle of the glitz and gloss, she spotted

the dull beige of a framed newspaper article. The headline read, *Country Icon Jailed for Drunken Crash.* Ellen knew the story, but she skimmed the article anyway. No one was hurt, but he'd been belligerent with the police and swung his fists.

George stared hard at the headline. "There it is. My ticket to rehab. It's the most important thing on this wall."

Ellen squeezed his elbow again. It was all she had to give. "I remember reading about it."

"To this day, I'm amazed I didn't kill someone."

"Or yourself."

"That too. Back then I didn't much care if I lived or died. My career was in the tank. Ginger wouldn't have anything to do with me. Instead of earning money, I was blowing it on fast cars, fast women, and bad habits. Caliente Springs wouldn't be in the hurt locker now if I'd been smarter."

Ellen couldn't help but think of Ben. He'd invested wisely, and she was grateful for the financial security. As for drinking, he had enjoyed a beer on a hot day, but that was all. She appreciated his temperance, but she wasn't about to condemn George. "It made you who you are today."

"True. But that colorful past of mine has consequences, ones I feel to this day. Like guilt over ruining Ginger's singing career. That woman is a canary, I tell you. I made amends to her when I got sober and she forgave me, but there were a lot of years in between our last album and that apology."

"She tried to go solo, didn't she?"

"For a while, yes. But her little brother with his big voice and bad habits stole the headlines and the airplay."

"Did she hate you for it?"

"I wish it had been that simple." His chin lifted as if he expected a slap. "She was determined to 'help' me. If you know anything about drunks, we don't take kindly to being helped. I was awful to her. She quit music altogether and focused on Caliente Springs until she got married. When that ended, she focused on her friends and working with animal charities."

"I don't want to be nosy, but what happened to her marriage?"

George patted her hand. "You can be as nosy as you want. You're my friend, Ellen."

She liked the sound of *friend*. Her ankle hurt, so she leaned more heavily on George. A picture of the Travers Twins at an awards show caught her eye. "What trouble did Ginger have?"

"Her husband left her after ten years. They just sort of fell apart. No kids, but she wanted them."

"That's hard." Ellen ached for Ginger. She was also curious about George. "You never married, did you?"

"Me? No. Never."

Ellen chuckled. "That was emphatic."

George laughed with her. "I could joke and say no woman in her right mind would have me, but the truth is, I was married to my career. I cheated on that too."

"What do you mean?"

"I had a love affair with Tennessee whiskey. There were women too. But in the end, those times were as empty as the JD bottles I polished off."

"JD?"

"Jack Daniels." He scrubbed his jaw with his long fingers. "My former best friend until I met the Lord Jesus Christ. It's kind of ironic, isn't it? Because of Jack, I meet Jesus." His wide mouth quirked into a sly grin. "That sounds like a song lyric."

"Write it."

"I just might do that. I'm a drunk and always will be, but God gave me a new life. I thank Him for it every day."

"I thank Him too. For—" *Ben and the kids.* She bit her tongue. It seemed wrong to mention Ben with George so close.

He turned his head, seeking her gaze when she wanted to hide. "You were going to say that you thank God for your marriage and your children."

"Yes."

"It's okay, Ellen. You can talk to me about Ben.

He's part of who you are, just like this wall is part of me. I regret a lot of the things I did, but when I stand up and speak in church or at an AA meeting, folks listen because I've been where they are."

"You're the real deal."

"Yes, ma'am," he said. "And so are you. We have some hard miles on us."

"And a lot of them too."

She and George both had more years behind them than lay ahead. No one lived forever, and nothing on earth hurt as much as losing someone you loved. Ellen couldn't face that pain again, and she wouldn't wish it on anyone, especially someone she cared about.

With her chin high, she stepped back from the wall. "It's getting late. I should head home."

"One more thing." George turned enough to face her without releasing his grip on her elbow. "As much as I enjoy watching old movies with you, I think it's time we went on a real date."

"Oh—"

"I hope you'll say yes, because I have something special in mind."

Her mouth must have been gaping, because George touched her chin with his knuckle and closed it for her.

"I'm doing a show in San Jose next Friday. It's a fundraiser for Home and Hearth. You know I'm on the board of directors."

"Yes. Julia mentioned it."

"We'd drive up in the morning and spend the night. Two rooms, just to be clear. What do you say?"

Yes . . . No . . . Yes. The words sawed on her vocal cords until she thought of what Julia had whispered in her ear before she left with Zeke. *"Be brave, Mom."*

That was easy for Julia to say. She was only twenty-eight. God willing, she'd fall in love, get married, and live a long time. *God willing.* Ellen didn't use those words lightly. No one knew what tomorrow held, or even what the next hour would bring. All anyone truly had on this earth was *now,* this moment.

Fear and courage played tug-of-war in her heart, until courage won and she turned to George. "I'd love to go with you."

That famous grin flashed on his face. "Well, good."

Humming one of his own songs, he steered her back to the recliner, picked up her crutches, and carried them in one hand. She retrieved her purse, and they walked arm-in-arm to her car. Julia had driven earlier, but Ellen was certain she could manage the short drive to the cottage.

George's thick brows collided over his nose. "You shouldn't drive with your ankle. I'll take you home and walk back."

"No. I can manage." The mild sprain was healing fast.

"Are you sure?"

"Positive."

Frowning, he propped his hands on his hips. "You really do have some Katharine Hepburn in you."

Pleased, she leaned the crutches against the car and took the keys out of her purse. She opened her mouth to say good-night, saw George watching her, and froze.

If she gave him a sign, he'd kiss her. She wanted that magic moment to happen, but then she smelled the grass and thought of lawn mowers. And when she thought of lawn mowers, she pictured Ben in their front yard, cutting grassy diamonds because she liked how they looked.

Angry tears flooded her eyes. She'd always love Ben, but she was tired of missing him. For once she wanted pedal-to-the-metal excitement, but that was crazy. And risky. Trembling, she looked down at her feet.

Drawing her close, George tucked her head under his chin. "There's no rush, Ellen. None at all."

No rush? What about the rush in her blood? The rush of desire affirming she was female, alive, and maybe not over the hill.

He held her tighter. "Don't say anything. You'll know when it's right, and it's not right tonight."

She almost laughed. "That sounds like a bad country song."

"Or a good one."

Easing out of his arms, she managed a watery smile. "Do you know how amazing you are?"

"I'm a real gem," he said with his tongue planted firmly in his cheek.

"You're solid gold. And you have the records to prove it."

"Don't forget the platinum ones." He winked at her, then opened the car door and stepped back.

Ellen climbed into the car and backed out of the driveway, but before turning down the street, she peered through the windshield. George stood in the headlights, a silhouette with one hand raised high in a kind of salute.

He was right about that first kiss. She wasn't ready, but she wanted to be. A shopping trip for the perfect outfit seemed like a good place to start.

"Look out, George Travers," she said out loud. "Because I'm going to knock you into next week."

Twenty

Everything Julia did with Hunter was a minefield, and being in church was no different. He liked to sit on the aisle and always took it, so when Ellen asked him to scoot to the middle of the pew, he hesitated.

Julia kept her voice low. "It makes sense. George is singing today. He'll join us in the middle of the service."

Hunter's mouth opened, but he closed it and moved to the center of the bench. She felt a little sorry for him. Courtesies that came easily to most people upset him.

Julia followed Max, and the three of them sat in a row. She'd been up half the night thinking about Hunter and had reached a conclusion. She had moved on with her life, and he needed to accept that fact. Maybe, if he gave up the false hope that she'd go back to him, he'd call off Uncle Maury. She needed to speak to him after the service. He was leaving for LA immediately, so she and Max were riding back with George and Ellen. The minute she arrived back at the cottage, she planned to call Zeke with whatever information she gleaned.

The worship team took the stage, the lights dimmed, and the chords of a song about love never failing echoed in the sanctuary. Tears pushed into Julia's eyes. What she believed now about love was a lifetime away from that cheesy Valentine. After another song, George walked out with his guitar and sang a boisterous version of "I'll Fly Away." The congregation caught fire, but it was Ellen's smile, untouched by grief and a testament to grace, that brought fresh tears to Julia's eyes.

When George finished, the minister stepped to the podium. "Let's open our Bibles to Daniel, chapter six."

Julia set her Bible in her lap and thumbed through the pages but couldn't find the book of Daniel. That happened to her all the time, but she preferred a hard-copy Bible to an app. At moments like this, she envied Zeke and his life-long exposure to God's Word.

For the next half hour, the pastor talked about Daniel in the lions' den. Julia silently asked God for a Daniel-like faith, because though Hunter wasn't a lion, she felt trapped by his personality. She soaked in every word until the final "Amen."

With George in the lead, the five of them made their way out of the sanctuary. After Hunter said his good-byes to the others, including a big hug with Max, he turned to Julia.

She wanted to be in control, so she spoke first. "I need to get Max's backpack. I'll walk you to your car."

They left the lobby and headed to the Lexus parked at the far edge of the lot, taking up two spaces to protect the paint from dings. She used to scold him for inconveniencing others, but today she welcomed the distance from the crowd.

When they reached the car, he started to open the passenger door. "It's hot. Get in and I'll run the A/C."

"No." The car seemed like a trap to her, or a cage, so she stopped by the trunk. "This will only take a minute."

"Sure. What is it?" He let go of the handle without a complaint. Maybe he really was changing. She hoped so, because it would make the future easier for everyone.

"I want to make sure we're clear on something."

"Is this about Max?"

"No."

He studied her, his eyes slightly narrowed. "So it's about Uncle Maury. And Zeke."

"No. It's about you and me."

"Then it's about Max."

As usual, Hunter needed to win, and he was using their son to do it. "Let's leave Max out of it."

"I can't. What you do affects Max, and that affects me."

Me. Me. Me. Along with *I,* it was Hunter's favorite word. But what about words like *you* and *us,* even *others?* People were pawns to him, even his own son. They'd quarreled enough in the past that she knew better than to fire back. The only way to win with Hunter was to refuse to play his game.

She forged ahead. "I've told you before that our relationship is over. Just to be clear, I'm saying it again."

"Fine. Whatever."

He was blowing her off, dismissing her, so she repeated herself. "It's over, Hunter. I'm moving on."

He leaned a hip on the Lexus. "It's not over, Julia. And you know it. You're just confused right now."

She wasn't the least bit confused. Daniel had faced a den full of lions; Julia was trapped in the same way but with a tiger, the most cunning cat in the kingdom. A creature that stalked its victims, lunged unseen, and fed on a kill for days.

Refusing to be Hunter's prey ever again, Julia swallowed a retort, spun on her heels, and started back to the church.

Hunter clamped his hand on her shoulder and forced her to turn around. "I will not lose you— *or my son*—to anyone. And especially not to a pious snot like Zeke Monroe."

There was no doubt now. Hunter had come to church for his own purposes, though maybe he'd heard the message of faith in the sermon. Forgiveness was his for the asking, but Hunter would never ask.

Julia didn't have the energy to deal with him now, so she stripped all the anger from her voice. "We don't have to agree, Hunter. But we *do* have to be good parents. Whatever happens, I won't interfere with your relationship with Max. You will always be his dad."

Hunter folded his arms over his chest. "This is because of Zeke."

"No. Not at all." The last thing she wanted to do was jump from one relationship to another. "This is about me and how I've changed. I want to be honest with you. And fair."

Hunter's eyes narrowed. "You're chasing after Zeke, aren't you? Just like you did in Berkeley."

"Fine!" She flung her hands in the air. "Blame Zeke. Blame me. Blame anyone but yourself. That's what you always do."

She turned to leave but caught sight of his hand slipping inside his coat. Her gaze shot to his cynical smile, and she knew whatever he was doing was meant to bring her to her knees. *Don't ask. Don't play his game.*

But the question burst out of her. "*What* are you doing?"

He withdrew his phone, tapped the screen, and raised the device to his ear. Staring at her with slitted eyes, he remained silent until whomever he called picked up.

"Uncle Maury. How are you?"

As badly as Julia wanted to walk away,

for Zeke's sake she took the bait and listened.

"About that visit to Caliente Springs," Hunter said more to her than to Maury, "I think you should move fast. Ginger Travers wants out now, and she thinks her brother will come around with a little persuasion." Pausing to listen, he leaned against his sporty car as if he didn't have a care in the world. "The week of September tenth? That should work. In fact, I'll take the whole week off. That'll give you some flexibility, and I can spend a lot of time with Max."

No. No. No. Her pulse pounded with the beat of a war drum. With as much nonchalance as she could muster, she listened as the conversation dragged on another five minutes.

"That's it," Hunter finally said to Maury. "I'll check with Ginger about the dates. You can expect a call from her or the GM. His name is Zeke Monroe. If you say 'frog,' he's supposed to jump."

Humiliating Zeke was vintage Hunter. It disgusted her. But even worse, this kind of behavior would rub off on Max. She couldn't stand the thought, but how did she stop it? She couldn't. But like Daniel, she could muster her faith, stand her ground, and rely on God to deliver them all. With the blacktop burning through the soles of her thin sandals, she watched every change in Hunter's expression for clues that would help Zeke.

The instant he finished with Maury, he made a

second call. "Ginger, it's Hunter Adams. I just spoke to my uncle."

Julia couldn't hear Ginger's side of the conversation, but Hunter's smirk confirmed her worst fears. She was firmly in his camp. Furious but not surprised, Julia listened until Hunter said good-bye, then she spun on her heels and headed to the church.

"Julia!"

She walked even faster. But Hunter shouted again, this time in a singsong. "You forgot something."

More bait. Another gambit to force her to bow to him. But if she didn't turn around, she'd come off like a pouting child. Chin high, she pivoted and saw Max's backpack dangling in Hunter's hand. In spite of the hot sun, her face paled at the thought of her son's clothes, his favorite stuffed bear. Ordinary things a father should love and respect, but Hunter didn't respect anyone, especially her.

He wanted her to grovel. She could feel it. If the backpack had belonged to anyone but Max, she would have stalked off. But her son needed his things. Forcing an air of calm, she walked back to the Lexus. When she reached the car, Hunter held the backpack even higher, flicked his wrist, and made it spin. She tried to grab it, but he jerked it away.

Slapping her hands on her hips, she glared

at him. "Just what do you think you're doing?"

"I'm reminding you that Max belongs in Los Angeles. Come home, Julia. I'll tell Uncle Maury that Ginger changed her mind, and Zeke the Freak can have Caliente Springs. The choice is yours."

No way would she make a deal like that. *Never.* "That's not going to happen. I signed a contract to plan a wedding. I'm staying and so is Max."

His voice came out in a purr. "I don't want to fight about this, Julia."

Of course he didn't want to fight. To Hunter, *not fighting* meant *you do what I want.* In his world, every choice was black or white; he won or lost. And he always had to win. But he wouldn't win today. With God's help, Julia could handle his threats.

Meeting his gaze with a forceful one of her own, she repeated her position. "I won't leave Caliente Springs until my job is done."

"Are you sure?"

"Positive."

"Fine." He tossed the backpack at her feet, forcing her to squat in front of him to pick it up.

Keeping her eyes locked on his, she lifted the backpack and stood tall.

Hunter climbed into the Lexus, started the engine, and powered down the window. Sunglasses in place, he gave her a cocky salute. "See you later, babe."

She stared back, watching until the Lexus cruised out of the parking lot. When the vehicle was out of sight, every muscle in her body went slack. Weak from the fight, she hugged the backpack tight and tried to pray. She knew she was forgiven and God loved her. He loved Hunter too, and that meant she needed to forgive him. That was surprisingly simple. The problem was knowing she'd have to forgive him so many times, because he'd always be part of her life.

Finally, after several moments, the emotions sank back below the surface and she returned to the church where her mom, Max, and George were throwing pennies into a fountain. When Max hurled a coin as hard as he could, Ellen and George grinned at each other with so much affection Julia caught her breath. Hunter had never looked at her that way, but Zeke had.

She called to the trio from ten feet away. "I'm back."

Ellen hurried to her. They were out of Max's earshot, but Ellen still spoke in a hush. "How did it go?"

"Awful." Keeping one eye on Max and George, she told her mom everything.

"I was afraid of that. Ginger called George a few minutes ago. He said he'd give me the details later, but I think you just explained it."

"Mommy!" Max waved to her from the pond. "We're making wishes. Can I have more pennies?"

"Sure." It felt good to indulge him in something harmless, so she dug in her purse for some coins as she walked with her mom to the pond. With Max occupied, Julia turned to George. "You know what's going on, right?"

He propped his hands on his hips. "Yes, I do. Zeke has orders to prepare for a visit from Maury Applegate the week of September tenth. That's a week from now. We have some time to prepare, but this problem is bigger than all of us put together. If you ladies are agreeable, I say we join hands and pray."

Julia nodded. "I'd like that."

When she called Max, he dropped the remaining coins with a kerplunk, dashed to her side, and gripped her hand. Ellen gripped his other hand, and they both offered their free hands to George.

"We're going to say a prayer," Julia told Max. "Like we do at bedtime, when we thank God for things."

"Like for food," Max said. "And for Daddy."

"Yes." She managed to sound cheerful for Max's sake, but she felt like Daniel thanking God for the lions.

They bowed their heads, and George began. "Well, Lord. Here we are, and we need your help."

There was nothing formal about the rest of his prayer, nothing poetic or profound. George prayed in the down-to-earth way Zeke used to pray in Berkeley.

Julia's mind drifted to the Bible buried in the cardboard box, a picture that had bothered her ever since she saw it. Even if he had a new Bible, he would have put the old one on a shelf or passed it along to someone. Even more telling, he hadn't brought up his faith a single time since she'd been in Caliente Springs.

Oh, Lord. What happened to him?

George finished, and Ellen asked God to give them all the courage to trust Him. Julia choked up, because she knew the personal struggle beneath her mom's prayer.

It was Julia's turn. Feeling awkward, she was grateful God could see past her stammering to her heart. "Lord, I'm worried about Zeke. Help him. Please." She prayed out loud for God to give Zeke the wisdom to cope with the problems coming his way, but in the quiet of her mind she prayed for his soul. *Father God, something is terribly wrong. He's cold and distant to you. He's hurting. Help me to know how to help him . . . if I even can.*

After a pause, George said, "Amen."

The breeze stilled, leaving only the gurgle of water cascading over the rocks. As they walked to the car, the calm certainty that she needed to speak to Zeke settled into Julia's bones. She sent him a text. Need to see you. Your house?

He sent back one line: Yes. ASAP. You OK?

Sighing, she typed back the only truthful answer she could give. Yes and no. We need to talk.

Twenty-one

With time to kill before Julia arrived at his house, Zeke decided to make short work of emptying his parents' storage boxes. As he stepped into the garage, his father's voice rang in his ears.

"It's Sunday morning, Zeke. Why aren't you in church? Get busy, son. Those boxes won't unpack themselves. If you'd stacked them in order, number one wouldn't be on the bottom, and you'd have that list. You'd know what's in them."

All good points, but to use one of Cowboy Chet's favorite words, Zeke didn't give a hoop-dee-doo about emptying the boxes in order. Between Ginger's phone call about Applegate's visit, the Bible on the workbench, and the mental picture of Julia sitting next to Hunter in church, he was in a sour mood when he slit open Box No. 12.

Bath towels. Old ones. Nothing but rags, thanks to a family of mice who had set up housekeeping sometime in the past. He shoved the box aside, took a marker, and wrote DUMP in big messy letters across the top.

Box No. 8 held his grandmother's good china. A family heirloom to be sure, and something for his sisters.

As he crossed out his dad's precise *No. 8* and wrote *Grandma M's Dishes,* he choked up. For all his irritation with his father, Zeke had good memories too. Even great ones. Like the Christmas the kitchen sink clogged and he and his dad had washed the dishes in the bathtub. To a boy, that was a riot. Somehow it had been a lot easier to be a perfect kid than it was to be a perfect man.

By two o'clock, the garage looked like a bomb had gone off. Crumpled newspaper overflowed from the recycle bin and littered the floor. Family treasures were piled against a wall to be sorted later, and stuff for charity was in a heap in the middle of the garage. The eight sealed boxes that remained stood in a sloppy stack with number one on the bottom.

Zeke's hands were black with newspaper ink and his mood matched when he sliced into Box No. 11. He was about to pull back the flaps when Julia's Outback rumbled up the street. Leaving the box, he strode down the driveway to meet her.

As she approached, a yellow dress swished around her legs with a lightness that countered the grim set of her mouth. Every instinct told him to draw her into his arms, but his hands were filthy. He held them palm out to show her. "I better not touch you."

She raised a brow. "You've been busy."

"I'm finally emptying the boxes." He motioned for her to follow him. "Let's go inside. I'll finish later. Where's Max?"

A pleased smile curved her lips. "At the cottage

with Grammie and George. When I left, my mom was on the couch with an ice pack on her ankle, George had his guitar out, and Max was teaching him the words to 'The Wheels on the Bus.' "

In spite of his grim mood, Zeke smiled. "They go 'round and 'round, as I recall."

"All through the town," Julia added.

"The memory's vague, but I remember singing that song as a kid on family road trips. My sisters and I used to make up silly verses, including one where a bug went splat-splat-splat. It drove my dad a little crazy."

He watched Julia survey the mess and the remaining boxes. "Why don't I help you finish?" she asked. "We can talk out here."

Zeke would have preferred to wash his hands and sit in the air-conditioned house, but his dad was right. The boxes wouldn't unpack themselves. On the other hand, Julia didn't belong in the garage in her pretty dress.

"You'll get dirty."

"I'll take my chances." She walked over to the box he'd slit open just before she arrived, reached inside, and unearthed an orange Nike shoebox.

Zeke recognized it instantly. Grinning, he crossed the garage and lifted it from her hands. "This box is mine. I forgot all about it."

"What is it?"

He set it on the workbench, wiped his hands on a rag, then lifted the lid. One by one, he placed the four Teenage Mutant Ninja Turtles in a row. Scratched and missing their weapons, Leonardo, Donatello, Raphael, and Michelangelo were heirlooms to him.

Julia smiled up at him. "I bet you played with these for hours."

He picked up Leonardo, his favorite, and maneuvered the toy into a fight stance. "I saved the world more than a few times with these guys. Too bad they're not real, because it looks like we're in for a fight with Maury Applegate."

"I'm afraid so."

"So tell me about Hunter." Zeke tossed another ball of newspaper toward the overflowing can. "I have a pretty good idea what happened thanks to that phone call from Ginger. He must have called her right after the service."

Julia huffed. "You don't know the half of it. He deliberately made the call right in front of me."

"So he's making it personal."

"Yes. It's just like I thought." She picked up Raphael, though Zeke doubted she knew he was the Turtle who usually threw the first punch. "Hunter's doing this to punish me. The trip to church was a sham, which I suspected. I made sure he knew we were through."

"So how did he take it?"

"Badly. But I think he finally believes me." She set Raphael back on the workbench and hopped up on a stool. In a tight voice, she told him about the confrontation in the parking lot, Hunter's phone calls, and finally about the backpack. When she finished the story, she laced her hands in her lap. "Hunter's a permanent part of my life because of Max. I pray about the situation all the time."

She looked at him expectantly.

Trapped! Zeke could admit the truth about his lost faith or deflect with platitudes. With his throat dry and tight, he turned away before he realized how it would look to her. Superheroes didn't dodge hard questions, but Zeke felt like Leonardo stripped of his mask and swords.

Finally he choked out, "That's good."

"Good?"

"Yeah. Sure." *Liar, liar, pants on fire.* Turning abruptly, he pulled another shoebox out of the carton, opened it, and saw a bunch of G.I. Joes. "Hey, look at these—"

Julia gently closed the box lid. "I'll look later. Right now, I'm worried about you."

"Me? Why?'

"You're different than you were in college. You used to talk about your faith all the time. It defined you. And now it's—it's gone. I don't know what to think."

Busted. Unable to meet her gaze, he turned back to the Turtles, arranging them just because he could. "You're right. I've changed. But it has nothing to do with you. It's between God and me."

"I don't understand." Her gaze shot to the things

piled on the workbench, including the Bible from the Berkeley box. When he repacked the other stuff, he had left the Bible out, unsure what to do with it. Julia nudged the worn book with her fingertip. "Before we broke up, you wanted to be a minister. I remember how committed you were."

"That was six years ago."

"What happened?"

"I changed."

"How?"

"I just did."

She waited for more. When he didn't speak, she pursed her lips. "You're stalling."

"Yeah," he admitted. "I don't like to talk about it."

Leaning forward, she laid her hand on his biceps, her fingers as gentle as a bird landing on a branch. There was something powerful in her touch, something more than what had come out of the Berkeley box. In college, they'd been friends and lovers. With Julia's new faith, they had the potential to be husband and wife, but only if Zeke could find his spiritual footing. Looking at Julia now, he very much wanted to find it . . . if he could.

"You win, Jules." He pulled back and nudged the Turtle named Michelangelo, the youngest and least serious of the brothers, away from the others. "When I went back to Chile, I wasn't the same person who left for college."

"We all change."

"I sure did." Sighing, he indicated the Bible. "Looking back, it started even before I met you. Every time something went wrong at St. John's, I took it as a sign that I wasn't doing enough. Intellectually, I knew I couldn't solve every problem, but I felt compelled to try. And I did. In Chile, I tried to work with my dad again, but every day was harder than the one before it. When I finally told my parents I'd changed my mind about going into ministry, my mom understood but my dad didn't."

"I can imagine."

"Yeah, he was pretty upset." Zeke made air quotes, then spoke in his dad's booming tone. " 'I'm *disappointed* in you, son.' "

"Ouch."

"I got angry too. We had a terrible fight, but I couldn't pretend anymore. I was sick of trying to be perfect, and I was sick of feeling guilty for failing. But it's even more confusing than that. Deep down I didn't really feel guilty for any-thing—except for not feeling guilty."

A dazed look crossed her face. "That *is* confusing."

His gaze drifted back to the box of old toys. "You'd understand if you knew my dad. When I told him I wanted to go into business instead of ministry, he said I was letting God down. That Jesus had died for my sins and it was my duty to

271

use my gifts to lead others to Christ. And it is. I believe that. But I was tired of trying to live up to that calling."

She thought a moment. "That sounds like burnout."

"Maybe. But how do you burn out on a God who loves you enough to die for you?"

"I don't know." Looking down, she picked a fleck of newspaper off her skirt. "I'm still new at this. I just know that God loves us."

A fresh heaviness dragged on his lungs. "I hope you never feel like I do now, because it's a lonely place to be. I haven't talked to God in a long time. I haven't prayed, read the Bible, or been to church. I'm not proud of myself for it, but I can't live a lie."

How could someone with Zeke's deep faith lose sight of God? Julia didn't understand. With all the pressures in her life, she didn't dare loosen her grip on her new beliefs. She made mistakes every day, battled with doubt, and sinned like every human being, but she knew in the most broken parts of her heart that God loved her the way she loved Max.

Zeke opened the shoebox she'd closed earlier and lifted out a G.I. Joe with a missing arm. He set it down by the Turtles then shook his head. "Back in Berkeley, I had all the answers. But then I met you." He looked at her with a wistful smile. "Do you remember playing Jenga with the crowd from Bread on the Water?"

"Sure," she said. "Game nights were a lot of fun."

"My life was a lot like Jenga. Every time I messed up, it was like pulling out another block. The tower finally collapsed. Our relationship was one of the blocks, but it wasn't the final one that made the tower fall. The tower fell because I stopped caring."

Julia was in way over her head. "Maybe you should talk to George."

"Not if I can help it." Zeke dropped the G.I. Joe a little too hard. "I love the guy, but we come from different planets when it comes to Christianity."

"But God's the same."

Zeke gave a defeated shake of his head. "It's okay, Jules. You can't help me."

"I could try."

Ignoring her, he lifted another shoebox from the carton and opened it to reveal a tangle of Transformers. Julia's brother used to play with those, and so had she. With a few twists of a person's wrist, a robot became a bulldozer. Looking at the toys now, she saw a connection to Zeke and God. A Transformer didn't change itself; it took a greater intelligence to move the pieces. Zeke had lost his faith because he thought the robot had to do the work by itself. And it couldn't. No wonder he was frustrated.

"Zeke." Her gaze flew to his face. "You're

trying too hard. You're not trusting God to do the changing."

"Jules, don't."

"But—"

"Forget it. You can't help me."

His dismissive tone hacked away at her confidence. Who was she to question him? She couldn't even find the book of Daniel. And yet something stronger than doubt pulsed through her. Courage. Faith. And especially compassion, because when she looked at Zeke, she saw both the confident Christian she'd known in Berkeley and the tortured man he was now.

Julia grasped his dirty hand in both of her clean ones. "God loves you, Zeke. He loves you just as you are. We don't have to *try* to be Christians. We *are* Christians, because we've accepted Christ. He did the work for us. He—"

"I get it, Jules." He jerked his hand out of her grasp. "I know the theology inside and out. I'm sorry to be blunt here, but you're new at this. It's *easy* in the beginning."

"Oh, no it's not."

"You're on a honeymoon right now. That's how it starts. But the road gets narrower. Believe me, I know."

"Easy?" Julia leapt off the stool and stabbed her finger into his chest. "How can you think for even a minute that it's easy to deal with Hunter? That it was *easy* to walk away from everything I had,

everything I believed. Everything I thought I *was*. Easy? Becoming a Christian was the hardest, most gut wrenching, most costly decision I've ever made. Don't you dare say it was easy, because it wasn't."

He dragged a hand wearily across his neck. "Sorry. I didn't mean to be a jerk."

"Well, you were." She crossed her arms over her chest. "You have *no idea* what it's like to become a Christian when it means giving up your whole life. You grew up believing. I grew up with church on Christmas and Easter. Looking back, I think my mind started to change in Berkeley, largely because of you. All those conversations about life and God and eternity stayed with me."

Longing flashed in his eyes, even desperation. "So what did I say?"

Something akin to panic stirred in her chest. She needed to get this right, but she didn't have the knowledge Zeke possessed or the ability to preach like Billy Graham. Or to pray like George. Or to serve the poor like Mother Teresa or to sing like Chris Tomlin. Julia was an empty vessel that needed to be filled every day.

A little shaky, she sat back down on her stool. "I can't tell you exactly what you said in Berkeley, but I can tell you my story."

"I'm listening."

The first words stumbled out of her mouth. "I was unhappy for a long time, but it wasn't until a big fight with Hunter that I finally cracked. The fight was huge. The worst one ever. He wanted to take Max out on his awful speedboat, and I said no. When he told Max to get in the Lexus, Max got excited and ran to the car. I don't have anything against speedboats, but Hunter thinks he's invincible. I couldn't trust him to keep Max safe."

"That's rough."

"It was. And it still is. But that day I couldn't compromise. I grabbed Max's hand and dragged him kicking and screaming to my car instead. We drove straight to my mom's."

Zeke was watching her. Studying her without saying a word, and so quiet she could hear each breath he took.

"My mom wasn't home, but the house still felt safe. I'll never forget walking through the front door and wanting to break down, but I had to take care of Max. He was okay after some cookies, so I let him play with the hose in the backyard. He loves that, and my mom doesn't mind."

She was rambling, but the next part of her story was the hardest to tell. "With Max safe and happy again, I started to shake all over. I could see the future as plain as day—me trying to protect Max, and Max becoming more like Hunter every day. My feelings were all bottled up. I couldn't cry or yell. I was numb. So I tried to pray. Nothing happened, so I got my mom's Bible out of her bedroom and opened to the only Scripture reference I knew."

"Which one?"

"Proverbs 3:5–6. My mom has it tattooed on her shoulder."

"Trust in the Lord with all your heart." Zeke rattled off the rest as if he'd said it a million times. "And lean not on your own understanding; in all your ways submit to him, and he will make your paths straight."

"You know a lot of verses by heart. In Berkeley it irritated me. Now I envy you that knowledge."

"Yeah, well." He shrugged. "Finish your story, okay?"

"Sure." She took a breath. "I read that verse over and over. The next thing I knew, my eyes were closed and I was telling God how I felt. I cried until I couldn't cry anymore. When my mom came home, I told her what happened and that I was leaving Hunter. She was great. She gave me a big hug, told me to come live with her, and said she'd watch Max while I packed. I went to the condo, threw our stuff in trash bags, then waited for Hunter to get back from the lake."

"Oh, man. How did he take it?"

"Just like I expected. He called me a coward, said I was ruining Max, rolled his eyes when I tried to explain. I hated him at that moment." Her voice fractured into a thousand pieces. "We'd fought before. Hunter couldn't see it, but this time was different."

"Why?"

"Because I was different." She patted her chest. "I didn't want to be Hunter's doormat, and I knew enough about God—in large part thanks to you—that I wanted to live differently. That meant facing the truth and trusting Him even though I was terrified. I needed a job and didn't have one. I knew I'd lose friends, and I did. But the hardest part was knowing Max would be confused and hurt." She choked out her last words. "I love him so much."

Zeke took a step toward her. "Jules—"

"Don't. I have to finish." Blinking fast, she wiped her damp eyes with her fingertips. "Because of what happened with Hunter, I know what it's like to look down a long tunnel and see nothing but darkness. You know that leap of faith people talk about?"

He nodded.

"It's terrifying. Worse than skydiving, because you don't pack your own parachute and check it twelve times before you make the jump. Everything I just told you is why being a Christian isn't the least bit easy for me."

"No, I can see that now." He slouched back against the workbench. "And I'm truly sorry for saying it was. But do you want to know something?"

"What?" She could breathe now, even think a little.

"I envy you."

"That's crazy."

"No. It's not. You have something, Jules. It's real and it's yours. It's not something you believe because it's how you were raised."

"Well, that much is true. I messed up my life all on my own." Now she was trying to trust God instead of herself. With her heart threatening to beat right out of her chest, she peered into Zeke's face. His eyes met hers. One hug. One kiss. One touch to tell him he wasn't alone.

She took a step in his direction, but he held his hands palms out. "I'm filthy, Jules. Don't touch me."

She didn't care about his hands, but his heart was another matter. Until Zeke made peace with God, he was on the same shaky ground she'd been on in college. If she truly wanted to live her faith, she needed to commit him fully to God. *But Lord, I love him.* As glorious and messy as glitter flying off a visor, her feelings sparkled and spun through her entire body.

But it was too soon for those feelings, and she didn't trust her instincts. If she stayed, Zeke would see the turmoil in her eyes. She might tell him how she felt, and right now he needed God far more than he needed her rattled emotions.

Shaking inside, she let out a slow breath. "I

think I've talked enough. I should head home and let you finish out here."

He nodded, relief plain on his face as he put the Ninja Turtles back in their shoebox and handed it to her. "These are for Max."

"But they're special to you. Are you sure?"

"Positive."

Julia recognized the need to change the subject and felt it herself. She took the Turtles from him. "Thanks. Max will love them."

Together they held the box, their fingers brushing for an instant.

Zeke stepped back. "I'll see you at work tomorrow."

She said her own good-bye and walked to her car. She didn't look at him again, but her fingers tingled with the memory of that single touch. Dirty or clean, she loved Zeke just as he was.

Twenty-two

When Zeke walked into his office on Monday morning, he couldn't believe who—or what—stood around his desk. Marketing was at it again. They must have conspired with John at the pro shop, because there were five life-size cutouts of golfer Phil Mickelson scattered around Zeke's desk. The pro shop used the cutouts to sell golf apparel.

There was no plaid in sight, but someone had taped a cartoon word bubble over the Phil in the middle. It read *Clone Attack!*

Julia came up behind him and stopped. "That's . . ." She paused to glance at all five pasteboard smiles. "That's a little scary, actually."

"Yeah. Like zombies."

After last night, Zeke felt like one. Instead of unpacking the last seven boxes in the garage, he had hauled a truckload of stuff to a Salvation Army drop-off. He had expected a weight to lift from his shoulders, but as he unloaded the boxes, each one had felt heavier than the last. When he climbed back in his truck, he'd been sucker-punched with a grief so strong he slumped helplessly against the steering wheel.

Hollow and hurting, he'd driven back to Pismo Beach to think and remember, even to look for

God. But he'd come back still full of bitterness.

Julia walked up to his desk, set down some papers, and picked up one of the cutouts by the elbow. "The zombies need to wait. We have a lot of work to do. Later you can figure out what to do with them."

"I already know. John's going to find one sitting in the backseat of his car, and the others are going to show up in Marketing when they least expect it."

Julia smiled. "Revenge is sweet."

Zeke picked up two at a time. He just wished he had a real Phil Mickelson clone to play golf with Mr. Carter. He gestured toward the papers. "Are those the paving quotes for Golden Point?"

"Some of them are." She slid a manila envelope out from the stack. "Open this first. It's fun."

Zeke sat down behind the desk and pulled out a sheet of drawing paper covered with green circles vaguely shaped like turtles. The words *Thank you, Mr. Zeke* were written in Julia's neat printing, followed by *From Max* in crooked letters, including a backwards R.

Giving Max the Turtles had been an impulsive decision, but the instant he saw the box in Julia's hands, he knew Max would treasure the toys. Little boys longed to be heroes; so did grown men. Zeke didn't know what the future held for Caliente Springs, or for himself and Julia, but he was ready to do battle for both, even if it meant wrestling an angel like Jacob did in the Old Testament.

He snapped off a piece of tape and hung Max's drawing behind his desk. "This needs to go on display."

Julia sat on the chair across from him. Before he could pick up the paving quotes, she broke in. "First, the Carter visit. Mr. and Mrs. Carter arrive Wednesday. I offered them a cottage, but he wants to stay in a room like his employees would."

"I like how he thinks."

"The four of us have a six a.m. tee time."

Wincing, Zeke shook his head. "He really does love golf. We'll beat the heat, but does that work for you with Max?"

"It's fine. My mom's ankle is a lot better. She's still taking Advil, but she can get around without the crutches if she doesn't overdo it. In fact, I'm taking her for a quick shopping trip this afternoon."

"Enjoy it." Julia worked a lot of extra hours and deserved the time off.

Leaning back in his chair, Zeke picked up the quotes for paving the path at Golden Point. For the next several minutes, they discussed the job bids. They were all high, so at Julia's suggestion they decided to check out the rose garden as a possible ceremony site.

Zeke came around his desk. "Let's go right now. Then you can get on with your day."

They left the office and passed through the lobby. It should have been crowded with people, but he could have shot off a rocket and not bothered a soul. "We need this wedding to be a hit."

"I have a new idea," Julia said as they walked. "One of the bridesmaids is on the staff of *Flops & Fortunes*. Have you heard of it?"

"It's a reality TV show." Contestants competed to see who could throw the most amazing party on a thousand-dollar budget. Weddings, reunions, surprise parties. Whatever created drama.

"We don't qualify for the show, but Jessica, one of the bridesmaids, wants to live-tweet on the show's official Twitter account. Let's hope we're in the fortune category and not a flop, because a million people are going to read a blow-by-blow account. It's a little risky, but I'm all for taking chances."

"Me too. How does Tiff feel about it?" Zeke pushed open the door to the sidewalk leading to the garden.

"She's all for it."

"And Ginger and George?"

Julia made a seesaw motion with her hand. "They're ambivalent, but they like the idea of publicity for the resort."

"Then it's a go."

"Yes. But I'll feel better when we nail down the ceremony site." She glanced up at the sky. "I wish I could convince Tiff to move it all indoors. It rarely rains here in September, but I have to be prepared. There's a contingency plan in place, and it would be gorgeous."

"Where?"

"The Sagebrush Room. It's very plain, but we'd flood it with flowers and candles. I love the idea, but Tiff's dead set on sunset at Golden Point."

They arrived at the rose garden, stopped under the entry arch, and surveyed a watered lawn surrounded by adequate but ordinary rose-bushes.

Julia spoke for both of them. "It's not bad, but it's not special."

"No." Zeke thought of the paving bids. Did he buy a new freezer for the restaurant, fix the backhoe, or pave the walk to the lookout? With an eye on the future, and the hope that Tiff's wedding would lead to a hundred others, he made a decision. "Let's go with Golden Point. I'll find the money for the paving."

Julia let out a breath. "Decision made. But the clock's ticking. Let's hope we don't run into any big problems."

Ellen usually enjoyed shopping, but today she hated every minute, every outfit, and every inch of her middle-aged body. The mirrors in the

Macy's dressing room weren't helping, either. Every time she inspected an outfit for George's show, she saw the fifteen pounds she needed to lose. The dress she was wearing now was the worst one yet. It skipped *curvy,* zoomed past *plump,* and went straight to *sausage.*

"Good grief," she muttered.

There were clothes everywhere—on hooks and hangers, draped over the cubicle sides, even piled on the chair. Nothing felt right, and Julia was back on the sales floor, hot on the hunt and dead set on finding poor old Mom the perfect dress. Fat chance!

Julia, on the other hand, had tried on five dresses and picked two, both of which looked smashing on her.

"Those were the days," Ellen said to the chubby woman in the mirror.

She turned to the side, sucked in her stomach, then gave up and let everything sag. Gravity wasn't kind to women her age. She supposed men struggled too, but George didn't. He was confident. Patient too. *And* he had a flat stomach. Her stomach wasn't flat and never would be again, though the Spanx-brand underwear was worth every penny.

Fed up, she pulled the sausage dress over her head and decided to go with a western look. Jeans were more her style, and denim seemed fitting for George's country music vibe.

Trying to be confident, she put on a brand of jeans she'd never heard of, a tailored white shirt, and a vest with swirls of silver, black, and purple sequins. She took a breath, faced herself in the mirror, and hated every inch. But what did she know? She had lost her fashion sense when she lost Ben.

Julia slipped into the dressing room with another armload of clothing.

Ellen channeled her inner Katharine Hepburn and struck a pose. "What do you think?"

"Hmmm."

Ellen knew what that meant. "You hate it."

"It's just too—uh—"

"Too Dale Evans."

"Who's Dale Evans?"

Ellen felt as old as dirt. "You know who she is." Or was. Dale was dead, God rest her soul. "She was married to Roy Rogers. The cowboy on the 1950s TV show."

"Oh, yeah." Julia strung out the words as if she were recalling the Stone Age. "Now I know who you mean."

Ellen stuck out one leg. "Maybe boots would help."

"Uh, no."

"A scarf?"

"Mom. No." Julia gave a slow, sad shake of her head. "Trust me. That outfit isn't you."

"Then what *is* me?"

Ellen didn't know anymore. In the flower shop she wore jeans and a green smock with pockets full of notes and twist ties. She dressed up a little for church, but no one noticed and she was fine with that. She liked her comfortable clothes and her comfortable life.

Perspiration beaded on her brow. This shopping trip was just too much for her. But if she couldn't shop, how would she survive the three-hour ride in George's Corvette, the backstage excitement, and the front-row seat for his show?

And afterward, that first kiss still waited to be taken. Only four days had passed since she twisted her ankle, but she and George had spent hours together. Considering the long talks they shared as well as those silences filled with intimate sparks, kissing him should have been as natural as breathing. Yet in spite of the closeness she felt, she couldn't seem to give him even a peck on the cheek. George, a scoundrel to the core, wasn't making it easy for her either. He flirted until she blushed, but always backed away. The next move was hers, and Ellen knew it.

Warmth flooded her cheeks. Flustered and fed up, she squirmed out of the vest. "I've had it! If I don't find something in two minutes, I'm calling off the date." She unbuttoned the white shirt and threw it in a corner.

Julia held up a different dress. "Mom, try this one."

Why bother? She was going to hate it.

To appease Julia, she reached for the folds of black silk. The fabric warmed against her fingers, and when she held it up by the shoulders, she didn't hate it. The dress was short but not too short, and the wrap-around style promised to disguise her tummy. The half sleeves would hide her chicken arms, but what most caught Ellen's eye was the bodice covered with iridescent beads.

Holding her breath, she lifted the dress over her head. The silk fluttered down her body, caressing her, until the hem brushed just above her knees.

"Don't look yet." Julia jumped to her feet and worked the zipper upward.

Looking down, Ellen watched the silk tighten over her hips, her waist, and finally her chest. There wasn't a single pinch or pucker, no need to suck in her stomach or think about a minimizer bra to go with the Spanx.

When Julia finished, Ellen turned to the mirror and her jaw dropped. Forget Dale Evans. And forget Katharine Hepburn. This dress was *her.*

Julia clasped her hands over her heart. "Mom, you're gorgeous."

The last person who had called her gorgeous was Ben. Ellen's throat swelled with a familiar lump, but this time it slipped back down. Looking at her reflection, she mentally gave Ben a wink, then settled into being herself.

"I like it."

"*Like* it?" Julia threw her hands up in exasperation. "Mom, you're stunning! George won't be able to take his eyes off you."

Ellen turned to the left, then the right. Her tummy didn't show at all. As for the rest of her, the curves were in all the right places. She'd never be a size eight again, but with the right shoes, she just might find the courage to kiss George.

Julia met her gaze in the mirror. The sparkle in her daughter's eyes was gone now, leaving behind a dull sheen of worry. "Can I ask you something personal?"

Ellen and Julia kept very few secrets from each other, but her relationship with George was a whole new topic. "Ask away. But I might not answer."

"That's all right. I understand." Julia spoke to Ellen's reflection in the mirror. "George likes you a lot."

"We're good friends."

"I can see that. I'm wondering if you'd like to be more than friends."

While Ellen pondered, Julia unzipped the dress and waited. Ellen stopped and started a few sentences, but she couldn't find the right answer even when she was wearing her everyday clothes.

"I just don't know," she finally said as she paid for the dress. "But I do know my ankle hurts and

I need to sit for a while. Let's get some coffee before we take on jewelry and shoes."

"I'd like that."

They walked out to the main part of the mall, found a Panera Bread, and settled into big chairs with a latte for Ellen and something mocha for Julia. As usual, Ellen burned her tongue. She was impatient that way.

While Julia waited for her coffee to cool, Ellen considered her earlier question about George. "You think about life and love differently when you're older."

"How so?"

With her tongue stinging, she recalled the twenty-something woman who wanted a husband, children, and a house. Her eyes had been on the future, not the past. Now she looked back as much as she looked forward, and she enjoyed the view. "I'm content with my life."

"That's nice, but is *content* enough?"

"It beats feeling like a gutted fish the way I did after your dad died."

Julia let out a sigh. "I want more than contentment, Mom. I want the sparks. The diamonds." She smiled almost to herself. "Even the glitter. I want to fall in love again."

"This is because of Zeke, isn't it?"

"Yes." Julia stared out the window at the foot traffic in the mall. Moms with strollers. Teenagers clowning around. A gray-haired couple holding hands. Sighing, she faced Ellen. "Zeke and I are still getting to know each other again, but I like him a lot. No. It's more than that. I'm afraid I'm falling in love with him again."

"I wondered about that." The little black dress Julia had just purchased said everything. "Do you know how he feels?"

"Not exactly. But I'm pretty sure he's as confused as I am." Julia slumped back in her chair and sighed. "I messed up so badly with Hunter. What if I'm wrong about these feelings for Zeke? He's different than he was in Berkeley. Instead of leaning on God, he's burned out and angry. Even bitter."

"That's not necessarily a bad thing."

"Really?"

Ellen tapped her shoulder with her index finger. "Been there. Done that. Got the tattoo. Those months after your dad died were brutal. The grief nearly broke me, but my faith came back stronger, like a rosebush pruned to a few bare branches. It was tough. Zeke's struggling right now. You're wise to be cautious, but don't forget that God knows him and loves him more than you can imagine."

The cappuccino machine spurted hot milk, and cups and plates clattered against a metal sink. Julia traced the lid of her coffee cup. "I just want to do the right thing for Max. And for Zeke. How do I trust God when there's so much at stake?"

Ellen was long past pie-in-the-sky expectations. "You accept the fact that sometimes life hurts."

"But Max—"

"He's in God's hands, just like you are." Ellen reached across the table and squeezed her daughter's hand. "You need to be brave."

"You too, Mom. I like George a lot."

"So do I."

Julia's eyes sparkled with mischief. "You're not too old to get married again."

"I'm also old enough *not* to get married. I like my freedom." She frequently had this conversation with friends her own age. A few of them dated and even belonged to online sites like eHarmony, but Ellen found the entire social scene confusing. What did men expect or want? She didn't know the rules anymore, or maybe there weren't any rules.

Julia tipped her head to the side. "But, Mom, don't you get lonely sometimes?"

"Of course." Ellen saw no point in being coy with her adult daughter. "I miss having a husband. I miss everything about being married."

They both paused, maybe to ponder what the words meant. Ellen missed the kisses and cuddling, the tender nights, but what she missed even more was talking over decisions. She could handle taking the car to the mechanic, but she hated the moment when the service manager asked her to sign a work order she didn't understand. Then there were the nights when the house was too quiet and she imagined she heard a prowler.

In general, her days were easy and dull, comfortable like an old pair of jeans. She liked her life, except for hot flashes like the one erupting now.

She grabbed a napkin and fanned herself. "I should have skipped the coffee."

Julia sighed with her. "I don't think the caffeine is doing it, Mom. I think you have feelings for George and they scare you to death."

"That about says it." She fanned herself harder.

Julia raised the mocha in a kind of toast. "To fabulous dresses, great shoes, and good men."

"To dresses, shoes, and men." Ellen touched her paper cup to Julia's.

"And to courage," Julia added. "For both of us."

Twenty-three

Thursday morning dawned clear and bright. The cool temperature was perfect for eighteen holes of golf, and even the fairways seemed greener than usual. Optimistic, Zeke steered the golf cart down the trail to the first tee. Mr. Carter sat next to him. The women were behind them in a second cart with Julia at the helm. Everyone was smiling, happy, and primed for a great day of golf.

So far, so good. With a little luck, Mr. Carter would be impressed enough to finalize the conference contract at dinner tonight.

When Zeke eased the cart to a stop, the men climbed out and met at the back to select their clubs. Mr. Carter chose a wood for a long drive on the opening par four, then watched Zeke's club choice. "Julia tells me you've been playing for just five months."

"That's right."

"I've been playing for forty years," he remarked. "How about we make this a real competition?"

"Sure." Zeke grinned. "What do you have in mind?"

"I'll spot you two strokes a hole. That should make it interesting for both of us."

Zeke figured he'd need three strokes a hole to be competitive, but the only thing he really wanted to win was Mr. Carter's business. Zeke would be lucky to break 110 today, but he could impress Mr. Carter in other ways. Etiquette. The condition of the course. Respect and courtesy.

He offered his hand and shook. "You have a deal."

Mr. Carter clapped him on the back, and they both turned to the women.

Mrs. Carter was tall, trim, and dressed all in white, including a visor that capped her silver hair. For some reason, she was glaring at her husband.

When Mr. Carter glared back, Zeke turned to Julia with the hope of gaining some insight. He couldn't read her expression, but she looked great in a pastel pink ball cap, white collared shirt, and a skort boasting pink, gray, and black plaid. The skirt-shorts combo showed off her legs, but what Zeke liked best was knowing she'd worn it for him.

Clearing his throat, Zeke focused on Mrs. Carter. "Are you ready?" Earlier, when a tee was tossed to determine who played first, it had pointed to her.

Mrs. Carter gave him a smug smile. "I'm ready. But I doubt you are."

Zeke raised a brow.

Mrs. Carter gave her husband a pointed stare. "Larry, you be nice to this young man. Do you hear me?"

Mr. Carter rolled his eyes. "Aw, come on, Doris. Lighten up."

"Golf is not war." She pointed a finger like the gym teacher she used to be. "It's a sport, and it's supposed to be fun."

"*Winning* is fun." Mr. Carter threw back his shoulders, put his hands on his hips, and looked at Zeke with a maniacal gleam. "You're dead meat, Monroe."

Cue evil laugh. Enter Golf-zilla! Zeke didn't mind at all. He just wanted Mr. Carter to have a great day of golf and to sign on the bottom line.

"You're on," Zeke said with a gleam of his own.

Four hours later, they were on the sixteenth green. The women had stopped keeping score for themselves, but Mr. Carter diligently counted strokes, smirking every time he gained on Zeke. Thanks to those extra strokes, Zeke was holding his

own. The eighteenth hole promised to be a white-knuckler.

"I'm impressed," Mr. Carter said as they approached the green to make their putts. "You've done well."

"I have a good teacher in our pro, John Rossmore." Plus Jules was wearing that cute plaid skort. Earlier, when he teased her about bringing him luck, she took credit with a little curtsy.

Mr. Carter pursed his lips. "So far, I like what I'm seeing here."

The day wasn't over, but Zeke breathed easier as he walked up to his ball. It was about twenty feet from the hole and the farthest out, so he putted first. Head down and feet square, he tapped the ball, watched it roll across the green, loop the hole, and fall in with a clunk.

"Yes," he said under his breath. No one cheered during a round of golf, but he indulged in a tiny fist pump. When he glanced at Julia on the sidelines, she gave him a thumbs-up.

Mr. Carter studied him with new admiration. "Nice shot, Monroe. You're giving me a run for my money."

"Good," Zeke shot back. "But it's only because of those extra strokes."

"That's part of the game." Putter in hand, Mr. Carter approached his ball. No one breathed as he lined up for the shot, looked at the hole, then down at the ball. He pulled the putter back and—

"Maaaah. Maa—AAAH!"

Ladybug!

Zeke turned white. Mr. Carter swung and sent the ball twenty feet too far. Stunned, he stared at the nearby bushes bobbing like a scene in *Jurassic Park*. It was all Zeke could do not to yell "run!" His hand flew to his belt for the radio, but the radio was in his office. He'd left it behind in deference to etiquette. He whipped out his phone instead and called Chet.

Julia, her face aghast, trotted to his side. "Was that—"

"Yes." The word hissed off his tongue.

Chet answered on the third ring. "I'm here, boss. And saddled up. I hate to tell you this, but—"

"Get to the sixteenth green. *Now*."

"Ladybug?"

"Yes. *Ladybug*." Zeke clenched his jaw to keep from saying more. "I'm with an important client, Chet. Hurry."

Zeke hung up. Now to figure out what to say to Mr. Carter, who was staring at the bushes with his hands on his hips. Mrs. Carter was seated in a golf cart parked on the trail between the bushes and the green. Julia was already approaching the cart. If Ladybug charged, he was sure Julia would slam the cart into gear and burn rubber to the clubhouse.

Ladybug bleated again.

Mr. Carter faced Zeke, his hands still on his hips and his face beet red. "Is that a *goat?*"

Zeke straightened his shoulders. "I'm afraid it is."

The bushes snapped and swayed. Ladybug stayed out of sight, but Orphan Annie trotted out from behind the hedge.

Mrs. Carter bounced out of the cart. "Oh, Larry, look. A goat! Isn't she cute?"

Mr. Carter wasn't amused.

Zeke strode toward him, his phone in hand so he'd look like he was doing something. "Our stable manager is on the way. I'm sorry for the interruption. The equestrian center is up there." He pointed to the hill shadowing the course. "The goats belong to Ginger Travers."

Mr. Carter scratched his head. "Do they *graze* out here?"

"No, sir. It's—"

Before he could finish, Ladybug popped out from behind the shrubs. She took one look at the shiny watch on Mrs. Carter's wrist and lowered her head.

Julia called to Mrs. Carter. "I think we should go."

"Oh, I'm fine," she called with her back to Ladybug. "I grew up on a farm. I love baby goats. They're just precious."

Julia turned to Zeke, her eyes wide with dread. Zeke stared at Ladybug, and Ladybug looked at Mrs. Carter. Or more precisely, the goat was eyeballing Mrs. Carter's backside with an evil gleam in her dead brown eyes.

"It wasn't that bad," Julia said to Zeke back at the pro shop. Actually it was horrible, but she wasn't about to point that out to him right now.

They were sitting on a bench shaded by the long eaves of the building. Zeke's knees were covered with grass, and he'd skinned both hands in a tackle worthy of an NFL defensive end, but the worst was over.

At least she hoped it was. The Carters, rather than ride back to the hotel with Zeke and Julia, had left quickly with Security Chief Rex Hayden.

Zeke leaned his head back against the stucco wall, banging it just hard enough to make a thump. "Don't kid yourself, Jules. Anytime a cowboy gallops a horse onto a golf course and lassoes a goat, it's bad."

"I still can't believe it."

The scene played through her mind. Zeke had tackled Ladybug before she butted Mrs. Carter, but not before she chased the woman a good forty yards. The former gym teacher managed to circle around and leap into the golf cart with Julia, which was fortunate because Ladybug squirmed away from Zeke. Finally, Chet, saddled up because he'd been checking the hills, arrived at a slow gallop, lassoed Ladybug, and scooped Orphan Annie onto his lap. With a tip of his hat to the Carters, he rode off as if goat wrangling were a daily occurrence.

Julia banged her head against the wall just like Zeke. "Maybe it's like trouble at a wedding. The worst things make the best memories."

"I hope so, but you should have seen Mr. Carter's face. I thought he was going to have a stroke."

"So did I," Julia admitted. She knew how badly Caliente Springs needed the Carter business, but she also knew Mr. Carter. When it came to his business, he demanded the best of everything. "We'll just have to wow him at dinner tonight. He's a good man. Eventually he'll laugh at this."

Zeke was quiet for a minute, then he leaned his head just enough to touch his cheek to the top of her head. "You're good for me, Jules."

He didn't seem to care if someone saw them. It was a slow time of day, and they were alone except for a blue heron standing in the pond and an old man on the putting green. The warmth of his cheek soaked into her hair, then her scalp. Their breathing synchronized, and she longed to hold him even closer.

His words drifted into her ear. "I'm glad you're here. Somehow you give me hope when things are crazy. But do me a favor, okay?"

"Anything."

He pulled back to put them eye-to-eye, and she saw the old twinkle that belonged to Glitter Man. "Whatever you do tonight, don't wear plaid. It's not as lucky as I thought."

Tonight wasn't a date, but it felt like one to Julia. As she walked through the hotel lobby to the steak house, her three-inch heels clicked with a happy beat on the marble floor. The hem of her little black dress brushed above her knees, the sleeveless bodice showed off her shoulders, and instead of her portfolio, she carried a tiny red purse with a bit of bling.

In spite of the Ladybug fiasco, tonight was going to be good for Zeke. Earlier that afternoon, when they were back at the office, he had asked her to call Mr. Carter to make sure Mrs. Carter was recovering from the chase. Mr. Carter let her know they were both just fine and laughing about the goats. He didn't say anything about the contract, but he indicated dinner would be more than enjoyable. When she told Zeke about the hint, the tension in his face instantly eased. If they could nail the Carter contract, he'd have some ammo against selling the resort to Uncle Maury.

But first they needed to finalize the contract. And fast. The Applegate visit was scheduled for next Wednesday, exactly one week from today.

Hopeful and relaxed, Julia walked into the steak house. Zeke was speaking to the maître d', his back to her and his hands in the pockets of a classic black suit. His hair was freshly cut, and the suit framed his broad shoulders perfectly. Even from behind, he looked like the man in charge. When she walked up behind him and tapped his shoulder, the maître d' politely disappeared.

Zeke turned to her and his eyes widened. Just like she hoped, his gaze skimmed slowly from her face to her toes, then back up to her tanned shoulders. By the time he met her gaze again, her cheeks were warm and his jaw was hanging open. "Wow."

"Not a scrap of plaid in sight," she said with a grin. "You look good too."

"Not as good as you." Giving a faint whistle, he looked her up and down a second time, his Adam's apple bobbing as he swallowed. "Do you have any idea how beautiful you are? You were beautiful in Berkeley, but now you're even more amazing."

Her cheeks heated past a blush to a tingle. "No one in college would recognize us, would they?"

"Probably not. And tonight I like the changes."

"Me too."

He glanced at his watch. "The Carters should be here any minute."

The maître d' returned, and the three of them chatted about work for another ten minutes. It wasn't unusual for the Carters to run a little late, especially Mrs. Carter, but after fifteen more minutes they still hadn't arrived. Zeke asked the maitre d' to seat them and bring the Carters to the table as soon as they arrived.

When she and Zeke were comfortably seated at a U-shaped booth, her phone vibrated. "It's Mrs. Carter." She managed a normal hello in spite of Zeke's concerned stare.

"Julia!" Mrs. Carter sounded out of breath. "I'm so sorry to call so late, but we flew out of there two hours ago and I couldn't get good reception until now. We're halfway back to Los Angeles."

"Oh no." Her gaze flew to Zeke. "Are you all right?"

"We're fine. But our youngest daughter went into premature labor and they can't stop it. The baby's nine weeks early. We need to be there."

"Of course you do." Julia mouthed *It's okay* to Zeke. But it wasn't okay. Her heart ached for the Carters.

Mr. Carter said something in the background. Julia couldn't make it out, so Mrs. Carter repeated it. "Larry says he'll call Zeke next week. We had a lovely time, but right now our lives are on hold until we know how baby Emma is doing."

"So it's a girl," Julia said.

"Assuming the ultrasound is right." Mrs. Carter choked up. "Our first granddaughter. I just love frilly little dresses."

"I'll be praying for you." *Like you prayed for my mom, brother, and me when my dad died.* "And I'll tell my mom about Emma. Keep us posted, okay?"

Julia ended the call, gave Zeke the details, and blew out a breath. "I'm sorry for everyone. Nine weeks early is rough."

"It sure puts things in perspective," he said

quietly. "A baby is a far bigger worry than a business deal."

They sat in respectful silence until Julia broke it. "I really thought we'd be celebrating the contract tonight. Instead"—she shrugged—"here we are."

"Two hundred jobs," he said, shaking his head. "I can't seem to catch a break these days. The harder I try, the more things go wrong."

He looked at the sparsely filled restaurant, his expression haggard and weary. She hated to see him this way, but at the same time, she recalled the conversation with her mom at Panera about new strength coming from brokenness.

She put her hand over his solid wrist. "We can't change what just happened, but the night doesn't have to be a total bust. How about a burned steak for you and a medium one for me?"

"Sure." He flung an arm over the back of the booth. "Why not?"

He signaled the maître d', passed on the news about the Carters, and ordered her favorite appetizer along with the steaks. They chatted through the meal about work, Tiff's wedding, and Ginger's latest worry, namely that summer temperatures would soar and the new asphalt would turn to glue.

Zeke traced the condensation on his water goblet. "The way things are going, it wouldn't surprise me. At this point, I'm ready for the San

Andreas Fault to shift, or for a tropical storm to roll up the coast, flood the hotel, and sweep it away in a mudslide."

Julia ached for him. "That's California for you. But as far as the wedding goes, we're ready for rain."

"Good. But what about the surprises we can't imagine?"

He sounded even more beleaguered than before. There wasn't much she could do to lighten his load, but she could reassure him about the backup plans for the wedding. "Let's walk over to the banquet room on the other side of the pool. I'll show you what I have in mind in case of rain."

They left the restaurant at a leisurely pace, exited the lobby, and ambled down a stone path to a brightly lit swimming pool. It was closed for the night, so they were alone.

As they walked around the deep end, Julia couldn't help but compare the color of the shimmering water to the geode she'd given to Zeke in Berkeley. Bright, clear, shining. The underwater lights cast a subdued glow, giving the water texture and depth like the geode, while inviting a person to dive right in.

When she stopped to breathe in the smells of chlorine and the warm night, so did Zeke. He touched her arm, turned her to him, and stared into her eyes. For the first time that day, the weariness drained from his face. Something powerful glinted in his eyes, something profound and human: The need to be understood. The desire to be loved. The instinct to connect in the most elemental, unspoken ways.

He kissed her then. Sweetly. Softly. The kiss brimmed with desire, but he tempered it with restraint. She softened against him, a shiver running up her spine. There was no doubt now. She'd fallen in love with him for the second time. Or maybe for the first time, because her idea of love now was light years beyond that cheesy Valentine's Day card. Love wasn't something to be enjoyed just for a season. It was meant to last a lifetime. A commitment of body, heart, and soul that made a woman vulnerable to terrible pain while promising the sweetest of joys.

Lord, what do I do? She'd fallen in love with a man whose faith was packed away in a cardboard box.

Intending to push back, she placed her hands on his chest but looked into his eyes instead. They were stormy blue, bright from the reflected light of the pool, and burning with undefined emotions.

He reached up and took her hands, knotting his fingers in hers. "Jules . . ." He breathed her name. "Something strong is happening here. Something good."

Her breath caught. "Yes."

"But we have to be careful." His voice rasped against the silk of the still air. "I'm not in a good place with God. I'm bitter right now, and that bitterness might be contagious. I don't want to do anything to risk the peace I see in your eyes."

"Too late," she said.

"Why?"

"Because I'm in love with you."

Lord, is that okay? I don't know what to do here. All she knew was that Zeke was looking at her like a man drowning in the ocean, flailing desperately against the sucking pull of a dark tide. *Lord, help him. He's lost, but he wants to be found.* Julia didn't have the power to rescue him, but she could be waiting for him on dry sand.

Zeke pulled her more tightly into his arms and tucked her head under his chin. Bending to her ear, he whispered. "Pray for me, okay?"

"I will."

Every night. Every hour of the day. Whatever it took for Zeke to find his way back to God and into her arms.

Twenty-four

The next five days bordered on torture for Zeke.

After they parted, he couldn't stop thinking about Julia. He loved her. He was certain of it. And this love was completely different from what they had shared in college. Deeper. Richer. Possibly forever. But he couldn't tell her until he was right with God.

At home, he took his old Bible into the house and tried to read it. Instead of finding peace in the familiar verses, he saw only his failure documented in savage underlining and margins full of pointed notes about resisting temptation. The Bible ended up in a drawer in his nightstand, hidden from view but not forgotten.

On Friday the front desk manager quit without notice, and the hotel computer system crashed.

On Saturday a water pipe broke on the fifth floor, damaged six rooms, and forced an elevator shutdown.

On Sunday a crazy person set a dumpster on fire and the main building had to be evacuated.

And on Monday, Hunter Adams checked in. Within six hours, he had complained about low water pressure, demanded regular clothes hangers instead of the anti-theft kind, made a noise complaint to security, and returned a room service meal because it was allegedly cold.

How did Julia stand the guy? Zeke didn't know, and he wasn't about to ask her, mainly because she was driving him a little nuts too. Every time they passed in the office, she gave him a worried look or an awkward smile. She'd taken to hovering over him, which he couldn't stand. She meant well, but the TLC made him feel like a baby that couldn't feed itself.

By Tuesday afternoon his teeth ached from a permanently clenched jaw. Helpless . . . that was how he felt. Seated at his desk, he was scouring the budget for extra money for Golden Point when a tap sounded on his door and he looked up.

Julia lingered at the threshold. "You skipped lunch. Can I get you something?"

"No."

"A burned hamburger?"

"No. But thanks."

"Coffee?"

"No. I'm good."

She bit her lip. "How about—"

"Julia. I'm fine."

He ached to call her Jules, but the nickname stirred up the feelings he needed to keep in check. Unlike in Berkeley when he'd given in to impulse, he was determined to keep his promise to be careful with their relationship.

He stood and palmed his keys. "In fact, I'm

going to get out of here for a while. I need to check on a few things before Applegate's visit tomorrow."

Without meeting her gaze, he left and drove to the pro shop. The instant he stepped through the door, John put his hands on his hips and glared. "Is it true?"

"Is what true?"

"That Caliente Springs is being sold to some big-shot developer from Los Angeles. I have alimony payments, Zeke. And a kid in college. Jobs like this are hard to find."

Zeke hated rumors. He hated them even more when they upset the good people on the CS staff. He sucked in a deep breath. "I'll be straight with you, John. What you heard isn't true, but there's some serious interest."

"Great. Just great."

"It's very preliminary." Zeke told him a little about Applegate's visit. "Don't start looking for a job yet. We need you here."

"Well, rumors are flying. I heard it this morning."

"From who?"

"Shirley at Katrina's. The guy who left that big tip ate dinner there last night. She overheard him on his phone."

Sabotage. Zeke was certain Hunter had deliberately dropped a rumor-bomb while Shirley refilled his coffee cup. He glanced at the wall clock and decided to visit Chet to see what he might have heard.

"I have to run," he told John. "Try to hang in there."

The instant Zeke walked into Chet's office, the old cowboy launched to his feet. "What's this talk about some yahoo snob from LA buying this place and firing everyone?"

"Where did you hear that?"

"From Ricky." A teenage stable hand. "He heard it from one of the lifeguards. And she heard it from—"

"Shirley at Katrina's." Zeke couldn't clench his teeth any tighter. "Here's the truth, Chet. All of it. Ginger is interested in selling, and there's a potential buyer. The key word is *potential.* This is nowhere close to being a done deal."

Chet snorted. "Boss, you're lying to me. I never thought you'd do that."

"*Lying* to you?"

"Yes, lying." Chet aimed a finger at the window. "I heard about the sale from that friend of Miss Julia's. He was here about an hour ago with her little boy. He's already acting like the boss."

"Well, he's not. I am." *At least for now.*

Zeke held Chet's stare, but his stomach sank to his feet. As a single guy, he could live on ramen and cheap canned soup. He was also free to pack up and move anywhere for the sake of his career. But that wasn't true for the two hundred employees under his wing. And it wasn't true for Julia. She was tied to Los Angeles, at least Southern California.

In his mind, Zeke heard his dad's booming voice. *"Your first job is to pray for your family. Your second is to feed them."* Prayer was already missing from the life he wanted to give to Julia and Max. Without a job, he'd be even more incompetent. For once, Zeke agreed fully with his father. Even if he made peace with God, he couldn't imagine pursuing Jules without the ability to put a roof over her head.

Chet snatched his hat off a hook. "I better get back to work."

"Same here." With Hunter on the loose, Zeke needed to do damage control. "Do you know where Hunter was going when he left here?"

"He's not gone. He and the boy went for a ride."

"Who's with them?" Guests weren't allowed to ride alone for safety reasons.

"No one."

Zeke stopped in his tracks. "Chet—"

"I know, boss. It's against policy. But Ms. Travers called me herself and said it was all right."

Zeke bristled at the arrogance from both Hunter and Ginger, but especially Ginger. She knew the rules and the reasoning behind them. The policies protected guests from harm and the resort from liability. But what alarmed him even more was the lack of concern for Max. He was only four years old. The minimum age for riders was six with a parent or guardian.

Zeke recalled Julia's story about the speedboat. Someone needed to check on Hunter and Max right now. "Which horses did they take?"

"Jed and Sugar Pie."

Max would be riding Sugar Pie, a sweet old mare reserved for children. Jed was a brown gelding, seasoned and reliable. Both horses could find their way to the barn blindfolded. "When are they due back?"

"Mr. Adams wouldn't say at first. I told him I needed to know, so he said maybe three o'clock."

Zeke glanced at his watch. "It's almost four. Did he leave a cell number?"

"I'll try it now." Chet stepped to his desk, made the call, but shook his head when Hunter didn't pick up. "Do you want me to go after 'em?"

"Yes. And I'm going to call Julia."

Julia was Skyping with Chelsea from Hot Pink Photography when Zeke called her cell phone instead of the office like he usually did. She let it go to voice mail but glanced down to read the text that immediately followed.

Call ASAP re: Hunter & Max.

With her imagination running amok, she finished quickly with Chelsea and called Zeke.

In a tone as cryptic as his text, he told her about

the trail ride. "It's probably nothing, but Chet's riding out on the Gator to check on them."

Julia was already out the door. "I'm on my way."

"I'll meet you at my SUV."

Driving as fast as she dared, she sped past Golden Point and veered to the stable just around the hill. When she pulled into the driveway, she saw Zeke waiting. She leapt out of the car and ran to him but stopped herself from hugging him. They were in full view of anyone who passed by, and she didn't trust herself to let go.

Her voice came out shaky. "Have you heard from them?"

"Not yet."

With his arm around her waist, they hurried down the path that led to the corral used to stage trail rides. When they reached the trailhead, she strained her ears for the clop of horses, Max's laughter, or the whine of the Gator. Fighting panic, she forgot all about being strong and reached for Zeke's hand.

Instead of clasping her fingers, he pulled her deep into his arms. "We'll find them, Jules."

"I'm scared."

"You're human. And a mom."

Lord, be with my son. Protect him. Please. She longed to hear Zeke pray the way he had in Berkeley, but all he did was hold her.

When his radio crackled with Chet's voice, he

kept an arm around her waist while he answered. "I'm here, Chet. So is Julia."

"Her boy is fine."

A heavy breath whooshed out of her lungs. Her whole body sagged, but Zeke's arm held her steady. Nothing mattered as much as Max's safety, but Chet's tone hinted at trouble.

"Adams is okay too, but we have an emergency out here. Jed was bitten by a rattlesnake."

"What?"

"You heard me, boss. I found them at the rock pile."

Julia gasped. The rock pile was a hill littered with boulders. A half-mile from the main trail, the area was clearly marked as off-limits and unofficially called Rattlesnake Ranch. Only a total fool—or an arrogant one—would ride past the signs. The rock pile offered a beautiful view of the resort, but it posed significant danger to horses, riders, and hikers.

Zeke's fingers tightened on the radio. "We're going to need Doc Cahill. I'll call her."

"Ricky already did. She's on her way."

With Max safe, Julia focused on Zeke. His expression turned murderous as Chet relayed details over the two-way radio. Ricky was already headed out to assist. When the young stable hand arrived, Chet would bring Max and Hunter back on the Gator, and Ricky would walk back with the horses.

"It's bad," Chet said in a low voice. "Judging by the fang marks, the snake was big and it bit Jed twice. I hope he makes it, boss. Because that horse deserves a lot better than the treatment he got today."

Zeke was used to problems like a broken freezer or an A/C unit on the fritz, but there was a big difference between a freezer and a horse. The freezer was just equipment. Jed was a four-legged member of the CS family.

"How's he doing right now?" Zeke said into the radio.

"He's on his feet, but judging by the swelling around the pastern, the snake injected its venom. It's better than a bite on the nose, but Jed needs treatment fast or we could lose him."

Zeke stifled an oath. This was Hunter's fault. And Ginger's. As soon as Max was safe, Zeke intended to go to war. But right now, Julia needed him. Turning, he pulled her back into his arms, and though he doubted God would listen, he breathed a prayer. *Thank you, God, for keeping Max safe.* That was all he could manage before his jaw clenched again.

The Gator hummed in the distance. Julia broke away and stared down the trail. Zeke stayed at her side as Chet steered the utility vehicle into the corral. Hunter sat on the passenger side with Max huddled on his lap, his dusty cheeks streaked with dried tears. The instant Chet cut the engine, Julia swept her son away from Hunter and into her arms.

Hunter eased off the seat, slapped dust off his pants, and glowered at Zeke. "I don't know what happened out there, but something spooked that horse. It nearly threw me."

Chet's hands fisted on his hips. "Now you just wait—"

Max, still clinging to Julia, swiveled his head toward Zeke. "There was a s-s-snake. It m-m-made that s-s-sound. The horse stopped, and then—then—" He buried his face against Julia's shoulder and sobbed.

Hunter's mouth pinched into a line. "Come on, Max. It wasn't that bad."

Not that bad? What planet was this guy on? Zeke opened his mouth to inject some reason, but Julia stepped in front of Hunter with Max tight on her hip.

"How dare you take *my son* on a ride like that!"

"Now wait a minute—"

"No. *You* wait." In spite of Max's weight, she stood ramrod straight. "*What* were you thinking? Didn't you see the sign? You can read, can't you?"

Splotches of red erupted on Hunter's lean cheeks. A tic pulsed in his clenched jaw, and his eyes narrowed to a squint. Zeke positioned himself next to Julia, and Chet circled around to his side.

Keeping an eye on Hunter, Zeke spoke to Julia. "Max has had enough distress for today. Why don't you take him to the bench under the tree?"

As she left, Hunter tracked her with his eyes. If he went after her, Zeke would cut him off. Both men stood with the sun beating down on them and Chet slowly tapping his boot in the dust.

After a glance to be sure Julia was settled, Zeke focused back on Hunter. "That hill is plainly marked as dangerous. I'm curious. Why did you disregard the sign?"

Hunter's mouth curled into a sneer. "What sign?"

Chet muttered under his breath. "It's there, boss. I saw it."

So Hunter was going to flat-out lie. Zeke knew this particular game. They had played it at St. John's.

After a long pause, Hunter skimmed his eyes over the empty corral and the run-down buildings behind it. "I don't think much of your facilities or your rental horses. They're skittish."

"Jed's been with us for five years," Zeke replied. "He's one of the most reliable horses in the stable."

"Not today. He nearly got me killed."

Chet jabbed a finger in Hunter's direction. "You stop right there, Mr. Adams. I told you myself to stay on the main trail. There's a reason those boulders are off-limits. Rattlers hang out there. We keep the main trail wide and clear, so riders can see what's ahead, like a rattler sunning itself."

Arms crossed, Hunter rocked back on his heels. "The trail to the rocks looked fine to me. Besides, I had a good reason to go up there. My uncle asked me to send him pictures of this place. That hill has the best view of the entire resort. I see a lot of unused potential here. He'll want to make some changes, I'm sure."

No wonder rumors were flying. Chet shot Zeke a look that said *I told you so,* then excused himself to go meet Doc Cahill.

As badly as Zeke wanted to rip into Hunter and his lies, he needed to take the higher ground to protect Julia from the man's vindictiveness. And to protect Caliente Springs. Who knew what lawsuit Hunter might cook up?

Professional and experienced, Zeke kept his voice neutral. "Whatever your reasons were for going to the rock pile, you disregarded instructions that were given for your safety. I'll need to file an incident report."

"Forget it." Hunter turned and strode toward Julia.

When Zeke saw the fight in her eyes, he held himself back. Regardless of his feelings for her, Max was her son and Hunter was Max's father. Julia was the expert here, but he took a few steps closer in case she needed him.

She spoke loudly enough for Zeke to hear. "Hunter, this kind of thing needs to stop. You had no business taking Max to those boulders, especially on a horse."

"Come on, Julia. Quit babying him—"

"I'm not!"

Smirking, Hunter clamped his hand on Max's shoulder and looked down at him. "Come on, son. Tell Mommy the truth. You weren't really scared, were you?"

Not scared of a hissing snake? Not afraid of a bucking horse trying to stomp it? Unable and unwilling to hold himself back, Zeke strode forward. Max's eyes, so like Julia's, brimmed with tears.

Julia shoved Hunter's hand away from her son's shoulder. "Hunter, stop it."

Ignoring her, he bent down and clasped Max's chin instead. "You're brave like Daddy, aren't you?"

Max's lip trembled, but he mustered the courage for a nod.

Hunter thumped him on the back. "Good. I'm proud of you, son."

How many times had Zeke heard his own dad say, *"I'm proud of you, son,"* when his feelings had been as messy as the ones inside Max? Too many. And he felt as helpless now as he had then. As general manager he had authority over this situation, but any reaction on his part would trigger an attack from Hunter. And that attack might not be directed at Zeke. Julia and Max were weaker targets.

Paralyzed, Zeke stood with his feet planted in the dirt, anger boiling in his belly and his temper ready to snap. He couldn't fix this situation. He couldn't help Julia. All he could do was breathe in choking heat and dust.

But then Max turned and looked into Zeke's face. "Is Jed going to be all right?"

When a boy asked a tough question, he deserved an honest answer. "I hope so. The vet is coming with medicine, but we'll have to wait and see." Like everything else about this situation, Jed's fate was beyond Zeke's control.

Max nodded solemnly and snuggled deeper in Julia's arms. Pale and drawn, she thanked him with a smile more in her eyes than on her lips. The urge to protect her pounded at him, but right now he couldn't even hold her hand or offer a word of support.

With his hands jammed in his pockets, Zeke cleared his throat. "Julia, why don't you take Max home? I'll finish up the report with Hunter."

She nodded and stood, wrapping her arm protectively around Max.

Hunter rested a hand on the small of her back, leaving it even when she bristled. He stared pointedly at Zeke. "I have other things to do. The report can wait."

"No," Zeke said. "It can't." *And get your hand off her.* "You're an attorney. You understand liability. I need a statement from you now."

Hunter shrugged. "It's over. Forget it."

"I can't. This situation is too serious to ignore." If Zeke needed to use words like *child endangerment,* he would.

A long moment passed. Finally Hunter shrugged. "Fine. Let's get it over with." He let go of Julia, sauntered past Zeke, then waited for them all to follow.

When Julia reached her car, she lifted Max into the booster seat. As she worked the buckle, he sniffed away the last of his tears. "Mommy?"

"Yes, honey?"

"I liked riding the white horse, but I didn't want to go to the big rocks."

"Kind of scary, huh?"

"I told Daddy, but he made me."

Her hands stilled on the seat belt. She wanted to strangle Hunter. Max couldn't tell the truth because Hunter would belittle him, and Max wanted his daddy to be proud of him. But Julia knew, when she confronted Hunter, he'd blame *her* for Max's fear. The only person who emerged from the tangle unscathed was Hunter, who didn't have to take responsibility for anything he didn't like. The destructive pattern needed to stop now, before Max really did turn into Hunter's mini-me.

She reached up and smoothed his hair. "The situation would be scary for anyone. That's a good time to remember that God looks out for us."

"Is He looking out for Jed?"

"Yes."

Please, God. Let Jed be all right. Julia didn't know why there were rattlesnakes in the world, or cancer or heart attacks. All she could do was trust that God knew best. Like the Bible said, now she saw through a glass darkly. Someday she'd see through that glass with perfect clarity. There would be no smoke and mirrors like the ones Hunter arranged to his own advantage.

Max gave a big yawn. "I want to go home."

"Me too."

Relieved to avoid another tough question, Julia drove to the cottage. By the time she pulled into the driveway, Max was asleep. She lugged him out of the booster seat, staggered to the door with her back breaking, and somehow managed to set him on the couch without waking him up.

Without Hunter in the picture, Zeke would have followed her home, carried Max, and listened to her vent about the terrible afternoon. Missing him, she fetched the bag of Milky Ways. There were only a few left, a reminder that her stay at Caliente Springs was more than half over. With the candy melting on her tongue, she hoped God knew what He was doing, because she couldn't imagine a future without Zeke.

Nor could she imagine a future without Hunter, constant interference, and perpetual strife, all with Max caught in the middle.

Twenty-five

As soon as the interview was over, Hunter sped off, and Zeke headed for the stable to check on Jed. When he reached the horse's stall, he saw Dr. Jennifer Cahill administering an injection while Chet cold-washed the gelding's leg with a hose.

"How does it look?" Zeke asked.

Dr. Cahill withdrew the syringe. "I gave him an anti-venom injection and started antibiotics. His overall condition is stable, but there's a great deal of swelling. I think he'll make it, but he could still go lame."

Zeke knew what lameness meant. At best, Jed would be retired as a trail horse. At worst, he'd be unable to walk and would have to be put down. All because of Hunter Adams and his arrogance. That man deserved a one-way trip to Rattlesnake Ranch.

Dr. Cahill ran her hand along the horse's fore-leg. "I've done all I can. Jed's in good hands with Chet here."

"Thanks, Doc," Zeke said.

She packed up her bag, told them to call if Jed needed her, and left the stable.

Zeke turned his attention to Chet. The lines around his mouth were deeper than usual, and though he was humming "Streets of Laredo," fury still burned in his eyes. When he rounded on Zeke, his voice came out hoarse.

"I have a mind to pound Hunter Adams into the ground. He almost killed one of our best horses, and then he tried to blame the horse."

"It's all in the report."

"Stupid fool," Chet muttered. "And he's a liar. He deliberately ignored what I told him. That's just not right, especially with two horses and a boy in his care." Chet cranked off the hose and scratched Jed's neck. "If Jed balked, it was because of the snake. You heard what the boy said. He heard the snake before Jed saw it."

The interview with Hunter played through Zeke's head. Twisted facts aside, there was no denying Hunter's responsibility. He could lie and deny all day long, but the evidence stood and Hunter knew it.

"I doubt he'll make trouble, and if he does, I have enough on him to protect us from a lawsuit."

Chet let out a snort. "We should sue *him* for endangering Jed."

As much as Zeke wanted to agree, a good boss didn't complain to the employees below him. He took his concerns up the ladder, which he intended to do as soon as he returned to his office. Ginger was about to get a very serious phone call.

Zeke gave Jed a pat on the neck. "Anything else before I leave?"

"Nope." Chet turned the hose back on. "I'll spend the night out here on a cot. Just don't let Adams or his uncle buy this place."

"I won't."

The promise weighed heavily on Zeke's shoulders, because he knew good and well he might not be able to keep it. The shackles of helplessness tightened even more as he walked out of the barn and took in the run-down buildings and thirsty hills. Everywhere he looked, he saw the ravages of drought.

He drove past Golden Point, worried the asphalt wouldn't be laid in time, and raked his hand through his hair. Once he was back in his office, he shut the door and called Ginger. "We had a problem at the stable this afternoon."

She gave a little laugh. "What did Ladybug do this time?"

"Nothing. The problem involves Hunter Adams." He told her about Hunter leaving the main trail, the snakebite, and the trauma to both Max and the horse. "Jed's not out of the woods, but Dr. Cahill's hopeful."

Ginger gasped. "That poor horse. And Max too. What a fright for everyone. How did this happen?"

"According to Hunter, you gave him permission to ride alone with Max. Despite Chet's instructions, he left the main trail. I don't know what you told Chet when you gave your permission, but—"

328

"Hold on, Zeke. This doesn't add up. Hunter called this morning to confirm his uncle's arrival. During that call, he said he was an experienced rider and asked if he could give Max a riding lesson. I know Max is underage. I admit I bent that particular rule. But I assumed they'd stay in the corral. Apparently Hunter had other ideas. I just didn't realize it."

"And Chet got caught in the middle. When Adams insisted on taking Max out on the trail, Chet assumed you knew the plan."

"I can see how the mistake happened, but I did *not* give Hunter permission to go to those boulders."

"Understood. But that's what he did, and he did it in spite of Chet's instructions."

"Hunter's a smart man, Zeke. I like him, and anyone can see how much he loves his son. Perhaps he just made a mistake."

"No," Zeke replied. "It was deliberate. He said he wanted to take a picture of the resort for Applegate."

Ginger paused. "What are you suggesting?"

"You can't trust him."

"Oh, I see."

"What?"

"This is personal for you."

Zeke needed to tread carefully. "It's true that I don't care for Hunter's personality." *Or his ethics.* "But I'm speaking strictly as a professional. In my opinion, he deliberately misled you and then misconstrued Chet's instructions."

"I don't care for your tone."

"My tone? I'm not following you."

"You've been honest, Zeke, so I'll return the favor. I have to wonder if you're being unfair to Hunter because of your feelings for Julia."

Zeke answered with a clean conscience. "You don't need to worry. The three of us have a history, but Julia's a professional and so am I."

"I realize that. But I'm not blind. If the tension between the three of you impacts either this presentation to Maury Applegate or Tiff's wedding, I'll be extremely disappointed in both you *and* Julia. Regardless of Hunter's activities— and I agree he behaved poorly today—I expect you to show him the utmost respect."

What a load of garbage. Even more galling, she sounded just like dear old Dad lecturing him to do more, try harder, and be better. He rocked forward in his throne of a chair. "I'll do my best. You know that."

"Yes, I do."

Somehow he set down the phone without slamming it. He'd just been ordered to kowtow to Hunter, and he didn't know which infuriated him more—the lecture or the order itself. He shoved back from the desk, sending the chair skidding into the wall, and snatched his keys. He needed to see Julia now. He needed her touch,

330

her calm ways, even a dose of her faith. Never mind the caution flag waving in his face.

But halfway across the room, his common sense prevailed. If Ginger saw his car in Julia's driveway, especially right now, she'd jump to conclusions that wouldn't be entirely inaccurate. Sighing, he went back to his desk, dropped the jangling keys, and sat. At least he could still use the phone.

"How are you?" he asked when Julia answered.

"All right." She sounded distant.

"Is Hunter there?"

"No."

"Good."

"He texted about Max after you made the report." She heaved a sigh that rattled right through him. "I'm done with him for the night. Would you like to come over?"

"Oh, man." Zeke dragged his hand through his hair. "I wish I could, but Ginger's watching us." He told her about the call. "I don't think it would be smart."

"No."

He heard running water and the clatter of dishes. "What are you doing?"

"Rinsing a plate." Her voice took on the mommy tone, a sign Max was listening. "We had mac and cheese for dinner."

Max piped up. "And chocolate milk."

Julia spoke over the rushing water to Zeke.

"Hold on, okay?" She told Max she'd be in the living room, remained silent for a few seconds, then murmured into the phone, "How's Jed?"

"Better. But he could still go lame. It'll be a while before we know."

"Max keeps asking about him." Julia dropped her voice even lower. "I still can't believe what Hunter did today. When I think about what could have happened—" Her voice cracked.

Every nerve in Zeke's body tensed. He loved this woman. Loved her enough to fight and die for her, but all he could do was sit in his office and twiddle his thumbs. More than anything he wanted to ride in on a white horse, play the superhero, and rescue her from Hunter, snakes, and all of life's turmoil.

And then it hit him. He couldn't comfort Julia in person, but he could give her the same words she had already given to him. He might not to be free to fight for her, or to rescue her like Han Solo or the Ninja Turtles, but he did have a voice. "I love you, Jules. I loved you in Berkeley, and I love you now. I'd rather say this in person, but I need you to know how I feel. Right now, it's all I have to give."

A soft sob filtered into his ears. "I love you too, but . . ." That last word dragged into a sigh.

Zeke stared out the window, his brow furrowed. "But what?"

"You have no idea how much I want to tell you

to forget Ginger and come over right now. How much I want to just *be* with you. It would be the easiest thing in the world to lean on you, Zeke." Her voice shook but didn't break. "But I can't do that."

"Why not?" He *wanted* her to lean on him. For once today, he wanted to feel like a man and not a mouse.

"We talked about this at the pool. My faith is still so new. I'm still learning how to lean on God instead of myself. You're having problems too."

True or not, he bristled at the reminder. "My problems are my own. I'm working on them."

"I know you are." She took another breath. "But we both need to find our way independent of each other before we can have the solid relationship I think we both want. We'd be fools to move too fast, especially with Hunter in the picture."

Catman again. Zeke threw back his shoulders. "I can handle him."

"I know you can." The confidence in her voice gave him a lift. "You were great today, Zeke. I appreciate everything you did, especially how you worked it so I could leave alone with Max. But I'm not sure you understand what it's like to deal with Hunter almost every day. He pushes for his own way *all the time.* He'll pick fights with you. He'll treat you like he did in Berkeley. He'll make you mad and—"

"I get it, Jules. He's a jerk."

"He's more than that. He's a constant presence in my life. You can't change that or fix it."

Great. The woman he loved didn't think he could protect her.

"It's hard," she continued. "The only thing holding me together is my faith. Without that foundation, I'm afraid Hunter will get to us both, and I don't want to add to your problems. If you and I don't see life the same way, we'll fight like we did in Berkeley, and—"

"Jules, stop."

"But—"

"Don't." Her dire predictions smacked into him like stones, accused him of being weak, and reminded him that he really wasn't the man she needed and deserved. The turquoise geode caught his eye and he stumbled back in time to Berkeley. "It's a faith issue, isn't it? I'm not the man I used to be."

"Oh, Zeke—"

"I get it, Jules. You want Mr. Perfect Christian."

"What?"

"You know. The guy I used to be. The guy who does everything right."

Her voice cooled. "I don't know what you mean. To me, a perfect Christian doesn't exist."

He did not want to have this conversation. Not now. Not ever, because every time, the words flayed him alive. "I don't want to argue with you about this, especially not after a day like this one."

"I don't either. I love you, Zeke. I love you too much to settle for less than the kind of relationship I think we both want."

'Til death do us part . . . Forever . . . A marriage built on a strong rock and not shifting sand. Promises a mere mortal couldn't keep.

"I have to be brutally clear," she said. "I've been a Christian for such a short time. I don't know very much about God, and frankly I'm a little bit scared by all the changes. But I know this. No matter how much I love you, there are two things I can't compromise on—Max and my faith."

The tone of her voice scraped him raw. He started to respond, but she wasn't finished with him.

"That's why you and I need to be just friends until you're at peace and I'm stronger in my faith."

He didn't move a muscle. There was nowhere to go, nothing to say, because deep in his soul, in the dark corner where he was still a child, he envied her conviction. Zeke wasn't that certain anymore. He was an adult who knew how it felt to be beaten up by life. Then again, so did Julia. She wasn't innocent or naïve in the least. She'd been beaten up too, but instead of spurning the message of the cross the way he did, she had run to it.

His fingers tightened on the phone. Bile rose in

his throat. Their future came down to one simple fact: he couldn't be the man she deserved until he found his way back to God, and he needed to make that journey alone.

"Look," he said as gently as he could. "We're not going to solve this tonight. You need to take care of Max, and I have some thinking to do."

"I suppose we both do."

They murmured quiet good-byes without saying *I love you.*

Zeke tossed down the phone and stood. Hands on hips, he glowered at the wall of diplomas and awards, the books, even the geodes. Every degree, every accomplishment—what did all that hard work really mean? Apparently nothing. He had given Julia and Caliente Springs his personal best, everything in his heart and soul, and where was he now? Not good enough. Rejected by Julia in the past for being too Christian and now for not being Christian enough.

He stood frozen in place, trapped and mentally shackled.

Isolated.

Helpless.

Desperate enough to shout a cuss word he almost never used. With his fists knotted, he glowered at a bare spot on the wall. One punch. Just one powerful swing of his arm . . . but perfect men didn't put their fists through walls. They didn't crack and cry, or beg and plead. They stayed strong.

Except Zeke wasn't strong enough. He never had been, and he wasn't now. He was sick of it—sick of failing, sick of trying. Sick of being angry and hiding it.

Turning away from the blank wall, he glared at the geodes and imagined hurling one through the floor-to-ceiling window. Geodes were just ugly rocks until someone broke them open the way he'd cracked them with his dad. There were a lot of ways to do it, but a true collector used a hammer and chisel, tapping a line around the circumference until the rock was ready to give way. Then with a twist of his wrist, the expert opened the geode and discovered a marvel of God's artistry.

Tap . . . Tap . . . Tap.

Every memory of every sin in his life stabbed into Zeke's chest. He'd always been so sure of himself, especially back in Berkeley, so full of confidence in his ability to resist sexual temptation. Guilt over his choices had churned into ambivalence, and ambivalence had thickened into resentment. Over the years the resentment hardened into the lifeless stone now in his chest.

Groaning, he dropped down on the couch, propped his elbows on his knees, and buried his head in his hands. He saw it now. With every personal failure, God had been chipping at his pride. Zeke was not now—and he never had been—the perfect person he believed he could be if only he tried hard enough.

As a boy, he'd secretly resented every word out of his father's mouth.

Tap . . . Tap . . . Tap.

As a college student, he'd given in to lust and love in spite of putting up the best fight he could.

Tap . . . Tap . . . Tap.

And here he was now, a guy with an MBA, insisting he could single-handedly pull Caliente Springs from the brink of disaster.

Tap . . . Tap . . . Tap.

Every one of Zeke's failings was common to man. Nothing extraordinary. And yet the humiliation of accepting his own humanity tore the skin off his back. Knowing full well surrender meant repentance and trusting God fully, even to the point of death and failure, he handed over his heart of stone. "Finish it, Lord. Crack it open."

He felt nothing. No tears. No joy. But a pinprick of light illuminated the dark place where he had fallen. Suddenly he knew exactly what he needed to do. It was time to open the rest of the boxes in the garage.

Twenty-six

After dinner Julia gave Max a bath and tucked him into bed with his favorite bear. He was exhausted and fell asleep instantly. But at two o'clock he woke up shrieking about a snake in his bed. She held him tight until he went back to sleep, her tears mixing with his. She'd been too churned up to even doze after that, so when she arrived at the office at eight o'clock she was worried about Max, furious at Hunter, and so full of love for Zeke that every breath she took whispered his name.

Last night's conversation had been painful and difficult but satisfying too. She could speak her mind and Zeke listened. There had been no manipulation, no twists and turns, no lashing out. They were two adults dealing with real life, and they were doing it with mutual respect. She loved him more than ever after that conversation, which made the outcome of today's meeting with Maury deeply personal to her. Whatever happened this afternoon, she and Zeke would face it together.

She set down her purse, woke up the computer, and glanced down the hall to his office. To her surprise, it was dark. There was no sign of him, so she checked her computer for messages.

One from Zeke popped up with a time stamp of 4:42 a.m. I'm taking the morning off.

"Today?" she said to the email. "With Maury coming?"

Worried, she reached for her phone but stopped. She didn't want to wake him if he was asleep. On the other hand, what if he had a stomach bug and needed Sprite and crackers? Just last week a twenty-four-hour virus had run through accounting. No matter the cause for his absence, she needed to know he was all right.

Keys and phone in hand, she drove to his house. His SUV was in the driveway, so she knew he was there. Rather than risk waking him with a knock on the front door, she slipped through the back gate, crossed the patio, and tried the sliding glass door. When it opened with a whoosh, she stepped into the kitchen and saw a rectangular oak table surrounded by four chairs, the perfect size for a family.

Her heart did a little flip, but she squashed it. This wasn't the time to think about their relationship. All that mattered was helping Zeke with today's presentation.

A hallway led to the bedrooms. The door to the master was only slightly ajar, so she pushed it open another couple inches. Thick shades dimmed the morning sun to gray, but the bed was hotel-white with Zeke in the middle on his side, shirtless in pajama bottoms, tanned, muscular, and sleeping heavily with one arm hanging off the side of the bed. His hair fell on the pillow like a crooked halo.

How on earth, or where in heaven, would she find the strength to be just a friend when she wanted so much more?

He rolled onto his back, all muscle and man, flesh and bone. She needed to leave, but as she took a step, her phone meowed.

Zeke stirred and she panicked. With one eye on his face, she killed the ringtone, but not before he opened his eyes and saw her. Ragged and scruffy, he swung his legs over the side of the bed.

"Jules?"

"Yes. It's me." She stuffed the phone back in her pocket. Hunter could wait all day for all she cared right now. "I saw your message, but I was still worried. I thought maybe you were sick."

"I'm fine."

"You need your sleep. I'll leave."

"Wait." His voice came out husky and low. Blinking hard, he studied her as if she were a dream, then he rubbed his eyes with his fists.

Wise or not, she drank in the sight of his handsome face, defined muscles, the hair on his chest, and every golden bristle on his jaw.

He lumbered to his feet but stopped short of approaching. "I was up most of the night. If I don't get some sleep, I'll be worthless for the meeting with Applegate."

They stood facing each other, silent but with their feelings rattling between them. His eyes fastened on hers, his expression intense and adoring, yet controlled. Her breath synchronized with his in a moment so raw her cheeks burned.

"You better go," he said, his voice more gravelly than before.

"Yes." She stepped away, then stopped. She knew better than to ask the question on the tip of her tongue, but her heart got the better of her. "Why were you up all night?"

"It's a long story and I want to tell you everything. Maybe we can talk tonight."

"Sure." She could see the bluish circles under his eyes, the gaunt look she recognized from all-nighters in Berkeley. "My mom will be home packing for George's show, so she can watch Max. I'll wait for you at the office."

"I'd like that."

"Good. I'll stay until you get there."

She turned to leave, but an invisible cord made her spin back around. In a flash she crossed the room, kissed his whisker-rough jaw, and shot out the door.

Zeke crawled back into bed, mashed a pillow over his head, and fell back to sleep with Julia's kiss warm on his cheek.

When the alarm went off at one o'clock, he felt

fortified in spite of unpacking boxes until four in the morning. The job was almost done. Several boxes of family treasures were waiting to be shipped to his sisters, anything worthless was in the trash, and the useable items were in more bags for charity. It felt good to have his garage back and even better to be rid of the boxes.

The heavens hadn't opened last night, but Zeke felt better than he had in years. Only Box No. 1 remained to be emptied. Last night, when he slit it open, he had seen a photograph of himself and his dad taken twenty years ago on a camping trip. Choking up, he'd gently closed the cardboard flaps. That box held his father's personal things and deserved special respect, so he'd set it on the workbench with the intention of unpacking it on Sunday.

God was doing something inside him, something Zeke didn't understand as he dressed in his best suit for the meeting. At least he hoped God was doing something, because with the Carter account still undecided and budget-busters like paving the lookout, Zeke needed all the help he could get.

When he arrived at the Travers mansion, George called a greeting from the far end of the porch. Seated in the swing and holding a glass of lemonade, he raised the tumbler in a mock toast. "To my stubborn sister."

Zeke knew better than to get between George

and Ginger, but George's support pleased him. "She means well."

"Women." George scowled at the spot on the lawn where Ellen had twisted her ankle. "They drive me nuts."

Zeke could sympathize. "So who's driving you crazier? Ginger or Ellen?"

"Ellen. God sure has a sense of humor. I'm about to go on Medicare, and she has me thinking like a teenager."

Zeke gave a sigh of his own. "Women."

"Can't live with 'em—"

"And can't live without them," Zeke finished.

George took a swig of lemonade, wiped his mouth on the back of his hand, and swirled the liquid and ice so fast it rattled. "Can you believe it? I'm even writing songs about her. Mushy ones."

Zeke didn't see the problem. In fact, he envied George. He and Ellen were single, financially secure, and relatively unencumbered by career and family demands. On the other hand, Zeke and Julia faced career challenges, maybe unemployment for Zeke, faith differences, and Hunter's claims to Max.

Frustrated by it all, he said, "You two are great together. What's the problem?"

"She had an awful time when her husband died. She's scared of going through that again, and I don't blame her." He drummed his fingers on the glass. "We're just friends now and that's fine, but I'm so tied up in knots I can't stand it."

Zeke couldn't resist. "You know what you'd say to me?"

George glared at him. "Punk."

Grinning, Zeke leaned against the railing. "You'd tell me to hang loose and trust God. And you'd mean it."

George offered up an ironic smile. "Yes, I would. Keep reminding me, okay?"

The front door opened and Ginger stepped onto the deck. Her gaze darted between the two of them. "You look like partners in crime."

"You bet we're partners," George told her. "Zeke's right about saving this place."

Ginger's mouth wrinkled into a frown. "You don't know that, George. You promised to listen *and* to be on good behavior."

Here it comes, the famous Travers Twins bickering. Sure enough, George raised the glass of lemonade in another toast.

"To Maury Snapple-gate—"

Ginger huffed. "George, really."

"May the best man win." With that, he chugged the last of the lemonade and slammed the glass down on the armrest.

A car engine rumbled in the distance. Zeke turned his head and saw Hunter's Lexus cruise to a stop at the end of the driveway. Hunter climbed out first, straightened his coat with a flex of his shoulders, and tugged his cuffs into place.

The passenger door opened next. Zeke had seen photographs of Maury Applegate when he Googled him. Most were business portraits with Maury in a suit and tie, or pictures of the grip-and-grin variety with Maury presenting an award. The photographs were all formal and posed, so when he climbed out of the car, Zeke expected to see a man with Hunter's demeanor.

But Maury Applegate surprised him. He was shorter than Zeke had assumed, balding with a fringe of white hair, and dressed in a plaid shirt straight out of the Sears catalog. A white goatee balanced his puffy red cheeks. Maury didn't look at all like a man made of money, but those men were often the most powerful of all.

Hunter led the way up the steps, greeted Ginger first, then made introductions. George nodded curtly to Hunter but greeted Maury with his trademark smile and a firm handshake.

Zeke followed suit. "It's a pleasure to meet you, sir."

"Likewise, Zeke." Maury squeezed back hard. "Those reports you sent were detailed and insightful. Good work."

"Thank you, sir."

"Call me Maury."

The warm greeting knocked Zeke off balance. He'd been expecting a shark, not a nice old man in a plaid shirt. There was something familiar about him, something Zeke couldn't place until Maury's eyes twinkled like stars at the North Pole. That was it—Maury Applegate reminded him of Santa Claus.

Zeke's heart sank. There was no way he could compete with Santa Claus. He'd do his best today, but the fight was even more uphill than he had realized. *God? Are you there? This is it.*

Forcing a calm he didn't feel, Zeke faced the group. "Shall we get started?"

Twenty-seven

When the office phone rang at 5:48 p.m., Julia nearly jumped out of her skin. She knew it wasn't her mom calling about Max, because they had spoken ten minutes ago. Max was convinced there were snakes in the yard and wouldn't go outside. Julia was mad enough to flay Hunter alive, but the only person she wanted to see was Zeke. Hoping to hear his voice, she snatched up the handset.

It was Kevin in maintenance. "Sorry for the bad news, Julia, but we ran into trouble at Golden Point."

"Oh no. What happened?"

"The paving machine broke down. The contractor has others, but he needs this one because it's small. He's waiting for a part. With a little luck, it'll be up and running on Monday."

Just five days before the wedding. "We're cutting it close." Too close for her taste. "Keep me posted, okay?"

When Kevin hung up, Julia rubbed her temples until she saw stars. No way did she want to disappoint Tiff, and Ginger would use the debacle as another reason to sell Caliente Springs. She would also consider the paving a foolish gamble,

348

a waste of money, and a black mark against Zeke's judgment.

Julia's cell phone chirped with a message. *Zeke.* The meeting had to be over. But when she picked it up, she saw an email from Mrs. Carter replying to a note Julia had sent earlier about the baby.

Little Emma is doing well, but she has a long way to go. Please tell Zeke how much we enjoyed our stay at Caliente Springs and even meeting Ladybug. Larry hasn't forgotten about the contract. So sorry for the delay, but I know you understand.

Absolutely. But Julia ached for Zeke. Patience might be a virtue, but she didn't have a drop of it left. Her phone went off again, this time with a meow. Stifling yet more irritation, she answered it. "Hello, Hunter."

"Hey, babe."

She rolled her eyes to the ceiling. *Zeke's right. You really are a jerk.* "The meeting must be over."

"It is for me. I begged off dinner, but Maury's going back to the house tonight." He paused, daring her to ask about the meeting.

Refusing to give him the satisfaction, she answered with a long silence of her own.

Hunter broke it as if nothing were wrong. "Let's have dinner tonight. You, me, and Max."

"No."

"I want to see him." Not a word of concern for the snake-bitten horse. Not even concern for Max.

Julia didn't bother to mention the nightmare. Hunter would tell her she was spoiling him, or worse, he'd tell Max to man up. She needed to run interference, but she also needed to be here for Zeke. "Tonight won't work."

"I'll come to the cottage."

"No."

"Why not?"

"It's just not a good time for a visit."

"I'm his dad. It's always a good time." His voice dropped low and deepened. "I have rights, Julia."

She remembered Hunter dangling the backpack in the church parking lot. He was threatening her again, but this time she had the protection of a security gate. "Of course you have rights. But so do I. Like I just said, this isn't a good night for a visit."

"Well, it's good for me. I'll be there in thirty minutes."

"No, you won't." She couldn't help feeling a little smug. "There's a gate."

"So? I have the combination."

"How—"

"Remember? I drove Uncle Maury to the Travers house for the meeting. Ginger gave it to me."

The fight drained out of her. She could call hotel security and risk creating a scene, or she could go home and deal with Hunter in private. At the cottage she was on her own turf, but leaving the office meant abandoning Zeke. With Max involved, there was no choice.

Forced to surrender, she stripped the hostility out of her voice. "All right. I'll see you there at seven."

"Good. And Julia?"

"What?"

"Uncle Maury liked what he saw today. He's going to consult with some investors." He paused, baiting her again. "Zeke played a solid game today. In fact, it was so good, he talked Uncle Maury into moving faster than he planned. Don't get too attached to this place. *Or* to Zeke, because he lost today. He'll be out of a job before you know it."

Zeke drove away from the Travers house with his voice hoarse from talking, his thoughts confused, and his heart heavy. Uncle Maury was more than Santa Claus. He was Yoda, Mr. Spock, and Cinderella's fairy godmother rolled into one nice guy. His current employees enjoyed well-managed 401(k) plans, excellent health insurance, and generous paid time off. He ran his redevelopment business ethically, including a program to assist poor people who were displaced.

But now Maury wanted to do something different. He refused to be specific, but he assured George and Ginger that he'd respect the history, land, and employees that made Caliente Springs unique. No bulldozers. No condos or outlet malls. If he kept his word, who was Zeke to stand in the way, even if it cost him his own job?

God, are you listening? I'm trying my best here, and it's not looking good.

He needed a dose of Julia's optimism. Eager to put his arms around her, he parked the SUV and walked down the deserted hallway to his office. Knowing she'd be waiting, he walked faster, but when he rounded the corner, he saw the dark lobby. She was gone for the night, her promise broken. He was sure she had a good reason, but the loneliness stung as he walked past her empty desk to his own office.

Just before he flipped on the light, a key turned in the lock on the glass door. As he stepped back into the hall, Julia slipped inside, pausing only to lock the door behind her.

"Jules—"

She hurried down the hall, dropped her purse on the floor, and hugged him hard. No questions. No words at all. Nothing but the comfort of her arms. He lowered his face and kissed her, drinking in the sweetness until she eased back with a sigh.

He cupped her head against his shoulder. "I thought you were gone."

"I was, but I saw your car in the rearview mirror. I can't stay long, but I had to see you."

Guided by the light from the window, he led her to the couch and they sat. He drew her close again, breathed in the scent of her hair, and wondered how in the world he could support her if he lost his job.

Julia broke the silence. "I didn't want to leave, but Hunter is on his way to the cottage. Max had a nightmare about snakes, and I'm afraid of what Hunter will say to him. I have to be there."

I'll go with you. But his presence would only add to the tension with Hunter. Helpless again and hating it, he muttered, "It's all right. I understand."

She snuggled against him. "It's not fair. You have a lot going on too. We were going to talk about whatever happened last night."

"It can wait." With his job in jeopardy, he didn't know what to say to her.

Pulling back, she laid a hand on his arm. "Before I leave, what happened today? Hunter told me Maury's calling investors."

"I'm not surprised. Applegate liked what he saw."

She waited for more. "And?"

"It's not good, Jules. At least not for me. Maury wouldn't share details, but he promised not to bulldoze the place. I have the feeling he wants to make it bigger and better." That was Zeke's vision too.

"Maybe he'd keep you on."

"I doubt it." Zeke knew what *he'd* do in Maury's place. "If you're going to make something brand-new, you have to clean out what's old. He might keep on specialized managers like Chet and John, but I'd be in his way."

"Or you'd be useful."

He stared at the shelves holding the geodes. The details were lost in the dark, and so was he. "George is still against selling, but Ginger is pressing hard. All that matters is doing what's best for them and the employees."

"But what about you?" Her voice came out small.

"You know the drill. I polish my résumé. Check out job search engines. Network. Whatever it takes."

Julia nodded. "What I learned from my own experience was to be open to change."

"I suppose so."

But deep down, he hated the idea of being in limbo. Especially now, when he wanted to offer Julia a diamond engagement ring, a wedding of her own, and a house with a white picket fence and a dog for Max.

The room was almost completely dark now, but he could still see the planes of her face. The longing to stay shone in her eyes. Knowing she needed to leave, he stood and offered his hand. "I'll walk you to your car."

"No. You stay here." She stood, rested her hands on his shoulders, and massaged the tense muscles. Mischief sparked in her eyes. "We don't want to start any rumors. And what I have in mind right now—"

"—just might start a lot of them."

He kissed her. Long and slow. Dark and sweet. They had a few miles to go before they took the next big step, but for now, this kiss was enough.

Ellen believed in simplicity, and dating a man like George didn't change that part of her personality. When he arrived at the cottage on Friday morning, she was ready to go with a small suitcase and the black dress in an opaque garment bag. He greeted her at the door as if he were a chauffeur, carried her things to the Corvette, and they took off down the highway.

"It's about four hours to San Jose," he told her. "We'll settle in at the hotel first. You can rest while I do a sound check, then we'll grab an early supper with some friends of mine from Home and Hearth. You'll be sitting with them during the show."

George could be a handful, but he was also a big old teddy bear. Ellen stole a look at his strong jaw and his big hands relaxed on the steering wheel. "You're taking good care of me."

"I try." He gave her a sideways smile. "After the show, it'll be just you and me. We can eat a late dinner somewhere nice or keep it casual at IHOP."

Candlelight appealed to her far more than a coffee shop, but her heart skittered at the thought of what candlelight implied. "Let's decide later."

Silence settled between them. It wasn't exactly awkward, but neither did it feel right.

After a couple of miles, George cleared his throat. "There's an old movie theater in downtown San Jose that plays classics. Maybe we should check it out."

Ellen stifled a sigh. She wasn't the least bit interested in seeing a movie. In the past two weeks, she and George had watched John Wayne in *Rio* this and *Rio* that, three Katharine Hepburn comedies, and all the Chevy Chase *Vacation* movies, which George thought were hilarious.

She was tired of movies and even more tired of ending each night with a gentle hug. George was a bona fide heartthrob, and when he gave her that special look, she lost her breath. *Courage.* Just one move on her part and the waiting would be over. He'd kiss her. But he wouldn't do it unless he knew she was sure.

That first kiss dangled like a ripe peach. Every day it grew brighter in color, softer to the touch, and sweeter from the extra time in the sun. Peaches were all she could think about as they wove through the hills toward the coast.

Keeping one hand on the wheel, George reached to turn on the sound system. "Music?"

"Sure."

While a playlist loaded, she looked out the window. Maybe she'd kiss him for good luck just before the show. If she got the kiss out of the way, she could enjoy his singing instead of fidgeting through the set list she'd helped him select. An oldie, "I Fall to Pieces" by Patsy Cline, played through the speakers now. Her eyes slid to George's profile. When his lips parted and he started to sing along, she nearly forgot to breathe.

He hooked a brow at her, then focused on the road while singing softly in his famous baritone. The moment etched itself on her heart—the lyrics, George crooning the soul-searing melody, the empty road, and the sky meeting the hills. Beauty exploded all around her. This moment was meant to be savored. *Life* was meant to be savored in all its fullness.

"Stop!" she cried.

George swung his head in her direction, then refocused on the highway. "Is it the song? Ellen, I—"

"No. Just stop."

"Stop what?"

"The car!" She pointed to a turnout with a historical marker. It was about a hundred feet away. "Right there."

George veered onto the gravel apron, the tires spitting rocks until the Corvette crunched to a halt. Swinging the door wide, Ellen burst out of the car like a butterfly emerging from a cocoon.

George climbed out too. "Ellen, what's wrong? Are you sick?"

She didn't dare hesitate. Shoulders square, she hurried around the hood of the Corvette. George met her halfway and stopped. Lines of concern fanned from the corners of his deep-set eyes. He was so much like Ben in all the best ways. But George was George, purely himself. And Ellen was herself too. Her heart hammered against her ribs. It was a brand-new rhythm, one that belonged just to them.

George placed his big hand on her arm. "Ellen, darlin'. I'm worried about you. I can take you back and still make the show."

"Don't you dare!"

He cocked his head to the side, clearly confused. Feeling rather smug, she draped her arms over his shoulders, traced his muscles with her fingertips, and swayed toward him, her face rising to his.

George's brows shot up. "Oh, I see . . ."

She expected him to take over, but he didn't move an inch. Instead he stared at her lips. She met his confident gaze with one of her own. "You're not going to make this easy, are you?"

"No, ma'am. I am not."

"Well, neither am I." She swayed an inch closer. So did George. When she moved another inch and stopped, he did the same.

She couldn't stand much more, but the power she possessed thrilled her. Bold as brass, she stood on her toes and matched her mouth to his. George did the rest. His arms tightened around her back, and he hauled her against his chest. His mouth moved with hers, exploring, tasting, enticing, until she was dizzy with the thrill of it.

Finally, when they both needed air, he drew back and kissed her temple instead of her mouth. "It's a good thing you did that, because I was about to die."

"Really?"

"Yeah." A deep chuckle shook his chest. "Tonight, when I sing a new song called 'Starting Over Twice,' it's for you."

"Oh, George." She choked up. "I'm honored."

"We're not kids anymore, Ellen. If I've learned one thing in the past few years, it's to honor the time God gives us." Stepping back, he gripped her hands, lifting them up to make a bridge of sorts. "I love you. I know this is fast, but I'm old enough to know the real thing when I feel it."

Ellen looked into his craggy face. Each rugged line told a story, and each story was a stone in the path leading to this moment. *Love.* She felt it too. It was a miracle, but she also knew the risks. She buried her head under his chin. "I love you too. It scares me, but I can't stop these feelings."

"Would you stop them if you could?"

"No." She pressed her lips to his Adam's apple. "But can we take things slow? Loving again . . . it frightens me."

"We'll take it one day at a time," he told her.

"I can handle that."

He looped his arm around her waist and led her back to the car, where he kissed her one more time. They climbed in and he steered back to the road, holding her hand while she thought about the tattoo on her shoulder. That verse had seen her through hard times and it always would. With her heart light, she watched the road as it took them straight into the future.

Twenty-eight

When Julia parked her Outback at the stable on Sunday afternoon, Max was strapped in his booster seat, rubbing his eyes and irritable because of yet another nightmare. She had done her best to dispel his fear, but she couldn't make it go away if he wouldn't even acknowledge it. Hunter praising him for being a big boy didn't help. The dreams about the snake occurred nightly now, so she had arranged today's visit with Chet. If Max saw Jed was safe, maybe he could put the snake out of his mind.

Her mom and George had extended their trip and were still gone. With Tiff's wedding just five days away, Julia would need to take Max to the children's program or leave him with a hotel babysitter tomorrow. Neither option would be easy if Max was afraid to leave the house. This morning she had tried a "kill the snake" game and brought in Zeke's Ninja Turtles for backup, but Max wasn't impressed with her skills.

As she climbed out of her car, he kicked his legs. "Mommy, no! I don't want to get out."

With her heart breaking, she peered at his tearstained face. She'd spent an hour coaching him about this visit. "But Max, we decided—"

He kicked even harder. "I don't want to see the horse!"

Chet walked up to the car and laid a friendly hand on her shoulder. "How about if I give it a try?"

"Thanks," she murmured. "I'm desperate."

Leaning forward, Chet pushed back his hat and put his hands on his knees. "Hey, partner. How would you like to visit Sugar Pie?"

Taken by surprise, Max stopped squirming. Julia popped the harness, swung him up to her hip, and smiled her thanks to Chet.

"That sounds like fun, doesn't it?" she said in her mommy voice.

Max's arms tensed around her neck, but he didn't squirm. His eyes were riveted to Chet's face. "You came to get us at those rocks."

"Yes, I did. That was pretty scary, huh?"

The color drained out of Max's face, but he didn't utter a sound or tighten his grip on her neck. Hopeful, Julia lowered him to his feet. He slid easily but held tight to her hand, his eyes as wide as saucers as they approached the barn.

They were ten steps away when she spotted Zeke. Dressed in Levi's, an olive green T-shirt, and hiking boots, he stepped out of the barn. Julia's heartbeat tripled, and for a moment she enjoyed the sight of sunlight streaking his hair, the smile on his lean face, and the apparent strength of his broad shoulders. This was the man she wanted Max to copy and admire. Zeke carried himself with authority, not arrogance. He was in charge and it showed, but he wasn't controlling or critical. And those biceps clearly visible beneath the snug T-shirt . . . her mouth went as dry as it had when he kissed her in the dark.

Tingling in spite of the heat, she told herself to get a grip. She could enjoy Zeke's company later. Today was about Max. If anyone could help her son get over his fear of snakes, it was Zeke.

Julia waved a greeting and smiled. "This is a surprise."

"For me too," Zeke replied. "A good one."

Chet's gaze bounced from Zeke's face to hers, and then back to Zeke. "I was just taking Miss Julia and Max to visit the horses. If you can handle it, I'd be obliged. We're shorthanded today."

"Sure, Chet. No problem."

The cowboy left, and Zeke faced Julia. "I just checked Golden Point. The prep work is done, and the contractor got the part for the paver. With a little luck, the work will be done by Wednesday, and the landscapers can bring in the potted trees. It's not done yet, but I think we're going to make it."

"I hope so." But she was still ready with a backup plan, especially since a tropical storm was forming off the coast of Baja and traveling north.

Max tugged hard on her arm. She looked down and saw his gaze riveted on Zeke. "You gave me the Ninja Turtles."

"That's right," Zeke replied.

"You're wearing a green shirt. The Turtles are green too."

Hands on his hips, Zeke spread his feet a little wider. "That's me"—he deepened his voice—"Turtle Man."

Max giggled. "You're not really a Ninja Turtle."

"No." Grinning, Zeke lowered his arms. "But I wanted to be one when I was a kid. Who's your favorite?"

"Michelangelo." Max tilted his face up at Julia. "That's the one you used to try to kill the snake. But it didn't work."

When Zeke lifted an eyebrow at her, she mouthed, *Later.* "We came to see how Jed's doing."

Max kept his eyes on Zeke. "The snake bit him. I saw it. Snakes can be anywhere, even in your yard."

Understanding washed away the playfulness on Zeke's face. Dropping to a crouch, he put himself eye-to-eye with Max. "I hate snakes."

Max let go of Julia's hand and inched closer to Zeke. "I do too."

"If you ask me," Zeke said just to Max, "rattlesnakes make the scariest sound in the world."

A weight lifted from Julia's shoulders. This was the kind of understanding Max needed, not the shame dished out by Hunter.

The three of them walked into the big barn with Max in the middle. When Zeke laid a hand on his shoulder, Max looked up and grinned, his first true smile in almost a week. Julia's breath caught, and in a flash of hope she imagined the three of them together in ten years, then twenty.

One step at a time. Giving herself a mental shake, she focused back on Max.

A carved wooden sign marked Jed's stall. As they approached, Zeke picked up Max and balanced him on his hip. When they reached the stall, he pointed over the half door to Jed munching hay. Julia stood on Zeke's other side, their shoulders brushing while he gave Max an update on Jed.

"The vet checked his leg this morning. He's going to be as good as new in about two weeks."

"Is the snake gone?" Max asked.

"That's a good question." Zeke glanced at Julia, giving her a chance to intervene. But there was no need. She trusted Zeke's judgment, so she nodded. *Tell him what you think is best.*

Zeke shifted Max further back on his hip, then looked into the boy's tense face. "That particular snake is dead. I've never seen one around the stable or near your house or the big hotel, but I'll be straight with you, Max. Snakes are part of nature. It's smart to stay away from the places they hang out, like those boulders."

Max turned to Julia, his arm still around Zeke's neck but relaxed now. "I'm never going near those rocks again."

"That's a good idea," Zeke told him. "But you know what?"

"What?"

"You don't need to be afraid. You just need to be smart, which you are. If you ever hear that sound again, walk away from it."

"I will," Max vowed. "I hate snakes."

When they walked back outside, Max squirmed to get down. The instant his feet touched the ground, he stomped on an invisible snake. Zeke stomped with him, and so did Julia. The stomping turned into a silly game with Max deciding he wanted to be the Ninja Turtle named Raphael because he was extra tough.

Laughing and joking, the three of them decided to go back and give Jed some carrots. The big horse gobbled them up, but when they fed some to Sugar Pie, she ate like the dainty old lady she was.

With Max distracted, Zeke nudged Julia a few steps away and whispered into her ear. "That snake episode really shook him up."

"More than you know." She told him about the nightmares. "Thanks for helping him. It's been tough on us both, and Hunter didn't help at all.

He told Max to be a man like Daddy. Can you believe it?"

"Unfortunately, I can." Something dark dimmed his expression. For a moment he studied her. "Are you doing anything right now?"

"No. Why?"

"How about coming to the house? When I cleaned out the rest of the boxes, I found some more Ninja Turtle stuff. I want Max to have it. Plus it'll give us a chance to talk in private. I promised to tell you about the other night."

"I'd like that a lot."

When Julia told Max they were going to Zeke's house, he ran out of the barn, snakes and horses forgotten. Zeke lifted Max into the car seat, and they drove separately with Zeke in the lead. When they arrived at his house, he opened the big garage door. The wall of boxes was gone, but she saw one remaining carton on the workbench. The Ninja Turtle sidekicks named Splinter, the Shredder, and April O'Neil were lined up next to it.

Zeke led them to the bench and handed the action figures to Max. "You'll need these to go with the Turtles."

"Thanks!" Max clutched the figures in both hands, making a jumble of plastic arms and legs. "Want to play Turtles with me?"

"Maybe later," Zeke said. "But you can play with them on the grass while I talk to your mom."

Max looked at Zeke as if he really were Turtle Man, then scampered to the landscaped mound in the middle of the lawn.

When he was settled, Julia shifted her gaze to Zeke. "So here we are."

Zeke glanced at the flattened boxes stacked against the wall, ready in case he lost his job and needed to move. Last week when he told Julia something was happening to him, he had expected to be in a different place mentally and professionally. A place of triumph, his career secure and his faith restored after defeating Maury and Hunter. Instead, his first step back to God had led him to his own Gethsemane. A lonely place of decision, where a man chose to fight for himself or die for the sake of others.

The more Zeke thought about everything Maury could do for Caliente Springs, the more he wondered if his return to faith would cost him his career. Without a job, he couldn't bring himself to even think about asking Julia to marry him. Some men might not care about supporting a wife and child, but Zeke did.

Julia pushed up on her toes and looked into the open box on the workbench, specifically at the upper half of a framed photograph of Zeke and his dad.

"Can I see it?" she asked.

Without comment, he handed it to her. He had

tried to go through his dad's things that morning, but the picture of that grinning kid had sucker-punched him. He'd come within an inch of taping the box shut again.

"What else is in here?" Julia lifted out a thick manila envelope. "I'd love to see more pictures."

He plucked the envelope from her fingers. Family photographs were his mother's domain, and he'd already divvied up the loose prints and albums with his sisters. He had no idea what expression was on his face, but Julia backed away from him. "I'm sorry, Zeke. I didn't mean to pry."

"You didn't." If he could share facing his father's disappointment with anyone, it was Julia. "This stuff belonged to my dad."

She looked at the box, trailed a finger down the smooth side, then traced the crisp No. 1 written on it. "I know what it's like to go through old things like this. Would it help if we did it together? You never know. We might find something special."

Zeke doubted it. The envelope in his hand held his father's sermon notes, and it weighed a thousand pounds. Expecting nothing but his father's disappointment, he worked the clasp open and slid out a stack of paper. When he saw the double-spaced type with notes written in red ink, his father's voice played in his head. *Don't let God down, son. Your behavior is your witness.*

Zeke held back a scowl, but his throat knotted over a tender lump. If his dad had walked into the garage at that moment, Zeke would have hugged him hard and resented him all at the same time. The envelope slipped from his hand back to the workbench. Letting out a slow breath, he raked his hand through his hair.

"What's wrong?" Julia asked.

"I spent my whole life trying to live up to what's in these notes." Years of trying to be perfect, hiding his failures, and wearing a coat-hanger smile. "I couldn't do it."

Take the resentment, Lord. I don't want it.

Julia studied his face for a moment, sighed with him, and reached back inside the box. "Let's see what else is here."

Zeke touched her shoulder. Not to stop her but to draw strength from having her at his side. He had bared his soul to her, yet she was here with him now. Encouraging him, helping him, her eyes so full of love he didn't know whether to stand taller or break down. "Thanks for being here."

Reaching up, she laid her hand over his. "I wouldn't be anywhere else right now. Let's finish this."

Spine straight, he reached in the box and lifted out the ceramic candy dish his youngest sister made in second grade. It was lumpy, crooked, and glazed a hideous orange. Grinning, Zeke held it up for Julia's inspection. "What do you think?"

"I think it's beautiful." She admired it a moment, then tipped her head. "Did you make it?"

"No, my baby sister did. My dad kept it on his desk for years."

Julia grinned. "The baby of the family and daddy's little girl. I bet she got away with murder."

"Definitely."

But Zeke never did. He'd been in training to be the family standard-bearer. For the most part, he had enjoyed the attention. And though the pressure to be perfect had left marks, it had also given him his achievements. With more gratitude than resentment, he set the candy dish aside and looked back in the box.

Pushing to her toes, Julia peered over the edge. "A cigar box. And it's made of wood."

"What about it?"

"Cigar boxes are always special. I don't know why, but they are."

Julia didn't know it, but she was looking at his father's junk box—a collection of pencil stubs, dried-out pens, rubber bands, and whatever other flotsam gathered on his desk. Zeke put on the most somber expression he could manage. When he spoke, his voice came out in the dark tone of a mortician. "Would you open it for me?"

"Of course."

Equally somber, Julia paused to trade a respectful look then opened the lid. Instead of looking into the box, Zeke watched her brows arch and collapse as she burst out laughing. The box held just what he expected along with toenail clippers and wart remover.

Julia shook her head. "There goes my 'special cigar box' theory. Wart remover? Really?"

Zeke picked up the half-used bottle and smiled. Apparently the Reverend Jacob Monroe was as human as anyone else. If he had checked the box before storing it, he would have tossed the wart remover, but he'd missed it. Made a mistake. Forgotten to double-check the way he had always told Zeke to do.

It's okay, Dad. I get it. No one's perfect. Not you. Not me. With his eyes suddenly damp, Zeke found it easy to love his dad—warts and all.

Feeling lighter than he had in years, he reached back into the storage box. His fingers hit a rock about five inches in diameter, coarse to the touch, and surprisingly light in weight. He knew the feel of it, the shape in his hand. As he lifted it out, he turned his palm to display the round stone to Julia. "I can't believe this. It's an uncracked geode."

"From your dad."

"Yes. I wonder where it came from." He thought a minute and decided his father had purchased it somewhere, maybe as a birthday gift for his son. "Let's open it." He called over his shoulder. "Hey, Max, I found one of those special rocks. We're going to crack it open. Do you want to help?"

"Yeah!" Max scrambled into the garage, the Ninja Turtles toys abandoned in the shade of a juniper bush.

Zeke cut the corner out of a spare cardboard box to use as a wedge to hold the geode. Then he fetched a hammer, chisel, and two pairs of protective glasses out of a plastic toolbox. They needed three, so he fetched his sunglasses out of the SUV and put them on. He gave the clear plastic pairs to Max and Julia, and they all crouched in the middle of the garage.

Max wrinkled his nose. "We look funny."

"We also look smart," Zeke replied. "The glasses will keep any rock pieces from hitting us in the eye." He'd been down that road once. Never again.

After smiling her appreciation to Zeke, Julia patted Max on the back. "That's a good safety lesson."

Zeke set the geode in the wedge, positioned the chisel, and tapped it with the hammer. He made three cuts, then turned to Max. "Would you like to give it a try?"

When Max's eyes lit up, Zeke motioned for the boy to scoot in front of him. Knowing the hammer was heavy, Zeke put his hand over Max's smaller ones, and together they made another cut.

When they finished, Zeke offered the tools to Julia. "Your turn."

She gripped the hammer and positioned the chisel but checked with him before making a cut. "Is this right?"

"Close enough." Perfection no longer mattered to him.

She gripped the hammer, shifted her fingers again, but still hesitated. "I don't want to ruin it."

"Here. I'll help." He put his hand over hers, and together they tapped the stone twice. At the third tap, the ugly rock split in two to reveal the purest, most stunning purple geode Zeke had ever seen.

Julia caught her breath. "It's beautiful."

"It's amethyst." The semi-precious stone was one of his favorites, in part because it made appearances in the Bible. In Hebrew, the word for amethyst was *ahlamah*, and it meant *dream stone*. The tie-in to Dare to Dream wasn't lost on him. In Greek, *amethyst* meant "not drunken," and that seemed fitting too. Zeke had been drunk on his own accomplishments, and he was done with that now.

He picked up the two halves of the stone, handed one to Max and the other to Julia. "These are for you."

Max said, "Wow!" and took the rock in both hands, but Julia refused to accept hers.

"I can't. It's too special."

"Take it." He pushed it into her palms.

"But—"

"Take it," he said again. "We'll find a special place to put it."

We. She must have heard, because her cheeks turned the color of rose quartz.

He didn't know what to say with Max present, so he kept it simple. "I'm not where I want to be, but I'm not where I was either. God's working on me."

Julia studied him for a moment. "It's part of being human, isn't it?"

"What is?"

"Being clay in God's hands. Seeing our weaknesses, trusting Him to change us." She ran her finger over the shell of the cut geode. "Some changes take a long time, but others are instant. One minute you're standing on your own two feet, and the next you're on your face in the dirt. Getting up takes a lot more time than falling down."

No wonder he loved this woman. She understood him in ways no one else did, and he understood her too. Their journeys had started in very different places, but now they were on the same path. For today, that was enough.

They shared a companionable silence until Max announced he was hungry.

"Me too," Zeke said. "Let's get pizza."

"Yeah!" Max leapt to his feet. "Let's pretend we're Ninja Turtles. Mommy can be April O'Neil and you can be Leonardo."

Zeke reached for Max and tickled him. "How about you? Who are going to be?"

"I'll be . . ." Max couldn't stop laughing.

"How about Donatello?" Zeke suggested. "He's good at science."

"Cool!"

While Julia gazed sweetly at her son, Zeke studied the soft line of her mouth, the tender dip of her chin, and he thought of a rock of another kind—the diamond he wanted to slide on her finger. His career was hanging by a thread, but his faith was coming back strong. If God moved the way Zeke hoped, he'd be shopping for that ring very soon.

Twenty-nine

On Monday morning, the paving contractor arrived at Golden Point with a machine that stank of oil, tar, and dirt. Julia was never so happy to see asphalt being laid in her life. She and Zeke visited the site together, traded high fives, and breathed easier. Later in the week, when the grounds crew brought potted trees and the decorators added custom touches in Tiff's wedding colors, the walkway would be lovely.

Later in the day, George and Ellen returned from their trip. They took over everything to do with Max, freeing Julia to focus solely on the wedding.

On Tuesday, Tiff and Ginger drove up from Los Angeles and made themselves at home in the mansion. Derek and his parents arrived later the same day and moved into the cottage two doors down from Julia's.

Even the weather was cooperating. It was Wednesday morning, and the forecast called for rain in the afternoon. With a little luck, the valley below Golden Point would perk up, the mountains would glisten, and Saturday's sunset would be one of the most beautiful in the history of Caliente Springs.

Wedding preparations zipped along with surprising ease now that the path to the lookout was done. A little too easily, in Julia's opinion, because a hundred things could still go wrong. She wouldn't relax until Tiff and Derek left for their honeymoon.

She was going over her to-do list when her phone flashed with Ginger's caller ID. Ginger never called before ten o'clock. On alert, Julia picked up the phone with one hand and a pen with the other.

"Julia, good morning!" Ginger never sounded that cheerful, especially not in the morning.

"What's up?" Julia asked.

"I hate to do this to your seating plans, but I'm bringing a date to the wedding as well as two additional guests to the rehearsal dinner. We'll need three extra seats total for the dinner."

Julia did a mental calculation. The rehearsal dinner was planned for eight o'clock at the Travers house on the back patio. Derek's parents were officially hosting, the evening was formal, and the menu included lobster and filet mignon. There were fourteen guests including herself, a courtesy extended by Ginger. The seating plan called for two tables of eight, one for family and one for the bridal party.

Julia saw an easy fix. "I'll bow out."

"Thank you, dear. You've been a joy to work with. I hope this wedding gives Dare to Dream a big boost, because you deserve all the success in the world."

"Thank you. It's been a pleasure."

More than a pleasure. A painful lump pushed into Julia's throat. This month at Caliente Springs had changed her life. But what happened next? When the wedding was over, she and Max would return to Los Angeles. What would happen with Zeke? There would be phone calls and FaceTime, but she wanted so much more.

Ginger's voice broke into her thoughts. "I'm sure we'll see a lot of each other in the future. The way George is carrying on with your mom, you might have to start calling me Aunt Ginger."

Julia was genuinely pleased. "They're great together."

"I think so too."

Ready for work, she peeled off a fresh Post-it. "So the man you're bringing . . . I'll need his name for the place cards."

"It's Maury."

The pen dangled over the note. "Maury Applegate?"

"Yes." Ginger paused. "I'm afraid I owe Zeke an apology for admonishing him to keep his personal life and business matters separate. Maury and I met for dinner in Los Angeles. What started as a business meeting turned into a delightful time."

"I've always liked him," Julia admitted.

"I'm sure you'll understand about the other two guests. Since Hunter is here with Maury, it seemed rude not to include him. And since Hunter's time with Max is so short, he asked to bring him. Derek's parents are fine with it."

But I'm not. Unless requested by the bride or groom, a four-year-old didn't belong at a formal dinner. Max especially didn't belong, and she didn't trust Hunter to look out for him. "I appreciate the invitation, but Max can be a handful." And a distraction to her. "I'll find a babysitter."

"Go ahead and bring him. Hunter tells me he's an exceptional little boy. If Max gets bored, we'll set him up with a movie in George's den."

Ginger meant well, but she didn't know very much about four-year-old boys. "Thank you, but I still think a sitter is best."

"Whatever you decide is fine. I suppose it's between you and Hunter."

Always. The never-ending tug-of-war. Rather than turn the rehearsal dinner into a war zone, she conceded a small battle to avoid a bigger one. "Well, if you're sure it's okay . . ."

"Oh, I am."

Julia made a mental note to order a children's meal. Lobster and filet mignon were far beyond Max's pallet. "I'll make it work."

"Thank you, dear."

"Anything else?"

"No, we're set."

Ginger paused. "A month ago, I would never have guessed George and I would be talking to a man like Maury. We met with him last night. I can't go into the details yet, but Maury's making phone calls."

Wincing, Julia pictured Hunter smirking at Zeke in triumph. If she and Zeke shared a future, Hunter's jabs would be part of their family landscape. Who wanted to live with that? She didn't. But maybe that was the challenge to them all.

To forgive daily.

To endure the stinging darts and arrows.

To love the unlovable.

She couldn't do any of those things without God in her life. Even with God, every encounter with Hunter presented a new challenge to forgive as generously as she'd been forgiven.

Ginger changed the subject to the wedding. They chatted awhile longer about the weather, both agreeing a little rain would be wonderful but that too much could lead to a muddy mess.

When the call ended, Julia pressed back in her chair. There wasn't a thing she could do about the weather or Hunter, but she could help Zeke fight for Caliente Springs. All she needed to do was pray, hope, and pull off the wedding of the century.

· · ·

With rumors finding him like smart bombs, Zeke stayed home on Wednesday morning to compose a company-wide email about the possible sale of the resort. He started the memo a dozen times and deleted each draft. If he didn't give solid facts, which he couldn't, anything he wrote would fan the flames of fear burning in every office and hallway. He needed to put out the fire, but all he could do was type and delete.

Fed up, he shoved his laptop aside and bowed his head. "Lord, I need a break here. I don't care if it's the Carter account coming through or Maury giving up. This ship is going down unless you do something."

And Zeke was going down with it.

He sat for a long moment on the couch, his neck stiff and his heart cold again. Did he need to pray harder? Fall to his knees? Cry and scream and pound the floor? He wanted to throw the laptop across the room. Instead, he put on his best suit and steeled himself to face the mayhem at the office. Maybe Julia could buoy him out of his dark mood.

He climbed into his SUV, set his phone on the console, and turned the ignition. He was backing out of the driveway when George's Corvette whipped up the street. There was only one reason George would come to Zeke's house. There had to be news about Applegate. Zeke pulled back into the driveway, pushed the car door open, and slammed it behind him.

George stood by the Corvette, his expression neither warm nor cold. "Get in. We're going for a ride."

"Let's talk here." Zeke tried to make a joke. "If you're going to fire me, I'd rather lick my wounds in private."

"Come on, Zeke. Humor me. Thanks to Ginger, Tiff, and two of the bridesmaids, the whole house stinks of hairspray, perfume, and salad dressing. I need some fresh air."

Zeke glanced at the gray sky. The clouds were building in the southwest, and the air was heavy with humidity rare to California. Maybe rain was a good omen. "Fine. Let's go."

They rode in silence with the radio on an oldies station. After a couple of miles, George steered down a dirt road that led to an abandoned campground. With the Corvette bouncing in the ruts, they veered around a hill and made a sharp turn. The road ended at a cluster of picnic tables and campsites marked by broken lines of white rock.

George turned off the ignition, and they both climbed out. The campground seemed like an odd place to go, especially with the threatening sky, and Zeke wondered why George chose it. But then he saw the hard set of George's jaw. Whatever he had to say, Zeke wasn't going to like it. In his mind, the picnic table in front of them took on the form of an altar, and he knew with utter certainty that he was the lamb brought to slaughter.

Mouth tight, George stared at something in the distance. It wasn't like him to hesitate, and the delay severed another strand of Zeke's self-control. "Maury's buying this place, isn't he? That's why you dragged me out here. You're going to tell me you're sorry, but—"

"You know," George drawled, "you can be a real pain in the butt. I'm trying to be fair to you."

"So you drag me out here—"

"I brought you here so we could talk without getting interrupted by your stupid phone, my stupid phone, or any other stupid thing. This isn't an easy conversation to have."

"So finish it." *Tell me I'm fired. Send me packing. Tell me I didn't do enough, wasn't strong enough or smart enough.*

George looked him square in the eye. "Ginger and I met with Maury last night. I can't give you the details, but I've changed my mind about working with him. He's a good man, Zeke. He has resources we need."

So Santa Claus had come to town, and it wasn't even December. Zeke squeezed the back of his neck until it hurt. There wasn't a superhero anywhere who could compete with the jolly man in red, but God could. Except God didn't hand out candy canes or say "Ho ho ho." He loved his kids, but he didn't spoil them.

But neither did he abandon them.

Zeke jammed his hands in his pockets. He felt no peace at all, nor did he sense God's presence. He didn't see God anywhere, but maybe God was watching from a distance, sitting on His throne, waiting for Zeke to make the next move.

Tap . . . Tap . . . Tap.

But the tapping felt more like a death blow. And the death blow had come from a man Zeke considered a close friend, a mentor, even a little like a father.

George planted a boot on the old wooden bench. "It's not over yet, Zeke. I wouldn't have said anything to you just yet, but Chet called Ginger about a rumor that you had already been let go."

"So is it true?"

George hesitated. "Everything is on the table right now. But I want you to know I'm your friend. If worse comes to worst, I'll fix you up with Home and Hearth again."

"Great. Now I'm a charity case."

"Forget your pride—"

"Pride?"

"Yes, pride."

Far more than his pride was on the line. His whole *life* depended on what George, Ginger, and Maury decided. A good job meant food on the table, a roof over Julia's head, and shoes for Max. His salary at Home and Hearth had been decent, but it was small compared to what he made now. He didn't need to drive a black Lexus, but he wanted very much to give Julia and Max a secure future.

"You don't get it, George." His voice scraped at his dry throat. "I have plans, hopes. This will change everything."

George folded his arms over his chest. "You're jumping to conclusions here. You don't know what the future holds."

"Neither do you."

"That's right."

"So?"

"So be patient. It's not over yet."

"That's easy for you to say." For Zeke, finding a new position could take months, and with Julia and Max in his life, he was tied to Southern California. So was she, because of Hunter. *Why, God? I did my best. I tried to trust you.* Fury crackled in his chest, caught fire, and threatened to explode in an outburst he couldn't control. Zeke didn't want anyone, not even George, to see him fall apart, so he turned his back.

"Get out of here. I'll walk home."

"Are you nuts?" George aimed one thick brow at the dark clouds. "It's going to rain. You'll get soaked."

"Go," Zeke said again, his voice rising. "I'm fine."

"You're angry. I get that—"

"Angry?" Whirling, he held out his hands, his arms wide and out of control. "You bet I'm angry. I had plans, George. Good ones. And now—"

"Hey." George clamped a hand on Zeke's shoulder. "The situation is complicated. You have to trust me."

Trusting wasn't something Zeke did easily. He was far more accustomed to *trying.* He pointed at his own chest. "I worked my butt off and it wasn't enough. It never is. *Never.* I've had it, George. I'm sick of trying. Sick of it all."

"I bet you are." George's voice came out softer now, almost songlike. "You've been running on your own steam for a long time. I've watched you, Zeke. You live like you're being chased by lions. But you know something? You can't out-run them. They're big and hungry, and if you run, they chase you. I know, because lions chased me for a lot of years. Sometimes you just have to stop and—"

"Drop it, all right?"

"Sorry, I can't do that."

"Sure you can." Zeke stabbed a finger at the car. "You just close your mouth and leave. It's easy."

George let out a snort. "Rant all you want, but I'm not budging from this campground. I care about you, Zeke. I care too much to keep quiet right now."

"Fine. Lecture me. Tell me I'm supposed to stand around and pet the lions while they tear me apart."

"You're a preacher's kid," George shot back. "You know the answer to that. But you're also human. So am I. Stop trying to run the show, because you can't." George jabbed a finger at the sky. "Do you really think you can control the weather?" Next he pointed at the hills. "Or earthquakes?" He hooked a thumb at his own chest. "Or how about booze, addiction, and the lies printed in the *National Enquirer*?"

"Fine!" Zeke shouted. "I get the point. Shut up, will you? *Just shut up!*"

George didn't say a word. Instead, he watched and waited for close to a minute. When he finally spoke, his voice came out so low Zeke had to strain to hear him. "I'm not the one you need to yell at. Tell God how you feel. Trust me, He can handle a grown man having a tantrum. He put up with Jacob and Moses, Job, and quite a few others —including me."

Zeke understood the concept of that kind of love, but he couldn't grasp it for himself. "My dad would say you're presuming on God's grace."

"Maybe I am," George said. "But in my experience, God would rather I presumed on His grace than walk around like a prideful buffoon. There's a balance, and I'm looking for it. But until I get to heaven, I'm going to hang tight to that grace and thank God for every bloody drop of it."

Grace. Zeke knew what the word meant in his mind, but his heart couldn't grasp something so generous. A drop of rain splashed on his cheek. When he looked up, another one smacked his forehead.

Tap . . . Tap . . . Tap.

George strode toward the Corvette. "Let's get out of here."

The rain increased from sprinkles to a shower. George opened the car door, but Zeke shook his head. He and God weren't finished yet, and he wasn't leaving until he had some answers. "Go on ahead. I'll walk back."

George wiped the rain from his face with his sleeve. "Don't be an idiot."

"I'm not."

"But—"

"Just go. I need to do this."

George studied Zeke's face for a full twenty seconds, getting wet himself before he climbed into the Corvette and drove slowly down the road, leaving Zeke with a choice. He could yell at God, curse at himself, cry like a baby, or suck it up, man up, and plug up every ugly feeling. That was what he usually did, what he always did. But with the rain pelting him, he couldn't find the air to suck up anything. "Why?" The single word scraped over his lips. The rain was falling harder now, bouncing off earth so dry it was rock hard.

Tap . . . Tap . . . Tap.

With the drops washing his face, Zeke became a child again, a lost child, a frightened child like Max dreaming about snakes. That fear was real and legitimate, but so was the majesty of a geode. Somehow fear and beauty coexisted in the complexity of the earth, sky, and stars. And so did shame and grace in the ceaseless throb of the human heart.

Zeke shed his coat, took off his tie, and let the water soak through his shirt to his skin. "I give up, Lord. Take Caliente Springs. Take—"

Everything.

But he couldn't spit out that final word. *Everything* included Julia. They loved each other enough to survive anything. Zeke believed that. But if he lost his job, Hunter would lord his money and career over them. Hunter—the jerk who destroyed Zeke's career. The fool who took his own son to snake country. The manipulator who pulled Julia's strings as if she were a puppet required to dance for him. How did Zeke protect the woman he loved if he couldn't even put bread on the table?

Tap . . . Tap . . . Tap.

"Lord," he prayed, "we're not done yet, are we?"

Soaking wet, Zeke drew in lungfuls of the heavy air. His battle with God still wasn't over, but nothing else would happen today. Chill bumps erupted on his skin, and he realized just how cold and wet he was. He thought of calling George, but his phone was sitting in his own SUV.

Flinging his soggy coat over his shoulder, he took a final look around his personal Calvary, then headed to the dirt road, stomping in a big puddle just because it was there. As he rounded the bend, he saw George's Corvette idling in the rain, the taillights bright in the gloom, waiting for him. Grinning, Zeke broke into a jog.

Thirty

At six o'clock on Friday evening, the wedding party gathered at the lookout for the rehearsal. George and Ginger were present, along with Derek's parents. Tiff and Derek's minister, an older man and the veteran of a hundred weddings, took charge. There wasn't much for Julia to do, so she wandered to the edge of the canyon and peered at the valley below. Thanks to the rain, the grass was neon green. With temperatures in the high seventies, tomorrow promised to be as perfect as today.

Tiff was going to have the wedding of her dreams. Maybe someday Julia would too, but Zeke had been strangely quiet since Wednesday. He hadn't mentioned the future at all, and she wondered if the rumors were getting to him—or worse, if they were true and he knew something he didn't want to share with her. They were both in limbo, waiting and facing circumstances bigger than they were.

Like Hunter. Earlier today, when she met him to hand over Max, she had barely managed to let go of her son's hand out of fear of what Hunter might say or do.

Tiff's laughter drifted to Julia's ears, and she turned back to the rehearsal, listening as the minister told Tiff and Derek what to expect. Love for his bride lit Derek's eyes, and Julia was sure Tiff's expression was just as bright.

The minister's voice rose above the happy chatter. "Tomorrow, this is when I'll say, 'You may now kiss the bride.' I don't think you two need any practice, but—"

"I think we do," Derek announced.

Tiff flung herself into his arms. He kissed her thoroughly, picking her up and spinning her around and around. Julia watched with tears stinging her eyes.

The rehearsal ended with a round of hugs, and the troop returned to their rooms to dress for dinner.

An hour later, Julia arrived at the Travers mansion. The same little black dress she'd worn the night she told Zeke she loved him swished around her legs, but she wouldn't see him tonight. Instead she would have to watch Hunter with Max while she smoothed out any wrinkles with the dinner.

She walked around to the backyard to check the patio and caught her breath at the sight of two round tables with crisp linens and centerpieces dripping with orchids. Thousands of tiny lights glistened in the trees and overhead arbor, and night-blooming jasmine scented the air.

Someday she wanted a night like this with Zeke. No, she corrected herself. Not *someday*. She wanted that night now. But she knew Zeke.

He wouldn't propose marriage unless he had a good job. And what would they do if a job offer took him away from California? Julia felt obligated to stay within driving distance of Hunter. As he was so quick to remind her, he had rights.

After a final inspection of the tables, she headed to the kitchen. She greeted the catering staff, verified serving times with the woman in charge, then checked on Max's meal. When she lifted the plastic cover, she was delighted to see bites of fruit arranged in the shape of a dinosaur, chicken tenders, plain green beans, and macaroni and cheese. Perfect. Exactly the kind of food Max liked.

Guests would be arriving soon, so she headed for the front door. As she crossed the living room, Ginger emerged from the hallway. Dressed in a beaded gold gown with her platinum hair sprayed to perfection, she glowed with her old star quality. George, dapper in a black suit, followed her into the room and left to pick up Ellen. Julia stationed herself at the front door to play hostess.

The wedding party arrived all at once. Jessica, the production assistant for *Flops & Fortunes*, snapped dozens of pictures and tweeted on the fly. The arrival was full of joking, nervous laughter, and back-slapping for the guys.

The doorbell rang again. When she opened

the door, Maury greeted her with a warm handshake. "You're as lovely as ever, Julia."

"Thank you."

They shared a quiet moment that honored the past without bringing it back to life.

She turned back to the door just as Hunter's Lexus cruised into the driveway. She tensed, but her irritation was tempered by the sweet anticipation of seeing Max in the suit she had bought for him. It was a little big, but he looked adorable in the plaid bow tie.

Hunter climbed out first, tugged on his cuffs the way he always did, then lifted Max out of the booster seat. His back blocked her view, but she saw him comb Max's hair first, then his own.

As they walked toward the house, Julia raised her arm to wave, but when she saw Max, she froze. Instead of the cute gray suit and plaid bow tie, he wore a black suit almost identical to Hunter's, tailored to his small frame and accented with a burgundy tie that also matched Hunter's. Even their shoes were the same. Instead of his favorite cowboy boots, Max was wearing little black wingtips.

Hunter's mini-me.

Julia managed to smile and wave, but the evening air took on a chill.

"This is wonderful," Ellen said to Susan Wilkins, Derek's mom. They were seated across from each other at the family table. A waiter was removing salad plates, and Ellen was enjoying the food, lively table talk, and having George at her side. The bridal party was seated at the second table. Tiff glowed the way a bride should, Derek looked both nervous and proud, and the air was full of joking, flirting, and just a hint of longing on the faces of the two bridesmaids who were single.

Ellen loved weddings, but this one sent pangs straight to her heart. As happy as she was for Tiff and Derek, she had lived through the years of Hunter's delays and Julia's disappointment. She was very grateful they hadn't married, but it irked her now to be seated with him. The only bright spot was Max fidgeting between them.

George gave her hand a squeeze. "I know what you're thinking."

"You do?"

"You're planning a day like this for . . ." He waggled his brows at her.

"Don't you dare say *us*," she teased back as she withdrew her hand. "I expect some serious romance before we take that step."

"And you'll get it, darlin'. Plenty of it. But for the record, I was going to say Julia and Zeke."

Ellen reached for his hand a second time. They held tight until a waiter brought them both filet mignon. A second waiter delivered lobster tails to Hunter and a children's plate to Max.

When Max saw the dinosaur made of fruit, he scrambled up to his knees. "It's a T-rex. That's my favorite."

He started to take a strawberry with his fingers, but Hunter stopped him. "We need to wait, son."

As much as Ellen disliked Hunter, sometimes he set a good example. Tonight seemed to be one of those times, so she relaxed.

While the waiter finished serving, George checked his phone. It wasn't like him at all, so she whispered, "Is everything all right?"

"It's better than all right." She waited for more, but he only shrugged. "Zeke answered a text. That's all."

"I wish he were here."

"He will be, but not until later." George met Maury's gaze and nodded.

"Something is going on," she said.

"Yep."

"What is it?"

"You'll see." For a man who bared his soul in his music, he could be a brick wall when he didn't want to talk.

Ellen huffed. "You're not going to tell me, are you?"

"Nope."

"Do you know how frustrating you can be?"

"Yep." But then he winked at her. "Get used to it, darlin'. I want a lot of years with you, and I'm not going to change. That's the bad news. The good news is that I don't want you to change either."

But change would come. A year from now, when Max was in school and Julia didn't need her so much, maybe Ellen would sell the house and move to San Luis Obispo. In the meantime, George was free to travel to Los Angeles whenever he wanted, and Ellen planned to sell the flower shop. It had been a placeholder in her life, something to fill the hours without Ben. She was done with it now.

Feeling wistful, she took in the tall orchids with a professional eye, then turned her attention to the meal and conversation. Derek's parents were gracious hosts, and Maury told jokes like Jay Leno. Ginger, poised as always, told Max how handsome he looked in his suit. He said thank you, then scooped up another bite of his macaroni and cheese.

Hunter signaled the waiter and asked for another champagne cocktail. In less than a minute, the waiter placed a crystal flute in front of him. A sugar cube fizzed at the bottom, and a twist of orange curled around the bubbles.

When Max saw it, his eyes popped. "Can I have one?"

Hunter shook his head. "Sorry, son. This kind of drink is for grown-ups."

Ellen let out the breath she was holding, but then Max scooted up on his knees.

"Please, Daddy? I want to try it."

Maybe she was too conservative, but Ellen saw no reason for a four-year-old to sample a cocktail. She fully expected Hunter to say no.

Instead he gave Max a wink. "All right. But just a sip."

Ellen opened her mouth to protest, but Hunter was already holding the flute to Max's lips. Instead of a sip, Max took a gulp. Hunter laughed, but Ellen saw no humor in the situation at all. Maybe she was crazy to worry. She'd grown up in an alcohol-free home and didn't know what other people considered normal.

Needing help, she put her hand on George's knee. He squeezed her fingers tight as if to say, *You're right. This isn't a good idea.*

She braced herself to step in, but Hunter set the glass down. "That's all."

"I want some more," Max insisted. "Please, Daddy! Pleeeeease."

Ellen laid a firm hand on her grandson's shoulder. "No, Max. Champagne is for grown-ups."

Instead of settling down, Max flung back his shoulders and gave her a snotty look. She arched her brows at him, her expression a warning Max knew well and usually respected. But not tonight. With his little nose in the air, he turned back to Hunter. "Please, Daddy. I like *your* drink the best."

Ellen seethed inside. Not at Max, but at Hunter,

who was beaming a proud smile as if to say, *Isn't he cute?* No. He wasn't. He was being a brat. Max needed to be corrected even if it meant taking him to another room.

He pushed up higher on his knees. "Daddy? Could I *please* have some more?"

Chuckling, Hunter raised the glass to his son's lips. "Oh, all right."

Ellen broke in. "I don't think—" The second gulp was over before she finished, so she sealed her lips.

"Hey, Hunter," George said in the rumble he used on stage, "take it from a pro. That stuff is going to hit the boy harder than you know. If not tonight, twenty years from now."

"He's fine," Hunter said. "Aren't you, Max?"

"Yeah!"

Hunter picked up the glass and drained it himself, thus solving the problem or making a point. Ellen wasn't sure which.

Still on his knees, Max bounced up and down like a little jackhammer. His gaze landed on Hunter's plate and the remains of the red lobster shell. A few bites of the white meat still remained. Max wrinkled his nose. "Eeeeew. That's gross!"

"Gross?" Hunter laughed again. "No way. Lobster is Daddy's favorite food. You should try it."

"Yuck!" Max's voice rang across the entire patio.

A couple bridesmaids, including the one with

Flops & Fortunes, nudged each other and whispered something. Ginger smiled benignly while Maury watched with a frown. Derek's parents traded a look of concern mixed with irritation. George pushed back in his chair, watching and waiting for Hunter's next move.

Ellen was on the verge of getting Julia when Hunter stabbed a bite of lobster with his fork, swirled it in the melted butter and held it in front of Max. "Here. Try it."

Max covered his mouth with both hands and shook his head.

"Come on, son." Hunter moved the fork to within an inch of Max's lips. "Be a big boy and try it."

With his hands firmly in place, Max stared cross-eyed at the dripping shellfish. Ellen knew this child. He loved his daddy and wanted to please him. But he had also consumed two chicken tenders, watermelon, a giant strawberry, most of the macaroni and cheese, a glass of milk, and those two gulps of champagne. Forcing lobster on him was both cruel and unwise.

She pushed out of her chair, dropped her napkin on the seat, and spoke to George. "This is ridiculous. I'm going to find Julia."

The rehearsal dinner was in full swing when Zeke stepped through the sliding glass door leading to the patio. He intended to signal George that he was here then slip inside to wait in the den. George's text had been cryptic, to say the least. Need to meet w/ you tonite. Come to the house around 10. Not knowing what to expect, Zeke had dressed for a business meeting, a formal dinner, or a funeral for his career. The timing was peculiar, but Maury was returning to LA on Sunday and the wedding was tomorrow.

Leaving the slider ajar, he raised an arm to wave at George, but Ellen, striding toward him, blocked the view.

She halted in front of him, her face tight and unsmiling. "Have you seen Julia?"

"No. I just got here."

A waiter holding a white towel and a water pitcher passed in front of them. "Miss Julia's in the powder room."

Ellen let out a groan.

"What's wrong?" Zeke asked.

"Hunter." Grimacing, she hurried past him and into the house.

Zeke stepped onto the patio but stayed in the shadows. Tiff and Derek were snuggled together and posing for pictures. Jessica from *Flops & Fortunes* snapped one with her phone, then turned and saw something that made her brows shoot up.

He followed her gaze to the family table and the back of Max's head. He was shaking it hard and covering his mouth with both hands. Next to him was Ellen's empty seat, her chair askew as if she had launched out of it. George too was focused on Hunter. Next to him were Derek's parents, both frowning, then Ginger, disdain radiating from her ramrod posture. Maury leaned toward Hunter and said something, but Hunter shook his head and raised his hand a little higher, giving Zeke a glimpse of a bite of lobster shining with drawn butter.

The lobster might have looked delicious to someone else, but Zeke winced. Call him a wimp, but shellfish made him gag.

Hunter lowered his chin, said something firmly to Max, then moved the fork even closer. When Max didn't budge, Hunter's brows slammed together. Zeke couldn't hear what he said, but the words or the tone convinced Max to lower his arms and open his mouth. There was no kindness on Hunter's face, only a look of triumph as he fed Max.

The boy's spine stiffened and his hands flew back to his mouth. His little shoulders heaved once, twice. By the third time, there was no holding back. The poor kid threw up all over himself.

Hunter leapt to his feet, grabbed a napkin, and swatted at the slime on his own coat. "You wimp!"

Zeke bolted out of the shadows and toward Max. George circled around the table, but Max, still gagging, flung himself at Hunter. "Da-da-daddy!"

403

The stench of vomit assaulted Zeke's nostrils from ten feet away, but what burned in his brain was the sight of Hunter pulling back from his own son, glowering at him as if he were disgusting. Which he was, but that wasn't the point. Max needed help. When he lunged for his daddy again, Hunter snatched him up by his armpits, held him stiff-armed, and set him down so hard that Max's knees buckled.

"Hey!" Zeke shouted. "That's enough."

Max whirled toward Zeke, bolted across half the patio, and flung himself against Zeke's legs. Scooping him up and into his arms, Zeke tucked Max's head in the crook of his neck, smelled the vomit, and held him even tighter.

Julia burst through the open slider. Her gaze whipped to the mess and Hunter wiping vomit from his coat with a fresh napkin. Pulling up short, she gasped. "Where's Max?"

"Over here," Zeke called.

Her gaze whipped to his, then dropped to Max. Striding forward, she snatched a napkin off a chair and hurried to them. "Poor baby," she said as she wiped her son's face. "It was just too much, huh?"

Max's fingers knotted even harder in Zeke's coat. Ellen arrived with a glass of water, handed it to Julia, and stepped back to give them room.

While Julia tended to Max, Zeke kept an eye on Hunter easing out of his coat with exquisite care. He folded the soiled garment in two, draped it over a chair, and planted his hands on his hips. "I don't know whose idea it was to feed the kid macaroni and cheese—"

"Hold on." George's voice boomed across the table. "You're the fool who gave a four-year-old a champagne cocktail. Then you shamed him into eating something he didn't want. No wonder he puked."

Hunter looked at George as if he were gum on a shoe. "Stay out of it, old man."

George took a step forward, his fists knotted, but Ellen laid a hand on his arm. Maury said something to Ginger, who whispered to George. He turned to Ellen, who nodded back. The four of them faced Hunter in a solid line, saying nothing. Derek's parents moved in and stood with them.

Hunter glared at Julia, his gaze razor sharp. "You're turning my son into a wimp."

With the soiled napkin in her hand, she turned to Hunter with her chin high. "It's time for you to leave."

"You're ruining him."

"Like I said," she repeated, emphasizing each word, "it's time for you to go. Max is done for the night. I'm taking him home."

"You—" A foul word spewed from his mouth.

Max heard the ugly word. So did everyone else, including Zeke. One punch to Hunter's jaw to even the score for Julia . . . just one bloody nose to avenge Max. He burned to take Hunter out in the most primitive way, but if he played Hunter's game, Hunter won. Caliente Springs was Zeke's territory, at least for the moment, and *he* made the rules.

As calm as ice on a winter lake, he spoke to a waiter. "Call Security. Tell them it's a Code Orange." An out-of-control guest.

Hunter put on a smirk. "Security? You're kidding me."

"No, I'm not." Zeke handed Max over to George. "Julia asked you to leave. We can do this the easy way, where you say good-night and we're done. Or we can do it the hard way, where Security escorts you back to your room."

Hunter chuckled softly, almost purring, then zeroed in on Julia. "I'm sick of this little charade of yours. You're turning *my* son into a sniveling brat. Or maybe it's in his genes—the ones he got from you."

Julia didn't say a word or make a sound. There wasn't a trace of fear on her face, only determination and maybe pity, because Hunter's taunts were nothing but lies. When she spoke, the words lilted out of her mouth. "I won't fight with you, Hunter. It's not good for you, me, or Max."

He flung out his arms. "You're ruining him, Julia. *Ruining him.*"

"This isn't the time for that discussion," she said calmly. "You're a guest at a party, and the party's over. It's time for you to leave."

Zeke had never been more proud of her. He was ready to jump in, but Julia didn't need him. If Hunter thought he was in control of the situation or this woman, he was dead wrong.

The lights twinkled in the arbor. Crickets chirped in the distance, and somewhere on the patio, a cell phone buzzed with a message. Hunter's eyes narrowed to slits. His shoulders pulled back, and his lips twisted into a sneer.

Without warning, he lunged at Julia. "You little—"

Zeke thrust himself in front of her. "Back off, Hunter. Now."

Air hissed from Hunter's nose. No one said a word. He stood motionless with all eyes on him, including the eyes of his own son nestled in George's arms. Hunter stared at the bridal party, then at the people standing with George and Ginger. When Julia stepped to Zeke's side, Hunter let out a snort. "You know what, babe? You're not worth this much trouble. If you want a wuss of a kid, fine."

Max let out a whimper, squirmed in George's arms, and reached out for Zeke. Zeke lifted him to his hip and held him tight. Julia joined them and put her arm around Zeke's waist. Three uniformed security officers stepped from the house onto the patio, silent but ready to intervene if Zeke gave the signal.

Hunter took in the uniforms and badges, gave a derisive snort, and shrugged. "You know what? I'm done here." He snatched up his coat and headed for the sliding door.

Zeke let out a relieved breath, but Julia raised her voice. "Hunter. There's one more thing."

He stopped at the door and turned. "What?"

"You can leave Max's backpack at the front desk. I'll get it tomorrow."

After the faintest of nods, Hunter Adams gave a shake of his head as if he couldn't quite believe what was happening. Or maybe he just didn't want to believe it. Shoulders rounded, he sauntered through the house and into the night.

Thirty-one

The ping of a spoon tapping a water goblet called everyone's attention to Ginger. With her hand light on Zeke's arm, Julia turned and looked with the others.

Ginger set down the spoon. "Ladies, gentlemen, I think that's enough drama for one night. Shall we get back to the party?"

"Definitely," Derek called out.

Conversations erupted, all of them riddled with phrases like *poor kid* and *who was that guy?* Julia pitied Hunter, but she knew his mind games would never stop. Tonight, however, the playing field had changed. And it had changed because of Zeke. Turning, she hugged both Zeke and Max as hard as she could. Zeke freed one arm, wrapped it around her waist, and the three of them hugged tight until Max wiggled.

"Mommy, I can't breathe!"

Laughing, she eased back. Max grinned and dived into her arms for a mommy hug. Julia savored every second of both the hug and Zeke's hand on the small of her back. Protecting her, not controlling her. Lifting her up, not holding her down.

When her muscles protested against Max's weight, she lowered him to a chair. Zeke slipped out of his smelly coat, pulled two more chairs around to make a crooked triangle, and they both sat with Max. Her boy needed fresh clothes, but his heart needed attention too.

"So," she said, deliberately matter-of-fact, "how does your tummy feel?"

"Okay," he mumbled. "But Daddy got mad at me."

"Yes, honey, he did." Julia finger-combed his hair. "But what happened wasn't your fault."

Zeke rested his forearms on his knees and leaned forward, putting himself on Max's level. "I can tell you one thing for sure. There's a reason the Ninja Turtles eat pizza."

"What?" Max asked him.

"Lobster is *gross!*"

"Yeah!" Max declared. "It tastes like boogers."

All three of them busted up. The gentle laughter floated over to George and Ellen, who approached holding hands. Just like Julia, Ellen ran her fingers through Max's hair. "How's my boy?"

He patted his tummy. "I feel better, but I made a really big mess."

"You know what?" Zeke sat tall, taking charge as if he were conducting a staff meeting. "We can clean the mess up easily. Getting sick like that can happen to anyone."

"Did it ever happen to you?"

"In third grade," Zeke replied. "A peanut butter

and jelly sandwich. Right in the middle of the school cafeteria. I remember that day every time I open a jar of peanut butter."

Max turned to George. "Did *you* ever throw up?"

George splayed his big hand over his heart. "Son, I've tossed my cookies more times than I can count. I used to call it doing the big spit."

"How about blowing chunks?" Zeke offered.

"Or—"

"George!" Ellen cut him off. "We get the idea."

"Ah, come on, darlin'. I was just getting to the good ones." He gave Max a wink. "I'll tell 'em to you later."

Ellen and Julia traded an eye roll while the guys snuck in a few more jokes. They were all laughing, especially Max. Thanks to Zeke and George, he would remember this night with humor instead of shame. And love instead of rejection from his own father.

With Max at ease, Julia turned to Zeke. Her mind cleared, and she realized she didn't know why he was here. Before she could ask, he gave her hand a squeeze then stood and said something to George.

George nodded then spoke to Ellen, who held her hand out to Max. "Your mommy and Zeke need some grown-up time. Let's get you cleaned up."

When Ellen, George, and Max headed for the

hallway, Zeke led Julia to George's den. A single lamp spilled a circle of light from the corner, casting a glow that didn't quite reach them. Zeke closed the door with a soft click, drew her into his arms, and kissed her so passionately that she melted against him, every thought forgotten and every worry set aside.

She could have kissed him like this all night, but muted voices reached her ears through the closed door. The party was breaking up.

Easing back, Zeke pressed his lips to her temple. "That was quite a scene. I thought Hunter would put up more of a fight."

"He couldn't win and he knew it."

"Smart man. If he'd laid a hand on you, I'd have—"

She kissed him hard and fast. "You were wonderful, Zeke. I'm so glad you were there for Max."

"Me too."

They stood in a relaxed embrace, alone with their thoughts and aware of the uncertain future. Twenty-four hours from now, Tiff's wedding would be over and Julia would go home. She had loved every minute of her time at Caliente Springs—the camaraderie at the office, the fun and challenge of the wedding, and most of all being with Zeke and falling in love.

Telling him good-bye even with the comfort of visits, phone calls, and FaceTime hurt too much to bear right now, so she focused on her best memories. "You and I make a good team."

Zeke hummed thoughtfully into her ear. "We're a lot more than a team, Jules. We're a couple."

A couple. Two people becoming one flesh for a greater purpose. Two people putting their individual desires second to the needs and desires of the other. Julia's hands tightened on his shoulders. "I just realized something important."

"What is it?"

"Hunter and I were never really a couple. We were two self-centered people using each other. I wanted what I wanted, and he felt the same way. I see love differently now. But that doesn't change the fact that I can't fully trust him with Max."

"Champagne and rattlesnakes?"

"It's deeper than that." The lamp in the corner persisted against the murky shadows, reminding her that light always trumped darkness. "It's about a father loving his children—or rejecting them. If Max isn't perfect, he can't be Hunter's mini-me, and that's all Hunter wants from any-one—a reflection of himself."

Zeke eased back but kept his hands on her waist. His fingers tensed on the black silk of her dress. "That part about being a reflection is a little too familiar."

"How?"

"It reminds me of my dad wanting me to be like

413

him. But my dad wasn't at all like Hunter. Maybe he pushed me too hard, but he cared more about my mom, my sisters, and me than he did about himself. If I'd thrown up like Max did tonight, my dad would have held my head and cleaned me up."

"That's what a real father does." Julia's vision blurred with the memory of her own dad and the knowledge that he would have liked Zeke a lot. And George too.

"We had our differences." Zeke gazed at the awards on George's wall. "But if my dad were still alive, he'd tell me to stay brave, walk tall, and fight a good fight. He pushed me hard, but I never doubted that he loved me."

Julia didn't know where Zeke stood with God right now, but she knew what she'd seen. "He'd be proud of you tonight. I know I am. Hunter behaved terribly, and you still treated him with respect. If that's not turning the other cheek, I don't know what is. How you handled him tonight came from someplace deep inside. It's who you are."

With a glint in his eyes, he tugged her body tight against his. "Don't give me too much credit. When he went after you, I came close to decking him."

"That's how I felt too. The way he went after Max, and the way he's gone after Caliente Springs—Oh!"

"What?"

"I didn't expect to see you tonight. Why are you here?"

Zeke eased back from Julia but didn't release her. "George sent me a text. It didn't say much, just to be here around ten. Either he and Ginger have reached a decision about selling to Maury, or they want more information."

"But it's Friday night—"

"George knows I'd rather get fired tonight than put it off until Monday."

"Oh, Zeke."

"Yeah, I know." His gut clenched at the prospect of starting over somewhere. "Maybe this is for the best. Your job here ends Monday, and we haven't talked about that at all. Maybe I'll find a new position in Los Angeles." *Or maybe not.* But he didn't say that.

"Something will work out. We can't untangle it tonight, but I'm hopeful."

Zeke wished he felt the same way. With Julia in his arms, he couldn't bear to think about geography and where a new job might take him. He would have far preferred to plan a marriage proposal, or even to pop the question right this minute. He could hardly stand the compassion in her eyes— or was it pity? His pride roared up, but in the next breath he remembered Hunter slinking away, a man brought down by his own arrogance.

Zeke glanced down at his polished shoes, recalled the muddy campground, and swallowed hard. *There but for the grace of God go I.*

He raised his eyes back to Julia's face. "I have to tell you what happened with George on Wednesday."

Surprise lifted her brows. "I've been wondering."

He told her about George preparing him for bad news, the rain, and how he broke down and cried out to God. "I reached the end of my own rope out there, and what I found was God waiting to pick me up when I finally let go. I'll never be a perfect man, but I love you, Jules. And I love Max. I might not have a job in an hour, but no matter what the future holds, I want to spend it with you."

"Oh—" Her eyes lit up.

The future . . . with you. Zeke hadn't planned to propose. Not at all. If he had, they'd be at Pismo Beach with an engagement ring in his pocket. Did he back down or take a leap of faith? There was no doubt in his mind. God had brought him to this moment, and the choice was plain. Trust himself or trust God.

Tap . . . Tap . . . Crack!

His heart split into two perfect halves, each one beautiful, matching but not identical, just like he and Julia fit together as a couple. Zeke didn't deserve her love at all. He was a broken-down preacher's kid. Joe Average who couldn't play golf worth beans. A general manager about to get canned. Yet the love in her eyes shone with the light of a thousand stars glittering in an endless sky. A gift from God to be cherished, esteemed, and protected. A gift to be treasured as long as they both drew breath.

When her fingers tightened around his, he dropped to one knee and cupped her hand. "The future is uncertain, Jules. But that's in God's hands, not mine. All I know is that we belong together as husband and wife. Will you marry me?"

Tears sprang to her eyes. "Yes! Oh yes . . . I'll marry you."

Zeke shot to his feet and pulled her against the length of his body, and they shared a kiss of passion, affirmation, and relief. Whatever the future held, God could handle it far better than Zeke. With that weight off his shoulders, he savored the warmth of her until he remembered he'd been summoned for a meeting. Slowly, he lifted his head. "I don't want to leave you, but it's after ten o'clock."

"The meeting—"

"Yes. I have to go." A walk to a guillotine. But with the promise that God would never leave or forsake him. He gave Julia another long, slow kiss then opened the door.

George called to him from the living room. "It's about time you opened that door. Zeke, get over here. Julia, you too."

They exchanged a confused glance then walked into the living room, where two couches and an armchair formed a horseshoe. George, Ellen, and Max were seated on the couch facing Zeke and Julia. Fresh from a bath, Max was clean, wearing a shirt too big for him, and close to falling asleep. Ginger sat on the second couch, her back to them, and Maury was seated in the armchair.

He indicated the empty spots next to Ginger. "Have a seat."

Julia sat in the middle, leaving the spot at Maury's right hand for Zeke.

As soon as Zeke settled, Maury cleared his throat. "You must be wondering why you're here."

"Yes, sir," Zeke replied.

Maury smiled at Ginger. "Would you like to deliver the news?"

"Oh, no!" she said. "You do it."

"George?" Maury asked. "How about you?"

"No, thanks." George gave Ellen's shoulders a squeeze. "I'm having way too much fun watching Zeke squirm."

No way would George joke unless something good was about to happen. Zeke's pulse started to race, but he kept his poker face on. "I admit I'm curious, but I'm not jumping to any conclusions."

Maury relaxed back in the chair. "That's one of

the things I like about you, Zeke. You think before you act, but you're not afraid to leap off a tall building when the situation calls for it. That's what you did when you made that first presenta-tion to me. I was impressed with both your honesty and enthusiasm."

"Thank you, sir."

When Julia nudged his foot, Zeke nudged her back.

"It's peculiar how life takes sudden turns." Maury drummed his fingers on the armrests. "I came to Caliente Springs because Hunter told me the resort was ready for the wrecking ball. There's some truth in that assessment. The infrastructure is old, but material things can be replaced or restored. What can't be bought is heart and soul, and that's what Caliente Springs has."

Zeke sat up straighter. "I fully agree."

"Of course you do," Maury said, his voice gruff. "You're the one who set that tone. When I paid Caliente Springs that first visit, you gave me the facts, but I came back under a different name and walked around. I also asked some friends to check in as guests. Do you know what we found?"

A dried-up golf course. A nasty old goat. Leaking faucets. But those things weren't all Caliente Springs had to offer. "I hope you found a friendly, well-run resort."

"We found a restaurant with good food and a happy staff."

"Katrina gets full credit."

"We played golf on a course that's brown out of respect for the environment."

"The drought—"

"Don't waste your breath," Maury said. "I know all about the drought. That's beyond your control, but others things aren't. You and your staff know how to make guests feel welcome. The rooms may have a leaky faucet or two, but the maids are careful and honest. The desk staff is friendly, the concierges respond like U.S. Marines, and the valets hustle like soccer players. That's what guests see and why they return. But that's not enough."

"No, it isn't." Zeke agreed with Maury completely. "We need an influx of new guests and big events. I'm working on that. Carter Home Goods is still up in the air, but—"

"May I interrupt?" Ellen asked.

Maury signaled her with a nod.

"I spoke with Doris Carter this morning," she said. "They want to come back next month. We didn't talk business, but I think that's a good sign."

"A very good sign," Maury said. "If Carter doesn't snap up the deal you made for that annual conference, he's crazy. And given the success of his business, we know he's a smart man."

There were few things Zeke enjoyed more than a true meeting of the minds. "I hope Carter Home Goods is the just beginning. I have a lot of ideas. Expanded children's activities and better use of that old campground, maybe for a stand-alone retreat center. The cottages serve a high-end clientele, but they're underutilized. We need to do more with them. I'd also like to expand the pro shop. And weddings—"

Maury held up a hand to stop him. "I like the way you think. Before you go any further, I'm going to turn the meeting over to George."

"Thanks, Maury." George removed his arm from Ellen's shoulders, hunched forward, and focused on Zeke. "You know we've been working on something big."

"Yes."

"This morning we reached an agreement. Ginger, Maury, and I are forming a new corpora-tion. Instead of bulldozing old places like this one, we're joining forces to save them. We plan to keep Caliente Springs just like it is, but to be viable, we need to do more. We want you to be a big part of that plan."

"I like what I'm hearing." *Like?* He wanted to leap off the couch and give everyone a high five.

"Of course more responsibility comes with a big raise and a new title. How does Chief Operating Officer sound?"

Like a prayer answered. A gift from God. And

immeasurably more than anything Zeke had dared to imagine. He remembered that morning a month ago when he was deciding on a new business card. Today the name choice was easy. He was clay in God's hands, a work in progress, but he knew exactly who he was. " 'Zeke Monroe, Chief Operating Officer' has a nice ring to it."

"We think so too." Maury steepled his fingers over his chest. "But we're not done here. As capable as you are, we think you'll need some help. This is where Ginger comes in."

Everyone focused on Ginger, who turned to Julia with the fond smile she usually reserved for Tiff. "We have a wedding tomorrow, don't we?"

Julia repositioned herself to face Ginger, crossed her feet at her ankles, and folded her hands. "Yes, we do."

"You've done a wonderful job," Ginger said. "In just thirty days, you pulled together an event I thought was impossible, and you handled the planning in a way that gave me confidence. The weather's beautiful now, but you were ready for rain. You saw to every detail, and you made it look easy in spite of the challenges. I want to personally thank you for your efforts. I expect tomorrow to be glorious."

"I hope so. But it's not over yet."

"No." Ginger's eyes twinkled. "But I think

tonight's little episode was that inevitable glitch you warned us about."

"It certainly qualifies," Julia said. "I have to admit, tonight wasn't something I'd like to see on social media. I'm rethinking our Twitter connection through Tiff's bridesmaid."

"Her name's Jessica," Ginger reminded them. "And no harm was done. I checked with Tiff. *Flops & Fortunes* has a policy against mentioning children, so Jessica ignored the entire incident."

"Good," Zeke said. "Max doesn't need that kind of attention." He already felt like Max's dad.

Julia smiled her thanks, then focused back on Ginger. "The wedding should be all about Tiff and Derek. It's their love that makes the day special."

"Yes, it is," Ginger agreed. "And you consistently kept their desires front and center. George, Maury, and I are all impressed with your ability. As you just heard, we have big plans for the future, including the addition of a full-time event planner for this resort. We'd like to offer you the position. You'd have to relocate, of course."

Julia grabbed Zeke's hand, but her gaze shot to Ellen. "Mom—"

"Yes!" Ellen shouted, jarring Max, though he didn't fully wake up. "I'll put the house on the market tomorrow. It's been our home for over twenty years, but I'm ready for a change and so are you." She turned to George and kissed him.

Zeke gave Julia's hand a meaningful squeeze. If there was any question about their being a couple and working together, he wanted to make his position clear. He whispered into her ear, "Are you okay with making a particular announcement?"

A pretty blush blossomed on her cheeks. "More than okay. I can't wait to share the news."

Neither could Zeke. He skimmed the circle of faces, including Max relaxed with sleep and cuddled in his grandmother's lap. Zeke would be a dad soon. And a husband. He hoped Julia didn't want to wait too long for a wedding, because they had already lost six years. It was time to start the future.

Pulse thrumming, he pushed to his feet. "I want to make something very clear."

"Go for it," George said.

"You're hiring Julia and me as a team, namely Mr. and Mrs. Zeke Monroe. I asked Julia to marry me and she said yes."

Ellen squealed and reached for Julia even with Max in her lap. The men traded handshakes and thumped Zeke on the back. Ginger hugged Julia too.

Somewhere in the celebration, Max woke up. Dazed, he rubbed his eyes. "Mommy? What happened?"

Zeke already felt like a dad, but relationships

needed time to grow. Right now, Julia was Max's anchor, so Zeke waited for her to take the lead.

When she dropped down next to Max, Ellen stood. Julia motioned for Zeke to take her mom's place, then turned her attention to Max, her expression serious. "Do you remember the purple rock Zeke gave us?"

Max nodded. "It's called a geode."

"It's special to all of us, so we're going to share it. Zeke asked me to marry him, and I said yes. You, Zeke, and me . . . we're going to be a family."

Max didn't fully understand the gravity of that commitment, but a wondrous smile lit up his face, and he scrambled to his knees to be closer to Zeke. "Can we play Ninja Turtles?"

"You bet."

"And can we break more geodes?"

Zeke clasped Max's shoulder the way his own dad used to squeeze his. "We can go hunting for them in the desert. I'll take you where my dad took me." His parents would have loved being grandparents.

"All right," Max said. "But Mommy?"

"Yes?"

"I'm hungry."

Laughter from the adults floated in the air. Ginger went to the kitchen and brought out a plate of cookies for Max. The group bantered and talked shop for almost an hour. No one wanted the evening to end, but eventually Max let out an eye-watering yawn.

George finally cleared his throat. "We all have a big day tomorrow. Before we say good-night, let's say a prayer for Zeke and Julia. And for Tiff and Derek too. These young couples have a lot ahead of them."

A hush replaced the chatter, and they all formed a circle with Max between Julia and Zeke. Everyone bowed their heads, and George prayed for blessings of health, peace, and growing faith for both couples.

The prayer hit Zeke hard. In his mind he saw the geode of his own heart, recalled the tap of God's hammer, and thanked his heavenly Father for loving him enough to never let go. Zeke couldn't think of a better way to start his new life with Julia.

But before they celebrated a big day of their own, they had another wedding to pull off.

Thirty-two

Julia couldn't have asked for a more perfect day for Tiff's wedding or for her own first day as Zeke's fiancée. They kept the news to themselves as they supervised the last-minute preparations, but having a secret only made their engagement sweeter. They exchanged several meaningful looks and a few kisses too. But this was Tiff's day.

With the ceremony ten minutes from starting, Julia stood at the entrance to the paved walkway. Any moment now, a stretch limousine would deliver Tiff and her bridesmaids, and a Lincoln Town Car would deliver George, Ginger, Maury, and Ellen. Julia would have enjoyed having Zeke at her side, but he was at the ceremony site, keeping an eye on the crowd, the musicians, and the PA system, as well as Derek and the grooms-men.

The guests were seated except for a few stragglers. Julia had heard nothing but compliments about the setup. Thanks to the grounds crew, the ugly black asphalt was lined with potted trees, flowers, and more twinkle lights than Macy's displayed at Christmas. Pink and rose-gold ribbons draped from white iron posts marked the path to Golden Point and matched the bridesmaids' dresses to perfection. Best of all, the view from the lookout was stunning thanks to feathery pink clouds, a turquoise sky, and the brilliant rays of the setting sun.

Julia glanced at her watch. Tiff and her bridesmaids were a little late, but that was to be expected. With a moment to spare, she used her two-way radio to call Zeke. His promotion would be officially announced in a month or so, but Ginger herself had leaked the news that Zeke was here to stay. He'd been getting congratulatory calls all day from people like Chet and John.

She raised the radio to her mouth. "Wedding Planner to GM."

"GM here. What's up?"

That voice. Even on a scratchy radio, the tenor of it thrilled her. "Just checking in. There's no sign of Tiff yet, but you know how brides bounce off the walls."

"Grooms too." Zeke lowered his voice. "And I don't mean Derek."

Happy goose bumps danced down her spine. "I hear there's another wedding in the works." *Ours.* She already had ideas for it. December, here at Caliente Springs with friends and family. Indoors with no threat of rain. Max included in the vows. Zeke in a tux. She would wear a strapless white gown . . .

"Jules? Are you there?"

"Sorry." *Not really.* She could hardly wait to

marry him. "I was planning that next wedding in my head. It's going to be—"

"Perfect?"

"In its own way, yes. But I was going to say beautiful." The limousine and the Town Car cruised up the road, the sun glinting off the polished chrome. "The bride's here. Gotta go!"

Julia walked to the limo to meet Tiff. The white-gloved driver opened the door, and the three bridesmaids emerged one at a time, bouquets in hand and smiles gleaming. Chelsea Robertson, the official photographer, and Jessica from *Flops & Fortunes* both snapped pictures as Tiff emerged. She was so beautiful in white that the earth itself seemed to hold its breath.

She met Julia's gaze and smiled. "I am *so* nervous!"

"You'll do great," Julia assured her.

George and Ginger approached. Ginger gave Tiff a gentle hug, told her she loved her, and left with Maury and Ellen to take their seats in the front.

George offered his tuxedo-clad elbow to the blushing bride. "Are you ready, darlin'?"

Tiff took a big breath, scanned the long walk, and gave a crisp nod. "Let's do this."

Julia led the group down the walkway to a spot she called the launch pad, a square of pavement shielded from view and perfect for staging the processional. The strains of music played by a string quartet plus a Spanish guitarist drifted to them, and she smiled her thanks to George for arranging the music.

When the bridesmaids were lined up, she radioed Zeke. "We're ready. Cue the musicians."

The quintet began the first song in the processional. Julia gave a nod to Bridesmaid No. 1, and she walked down the aisle one slow step at a time. The other bridesmaids followed, leaving Tiff, George, and Julia on the launch pad.

George patted Tiff's hand then faced Julia. "Tiff and I have this covered. Why don't you join Zeke?"

"Yes," Tiff said. "I'm-I'm fine. Well, sort of. I'm just so nervous! What if I trip or—"

"I've got you." George patted Tiff's hand the way Julia knew her own dad would have patted hers.

With a lump in her throat, she slipped around to the back row where Zeke was waiting for her.

Side by side, they held hands, squeezing tight as they took in the smiling bridesmaids, the lush bouquets, and the white arch dripping with peonies, hydrangea, and long trails of miniature ivy. The minister stood front and center with Derek and his groomsman lined up to his left, their black tuxes a swaggering contrast to a sky mottled with feathery pink clouds. The photographer snapped pictures then sat in the front row.

Anticipating Tiff's bridal march, Julia held her breath, ready to stand at the first elegant notes of Pachelbel's *Canon in D.*

Silence settled over the crowd. The violinist raised his bow, but something caught his attention and he stopped with his eyes riveted to far side of Golden Point. Straining forward, Julia followed his gaze down the line of bridesmaids, all standing at attention except the bridesmaid closest to the edge of the lookout, where the incline sloped gently.

Looking down with her mouth agape, the bridesmaid scooted back, her arms outstretched as though she were tugging on her bouquet.

Julia and Zeke jumped to their feet, exchanged horrified glances, and leaped to the worst possible conclusion. Sure enough, Ladybug was chomping on the bridesmaid's flowers. Apparently she didn't like the taste of hydrangeas, because she spat them out and went after Bridesmaid No. 2.

Zeke bolted past Julia. "I'll get Ladybug. You guard Tiff."

Julia ran back to the launch pad. Some glitches turned into wonderful memories. Others were truly disasters. If Ladybug flattened Tiff or ripped her dress, stole the bridal bouquet or ate the rings, it would be impossible to recover. Julia's first wedding for Caliente Springs would go down in history for all the wrong reasons; Zeke would have some serious explaining to do about

Ladybug; and worst of all, the most important day of Tiff's life would be ruined.

Breathing hard, Julia rounded the corner to the launch pad. Tiff saw her and paled. "Oh, no—"

"It's going to be fine," Julia assured her.

"Did Derek . . . back out?"

"Oh no! It's nothing like that." He was probably chasing Ladybug with Zeke. "We've had a little interruption. That's all." Somehow Julia kept her voice almost normal. "You've met Ladybug, haven't you?"

"Aunt Ginger's *goat?*"

"Yes." Julia gave George a desperate look. "She . . . crashed the wedding. Stay here with George."

He muttered something not very nice about Ladybug and goats in general. "I'll protect you, Tiff. If I have to wrestle that goat to the ground—"

"You two stay here," Julia ordered.

She ran back to Golden Point, silently praying that Zeke had Ladybug in custody. But instead of seeing him calmly escorting the goat away from the ceremony, she walked into total mayhem.

Guests were on their feet. The ones in the front rows were crowded in the outside aisle, and the minister was sprawled on the ground with the remains of the flower arch on top of him. Ladybug—who was being chased by Zeke, Derek, and the groomsmen—was chasing all three bridesmaids down the main aisle. A white cord that moments ago had marked the family section dangled in the shape of a noose from Zeke's hand.

Zeke and the groomsmen picked up speed. But so did Ladybug. At the end of the aisle, the bridesmaids scattered. Only Julia stood between the goat and the bride. Preparing to take a hit, she spread her arms, balanced on the balls of her feet and stared Ladybug dead in the eye.

The goat lowered her head. "Maaaah. Maa—AAAAH!"

"Don't you dare!" Julia shouted back.

"Maa-AAAH!"

Julia braced for the hit. Ladybug picked up steam. Just before the goat butted into her, Zeke lunged forward and snagged Ladybug's rhine-stone collar. She twisted and bucked, but Zeke held tight with both hands. Julia wrangled the cord over Ladybug's head and tightened the loop. When the groomsmen and Derek crowded behind her to make a human wall between Tiff and Ladybug, Julia finally let out her breath. Zeke took the rope from her, shortened it to six inches, and held Ladybug tight.

Ginger and Maury shoved their way through the crowd. Ginger broke through first, strode up to her pet, and waved her finger in the goat's face. "Ladybug, shame on you! I can't believe what you just did. Look at this mess!

433

And it's Tiff's wedding. Bad goat! Very, very bad!"

While Ginger babbled apologies to anyone who would listen, Julia surveyed the damage. Guests were scattered all over the lookout. The sun was dropping fast, and gray shadows were growing longer by the minute. Crushed flowers and broken stems littered the aisle, and the only sound to reach her ears was a shell-shocked silence punctuated with murmurs of "Poor Tiff."

No. Tiff's day would not be ruined by a goat. Not if Julia had anything to say about it.

She spun toward Zeke, who was handing Ladybug off to the lead member of the set-up crew. Four other workers stood by ready to take orders. Zeke turned to her, grim-faced, but his eyes glinted with raw determination. They were partners, a team, a couple. They didn't need words to back each other up. With a single crisp nod, they united in their cause. Tiff's wedding would be as wonderful as they all dreamed, or Julia and Zeke would go out together in a blaze of glory.

"Let's do this." Zeke turned to the set-up crew. "Gentlemen, this wedding is on. Do whatever it takes to clean up the mess before we lose daylight."

As the men hustled away, Julia waved frantically to Ellen approaching with the mangled bouquets in her arms.

Julia turned to Ginger. "Will you check on Tiff? Tell her—"

George called from five steps away. "Tiff's fine. Derek's with her." He joined the group, and the six of them huddled together.

Julia turned to her mom first. "The flowers—"

"I'm on it." Ellen indicated the blooms and greenery piled in her arms. "The arch can't be saved, but I can pull together three nice bouquets."

"How long?" Julia asked.

"Thirty minutes."

"The sun's setting," she reminded them all. "Can you do it in fifteen?"

"I'll help," Ginger said.

George rested his hand on her arm. "Sis?"

"Yes?"

"We have five hundred people standing around. And they're going to be talking about poor Tiff until we get this mess cleaned up. We need to change the mood. How about I borrow a guitar and we do some entertaining?"

The Travers Twins hadn't performed together in close to thirty years. While the bad blood of the past was long gone, scars remained. Julia held her breath while Ginger studied her brother's face. Her eyes turned misty as she kissed his cheek. "You're on, partner. How about 'Diddly Down' for old times' sake?"

"You got it, sis."

Side by side, they strode to the front of the

lookout. George borrowed the guitar from the quintet, tested the microphone, then called for attention. "Ladies and gentlemen!"

The murmuring changed from pity to surprise.

"I'm George Travers." He strummed a chord and leaned back to give his sister center stage.

"And I'm Ginger Travers."

A smattering of applause turned into an ovation. When it calmed, George cracked a smile. "That goat you just met is Ladybug. She's sort of a pet around here. While the crew puts this wedding back together, Ginger and I are going to sing a few songs, starting with a toe-tapper you all know well."

Someone let out a hoot of approval. George played the first notes of "Diddly Down," and his voice blended with Ginger's in perfect harmony, as if they had just rehearsed. Sometimes the years didn't matter at all.

Julia reached for Zeke, and they hurried to the launch pad. The bridesmaids and groomsmen were huddled together, talking rapidly as they waited for word about the wedding. Julia thought briefly of Jessica and *Flops & Fortunes*, but there was nothing she could do about that exposure now.

Tiff and Derek stood on the far side of the asphalt slab, their arms around each other as the minister tried to console them. Tears streaked Tiff's face, and Derek's tux was askew. The words to "Diddly Down" floated in the air, but no one noticed.

"Attention please," Julia called to the group. "We just had a wedding crasher. Ladybug made a mess, but this wedding is going to happen. And it's going to be spectacular for just one reason. Derek and Tiff love each other. That's why you're all here, and that's what we came to celebrate."

Relief and joy washed over Tiff's face. Derek planted a kiss on her temple, squeezed her waist, then faced Julia. "What do you need the guys to do?"

"Not a thing," she replied. "The set-up crew is taking care of the mess. Ladybug is on her way back to the stable, and my mom's making new bouquets. George and Ginger are entertaining the guests, and there's just enough daylight left for the ceremony."

Tiff sniffed back her tears. "My makeup—"

Julia handed her a tissue from her pocket then turned to the maid of honor. "There's an emergency basket in the limo. We have hairspray, lipstick, safety pins, even super glue. Will you get it for us?"

The bridesmaid scooted away on her high heels. Derek gave Tiff a last lingering look and left with the minister and his groomsmen. Zeke, radio in hand, checked on the clean-up and received good news.

"The crew's almost done," he told her. "I'm going up front. Radio when you're ready, and I'll signal George to wrap up the show and come back to escort Tiff."

Julia smiled her thanks then turned her attention to the bridesmaids who were repairing their hair and makeup. Fresh lipstick did wonders for everyone, and within minutes the group was laughing, even Tiff. Ellen arrived with three bouquets even prettier than the original ones. Tiff threw herself into Julia's arms and hugged her hard.

Ten minutes later, with no sign whatsoever of Ladybug or the mayhem, Tiff walked down the aisle on George's arm.

Zeke and Julia watched from the back row, their fingers laced and shoulders touching. The setting sun shimmered into liquid gold. The rays bounced off the coastal mountains and turned the distant valley into a bottomless sea of light. At the precise moment Tiff and Derek spoke their vows, the clouds burned bright pink. When they kissed as husband and wife, the crowd erupted with cheers and applause.

Julia let out the breath she'd been holding and sagged against Zeke.

Drawing her against his side, he whispered into her ear. "Maybe it's true."

"What?"

"That the biggest problems make the best memories."

"I think maybe they do," she whispered back. "But just for the record, you and I are getting married indoors."

"Ladybug isn't invited?"

"Not a chance."

Epilogue

Five Years Later

"Are you hoping for a boy or a girl?" George asked Zeke.

The two men were standing at the grill, chatting while Zeke flipped hamburgers for the twenty or so guests invited for today's gender reveal party. The party was Ginger's idea, but the event was being held in the backyard of the suburban home Zeke and Julia had purchased a year ago. With another baby on the way—this would be their second in addition to Max—they had given up the manager's house at Caliente Springs for a neighborhood with schools, shopping, and a nearby pediatrician.

Today's plan called for Zeke and Julia to say the blessing over the meal then open a giant box of balloons and send them soaring. The balloons were either pink or blue. No one knew except Julia's doctor, the ultrasound technician, and Ginger, who had planned the party now in full swing with guests like Chet and John from Caliente Springs and friends from the church Zeke and Julia attended.

Zeke considered George's question. "We already have one of each, so I don't have a preference."

George clapped him on the back. "Either way, Ellen and I are going to be thrilled."

George and Ellen had been married four years now, almost as long as Zeke and Julia. George and Zeke were closer than ever, and Zeke called Ellen "Mom" like Julia did. Ginger was part of their family too.

And then there were his kids. Max was nine now, smart as a whip, and a budding geologist. Hannah was two years old and too cute for words.

At the heart of it all was Julia.

His wife.

His partner.

His best friend.

And soon to be the mother of another son or daughter. She was the most beautiful woman in the world to him. Strong, kind, and smart, she was the anchor that kept their growing family steady.

Life was sweet these days. Thanks to Tiff's wedding, *Flops & Fortunes* had bestowed Caliente Springs with "platinum fortune status" and done a full network TV show on the resort.

Today the hotel was booked two years in advance with weddings and conferences.

Zeke was proud of the accomplishments, but even more exciting was the men's group he led at church. He shared his burnout story often, and more than a few men had found strength in it.

Not even Hunter could mar the goodness in Zeke and Julia's life. With time and prayer, they had accepted him for who he was, though Hunter remained aloof to them and even to Max. Zeke and Julia invited him to Max's birthday parties, but he didn't come. Instead he sent cards with money. Over the years, phone calls had dwindled from weekly occurrences to rare ones. It had been a slow pulling away, and Max had accepted Hunter's role in his life as Hunter chose to define it. With Zeke to fill the gap, Max had adjusted well.

Zeke loved being a father. Hannah called him Daddy, and Max called him Dad. Beautiful words indeed.

Proud and content, he added the burgers to the buffet table then signaled to Julia. Grinning, she rounded up Max and Hannah and came to stand at his side in front of their guests. Zeke hoisted Hannah to his hip, grinned at Max, then laid his free hand on Julia's belly. "How's the little one?"

"He's doing great." She was sure it was a boy.

"Or she is."

"We'll know in a few minutes."

Zeke gave her tummy a pat then called for attention from the crowd. "Julia and I want to thank you all for coming today. We especially want to thank Ginger for pulling the party together."

Applause broke out, led by Maury. Nothing romantic had developed between him and Ginger, but they were good friends.

"This is a special day for us," Zeke continued, "and it's a joy to share it with every one of you. If you're so inclined, would you bow your heads for a short prayer?"

Julia gripped Max's hand, then put her arm around Zeke's waist and leaned into him. Max scooted nearer, and Hannah cuddled into his chest. With his family tight and close, Zeke took a breath. "Father God, we thank you for the food, our friends, and our growing family. We ask you to bless this meal to our bodies and this fellowship to our hearts. We also ask you to bless the baby on the way. Boy or girl, help us to love this child just as you love us. Amen."

The instant he finished, Ginger leaped to her feet. "It's time! Go open that box."

The four of them approached a white box the size of a washing machine. Zeke passed Hannah to Julia, and they split up into two teams. With the girls on one side of the box and Zeke and Max on the other, they placed their hands on the flaps and braced to pull.

Zeke locked eyes with his wife, a unique woman who cared for others and loved God with her entire being. His chest swelled with more love than his heart could hold. "On the count of three?"

She nodded, and in unison they shouted, "One!"

The crowd joined in. "Two!"

And louder still . . . "Three!"

With little Hannah squirming, Julia, Zeke, and Max opened the box. A dozen bright blue balloons shot out of the box and soared into the sky.

"A boy!" Julia cried.

The crowd erupted with cheers and applause. Max gave a fist pump, and little Hannah clapped because everyone else was clapping. Zeke came around to Julia, tucked her against his side with Hannah between them, and pulled Max close. With his heart brimming, he gave thanks to his heavenly Father for entrusting him with the precious gift of a family to love, protect, and lead. That was what a husband and father did, and with God first in his life, Zeke embraced the call.

Acknowledgements

"God is stretching you as a writer."

I can't tell you how many times my friend Sara said those words to me over the year it took to write (and rewrite) *Someone Like You*. Stretching feels good when we stand on our toes and raise our arms as high as we can. That gentle pull releases tension and makes us hum with pleasure. But there's another kind of stretching, the kind my son experienced in physical therapy for a knee injury. That kind of stretching pushes us well beyond the limits of our respective comfort zones.

The stretching involved with *Someone Like You* falls into the second category.

This was a tough book to write, and I wouldn't have survived it without the love, help, and prayers of family, friends, and writing colleagues.

Sara Mitchell, play the tape. Play it every day and believe it. When my creative mind shut down, you came alongside me in a way no one else could. You shared your ideas, logic, wisdom, love, and faith. Adjectives and adverbs too! I couldn't have written this book without (wait for it) . . . *someone like you*.

Deborah Raad, *thank you* doesn't begin to express my gratitude. You brainstormed with me, read lousy first drafts, and proofread when I couldn't tell a comma from a question mark. When I lost enthusiasm, you encouraged me. When I felt like banging my head against the wall, you laughed with me at Panera. Friends forever!

To my editors at Bethany House Publishers: Charlene Patterson, I owe you a huge debt of gratitude. No editor wants to write an eight-page revision letter. And Raela Schoenherr, thank you for supporting me through this process. You both know the first version of this book was a mess. Your insights made all the difference. I also want to thank editor Jessica Barnes for catching some very embarrassing mistakes and making the writing shine. More than any book I've written (and this is number seventeen), *Someone Like You* was a collaborative effort. Thank you all from the bottom of my heart.

A host of other people helped bring this story to life with their prayers, encouragement, and insight.

Monica Mynk, friend and fellow Kentucky author, when I was at my wit's end, you offered to read through the mess I thought was a book. Your insights breathed life into those early chapters. Thank you!

More gratitude goes to my agent, Pattie Steele-Perkins. Pattie, we've been together a lot of years now. Your sage advice and encouragement are constant blessings to me.

And to my prayer partner, Ginger Burns: I didn't realize it at the time, but the seeds for this story were planted in the Centerpointe prayer room. I miss you, friend!

My parents are no longer on this earth, but their encouragement echoes in my mind every single day. So does my dad's wisdom and my mom's insight into people. I wouldn't be a writer today without their special blend of logic and empathy.

I'm so grateful for my family.

A big thank-you goes to Mom and Dad Scheibel, Peggy, Kathy, and Patti. I love you all. Another shout-out goes to Gary and Katie Hailey, my uncle and aunt. Katie, you've been in my life longer than anyone else. To my stepdad, George McLeary, thank you for loving my mom and joining our family. And last, a big hug to my brother, John, and his wife, Angie. Time and miles mean nothing when you're as close as we are.

To my sons and their wives: Joe and Meredith, you made me a grandmother for the first time and in a spectacular way. Twin girls! Big hugs to Kennedy and Corinne. Grandma loves you. Dave and Whitney, you inspire me with how you love and support each other. That love shows in everything you do. I'm proud of you both and am overjoyed to be your mom.

And finally to my husband, Michael: There's a reason this book is dedicated to you. Four words:

dorky pink hair bow. (Here's the story for those who don't know it: When I saw the cover for my second historical, I didn't like it at all. "It's all wrong!" I complained to Mike on the phone. "My heroine would *never* wear that dorky pink hair bow." Two hours later, he walked through the door with a bouquet of pink roses wrapped with dorky pink ribbon.) Honey, you're the best. I cherish your prayers, your wisdom, and every minute of our marriage.

A lot of thought goes into the title of a book. I was particularly pleased with *Someone Like You* because it works on so many levels. Sara got the first shout-out, but those three words apply to every person on this list. I couldn't have told this story without the support of each and every one of you.

I've been blessed in so many ways. With my heart full, I bow my head to the greatest Some-one in my life and say, "Thank you, Lord Jesus, for your grace."

About the Author

Victoria Bylin is a romance writer known for her realistic and relatable characters. Her books have been finalists in multiple contests, including the Carol Awards, the RITAs, and *RT Magazine*'s Reviewers' Choice Award. A native of California, she and her husband now make their home in Lexington, Kentucky, where their family and their crazy Jack Russell terrier keep them on the go.

Learn more at her website:
www.victoriabylin.com.

Center Point Large Print
600 Brooks Road / PO Box 1
Thorndike, ME 04986-0001 USA

(207) 568-3717

US & Canada:
1 800 929-9108
www.centerpointlargeprint.com